Hearts in Hiding

Hearts in Hiding

a novel

BETSY BRANNON GREEN

Covenant Communications, Inc.

Published by Covenant Communications, Inc.
American Fork, Utah

Printed in the United States of America
First Printing: May 2001

08 07 06 05 04 03 02 01   10 9 8 7 6 5 4 3 2 1

ISBN 1-57734-823-0

Library of Congress Cataloging-in-Publication Data

Green, Betsy Brannon, 1958-
    Hearts in hiding / Betsy Brannon Green.
       p.   cm.
    ISBN 1-57734-823-0
    1. Government investigators--Fiction. 2. Witnesses--Protection--Fiction. 3. Undercover operations--Fiction. 4. Mormon women--Fiction. 5. Georgia--Fiction. I. Title

PS35607.R43 H42 2001
813'.6--dc21
                          2001028117
                            CIP

For Butch,
my romantic interest

CHAPTER 1

When the clock finally reached five o'clock, Kate gratefully turned off her computer. She had typed seven wills that day and felt like dying herself. The small, windowless room she worked in was stuffy and warm. She stood and pulled the long hair off her neck for a few seconds, then neatly arranged the completed documents on her desk. When she returned tomorrow morning, these would be gone and a new stack would be in their place.

With a sigh, she walked through the copy room and lounge, then down a long hallway lined with offices. Finally she entered the cool reception area and waved to Felicia. The girl couldn't type, or even spell, but she sat in this lovely room all day and greeted people as they came in. Her nails were perfect, her makeup professional, and her clothes expensive. Every time Kate walked past Felicia, she was reminded that life was not fair.

As she stepped out onto the crowded sidewalks of downtown Chicago, the oppressive heat choked the air from her lungs. Gasping for breath, she joined the throng of tired people heading home. The lot where she parked her car was three blocks away, and her advanced pregnancy, combined with hours of sitting at a desk, had left her ankles swollen and her feet numb. As usual, she hadn't even stopped for lunch. Rubbing her lower back, she promised herself that she would take a break tomorrow, even if it meant working late and returning to an empty apartment after dark.

When she opened the door of her car, the heat rushed up to meet her. Reluctantly she slid onto the hot upholstery and pitted the air conditioner against overwhelming odds. She rolled the window down and backed out of her parking space, vaguely aware of a dark blue sedan that pulled out at the same time.

As she waited for an opening in the traffic, she checked the rearview mirror and noticed the blue car behind her. She didn't give it another thought as she negotiated through the busy streets. But several minutes later, she could see that the car was still there. Slightly disturbed, she studied the sedan. The two men riding in the front seat were the vehicle's only occupants. Kate reduced her speed, assuming that it was an unmarked police car. When she reached her apartment building, she pulled in front and took advantage of the valet parking service offered for five dollars. The blue car drove by slowly, and neither man looked in her direction. Leaving the keys in the ignition, Kate stepped out of the car.

"Good evening, Mrs. Singleton," one of the valets greeted her. "Sure is hot today."

"It sure is," Kate agreed and handed him a five-dollar bill. "You'll put the keys in my box?" He nodded and she went straight to the elevator. When the door opened on the third floor, she stepped off and walked down the hall, digging in her purse for the keys to her apartment. She didn't notice the man standing at the end of the hallway until she stopped at her door. She looked up, startled by his presence. He nodded briefly as he took a long drag on a cigarette. He was probably waiting for Claire, the girl who lived next door. She dated all kinds of men and Kate made a mental note to tell her that they couldn't smoke in the hallway.

She opened the door to her apartment and hurried inside. Out of habit she turned on the light and quickly surveyed the room. Everything was just as she left it, unfortunately. The place was a mess, and lately she never seemed to have any energy when she got home. Carefully she locked the door behind her, then walked into the kitchen. Ignoring the dishes piled in the sink, she drank orange juice straight from the carton. Nibbling on the last bagel she pulled from a bag in the almost empty refrigerator, Kate pushed the play button on her answering machine and sat down at the counter to listen.

There was a call from her mother and one from the dry cleaners reminding her that she still had not picked up the clothes she dropped off two weeks before. There were three hang-ups and then a message from Tyler Thornhill, Tony's partner.

"Kate," Tyler's voice said breathlessly from the machine. "It's very important that I talk to you right away. Call me on my cell phone as soon as you get this message."

Kate was mildly alarmed at Tyler's message. Her husband's partner never got upset, never yelled, never panicked. His frantic voice on the answering machine was cause for concern. She was reaching for the phone to call him when the doorbell rang. Groaning, she stood and walked to the door.

"Who is it?" she asked cautiously, squinting through her peep-hole. The two men from the blue car were standing in the hallway, looking grim and official.

"FBI, ma'am," one responded.

"I'll need to see your identification," she said calmly. They both held up credentials for her review. She was familiar enough with the real article to know that they were authentic. However, she got a pen from her purse and wrote down the numbers. "I'm calling to check on this," she told the men.

"Ask to speak to Mr. Evans," one of them said, referring to the Special Agent in Charge. This was an unexpected and painful surprise. She had not talked to Mr. Evans since the memorial service. She knew the number by heart, but dialed it with trembling fingers. She was put straight through, and Mr. Evans verified that the agents had been sent on official business.

With rising anxiety she walked back to the door and opened it. "Come in," she invited the men warily.

"Thank you, Mrs. Singleton," the same agent answered. He was tall, with black skin, graying hair, and kind eyes. The other man was younger but had the hard look of a seasoned agent. "My name is Agent Thomas, and this is Agent Roberts. We're sorry to bother you."

"You've been watching me today," Kate stated.

"We have been watching you for several weeks," he admitted, startling a gasp from her. "Today we changed to open surveillance."

"Why?" she asked as a shiver ran up her spine. "Does this have something to do with Tony?"

"I'm not at liberty to discuss the details with you, Mrs. Singleton," Agent Thomas told her. "But I am instructed to escort you to the Bureau office downtown. If you have any medications that will need to be taken within the next twenty-four hours, please bring them with you." His voice was calm, but it held an undercurrent of urgency.

She looked up sharply at this remark. "Am I in some kind of trouble?"

"Mr. Evans will explain everything." His gaze skimmed the room, and her eyes followed his. Perhaps it wasn't safe to talk in the apartment.

"But you're saying I will be gone for twenty-four hours?" she asked.

The agents exchanged glances. "I don't know when you'll be allowed to return," Agent Thomas replied.

"I see," Kate answered uneasily as she walked into her bedroom.

Agent Thomas stood in the doorway while she went into the bathroom and put her toothbrush into her purse. The dress she had worn to work was wrinkled, but she didn't want to ask for time to change. Taking one last look around the room, she had the odd feeling she would never see this apartment again. Despite the length of time she had lived there, she didn't feel particularly attached. The good memories she would take with her, the bad ones she was glad to leave behind. She closed the door and returned to the living room.

"I'll turn off the kitchen lights," she began, but Agent Thomas shook his head.

"That won't be necessary," Agent Thomas said, moving toward the door. "Stay close behind me," he instructed as he looked out into the hallway.

Kate and the younger agent followed. The man with the cigarette was still at the end of the hall and nodded to her again as they walked by him. When they reached the main floor, Agent Thomas turned toward the back of the building. They passed several janitorial closets and a security desk. Finally they stepped out onto a loading dock.

The dark blue car was parked beside it, and Agent Thomas held the door for Kate while the other man climbed in behind the wheel. Then they rode in silence through the busy Chicago streets.

An hour later Kate found herself sitting at a conference table in a large room at the FBI field office with Agent Thomas and his partner seated across from her. They waited for several minutes before the door opened and three men walked into the room. The first was an older man whom Kate recognized as William Evans, the Special Agent in Charge, or SAC, of the Chicago field office. The second was Tony's partner, Tyler Thornhill. The third was a stranger. He was tall, over six feet, with dark hair and somber eyes. His intimidating appearance was emphasized by the fact that he needed a shave. He glanced at Kate briefly, then took a seat at the far end of the table.

Tyler gave her a shrug and sat beside Agent Thomas. Mr. Evans claimed the chair to her right. "We very much appreciate your coming to meet with us, Mrs. Singleton," he began in a diplomatic tone.

"Agent Thomas was quite insistent," she answered blandly.

Mr. Evans smiled. "Yes, well, the matter we have to discuss with you is urgent and classified. It's better to handle such things in a secure environment." He looked up as if he expected her to object or demand an explanation. When she didn't, he continued. "Do you know anything about the case your husband was working on right before his death?"

Kate restrained a laugh. "Tony never discussed his cases with me."

Mr. Evans nodded as if her response was exactly what he had expected. "Well, I am going to tell you a little bit about it." He leaned back in his chair and studied her carefully. "This will be strictly confidential." She raised an eyebrow. "You've heard of money laundering?" Kate nodded. "Most people have. Few, however, understand how widespread and insidious it is. I'm going to give you a brief explanation."

Mr. Evans steepled his fingers. "All illegal activities, from prostitution to drugs to extortion and robbery, generate money that is hard to spend. Large cash deposits into banks and other financial institutions are reported to the government. If people use cash to buy stocks or bonds or million-dollar houses, they draw attention to themselves. So criminals need a way to wash or launder the illegal money they make through a legitimate enterprise. Many businesses are used for this purpose. Vending machine companies, restaurants, arcades, anything that deals in large amounts of cash. Once the money is run through one of these businesses, it can be deposited into legal accounts. Do you understand?" Kate nodded again.

"Your husband was working undercover to expose a very big money-laundering operation. They handle money for several of the largest drug dealers in the Miami area, and by stopping them, we could have significantly interrupted drug traffic as well. It was an extremely important case, and the people he was dealing with are very dangerous."

Kate's heart rate accelerated. "What really happened to Tony?" she asked weakly.

Mr. Evans spoke bluntly. "He was shot in the head. Execution style."

Kate shuddered, fighting the nausea that threatened to overwhelm her. Tyler cursed and jumped to his feet, his chair slamming into the wall behind him. "Why did you have to say it like that?" he shouted at his boss.

"Because I want to make sure before we go any further that Mrs. Singleton realizes that we are talking about violent, ruthless men," Mr. Evans said calmly, then added with a touch of annoyance, "Sit down, Tyler."

"You found his body then?" Kate asked bravely. When they had originally told her of his death, they had just said that he was killed in the line of duty, but his body was not available. There had been a memorial service but no funeral, and she knew that Tony's parents would want to have him buried properly.

"Not exactly." For the first time, Mr. Evans seemed slightly uncomfortable. "They sent us a video of the event and said that his body will eventually 'turn up.'" Kate closed her eyes against this news. "I know that this information is painful for you. All of us who knew and worked with him share a portion of your grief." Mr. Evans paused momentarily. "Tony's death also disrupted our investigation.

We've sent another agent in, but it will take months to get him into a useful position."

Tyler shifted impatiently in his chair momentarily drawing Mr. Evans's attention. The older man leaned forward. "We received some disturbing information recently regarding you, Mrs. Singleton," he said.

"From a drug addict who can't even remember his own name!" Tyler interjected angrily.

Mr. Evans addressed him directly. "I believe that our information is accurate. But regardless, we can't take chances with her life. We owe Tony that much at least."

"What kind of information did you receive?" Kate asked nervously.

"A contract has been issued on your life," Mr. Evans said bluntly.

"A contract? Like the way they killed people in *The Godfather?*" Kate's tone was incredulous.

"I'm afraid that this is not Hollywood, Mrs. Singleton. These are evil people with millions of dollars at stake, and they will destroy anyone who stands in their way."

Looking into his serious eyes, Kate felt close to tears at the suddenness of this revelation. "How could I possibly be a threat to them?" she managed to ask.

"That we don't know," Mr. Evans responded. "It makes me wonder if they have reason to believe that Tony told you something or left incriminating evidence at your apartment."

"Impossible." Kate shook her head.

"In any case, we feel that we must take some drastic protective measures," Mr. Evans told her firmly.

"What is it that you intend to do?" Kate asked with trepidation.

"We want to help you disappear."

A nervous laugh escaped before Kate could stop it. "You can't be serious. I have a job, a family, a life! I can't just leave! Especially now."

Tyler seemed pleased with her response, but Mr. Evans continued to press. "Believe me, Mrs. Singleton, we wouldn't ask if we felt there were other viable options. I realize that it may seem to you like we are overreacting," he said earnestly. "But . . . I did see them kill your husband." She flinched. "And we cannot guarantee your safety unless you cooperate with us completely," he finished quietly.

"How can a person just disappear?" she whispered.

Mr. Evans smiled grimly. "We are experts in that area, after all, and we have formulated a very elaborate plan, which is why we've kept you under surveillance for the past three weeks. As far as most people know, your life will carry on as always without interruption. We have an agent who resembles you, and she'll assume your life."

"She won't fool anyone," Kate mumbled, unimpressed.

"You'd be surprised," Mr. Evans said with a ghost of a smile. "The dry cleaner, the valets at your apartment building, coworkers who work on other floors . . ." He shrugged. "The agent has similar coloring and build, she will appear to be pregnant, and she will be wearing your clothes. She'll have your keys, your identification, your cleaning receipts. Most people who have limited contact with you won't even notice. The people who have to be given an explanation will be told that you are going into the witness protection program."

"If this other woman takes over my life, what will happen to me?" Kate asked.

"You will become someone else."

"Will I ever be able to come back?"

"The best way for us to insure your safety is to arrest the criminals who want you dead. We're working on it, but it may take a long time."

"How long?"

"Weeks, possibly months." When Kate didn't respond, he reached across and patted her hand. "I wouldn't ask you to do this unless I believed it was absolutely necessary."

"So, I have no choice," Kate said tonelessly.

Tyler refused to remain silent any longer. "Of course you have a choice! There's no reason for you to even consider this outrageous proposal!"

She was surprised by his vehemence. "What option do I have?" she demanded.

"Marry me," he begged. "I'll take you away somewhere safe. No one will ever find you. I'll protect you and make you happy."

At this, the dark-haired man sitting at the end of the table made a derisive sound. Kate glanced at him and saw that his eyes were hard in spite of his obvious amusement.

Returning her attention to Tyler, she smiled. "You know I can't marry you. We've had this conversation before, and I don't want to go through all the reasons here. Besides, I think Tony would want me to cooperate with Mr. Evans."

"Tony!" Tyler said disdainfully. "He certainly always had your best interests at heart."

Kate's voice was suddenly cool. "Let's not get personal, Tyler."

Mr. Evans wasn't happy with Tyler either. "Mr. Thornhill," he warned, "you will be asked to leave this meeting if you make one more unsolicited comment. You are advising Mrs. Singleton against the decision made by your superior, which places you in a very grave situation."

"We are talking about Kate's life and her future happiness," the agent grumbled. "My standing in the department pales in comparison."

Turning back to Kate, Mr. Evans continued. "Mr. Thornhill is a good friend. He's loyal to you and that's commendable. But he doesn't have the resources to protect you adequately, and if he pursues this trend toward insubordination, he may not even have a job. The safest place for you and your unborn baby is in our protective custody."

Kate nodded unhappily. "I'll do whatever you tell me to."

"I can't believe you're going to agree to this," Tyler said sharply. "Think of your child!"

"Sit down before they throw you out of here," Kate ordered him. "You don't have to remind me that I am responsible for a child. I have thought of little else for months. Right now, safety is more important than happiness, and I think there's no question that the FBI is in a better position to help me than you are."

Tyler's expression was desperate. "You see how well they protected Tony!" he jeered.

"Mrs. Singleton has made her decision, Tyler. Now we will ask you and Agent Roberts to leave the meeting. The rest of what we have to say doesn't involve you."

The younger agent who had escorted Kate from her apartment stood up promptly, but Tyler's face flushed with fury. "You aren't even going to let me help?"

"Your help is unnecessary. Everything is taken care of, and the fewer people who know the details, the better."

"You don't trust me," Tyler accused him, his voice rising. "I don't believe this!"

Mr. Evans had finally reached the limit of his patience. "Get out of here, Agent Thornhill, before I have you fired! Do you understand?"

"I understand plenty. And don't think I'm going to just sit by and let this happen."

Mr. Evans reached for a cell phone in his pocket. He pressed a button, then spoke. "Please prepare the paperwork necessary to end Mr. Tyler Thornhill's employment with the Bureau, and remove him from the active duty list. Have a check prepared for the appropriate severance pay, and send two security officers to the conference room. I'll collect his keys and his badge."

Everyone listened in stunned silence. Tyler's face paled. "I didn't mean . . ."

"You didn't mean to get fired?" Mr. Evans demanded. "Then you should have done what I told you to. Your behavior here today has been inexcusable."

"I'm sorry." Tyler glanced down the table at the dark-haired man who needed a shave and flushed when the man smirked back. "I care deeply about Kate—uh, Mrs. Singleton," he amended quickly as his face darkened with embarrassment.

"Please," Kate appealed to the older man. "He and Tony were very close, like brothers really. I wouldn't want his concern for me to cost him his job."

Mr. Evans sighed and nodded as two uniformed security men came through the door. "Very well, I'll give you another chance," he said to Tyler. "Only because Mrs. Singleton asked me to," he added, his voice rising with anger. Turning to the security men, he addressed them. "Would you gentlemen escort Mr. Thornhill to my office?" Everyone watched as Tyler followed the men out of the room. The look on his face was one of absolute defeat.

A few tears slipped out from beneath Kate's dark lashes. The man at the end of the table made a growling sound, then stood. Seconds later he handed her a wad of Kleenex.

After the man had returned to his seat, Mr. Evans continued wearily, "Mrs. Singleton, I'd like to introduce you to Agent Iverson. He is the agent who has been assigned to protect you."

Kate looked at the man and he nodded briefly. "Tell me what you have planned," she requested, turning back to Mr. Evans.

"The criminals who want you dead have sophisticated methods for locating people." Mr. Evans tapped his pen against the table. "So we have been very thorough in devising our plan. Agent Iverson was with the Bureau office in D.C. and has been reassigned to me."

Kate watched as the men exchanged glances. "The two of you will move to a small town in Georgia called Haggerty. It has a population of six thousand and is fifteen minutes away from Albany. They recently had an opening for a police chief. Agent Iverson applied for the job and was hired. As far as the townspeople know, you are a young couple moving in because of this change in employment."

This was unexpected. "Agent Iverson and I will be posing as husband and wife?" Kate asked.

"Actually, you will be married." Ignoring her sharp intake of breath, he continued. "Agent Iverson was carefully chosen for many reasons. He shares your faith." Seeing Kate's blank stare, Mr. Evans quickly explained himself. "I mean that you both belong to the Mormon Church. He is familiar with this case since he has provided support and review for the past six months. He knows the players and has been wanting a field assignment." This remark drew a scowl from Agent Iverson.

"Our first line of defense is Agent Roper, who will take your place as Kate Singleton Iverson. Agent Iverson has sold his home in Washington and told friends there that he has been transferred. A rumor was started that he is marrying a Mormon girl as arranged by your Church."

"Our Church doesn't arrange marriages," Kate felt obligated to point out.

"It's just a rumor. And fortunately for this particular situation, people are willing to believe almost anything about your religion."

Kate glanced down at the agent and he frowned back. "Anyone checking on Agent Iverson after he leaves Washington will find that he flew to Chicago, where he married Kate Singleton. Tomorrow he will begin a long-term assignment in Afghanistan with his new partner, Tyler Thornhill."

Kate looked in confusion at Mr. Evans. "But I thought you said that he and I would be going . . ." She tipped her head toward the end of the table, indicating the dark-haired agent.

"You will be with Agent Iverson, but the Bureau records will show that he has gone to Afghanistan with Tyler." Mr. Evans shifted in his chair. "Let me mention here that Tyler volunteered for the assignment to protect you, but we felt that he was too close to the situation and too emotionally involved. After your safety is established beyond any doubt, you and Agent Iverson can have your marriage annulled. If you were to marry Tyler, his feelings for you would complicate matters. Therefore, we must remove him completely from the picture."

Kate nodded her understanding.

"Agent Roper will continue your life. She will go to work at the law firm, attend your church, and shop at the local grocery store. Occasionally she will receive letters and postcards from Afghanistan signed by Agent Iverson. She will be heavily guarded for her own safety. If we are extremely fortunate, there will be no further search for you."

"But you don't expect things to be that easy," Kate guessed.

Mr. Evans shook his head. "No, they will probably discover the switch within a few weeks. What I hope is that we'll have enough time before then to get you established in your new life. It has taken us almost three weeks to set in motion a very complex plan. The FBI has an agent stationed in New York City named Drew Johnson," Mr. Evans pushed a single sheet of paper across the table to Kate. "His wife's name is Niki and they have been married for two years. Her father is a state senator and she has always lived a pampered life."

Kate glanced briefly at the biological data about Niki Johnson and then returned her attention to Mr. Evans. "After their marriage, Agent Johnson tried to maintain the standard of living that his wife had been accustomed to—nice cars, jewelry, expensive clothes, an apartment in Manhattan, furniture, symphony tickets . . ." Kate nodded. She got the picture.

"They lived well beyond their means and at the end of their first year of marriage they were heavily in debt. They couldn't even make minimum payments, so they quietly declared bankruptcy. It only took them a few months to get into financial trouble again. Since he couldn't borrow money the conventional way after the bankruptcy, he got loans with dangerous people. When a random audit of some of the Agency accounts in his department showed a shortage, he was put on leave pending an investigation. His father-in-law, the state senator, wants the Bureau to sweep it all under the rug."

Mr. Evans paused and gave Kate a hard look. "The FBI doesn't buckle to political pressure, but the good senator was in luck. We had been looking around for just such a situation." Mr. Evans smiled slightly, as if pleased by the couple's misfortune, Kate thought. Then he added, "As an extra bonus, Agent Johnson was raised in the Mormon Church, and his wife joined shortly after their marriage."

"We're using their names?" Kate rubbed a finger across the paper in front of her.

"The Johnsons have been very cooperative. They have new identities, new jobs, and a second chance. Of course the senator is taking credit for the whole arrangement. Agents in New York, posing as professional movers, packed all their furniture, clothing, pictures, jewelry, and personal items. Everything was taken to a warehouse in Atlanta and examined. Additions and subtractions were made and the result will be delivered to your new home in Haggerty tomorrow."

"Tomorrow?" Kate whispered.

"The cover story is that the senator pulled strings in Washington and got his errant son-in-law a job as police chief in the small Georgia town. Arrangements were made to sub-lease their apartment and purchase a house in Haggerty. The Johnsons left New York this morning. You and Agent Iverson will arrive in Haggerty tomorrow. You will unpack your boxes, arrange your furniture, and act like any young couple starting life over again. It's understandable that Niki and Drew's marriage might not be a particularly happy one, but marital discord will attract unwanted attention and so . . ." He paused and looked at Kate.

"Unfortunately, Niki Johnson is not pregnant." Mr. Evans frowned at Kate as though this was rather inconsiderate of her to produce this obstacle. "However, we have created a series of doctor visits to make it look as though she was. Your medical records have been sanitized and will be forwarded to an obstetrician in Albany. Agent Iverson has all the information. Do you have any questions?" Kate glanced down the table again at her future husband, then back at Mr. Evans.

"None that I can think of right now." Her feet were throbbing and her head was beginning to ache.

His face relaxed slightly. "I know that you're tired, but we still have a great deal of work to do. We need to go ahead and get your marriage to Agent Iverson recorded. I have the judge waiting if you are ready." Kate nodded and Mr. Evans made a quick phone call.

Kate looked once again at the data sheet on Niki Johnson that Mr. Evans had given to her, but before she had a chance to read past the fact that her new birthday was July 11th, the probate judge was walking through the door. There was no formal ceremony and he didn't say the regular things about love and honor and till death do us part. He just asked Kate and Agent Iverson if they were entering this marriage of their own free will and then had them sign several pieces of paper. Mr. Evans and Agent Thomas added their signatures as witnesses. Once that was completed, the judge left and Mr. Evans walked over to Kate.

"Now it is time for you to actually become Niki Johnson. You will need to give me your jewelry, even your wedding band," he said regretfully. Kate struggled to remove the ring from her swollen finger. "You will go downstairs where your appearance will be altered to resemble Niki as much as possible. Agent Iverson will be taking care of some details while you change. Then Agent Roper will put on your dress and be escorted back to your apartment."

Kate nodded. "I really appreciate all that you are doing for me." The scope of the protection plan was overwhelming.

"Tony was a good man. We don't intend to let him down again."

"Would it be possible for me to talk to Tyler for just a minute before I go?" Kate asked at the door. Mr. Evans frowned but led her down the hall. Tyler looked up hopefully when she walked into Mr. Evans's office.

"I haven't changed my mind," she clarified immediately, crossing the room to stand beside Tony's partner. "I'm going to cooperate with Mr. Evans."

"Why won't you marry me, Kate?" Tyler pleaded. "Tony and I were more than partners, we were friends. Don't you think he would want me to raise his child since he can't? Don't you know that I would do my best to make you happy?"

"I know that you would try, but I don't love you. It would be wrong for me to take advantage of you like that."

"You can't take advantage of me! I know how you feel and I don't care!"

Kate smiled at his tenacity. "Hopefully this will all be over soon and we can resume our friendship. If I ever develop any deeper feelings for you, I'll reconsider. But for now I'm going to do everything Mr. Evans tells me so that I can stay alive."

"You've made up your mind? There's nothing I can say to change it?" he asked.

"I've made my decision."

Tyler pulled her close and whispered into her ear. "I don't like this whole setup, Kate. Something stinks."

"You don't trust Mr. Evans?" she asked in alarm.

"It's not that I don't trust him. I mean, I don't think he's dirty or anything. But he is in charge of this field office and that's like being the king. Tony's undercover operation was particularly odd. Washington was misled about some of the details and there were too many questionable aspects. Tony didn't have a regular reporting schedule, and even though I was his partner, I didn't know much about his cover. No one did. He reported only to Mr. Evans. And now he's dead."

"You don't think Mr. Evans can protect me?"

"I'm not sure that your protection will be the most important thing to him. The operation is what he cares about. He may consider you dispensable, just like Tony."

"He let Tony die?"

"Mr. Evans was the only one who knew what was going on and he didn't pull Tony out when he could have." Tyler leaned his head against her shoulder. "And now they're shipping me off to a place where I'll be completely unable to help you. Your life will depend on him and a stranger." He took a card out of his pocket and slipped it into her hand. "If anything should happen and you feel you're not safe with them, call my parents at this number. They'll know how to contact me, and I'll move heaven and earth to get to you," he told her sincerely.

Kate leaned forward and kissed him gently on the forehead. He closed his eyes as her lips brushed his skin. "You're a good friend, Tyler." She turned to find Mr. Evans watching them closely. His gaze followed her hand as she tucked the card in her purse.

Once they were in the hall, he introduced her to a thin woman named Angela. "She will take you downstairs for your transformation," Mr. Evans said lightly. Eyeing the leather bag she clutched in her hand, he added, "And I'll need your purse."

"I have some vitamins," Kate said reluctantly. She thought about the pictures of Tony that were in her wallet and the number she could use to contact Tyler's parents.

"We'll transfer them into a different bottle with Niki Johnson's name on it," he said firmly as he removed the purse from her hands. "And you are not to contact Tyler Thornhill under any circumstances. The Bureau will provide you with all the protection you need. Involving anyone else is unnecessary and dangerous."

Letting go of her purse was more painful than Kate had expected. It was her last connection with Tony and the past. By giving the worn leather bag to Mr. Evans, she knew that she was relinquishing control to them completely. She wondered if that was wise but didn't resist. Instead she followed the other woman through several hallways and down a flight of stairs. They finally entered a small room where two huge satchels were stacked on a big metal table.

Angela asked Kate to go behind a screen in the corner and take off her dress. "You'll need to remove everything. New clothes will be provided. Put your old clothes in here." Angela handed her a plastic sack.

Behind the screen, Kate found a thick bathrobe folded neatly on a chair. She undressed quickly and put her old clothes in the sack. Angela then took the sack and handed it to someone waiting in the hall. Next, she settled Kate in a chair under a bright fluorescent light and opened the black suitcases.

"This is Niki," she said, handing Kate a black and white photograph of a woman stepping out of a taxi. "It's a surveillance photo and you can't see much, but Niki is about your size. Her eyes are green instead of blue and her hair is more blonde. There's nothing we can do about your eyes, but we're going to change your hairstyle and lighten it by several shades. First, I'm going to give you a little body wave. Get another one in six weeks."

As Angela wrapped Kate's hair in plastic rods, she continued, "You'll also need to have your roots touched up and your hair trimmed every two weeks."

Kate looked startled. "I never get my hair cut that often."

"Maybe not, but Niki Johnson does and she's used to sophisticated New York City stylists, so don't settle for someone who gives permanents in her kitchen."

While the body wave was being timed, Angela painted Kate's nails. Kate asked for a demure pink, but Angela chose blood red. "Niki is flamboyant. You've got to try to think like her. Get your nails done every week and never miss an appointment."

When the manicure was complete, Angela finished Kate's permanent and proceeded to lighten her hair. She then cut Kate's hair to shoulder length and styled it. Studying Kate's reflection in the mirror, Angela gave her a satisfied smile before turning to her makeup case. As she gave Kate a crash course on makeup application, Angela lifted a tray in the makeup case and showed Kate a list. "You don't have to remember all this tonight. I've written it down."

"Thank you," Kate told her gratefully.

Angela walked to a desk in the back of the room and picked up a thick, sealed envelope. "This is the detailed dossier," she said, handing it to Kate. "Study it carefully. It tells you everything you could ever want to know about yourself." Kate stared at the envelope. "I don't know where you're going. They only told me what I needed to know to help you prepare." Kate nodded. She was familiar with the "need to know" concept.

"Now let's get you into some of your new clothes." Angela pulled out a tailored pantsuit. "All your clothes came from New York. The maternity clothes are new, but they've been dry-cleaned a couple of times to make them seem used. After the baby comes, you'll probably be able to wear some of Niki's regular stuff. But if anything doesn't fit, get rid of it and order new things. That's what Niki would do," Angela informed Kate as she buttoned the beautiful outfit. The material was cool and soft against Kate's skin.

Angela held up a large hand mirror and a gasp escaped Kate's lips. Kate Singleton was gone, and a fashionable woman had taken her place. "I barely recognize myself," she breathed, touching her wavy blonde hair.

Angela laughed and handed her an elaborate wedding ring set, a diamond watch, three bracelets, and a pair of gold hoop earrings. "Put on this jewelry," she said. "And here's your purse." She slipped the beige bag over Kate's shoulder. The leather was soft from gentle use but not scuffed and cracked like the one she was passing on to Agent Roper. "Your vitamins are inside. Look through it so you'll be familiar with the contents. It's yours now."

Kate opened the purse and found a small cosmetic bag, a spritz bottle of French perfume, and a prescription bottle with Niki Johnson's name on it. The wallet was large and had several compartments. One section contained pictures of strangers.

"Their names are written on the back. Refer to your dossier to find out their relationship to you," Angela instructed. "When we're finished here, we'll get some pictures so a New York State driver's license can be made for you. It will be delivered with your furniture to Haggerty tomorrow."

Kate nodded and continued searching through the wallet. There was a pad of checks printed in her assumed name.

"Niki has her own checking account. The balance is here." Angela tapped the top of the ledger where a number was written in pencil.

"That says $25,000," Kate pointed out so the error could be corrected. She had a little over $2,500 in her savings account.

Angela laughed. "That's not an error. Agent Roper has your money now. You are Niki Johnson, and her father makes sure she has plenty of spending money."

"You mean I can spend this?" Kate was incredulous.

"You *have* to spend it. I told you, Niki is not thrifty. She needs money for haircuts and perms and manicures. And she's a compulsive shopper."

Kate was daunted. "Do I really have to be just like her?"

"You don't have to be as bad as she was," Angela relented. "They are supposed to be reforming, although no one really expects them to. So a little restraint won't seem suspicious to anyone watching. But don't scrimp, because she wouldn't."

Kate opened another compartment and found over a thousand dollars in cash. At her questioning look, Angela was quick with more instructions.

"Never go anywhere without cash. If your cover were to be blown suddenly, you might need it. Also, the jewelry is very valuable and easy to pawn," Angela added. "Consider it your insurance policy." Kate swallowed at this reference to reality.

Carefully arranged in another section were several credit cards. "Niki had them all. Your accounts basically have no limit. Use them as you need to, and consider it part of your job."

"How can the Bureau afford to give me all this money?" Kate asked and Angela laughed.

"Believe me, you're a bargain. All the expenses will come out of the assets they seize when the criminals are arrested." Angela looked at her watch. "Well, they're going to be wondering where we are." She put both hands on Kate's shoulders and squeezed. "I usually get more time with folks than this. Do you think you're ready?"

Kate shrugged. "I guess I'd better be."

"You're going to do fine. I didn't mean to scare you. I just mentioned the cash and jewelry because, in the end, we're all responsible for ourselves. I want you to be prepared if something goes wrong. Which it won't!" she promised cheerfully. "Now let's get some pictures."

Angela led Kate over to a booth similar to ones she had seen in malls where photographs could be made instantly for a small price.

Once Kate was settled inside, Angela asked her to smile. "And try to look happy," she coaxed. The machine quickly snapped several photographs, then Angela told Kate she could step out of the booth.

"I don't know how I can ever thank you," Kate began, tears gathering in her eyes.

"When all this is over, come back and see me. We'll let Niki take us out to lunch," Angela answered with a smile.

CHAPTER 2

Angela called Agent Thomas and he led Kate back to Mr. Evans's office. Tyler was gone and Agent Iverson was sitting in a chair in front of the desk. He was clean-shaven and looked a little less frightening.

"Well, Niki!" Mr. Evans stood up. "You look lovely!"

Kate avoided Agent Iversons gaze although she knew he was studying her. "I feel ridiculous."

"You'll get used to it in no time," Mr. Evans assured her. "I see you've got the dossier." He glanced at the envelope clutched in her hand. "I apologize for the necessity of taking your personal items, especially the photographs. But Niki Johnson has no connection with Tony. Pictures of him in Agent Roper's purse will strengthen her cover. They could ruin yours."

"We need to go." Agent Iverson rose from his seat.

Kate suddenly felt terrified at the thought of leaving the safety of the federal building. "Agent Thomas will be going to Haggerty, too," Mr. Evans said, indicating the tall black man. "He'll be working as a sewer maintenance man for the Street and Sanitation Department." Kate wrinkled her nose at this announcement, and the Special Agent in Charge smiled. "It's perfect actually. It gives him an excuse to be in all kinds of strange places day or night. Another agent will be posing as his wife; she will eventually be hired as your maid."

Kate shook her head. "I couldn't possibly have a maid."

"It's the only way we can have someone in your house on a daily basis without causing suspicion," Mr. Evans assured her. Kate decided she was too tired to argue. Instead she simply shook hands with

Agent Thomas, then followed Mr. Evans into the hallway.

Niki's bracelets jangled cheerfully as she walked down the stairs. Kate resisted the urge to cry when they reached the back door. She looked through the cloudy glass and saw a dark gray sedan with heavily tinted windows parked near the building. Agent Iverson went out first and unlocked the car so she could climb in quickly. Mr. Evans stood beside her as she adjusted the seatbelt.

"I want to remind you of what I said earlier. You are not to contact anyone. Not your employer, not your mother, and not Tyler Thornhill. Your mother will be given an explanation. I regret the pain this separation will cause you, but any contact would endanger you both. You'll have Drew." He inclined his head toward Agent Iverson. "Agent Thomas and his partner will be close by. And you know my number."

Kate nodded as he closed the passenger door. He stood beside the car, exchanging a few words with the dark-haired agent, then waved and went back into the building. Seconds later Agent Iverson swung into the driver's seat, and they pulled out into the dark streets of downtown Chicago.

Traffic was light as they made their way to the airport. Numb and exhausted, Kate stared out the windshield.

"I guess I should thank you," she said finally when it became obvious that Agent Iverson was not going to initiate any conversation. "You're going to a lot of trouble for me."

He glanced over at her. "I'm not doing anything for you. I'm just following orders," he said bluntly.

Kate swallowed, surprised by his lack of diplomacy. She assumed from his attitude that he wasn't happy about leaving his previous assignment. "It must have been interesting to work in Washington," she tried again.

"Not particularly." He concentrated on the road.

Kate laughed nervously. "We're married and I don't even know your first name. I can't keep calling you Agent Iverson," she pointed out.

"You can call me Drew," he said without looking at her. "You have enough to learn about the Johnsons. There's no point in clouding things with personal information about me."

Kate's lip trembled as she turned away from the agent. She had only asked for his name, and he refused to tell her. His reason for not giving it might be valid, but it wasn't as if she had asked for a detailed biography of his life. Leaning her head against the window, she stared out into the night. "Oh Tony," she thought to herself. "What have you gotten me into?"

* * *

She awoke slowly from a deep sleep. A strange man was saying something over and over. "Niki! Niki!" Agent Iverson called firmly. "You need to wake up. We're at the airport and our plane leaves soon." Dazed, Kate followed her new husband through the almost empty terminal. They walked for what seemed like miles to the gate.

Kate had assumed that they would fly to Atlanta or Albany, but the sign at the boarding area said Chicago to Chattanooga. She waited until they were settled in their seats on the plane before she questioned her escort. "The Johnsons left New York early this morning," he said as he glanced at his watch. "Actually yesterday morning. Two agents met them in Washington and are now driving their car down to Chattanooga. We'll pick it up there and go on into Haggerty."

Kate glanced at the plane tickets in his hand. The names on them were Frank and Sally Beckett. Leaning her head back against the seat, she sighed. "Remind me from time to time who I'm supposed to be. I can't keep track."

Kate slept fitfully during the flight. They reached Chattanooga at two o'clock on Friday morning. The older couple who met them hugged both Kate and Agent Iverson as if they were long-lost relatives. There was no one in the airport waiting area to notice, so Kate wasn't sure why they were making such a production, but she accepted the enthusiastic embraces. After a restroom stop, they claimed an assortment of luggage that Kate had never seen before. With the suitcases loaded on a rented dolly, they rode an empty tram to the short-term parking lot.

The older man told the driver to stop beside a silver minivan with New York license plates and helped Agent Iverson load the suitcases inside. Then the older couple got into the front seats, and Agent Iverson climbed in and sat on the middle bench beside Kate. Space was limited and he was pressed tightly up against her. His arm was rigid with tension, and Kate could tell that he was anxious to put some distance between them.

As they drove, the woman asked about their trip. Kate looked out the window and let her bodyguard answer. The man passed back a map and a set of keys. Several miles down the road they pulled into a gas station. Agent Iverson got out and started filling the tank. The older couple went inside as if they were going to use the restroom. Agent Iverson paid with a credit card at the pump and got into the driver's seat. In a few minutes they were traveling down Interstate 75 toward Albany, alone.

"There should be some pillows and a blanket on the back seat," the agent said as he studied the sparse traffic. "Try to get some sleep. It will be quite a while before we get there."

Kate looked into the back and saw the bedding stacked neatly in one corner. Gratefully she stretched out and fell into a deep, dreamless sleep. She was awakened hours later by Agent Iverson. They were parked in front of a Cracker Barrel.

"I thought you might be hungry," he said as she sat up and tried to get her bearings.

"I'm starving," she admitted. "Am I Niki again or still Sally?" she whispered, leaning close enough to the agent to smell his aftershave.

He pulled back slightly. "You're Niki from now on," he informed her. "You might want to bring your makeup case inside and work on yourself. We'll be in Haggerty soon."

Kate was mildly insulted until she glanced in the rearview mirror. Her new hair was standing up all over her head like a blonde tumbleweed, and she had mascara smeared under both eyes. With an effort, she pulled herself into a semi-standing position. Her feet felt like blocks of concrete and she needed to use the bathroom badly. She hobbled to the ladies' room and repaired her hair and makeup as much as possible without getting out Angela's list. When she joined Agent Iverson at a table in the nonsmoking area, she felt almost human.

He called the waitress over and they ordered. Then they sat in silence, waiting for their breakfast. Kate studied the people around them. Agent Iverson stared at a magazine. Kate's cereal and orange juice were delivered quickly, but the agent had to wait almost twenty minutes for his Country Boy Special. By the time his plate finally arrived, he was too irritated to eat it.

Once they were driving back down the interstate, Kate looked closely at the van's interior. It was nice and roomy, perfect for a growing family. This thought forced a nervous giggle from her. Agent Iverson gave her a sharp look, then turned back to the road.

"Something funny?" he asked humorlessly.

"I've been wanting a van like this ever since I found out I was pregnant, but I couldn't afford one."

"And they say dreams don't come true," he muttered.

She gazed over at the FBI agent. "Have I done something to offend you?" she asked abruptly.

"I barely know you."

"That's what I thought," she concurred. "That I haven't known you long enough to offend you. But you seem to be mad at me."

He appeared startled by her statement. "I'm not mad."

"Of course you are. And none of this is my fault. I'm just doing what Mr. Evans asked me to." She felt so much stronger after a few hours of sleep.

The scowl on the agent's face deepened. "I never said you were to blame for anything."

"Well, if we can't convince the people in this town that we are really Drew and Niki Johnson, then my baby is not safe. So if you can't do this, tell me now and we'll call Mr. Evans. Otherwise, the whole plan will be ruined and it will be *your* fault."

His expression went from startled to angry. "If you're looking for someone to blame for this situation, try your husband."

"Tony?" Kate asked, surprised.

"The renowned Agent Singleton. He didn't do anything by the book. He withheld information, missed check-ins, and went under-cover way too deep. Then, instead of pulling out when things got dangerous, he got himself killed, endangering your life in the process.

Now hundreds of people have been drawn into this elaborate scheme—all because Tony Singleton couldn't follow the rules."

"If you disliked Tony, why did you take this assignment?"

"I wanted something more interesting than reading other people's mail and eavesdropping on phone conversations. But I did not want to get married to a stranger, I did not want to be a small town policeman, and I certainly did not want to be Drew Johnson."

"You don't like him either?" Kate guessed. She was beginning to wonder if Agent Iverson liked anyone.

"I detest him. He's the worst kind of agent."

"Worse than Tony?"

"Much worse."

"What could be worse than an agent who can't follow the rules?" Kate demanded, her voice heavy with sarcasm.

"One who is a member of the Church and a thief," Agent Iverson replied grimly.

Kate inhaled deeply. "Well, maybe if you keep me alive, next time they'll assign you to protect someone important, like a foreign diplomat or even the president."

He scowled at the road. "My assignment doesn't have to be prestigious. I just don't want to write tickets and eat doughnuts for the rest of my life."

"Hopefully we won't be stuck together for the rest of our lives. But, just for the record," she paused and he raised an eyebrow, "I didn't want to marry you either."

His face expressionless, he stared straight ahead, and Kate turned her attention to the dossier on Niki Johnson. According to the stack of papers in her hand, she had a bachelor's degree in modern art and loved classical music. She was a health nut, ate almost no meat, and walked several miles every day. Kate groaned out loud.

"What?" Agent Iverson asked from the driver's seat.

"Niki is a vegetarian and she walks. A lot."

The tension around his mouth seemed to fade. "Drew wears little hankies that match his ties in his suit coat pockets."

"Oh," Kate breathed.

"And this haircut." He ran a hand across his head.

"Actually, I like your hair." Kate studied him carefully. It was short all around the bottom and long on top, parted on the side and moussed.

"It's so . . . finicky. I usually get my hair cut every couple of months. This thing has to be trimmed every two weeks," he reported dourly.

"I'll make you an appointment when I set one up to have my roots done."

"Your roots?" Agent Iverson looked bewildered.

She touched her hair. "In case you've forgotten, this color isn't natural. As my own hair starts growing out, I'll need to get my roots touched up. Angela said to find a hairdresser right away and set up an appointment. Nails too."

Agent Iverson exhaled deeply. "I guess you'll need to make me one of each."

"You want a manicure?" It was Kate's turn to be shocked.

The agent held up his hand for her inspection. "Drew gets his nails trimmed and buffed once a week."

Kate laughed and it felt good. "I think we just had a civilized conversation."

They were quiet as they passed a sign that read *Haggerty City Limits,* then Agent Iverson spoke up. "You're right. We can't be at odds with each other. This is a small place, and we're going to be the talk of the town for a while as it is. We don't need to draw any more attention than necessary. I'm sorry if I've been rude."

"I accept," Kate said generously. "And who knows. After a few weeks in a small town, Drew might decide he doesn't like those little hankies so much anymore. Or Niki might even lose them in the wash."

"Drew's suits cost several thousand dollars each. I don't think you're supposed to throw them in the washer," he said dryly.

"I'll bet Niki doesn't know that," Kate predicted. Looking out her window, Kate admired the houses scattered along the roadside, separated from each other by planted fields and pastures. Everything looked so peaceful and serene. It was hard to imagine that danger could be lurking around any tranquil corner.

Finally they came to a four-way stop facing a lovely town square complete with a fountain, park benches, and rose-covered arbors at each corner. There were three more identical intersections around the square. When she saw the library, a drug store, and an appliance repair shop, Kate realized that this was the business district of Haggerty.

"There's City Hall." Agent Iverson pointed out an old, two-story brick building with marble steps and four white columns. "And this lovely edifice is the Haggerty police station." He stopped in front of a short cinder-block building completely without grace or style. "It was built in the 1960s and hasn't seen a drop of paint since." He smiled at her for the first time. His smile so transformed his face that Kate was too stunned to pay much attention as he waved a hand toward the small antique furniture gallery, ladies clothing boutique, and auto parts shop.

"No grocery store?" Kate composed herself enough to ask.

"There's a Wal-Mart SuperCenter about a mile out of town and a convenience store straight down Walnut Street for emergencies."

Kate was surprised by his knowledge of the area. "How many times have you been here?"

"Only once to interview for the police chief's job, but Mr. Evans gave me some maps to study. When they notified me that I'd been hired, an agent posing as the Senator's secretary flew down to pick out our house and handle all the details. She brought back the paperwork, and we closed the deal in D.C."

"Didn't people think that was odd?"

"These people think everything about Drew is odd. He's from New York, he's been kicked out of the FBI, he's a Mormon."

"He wears little matching hankies in his suit pockets and has a fussy haircut," Kate provided helpfully.

"I used your pregnancy as an excuse," he retorted, and Kate decided to make it her mission in life to trick him into moments of good humor.

By this time they had circled the Town Square. Agent Iverson turned onto Maple Street and drove up two blocks. He pulled to the curb in front of an old home with gables, a turret, gingerbread lattice-work, and a wrap-around porch. It also had peeling paint and crooked shutters. The yard was a jungle.

"Here we are," he announced unnecessarily.

Kate looked up in wonder. "It's not at all what I expected."

"We were supposed to get a new house in a subdivision west of town, but the agent pretending to be the Senator's secretary said that none of those houses would be ready in time." He stared at their new home in disgust. "She and I dated for a while, and it didn't end friendly. That may have had something to do with us getting a fixer-upper."

Kate studied the house and tried to fathom Agent Iverson with a social life. "It's a neat old place," she said finally. "It just needs some work."

"You're about to have a baby, and I'll be trying to get settled into a new job. This is not a good time for us to take on a home repair project of this magnitude," he grumbled.

"I think it has character." Kate stared wistfully at the big old house.

He sighed with resignation. "As I recall from the paperwork, it was built in the early 1900s and has been vacant for almost ten years. A guy from Macon bought it a couple of years ago, hoping he could fix it up and sell it to some yuppies willing to commute to Albany. He put a new roof on, then replaced the old plumbing and electrical wiring before he ran out of money. He tried to unload it but couldn't find a buyer. We got it for almost nothing," the agent said as he stepped out of the van.

Kate waited patiently for him to come around and open her door. As her feet touched the ground, she heard a sound from the direction of their new home. She looked up to see an elderly woman standing on their front porch. The screen door slammed shut behind her, which seemed to suggest that she had just come out of their house.

"Helloooo!" she called and waved. "You must be the Johnsons." She walked forward to the edge of the porch. "I'm Eugenia Atkins, but just call me Miss Eugenia. Everybody does." The woman was fairly tall and solidly built. Her white hair looked like she had raked it back from her face with her fingers. As they approached the porch, Kate could see that it was held in a loose bun at the back of her head with an assortment of rusty bobbypins.

"I'm Drew and this is my wife Niki," Agent Iverson said smoothly. Kate held her breath, half expecting the woman to point her finger and scream, "Liar!"

But instead the older woman merely held out her hand to Kate. "You poor dear! You must be exhausted after that long drive. I live next door," she said, pointing toward a white house surrounded by spectacular flowers. "When I heard that you were coming today, I couldn't believe my ears! What man in his right mind would bring his pregnant wife to this house?" She gave Agent Iverson a stern glance.

"I didn't have any choice. I start work on Monday," he defended himself stiffly.

"Well, be that as it may, I felt a Christian obligation to take matters into my own hands. Go ahead and get your luggage. I'll take Niki inside," the woman instructed. The entryway was spacious with a hardwood floor, an antique chandelier, and water-stained wallpaper. "When the Rileys built this house, it was a showplace," she said as they stepped into a big, open room. "Their daughter, Miss Imogene Riley, was my piano teacher. This is the living room, and her baby grand piano sat right here." Miss Eugenia pointed to a corner by the front windows.

"After her parents died, the house fell into disrepair. Miss Imogene didn't mean to neglect things, but money was a problem and she was easily distracted. Since she was a spinster, there were no heirs to dispose of the property when she died. Finally a speculator got it for the back taxes." Miss Eugenia shook her head. "This is a good, well-built house, but the young people today want one of those new, cookie-cutter houses out on Highway 11. They think that being closer to Albany and the Wal-Mart is better than being in town." The older woman obviously didn't share their opinion.

Agent Iverson came in with a load of suitcases. "I'm giving Niki a tour. I hope you don't mind," she told him as she walked through a set of French doors into the dining room without waiting for a reply. "That man who bought it did have the floors refinished," Miss Eugenia pointed out and Kate admired the glowing wood. "You don't find floors like this anymore. Solid oak."

They left the dining room and entered a small area with cupboards on both sides that reached from the floor to the ceiling. "This is the butler's pantry. Nowadays most people use it for extra storage." They stepped onto a bare wood subfloor as they walked into the kitchen. The wallpaper had been pulled off and several patches of new sheet rock dotted the room. Beautiful glass and cherry wood cabinets were in place above, but old yellow-flecked countertops and cupboards with chipped light green paint surrounded the bottom.

The counters were covered with casserole dishes, pie plates, and china platters wrapped in aluminum foil. "The matching bottom cabinets are in the storage shed out back. The contractor bought them but never had them installed. You'll have to buy new counters and a sink. The kitchen hasn't been remodeled since the fifties." Miss Eugenia touched a crack in the old veneer. "But it's clean. A few of your neighbors worked all day yesterday."

"That was so kind of you," Kate began. "And what is all this stuff?" She pulled back the foil from a white dish.

Miss Eugenia laughed. "Oh, everybody just wanted to welcome you to Haggerty. Most of it will freeze." She leaned forward. "The fruit salad in that pink bowl?" Kate glanced down the counter and nodded. "That's from Miriam Long. She doesn't keep a clean kitchen, so you may want to discard it." Kate looked at the older woman in surprise. "Cats," she whispered.

Surveying the assortment of dishes, Miss Eugenia continued, "There are little notes on each dish that tell you who made them and how they should be served. I've made a list of everything that's been delivered so far." She waved toward a piece of notebook paper on the counter. "You'll want to add other things to the list as they arrive so you can write thank-you notes later." Kate nodded, her head spinning. "As you eat things, Miss Polly next door will take dishes back to the Baptists, and I'll return things to the Methodists."

Miss Eugenia placed her hand against the side of a large pan. "Your furniture is being delivered today?"

"Yes, I believe so." Kate looked toward the front of the house, willing Agent Iverson to appear.

"Good. These things need to be refrigerated," Miss Eugenia said, walking out of the kitchen as Kate followed. Pointing at the connections hanging from the wall, Miss Eugenia announced, "This is the laundry room. The washer and dryer go there. And this door leads to the back porch, but I wouldn't recommend that you walk on that wood. It's mostly rotten," she warned as Kate glanced out the window.

They left the laundry room through a different door and went down a hallway on the other side of the house. "Old Mr. Riley used this room as an office." She pointed toward a closed door to their left. "We didn't clean in there because it's locked." She paused as if she expected Kate to offer an explanation for this. When Kate failed to respond, she turned to the right.

"The speculator was going to put what he called a 'powder room' in here." Miss Eugenia pushed open a door under the stairs. "When the Rileys lived here, it was a closet." Kate glanced in and saw unfinished sheet-rock walls, a sink, a toilet, and a tile floor in the small space. "In the old days, this was a guest bedroom," Miss Eugenia explained as they walked by a good-sized room across from the living room. "You could use it as a den or a family room."

They heard voices on the front porch and went out to find Agent Iverson talking to a man dressed in white coveralls. A moving van was parked in the gravel driveway. "Movers are here," he said unnecessarily.

"Tell them to bring in the kitchen appliances first. We have pounds of food about to ruin," Miss Eugenia instructed the two men. Then she turned and walked to the back of the house.

Kate only had time to give the agent a wide-eyed look before a man came through the door carrying an overstuffed leather chair. "In there, I guess," she told the man, pointing toward the one-time guest room that her new neighbor had said would make a good den.

Agent Iverson stepped close to her. "There's a big bedroom upstairs with an adjoining room. The little room would make a good nursery. So when you see anything labeled 'master bedroom furniture,' tell the movers to put it there." Just then a mover came in carrying part of a computer system. "That goes in here," the agent said as he walked down the hall toward the office and produced a key.

Kate stood by the door and watched as various things were brought inside. She heard Miss Eugenia from the back instructing the men not to scratch the floors. The master bedroom furniture was Swedish pine. It was lovely and sturdy but looked completely out of place in the old house. The black lacquer dining room set was even worse. The upholstered living room furniture was white and the tables were painted iron and glass. Kate arranged everything as logically as possible in the big room, leaving the corner where the Rileys' piano had been empty. There was an extra bedroom suite that Agent Iverson directed the men to set up in the room across the hall from the master bedroom. At lunchtime Miss Eugenia insisted that everyone stop for boiled ham sandwiches and pecan pie.

Kate saw that Miss Eugenia had the kitchen in good order. The wooden table and chairs had been arranged near the window on the far side of the room. Empty boxes were stacked by the door, the appliances were all in place, and the casseroles had disappeared. Kate noted that the energy use disclosure statements were still attached to the appliances, and when she opened the refrigerator, her suspicions were confirmed. It was brand new and full of assorted foil-covered dishes.

"Mercy, these appliances must have cost the earth," Miss Eugenia said from behind her.

"The ones at our apartment were built in," was the best excuse she could come up with.

Miss Eugenia had fixed a plate for everyone with a sandwich, sliced tomatoes, and deviled eggs. She had also poured large glasses of iced tea. Kate dumped hers and Agent Iverson's back into the plastic pitcher, explaining that they didn't drink tea.

"You don't drink tea?" Miss Eugenia demanded. "Then what in the world do you drink?"

"Water, milk, Kool-aid," Kate said. "Anything without caffeine."

"Then you don't drink coffee either?" Miss Eugenia put a hand to her chest.

Kate shook her head.

"I declare," Miss Eugenia exclaimed. "And this is because you're Mormon?" the woman clarified and Kate nodded. "I don't really know anything at all about your church. You don't wrestle snakes or anything like that, do you?"

"Oh no!" Kate worked hard to control a laugh.

Miss Eugenia didn't smile, however. "Good. That kind of thing is very dangerous," she said quite seriously.

After lunch Miss Eugenia washed the dishes by hand in the old sink and then continued unpacking boxes. Kate tried to help, but the older woman insisted that she sit down in one of the kitchen chairs and prop up her feet. Occasionally she would ask Kate's opinion on the placement of various items, but mostly she just put things where she wanted to.

The movers left at three o'clock and Agent Iverson convinced Miss Eugenia to go home and rest. "You've worked yourself to death for us already," he told her as they walked to the back door.

"You need groceries," she pointed out.

"Yes, ma'am. We'll go to Wal-Mart as soon as I take these boxes to the alley."

Miss Eugenia nodded doubtfully. "The telephones are working. I've left my number on the refrigerator if you need me."

"Thank you for everything," Kate said as she gingerly put weight on her feet.

Agent Iverson almost had Miss Eugenia out the door when she thought of something else. "I know a handyman who can help with painting and wallpapering. He's old, but he does good work. His name is Ellis Harper and I'll call him if you'd like." Kate heard the agent accept her offer and then close the door firmly behind her.

When he walked back in, she had to laugh at the look on his face. "I thought we would never get rid of her," he whispered, checking over his shoulder as if he expected to find that she had sneaked back in.

"She was very helpful," Kate replied, tempering his remark.

"Yeah, I never would have thought of going to the grocery store," he muttered. "I've got to get the computer assembled." He turned toward the office. "That's how I'll communicate with Chicago," he added. "It shouldn't take long, then we'll go shopping."

Kate stood in the office doorway as he unpacked a monitor from the original box and set it on a black metal computer desk. The room was dark and creepy. Cobwebs laced the bookshelves, and the ancient drapes were rotten and hanging at crazy angles off their rusted metal rods. When Agent Iverson pulled a swivel chair out of a large box, he rolled it over to her. She sat down and watched him work.

When he plugged in the system, the screen glowed ominously in the dim room, reminding Kate of the sinister reasons for their move to Haggerty. Agent Iverson knelt down in front of the monitor and entered several numbers. He signed onto the Internet and ran through a series of chat rooms.

"Is that how you contact Mr. Evans?" Kate asked.

He looked over at her with a startled expression, as if he had forgotten her presence. Then he twisted, blocking the screen from her view with his body. "The less you know about that, the better," he answered sharply.

She stood and put the chair between them. "Let me know when you're ready to go to the store." She pushed the chair toward him and went upstairs.

She found the master bedroom filled with Swedish pine furniture and scarcely had time to lay down on the bare mattress before he appeared in her doorway. "I didn't mean to . . ."

Kate looked at him with accusing eyes. "You yelled at me."

"I didn't yell."

"Yes you did."

He rubbed the back of his head. "You surprised me," he admitted reluctantly. "And it would be dangerous for you to know the contact procedures."

Kate swung her feet over the side of the bed and started buckling her sandals. "You don't have to tell me all your little spy secrets. Just don't scream at me."

The agent scowled. "My little spy secrets just might keep you alive," he pointed out.

"Yeah, they worked great for Tony," Kate said with a disrespectful smirk as she brushed past him and walked downstairs.

* * *

She spoke to the agent only when absolutely necessary during their shopping trip, but by the time they got home, Kate was too exhausted to fight. She forced herself to eat the chicken salad sandwich that Agent Iverson prepared for her and then went upstairs. The agent followed close behind her.

"These are your things." He pointed toward an expensive set of luggage in the master bedroom. "I'll help you get some sheets on your bed," he offered, opening a box labeled *linens*.

"I can manage," Kate said stiffly, but he ignored her. In seconds he had located a matching set of light green sheets and they worked on opposite sides to spread them over the mattress.

"If you need me, I'm right across the hall." She gave him a weary nod and he closed the door, leaving her alone in the big room.

She was pleased to find that the master bathroom had been mostly remodeled. The large garden tub was inviting, but she was afraid that getting out of it might be a problem. Instead, she took a shower in the separate glass stall. Feeling slightly refreshed, she put on a pale blue nightgown and crawled between the cool cotton sheets.

The baby shifted and Kate cradled her unborn child, grateful for the company. Closing her eyes, Kate thought of Tony. It was his fault that she was living in a strange house, hiding from murderers and married to a man who wouldn't even tell her his first name. She wanted to be mad at Tony but couldn't muster the energy. So she burrowed into the soft pillow and fell into an exhausted sleep.

CHAPTER 3

The next morning Kate woke up refreshed but disoriented. It took her a few seconds to remember where she was and why. When the memories rushed back, she shivered under the thick comforter and pressed her face against the goose-down pillows. But the sound of a door slamming downstairs impelled her to get up. After making the bed, she spread open all four suitcases at once and filled the dresser drawers.

She unpacked the maternity clothes and started to hang them in her closet. Then she thought, *What would Niki do?* and she promptly took the clothes down, placing them in a pile on the end of the bed to be sent to the dry cleaners. One seersucker sundress had managed to avoid wrinkling for the most part, so she put it on.

Several of the boxes stacked against the wall under the windows contained clothes as well. Most were outfits that she couldn't wear until after the baby was born so she didn't bother to unpack them. She opened another box and removed a sterling silver brush and mirror set, some knick-knacks, and several family photos. Her hand trembled as she pulled out a computer-generated wedding photograph of herself and Agent Iverson, both smiling happily.

Shaken by the picture, she put it on the nightstand beside the bed. Then she closed the empty suitcases and stowed them in the closet along with the boxes full of clothes. Downstairs she found Agent Iverson eating cereal in the kitchen. Miss Eugenia was sitting across the table from him. Sighing, Kate sat down beside her.

"Well, good morning, Sleeping Beauty," her neighbor greeted her.

"I've been up," Kate defended herself. "I was unpacking." She looked down to see some old photographs lying on the table. "What are those?"

"Pictures taken in this house years ago!" Miss Eugenia proclaimed proudly. "Drew said that you're going to do some extensive renovations, and I'm hoping that you can restore the house to its original grandeur. These pictures should give you an idea of what it looked like in 1935." She pointed to a small girl sitting in a row with several other children. "That's me." She passed the pictures to Kate. A baby grand piano was clearly visible in the background.

"My sister Annabelle just built a house over on Highway 11," Miss Eugenia continued. "She got her wallpaper and paint from a little shop in Albany. The owner is a local girl and she's a real interior decorator. Annabelle says they can match any wallpaper pattern. You can also get blinds, curtains, and carpet. And if you order everything through her shop, the girl won't charge for her interior decorating services."

Before Kate could respond, an elderly man came in through the back door without knocking and shuffled into the kitchen. He was tall and thin, and his white hair looked like he'd forgotten to comb it. Miss Eugenia introduced him as Ellis Harper and then asked where they wanted him to start.

"We haven't really had a chance to talk about that yet," Agent Iverson said slowly. "But I guess the nursery should be our first priority."

Kate felt the blood rush to her face as Miss Eugenia turned to her. "Of course it should. How much longer do you have?"

"Six weeks," Kate and Agent Iverson said in unison.

"You don't say! Do you have a doctor in Albany?" she wanted to know.

"The doctor from New York recommended a Dr. Tremayne. Niki's supposed to call on Monday for an appointment," Agent Iverson answered.

Miss Eugenia waved her hand. "Never heard of him. But it's been years since I needed an obstetrician!"

"How many children do you have?" Kate asked, trying to be conversational.

Miss Eugenia shook her head. "I had several miscarriages during the early years of my marriage. Finally I carried one baby to term, but she was stillborn."

"I'm so sorry." Kate sincerely regretted her innocent question.

"Well, it was a long time ago," Miss Eugenia responded simply. Then she said she had to be on her way since there was a meeting of the Haggerty Garden Association in an hour. Kate asked directions to the closest dry cleaners and Miss Eugenia offered to drop their clothes off on the way to her meeting.

Kate went upstairs and returned with her arms full of designer maternity clothes. "These don't look so bad to me." Miss Eugenia looked closely at the clothing. "A warm iron would take out the wrinkles."

Kate gave her best impression of a disdainful look. "I'd rather have them done professionally."

Miss Eugenia raised an eyebrow. "I do declare. Well, you might want to keep at least one dress if you're planning to go to church tomorrow. We only have one cleaners here in Haggerty, and they can't turn things around in an hour like the city places do." She watched as Kate dug through the pile and pulled out a pale blue dress that she hoped would fit. "You need to stop by the cleaners soon and give them all your preferences," Miss Eugenia continued as Agent Iverson picked up the clothes to take to her car. Kate stared at her blankly. "Like whether you want them to sew on loose buttons and what kind of starch the Chief wants in his uniforms."

Kate turned helpless eyes to the agent, who spoke for her, "Heavy starch in this humidity." She knew his charming smile was intended to cover for her ignorance.

Miss Eugenia watched Kate suspiciously as she turned toward the door. "Just go by there one day soon."

Feeling that she needed to redeem herself, Kate followed. "We also need to find a hairdresser. Drew and I used the same salon in New York." Miss Eugenia swung her eyes to examine the new police chief, but he refused to meet her gaze.

"The preacher's wife goes to some place in Albany. I'll ask her for the name tomorrow," Miss Eugenia offered at last.

Agent Iverson ran a hand across his stylish hair. "Driving into Albany will be a lot of trouble. I might just get it cut off," he said hopefully.

"Oh, Drew, I love your hair," Kate protested, and his mouth tightened with irritation. After accompanying Miss Eugenia to the door, Agent Iverson came back and asked why she made that remark about his hair. "It sounded like something Niki would say," she told him with relish.

They went upstairs to the nursery where Ellis Harper had set up a ladder and was looking around like he'd never seen walls before. Kate gave the agent a worried glance, then walked over to the large, curved window that was part of the turret and sat on the built-in seat. The woodwork in the room was chipped and scarred.

"You folks picked out your wallpaper and paint for this room yet?" he asked.

"Not yet," Agent Iverson answered.

"Well, for today I'll just scrape loose paint and patch. It'll need a primer coat before we repaint the woodwork anyway," he mumbled.

There was a knock on the front door and the Johnsons descended the stairs together. Through the rusty screen, Kate could see a plump, elderly lady. She was wearing a loud floral print dress with a deep ruffle around the neckline and her hands were clutching a pie plate. "Welcome to Haggerty!" she exclaimed breathlessly as Kate opened the screen door. "I'm your neighbor on the other side, Pauline Kirby, but folks call me Miss Polly."

"I'm Niki and this is Drew." Kate found that the lie was getting easier.

"It's a pleasure to meet you," the older woman told Kate. "Chief." She lowered her lashes and blinked, blushing like a young girl.

"It's nice to see you again, Miss Polly." The agent gave her a charming smile. "We met when I came to interview for my job," he explained to Kate briefly.

"I made you a lemon meringue pie." She lifted the plate for their inspection.

"That was nice of you." Agent Iverson took the pie from her chubby hands, and she peered over his shoulder into the room beyond. "Would you like to come in?" he offered, following her gaze.

Within seconds, she was in the den. "I've never seen furniture from New York before," she explained with a nervous laugh.

Kate looked at the furniture and boxes piled haphazardly in the middle of the room, then turned back to their neighbor. "I wish you hadn't gone to the trouble to make us anything to eat. Our refrigerator is full already."

Miss Polly's mouth turned down at the corners. "No one makes lemon meringue pie like I do," she said piteously.

"I've got a sudden urge to try some." Agent Iverson stepped between the two women. He took Miss Polly's arm and led her toward the kitchen. "Would you like a piece, Niki?" he asked, giving her a pleading look. Against her better judgment, Kate followed.

The pie was wonderful, and Miss Polly turned out to be a font of knowledge. She described the people who lived on Maple Street and told them who was Methodist and who was Baptist.

"Not that it really matters, except at revival time!" she said with her irritating little giggle. Then she explained that the former police chief had retired so that he could run for mayor in November. "Mayor Witherspoon has been in office for fourteen years, so he will be hard to unseat. But if anyone can do it, Booster McMillan can." Kate couldn't imagine voting for anyone named "Booster," but she kept that opinion to herself.

Miss Polly said that the Methodists had a new preacher from Biloxi whose wife obviously dyed her hair. At this statement, Miss Polly's eyes strayed to Kate's bleached head, and the older woman blushed crimson. Standing abruptly, she invited them to come to church with her and the Baptists on Sunday. Agent Iverson declined, saying they would attend the Mormon Church in Albany. Miss Polly's mouth formed a perfect circle.

"Is that one of those churches where people speak in tongues and roll around on the floor?" she asked breathlessly.

"No. And we don't wrestle snakes either," Kate anticipated her next question. After they had walked Miss Polly to the front and firmly closed the door behind her, Kate rolled her eyes. "And I thought Miss Eugenia was nosy!"

"Miss Polly is in a league of her own," Agent Iverson agreed, watching through the screen as Pauline Kirby walked across the street and knocked on the door of the blue house directly in front of them. Turning to Kate, he sighed. "I guess we'd better start arranging this mess." He gestured toward the den.

Kate followed him and surveyed the room from the doorway. There was a large couch, a recliner, a big-screen television, and a sectional entertainment center. Various pieces of electronic equipment were stacked to one side along with two end tables, a coffee table, a bamboo chair, assorted boxes, and a three-foot statue of a naked man holding a fishing pole. He picked up the statue.

"I think the first step will be to put this fellow in the closet." Kate smiled and pulled the bamboo chair into the doorway and propped her feet on a box. "The couch here?" he asked, indicating the wall that the den shared with the spooky office.

"I guess," Kate said and he pushed the couch into place. "The television will have to go there." She pointed toward the large space between the windows that overlooked the front porch. Agent Iverson wiggled the heavy wood sections of the entertainment center to the designated spot. By the time he had the television centered in the middle cabinet, sweat was dripping off his face.

"Do you want me to ask Ellis to come help?" Kate offered.

"I'm sure he could lift at least a pound," he snorted, giving her a disgusted look. Kate laughed and settled back in her chair. "What about this recliner?" he demanded. Kate had him try three different locations before she was satisfied. "Are you doing this on purpose?" he asked suspiciously.

"Of course not. I just want everything to look nice." Kate stood and pushed the bamboo chair into an empty corner, then placed the end tables while he rolled out an area rug. They each took a side of the coffee table and put it in front of the couch. While Agent Iverson tried to connect the television to the VCR and stereo, Kate dug through boxes. She found accent pillows for the couch and rearranged them several times. Then she scattered magazines addressed to Niki in New York on the coffee table.

The agent finished with the television, but the reception was poor. He said he'd call to have cable installed on Monday. Then he opened a box of books and started filling the bookcase section of the entertainment center. When he came across a Book of Mormon, he held it up for her inspection. "At least they had a copy," Kate defended the Johnsons.

"Yeah, and it looks like they wore it out, reading and studying." The book appeared to be brand new and it was unlikely that Drew Johnson or his wife had ever even turned one page. Agent Iverson put it on the shelf.

Kate unwrapped pictures and photographs and vases and candy dishes. In one box she found a small painting of three undressed women standing in a grocery store line. "What is it they had with naked people?" Kate whispered as she showed him the portrait.

The agent shrugged. "Maybe naked is chic in New York. I'll put that with the fisherman." Kate handed him the picture and continued unpacking.

"I hate to say this," she said as she pulled a long, black onyx cylinder bud vase from a box. "But the Johnsons had awful taste." Agent Iverson murmured his agreement as he lined books up precisely by size. Kate pulled out a small figurine made of rusty cast iron. "Maybe we can have a yard sale," she suggested as she set the ugly piece on the bookshelf.

"I don't think Niki does yard sales." His tone was almost friendly as he glanced down at her. Then his expression changed. "What's that?" He pointed to the little statue.

She looked back at the entertainment center. "Twisted metal?"

"I think it might be another naked person," Agent Iverson said awkwardly.

Intrigued by his discomfort, Kate studied the figure carefully. "Really? I don't see it." She tilted her head to get a different perspective. "Male or female?"

The agent reached for the object in question. "Let's put it up, just in case."

Kate took a nap after lunch, and when she woke up, he suggested they take a walk around the neighborhood.

"It's what Niki would do," he assured her as she stuffed her swollen feet into designer tennis shoes.

They met several more of their neighbors as they strolled up and down the quiet street. Everyone was old except for one young couple three blocks down and across the street. They said they had bought their house cheap and intended to fix it up. Kate was pleased to see that someone in the younger generation could appreciate the beauty and charm of the older homes.

"Oh, yes," the wife, a court reporter, said cheerfully. "We'll make improvements and sell it, then we can buy a new house out on Highway 11."

After dinner, Agent Iverson went into the den to watch a video, and Kate got ready for bed. She woke up suddenly in the early hours of the morning, trembling with apprehension. She listened carefully, trying to determine what had awakened her. Creeping to the window, she looked out at the moonlit night. There were no strangers lurking at the street corner, no gunmen on the windowsill. When she opened the door of her room, she could identify the faint sounds of the television downstairs. Then she climbed in bed and drifted back to sleep, comforted by the knowledge that Agent Iverson was keeping watch.

* * *

On Sunday morning Agent Iverson woke Kate up by knocking on her door. "We need to leave in an hour," he said through the hundred-year-old wood.

Kate took a shower, then fixed her hair and applied makeup by following the instructions Angela had written down for her. The blue dress was a little short, but otherwise fit perfectly. Agent Iverson was wearing a gorgeous charcoal gray suit. His tie was unquestionably silk and a matching little hanky peeked smartly from his breast pocket. Kate wondered vaguely if the real Drew Johnson had ever looked so good in the same outfit.

The agent glanced up at her when he heard her walk in and after a quick perusal, his face darkened. "I know the dress is a little short, but all the others are at the dry cleaners," Kate explained. "And I don't usually wear this much makeup or jewelry, but Angela said Niki always does," she continued breathlessly, dismayed by his negative reaction to her appearance.

"It's okay," he said, adjusting his expression.

"You don't think I'll shock people at church?" She was uneasy now.

He shrugged. "Probably. But we're not supposed to be good Mormons anyway."

Kate tugged at her skirt all the way into Albany. As he parked along the side of the church, Agent Iverson assured her that her dress was fine.

"I was just surprised," he explained as he helped her out of the van. "You looked different this morning."

"Different?" Kate was still uncertain.

"Better," he admitted grudgingly.

She exhaled deeply. "The way you stared at me, I thought I looked like a hooker."

He shook his head in despair as they walked into the chapel. The meeting had begun and the only available seats were on the front row. Kate felt terribly conspicuous when she realized that the man standing at the pulpit was waiting for them to sit before he said the opening prayer.

"I feel like everyone is staring at us," she hissed after the "Amen."

"They are," he responded rigidly. After sacrament meeting, the bishop came up to them to introduce himself as Bishop Sterling and ask if they were visitors. Agent Iverson introduced Kate and said that they were new members of the ward. "I thought our membership records had been sent. I'm surprised you haven't received them." A crease of worry formed between the agent's dark brown eyes.

Bishop Sterling blushed. "Oh, yes. I recognize the names. We received your records and I called your former bishop. And, well . . . we didn't really expect to see you."

It was the agent's turn to be embarrassed, but Kate stepped in quickly. "With our move and the baby coming, we've decided to get involved in church again."

The bishop smiled. "Well, we're very glad to have you. The Gospel Essentials class meets back by the nursery." The bishop led them around to a small classroom where two sets of missionaries and an investigator were already sitting in the available seats. The bishop got folding chairs from another room, and Agent Iverson opened them up in front of the door.

The lesson was on faith and Kate thought it was well presented, but Agent Iverson sat in sullen silence throughout the class. Afterwards, the elders quorum president found them in the hallway and invited Agent Iverson to priesthood.

"I understand that you have been a prospective elder for eleven years," the man said and the agent's face darkened again. Seeing this, the man hastened to add, "I didn't mean to offend you. I was just hoping that we could help you prepare to receive the Melchizedek priesthood."

When they got into the van to drive back home, Agent Iverson stared ahead in angry silence. Kate finally had to speak. "So, what are you mad about now?"

"I was ordained an elder when I was nineteen and served a mission in Argentina. But because of Drew Johnson, I have to pretend like I never made it past the office of a teacher."

"That's too bad," Kate said sympathetically, hoping to assuage his anger.

"They think that I haven't been a full tithe payer a single year in my entire life. According to my records, the only calling I've ever held was secretary to the deacons quorum, and I have to sit in the Gospel Essentials class hearing lessons I learned when I was ten years old."

"Faith is a pretty basic gospel principle," Kate pointed out. "It won't hurt you to review a little. Besides, they probably didn't solve any deep mysteries in the Gospel Doctrine class."

He gave her a surly look. "It just galls me to have to act like a slacker," he grumbled.

"You're proud of your righteousness!" Kate accused.

"What do you mean by that? I should be proud that I'm righteous!" he responded.

Kate's eyes narrowed. "I would have thought that someone as righteous as you are would remember that the Book of Mormon warns repeatedly against pride, saying that it leads to destruction. But if you didn't feel that you were stretched spiritually at church today, maybe you can answer a couple of questions for me now." He nodded warily. "Where are the ten tribes?"

"What do you mean by 'where'?"

"I mean in what location could they be found, say, right this minute."

"I think they are on the earth, scattered in with everyone else," he said finally.

"I guess that is the popular theory. My great-uncle believes that they were literally taken to the land northward, which could be a hidden part of the earth but could easily be another planet. After all, the ten tribes would amount to millions of people by now. My great-uncle also believes that they have their own scriptures and prophets, and that they will return as a group after the millennium begins."

"That's a dramatic theory," Agent Iverson answered thoughtfully.

"Then there is the question of whether you pay your tithing on your gross or net income."

"Gross," he replied promptly.

"What about gifts?"

"Pay ten percent of any cash you receive."

"But what if my mother gives me a coat for Christmas? Should I ask her how much it cost and pay ten percent of that?"

"When you nitpick, you lose the spirit of the law."

"Oh, but if you don't pay ten percent of your increase annually, then you aren't a full tithe payer, Drew."

"So, what's your point?" he asked as they passed the city limits sign.

"My point is that you aren't too spiritual to learn more about faith, the Lord knows you pay your tithing, and you don't have the answers to every gospel question."

"Thank you, Sister Johnson, eight months pregnant and wearing a miniskirt to church," he said derisively as they pulled into their driveway.

Kate flushed and tugged on the hem of her dress, but before she could respond, Miss Polly was knocking on the windshield. Agent Iverson rolled down his window, and she invited them to Sunday dinner. Since there was no way to graciously decline, they accepted. Miss Polly smiled, taking the police chief's arm as they walked over to her house. Kate trudged resentfully behind them.

Dinner was a veritable feast of fried chicken, creamed potatoes, congealed salad, steamed asparagus, glorified brownies, and Italian cream cake. The food was so good that Kate could almost overlook the presence of the insufferable Baptist preacher who was also a guest. He baited them with questions, regaled them with his dubious wisdom, and misquoted New Testament scriptures throughout the meal. During his second piece of cake, he asked if they had been saved.

"We believe that the Atonement of Jesus Christ saved all men from eternal damnation," Agent Iverson responded calmly.

"Yet you think that you can earn a place in heaven with good works." The man's eyes narrowed with hostility.

"We believe that righteous living and adherence to the Lord's commandments are necessary to reach the highest degree of glory."

"You think that you can be a god, equal to the Eternal Father!" the preacher thundered. "Such blasphemy!"

"We believe that children grow up to be like their parents. Because we are children of God, we believe that we can achieve Godhood. However, I will never be equal to our Heavenly Father." Turning to the hostess, he smiled. "Miss Polly, this was unquestionably one of the finest meals I have ever eaten. We appreciate your hospitality, but I need to get Niki home so she can rest." With the briefest of nods to the preacher, he helped Kate to her feet and they left.

Inside their own home, Kate addressed the agent with newfound respect. "You handled Brother Paul very well."

He started to reply but was interrupted by a banging sound from the back. Agent Iverson hurried down the hall with Kate close behind him. He pulled open the door to find Miss Eugenia with her fist ready to pound again. "Is something wrong?" he asked tensely, searching the backyard with his eyes.

"That's exactly what I wanted to ask you. I tried to bring some fig preserves over earlier, and your doors were all locked."

"We were gone to Albany, so of course we locked our doors," Kate said irritably. She was tired and wanted to lie down.

Miss Eugenia was astounded. "Nobody in Haggerty locks their

doors during the day."

Agent Iverson gave her a stern look. "That is a very unwise practice. You should lock your doors day and night, even when you are at home, and tell your friends to do the same. This is a dangerous world we live in and getting worse all the time."

"Well, I do declare," she said as he took the fig preserves.

"Niki needs to take a nap now," he said as he led Miss Eugenia across the porch and into the backyard. As she went upstairs, Kate wondered how long it would take him to get rid of her.

After a long nap, Kate came down and found Agent Iverson working on the computer. She stayed in the hall and kept her eyes averted from the screen while she asked if he'd like anything for dinner. "Some of whatever you're having will be good," he answered, glancing up from his work. She heated a chicken casserole in the microwave and as they ate, Agent Iverson told her that a very sophisticated security system would be installed on Monday.

"Since no one here even locks their doors, they are bound to think a security system is odd. We'll use Northern paranoia and my late hours as an excuse," he explained. "The men who come to install it will be wearing uniforms from a local company that sells systems for $99 down and $21 a month."

"But our system costs more?"

"Much more. It won't have audible alarms. The way our neighbors walk in and out without knocking, someone would be setting it off all the time. So they are going to install a system of hidden cameras around the outside of the house and in all the ground-floor rooms. The cameras will be monitored twenty-four hours a day by agents in Chicago. There will be silent alarms that notify the surveillance team every time an exterior door or a window is opened so they can check the appropriate cameras," he continued, and Kate tried to absorb the information.

"So, people will be watching us all the time?" she asked with apprehension.

He nodded. "Only when we are downstairs or outside. The private areas of the house won't have any cameras."

"I guess I should be grateful that I'll still be able to bathe," Kate murmured gloomily. Out of the corner of her eye she saw Agent

Iverson smile briefly.

They washed the dishes, then went for their evening walk. When they got home, Kate sat on the couch in the den and massaged her tired feet. "Why couldn't Niki have liked to cross stitch or oil paint instead of exercise?" she asked as she turned her face to the ceiling fan.

"It could have been worse," Agent Iverson said with a grim smile. "Be glad she wasn't into tattoos or martial arts."

"Or silly silk pocket hankies," she retorted as she picked up her shoes and headed for the stairs.

* * *

On Monday morning Kate got up early after a fitful night's sleep. Every time the wind blew or a board creaked, her eyes flew open expecting to see a masked intruder with a gun or knife, ready to kill her. She felt better after a shower. Then she dressed, after putting on about half the amount of makeup Angela recommended.

Since it was Agent Iverson's first day as police chief of Haggerty, she wanted to make him a good breakfast. Not finding an apron in all the Johnsons' kitchen supplies, she tucked two dishtowels around her clothes and began frying bacon. She had several pieces blotting on a paper towel, eggs scrambled, orange juice squeezed, and toast buttered when Miss Eugenia pounded on the back door.

"All this knocking and door locking is going to take some getting used to," the old woman grumbled as she took a seat at the table. She was wearing a nice Sunday dress and knee-high hose with about two inches of veined leg showing in between. A coffee mug was cradled in her age-spotted hands. "I brought my own since you don't make coffee, even for guests."

"You wouldn't want to drink a cup of coffee I made," Kate assured her, placing the plate of toast on the table. Whatever response Miss Eugenia was about to make was lost as Agent Iverson walked into the room. His uniform was made of lightweight khaki. The top button was open, and his dark, shiny hair was styled to perfection. He stopped abruptly when he saw them staring.

"What? Do I look ridiculous?" He glanced down nervously at his crisply starched shirt.

"Oh no," Kate assured him, her mouth suddenly dry.

"No one can resist a handsome man in uniform," Miss Eugenia sighed. "You are going to break every heart in this town."

Agent Iverson grimaced as he sat down at the table. "Is all this for me?" he asked, pouring a glass of orange juice.

"Unless Miss Eugenia wants some," Kate offered politely.

"Mercy no! I couldn't eat a bite," Miss Eugenia said as she filled her plate.

"I hope you like your eggs scrambled," Kate watched him anxiously.

"Scrambled is fine. You're going to call the doctor today, right?" he asked Kate as he spooned the eggs onto his plate.

"First thing."

He nodded. "Good. I'll call the cable company."

"And I'll call Happy Goodwin at the decorator shop in Albany," Miss Eugenia offered. "Annabelle says she's married to a boy from North Carolina, and he has a job and a house in Raleigh. I swear that's the strangest sort of marriage I've ever heard of." She considered this for a minute, then shook her head. "Anyway, she might have some sample books she could send for you to look at. I'll see if anyone is going into town and can pick them up." Miss Eugenia paused long enough to bite into her third piece of bacon, then she took a slice of toast from the stack and asked, "Where are those fig preserves I brought you yesterday?"

Kate got the preserves out of the refrigerator and handed them to their guest. "Did you say her name is Happy?" she asked as she watched Miss Eugenia slather fig jam on her toast.

"Her real name is Hepsibah, but she's gone by Happy since she was a toddler. Her mother is my third cousin on my father's side," Miss Eugenia added as she took a big bite.

Agent Iverson finished his meal and stood. "I guess I'd better go," he said as he moved toward the door. Kate followed him into the laundry room and asked if he'd be coming home for lunch. "I'll call and let you know when I see how the morning goes. And remember that the security system will be installed today." She nodded. There was an awkward moment, both of them standing there, married yet strangers.

"Oh, you two don't mind me," Miss Eugenia called from the table. "I've seen young people kiss before." Kate flushed and Agent Iverson paled.

"It's what Drew and Niki would do," Kate whispered with a shrug. The agent nodded solemnly and bent his head to her. Kate closed her eyes and received a quick peck on the forehead. Her eyes flew open and she watched him leave, feeling strangely cheated.

Miss Eugenia left as well, saying she had a Christian Women Supporting Foreign Missionaries meeting. After the breakfast dishes were washed and put back in the appropriate cupboards, Kate looked through the freezer and picked out a casserole for dinner. Then she called the doctor in Albany and made an appointment for Wednesday afternoon at three o'clock.

Ellis Harper arrived at nine o'clock lugging a can of primer and several drop cloths. He told Kate that Melba Fishburn, Haggerty's only beautician was going into Albany that morning to pick up some permanent waves. On her way home, she would swing by Happy Goodwin's store for the sample books.

Kate went upstairs with Ellis and helped scrape the woodwork in the nursery. The FBI agents, disguised as security system installers, arrived at mid-morning. Kate let them in and they took boxes of equipment into the office. One man sat down at the computer while another went around placing small, clear discs in various locations. Kate watched in fascination.

"No wires?" she finally asked the man who had barely acknowledged her presence.

He looked up, surprised by her comment. "Wires have been obsolete for over a decade," he said mildly. "These little discs contain computer chips. They talk to each other and the console." He pointed in the direction of the office.

"Wow," was all Kate could think of to say. Agent Iverson never did call although he did come home at lunchtime. When he expressed concern about Kate being exposed to paint, she assured him that the open windows provided plenty of ventilation although he didn't look convinced as they walked to the kitchen. Closing up the primer cans,

Ellis followed them downstairs.

Kate offered to make the handyman a sandwich, but he said he believed he'd eat with their neighbor, Miss Eugenia. After he left, Kate invited the other agents to share their lunch, but they declined, giving Agent Iverson a peculiar look.

"We're just about finished here," the disc placer said. Kate walked into the kitchen, leaving Agent Iverson alone with his coworkers. The men left a few minutes later and Agent Iverson joined her at the table.

"They certainly did act weird," she commented as she watched the security van pull out of the driveway.

"I guess they aren't used to friendly potential murder victims." He took a sandwich from the plate in the center of the table.

Kate's eyes narrowed. "You mean they expected me to be wringing my hands?"

"Something like that," he agreed.

"Sounds like they don't have much confidence in Mr. Evans," Kate mused and glanced up to catch a fleeting smile on the agent's face.

"Acting nervous and scared won't help anything. The best thing you can do is work hard at being Niki," he advised.

"That's what I'm trying to do," Kate nodded. "Think Niki." Anxious to keep the conversation going, she searched for another topic. "So, how many deputies do you have?"

"I have patrolmen, not deputies. Two of them."

"And their names?"

"Winston Jones and Arnold Willis."

"Are they nice?" Kate pressed and he looked up from his plate.

"Winston has been on the police force for five years. He wanted the chief's job, and his plan is to make me so miserable that I will quit and go back to New York. Arnold started two months ago. He's nineteen, scared of his own shadow, and gets embarrassed when he has to say things like 'toilet paper' or 'female.'" Kate refilled their glasses with milk. "Add to that the fact that the old chief didn't really want to quit but had to in order to run for mayor. He spent all morning sitting at my desk, talking on my phone."

"All morning?" Kate asked with her mouth full.

"Every single minute," the agent confirmed. "And the dispatcher is indescribable. You'll have to see her to believe her." He swallowed the last bite of sandwich and drained his glass. "You'll get your chance on Saturday. It seems that we got here just in time for their annual Haggerty Police Department Bowling Tournament."

"Do you bowl?" Kate asked.

"Only when I absolutely have to," the agent answered grimly.

Melba Fishburn dropped off the wallpaper sample books just as Agent Iverson started back to his office. She flirted outrageously as she offered him a ride, which he declined. Kate watched from the front door as he finally freed himself from Melba and headed toward town. Then she took Happy Goodwin's books upstairs and looked through them until she fell asleep.

When her eyes opened, the room was completely dark and she could smell dinner cooking. After running a toothbrush across her teeth, she went downstairs to find Agent Iverson standing over a skillet.

"I'm sorry I overslept. I was going to heat up that ham casserole." She waved toward the pan covered with condensation on the counter.

"Don't feel obligated to make my meals," the agent said without looking up from the frying pan. "I'm used to cooking for myself."

Kate was stung by his comments. During their brief marriage, Tony had been gone so much that she rarely had a chance to cook for him, but she wanted Niki Johnson to be a good wife and was hurt by Agent Iverson's rejection of her efforts. Discouraged, she sat silently and watched him work. Finally the agent placed two plates on the table.

"It's a Creole recipe. Try it," he instructed as he went to get glasses and the milk. The food was good and she was starving so she decided to forgive him. While they ate, she told him that she and Ellis combined had scraped and sanded several feet of woodwork in the nursery. "Wouldn't you rather sit on the couch and watch game shows until the baby comes?" he asked.

"After six weeks of daytime television I'd be brain-dead," she dismissed his suggestion. "I've always thought it would be fun to do this." She waved her fork around at the bare walls. "To fix up an old house. But since this is temporary, I'm not sure how far to go. Angela told me the money Mr. Evans put in Niki's account was mine to spend, but the Bureau has gone to so much trouble to protect me, I feel guilty spending their money."

"They've gone to a lot of trouble to protect an important undercover operation. You're safety is only one element of that. Consider the money they've given you compensation for your cooperation," Agent Iverson advised.

"Eventually I'll have insurance money and I can repay them."

"Working on this house and spending money like crazy is part of your cover. And we're the ones who have to live here." He looked up at a bulge in the ceiling that almost guaranteed a serious leak in the new roof.

Kate finished her dinner and sat back to give her digestive system room to work. "I was thinking that after all this is over, I might want to buy this house from the government." He looked up sharply. "Chicago isn't my home. We moved there because that's where Tony was stationed. I could always move back to Utah, but after I get this place fixed up, why sell it? Do you think they would let me?"

"Let you what?" He didn't seem happy about the topic.

"Buy this house."

"I guess it will depend on how well this case turns out. If they are successful in arresting the people who want to kill you, they probably won't care where you live. If not, you may have to spend the rest of your life in hiding." His words seemed unnecessarily harsh, and Kate recoiled slightly. He sighed. "Do whatever you want to the house. Every improvement you make will increase the value for whoever eventually owns it."

After their walk, they inspected the house, room by room. Agent Iverson didn't say much, but his face was grim as he reviewed the overall condition of their new home. When he saw the meager improvements Ellis had made in an entire day, with Kate's help, he was visibly angry. He leaned against the wall and looked out the window. As Kate watched his face, bathed in moonlight, she had to force herself to concentrate on what he was saying.

"Finishing the kitchen is a priority and clearly beyond Ellis Harper's capabilities," he grumbled. "At the rate he's going, the ten tribes will be back from wherever they are before he applies a coat of paint."

Kate had to laugh. "But he does a very good job. He scrapes and sands and fills in each little hole. When he gets finished, it will look like new."

"It would be cheaper and more time efficient to buy new baseboards!" Agent Iverson's tone was exasperated. "I'm going to call around tomorrow and see if I can find somebody who can get this house livable." He watched as a spider descended gracefully from the ceiling. "I guess I'll call an exterminator, too."

When they got back downstairs, he gave her a furniture catalog from a store in New York. At a glance Kate could see that everything was absurdly expensive. "Mr. Evans said for you to order the nursery furniture from there."

"I had some things on lay-away at Wal-Mart in Chicago," she told him as she flipped past a crib that cost over $500.

"Niki only buys the best." He pointed to the glossy catalog.

"I am just about to get sick and tired of Niki," Kate mumbled as she saw a handmade baby blanket for $175.

He touched her arm. "Niki has probably never been in a Wal-Mart and the term 'lay-away' would be completely foreign to her. If anyone is watching us, a trip into Wal-Mart to put a cheap crib on lay-away could sign your death warrant," he said seriously. Kate looked at his hand, dark against the pale skin of her forearm. Drew Johnson's wedding ring sparkled in the dim light. "You were given this cover for a reason, and you have to stay in it."

Kate caught her breath, unsure if it was fear for her life or the warmth of his hand that was giving her breathing difficulties. "All right," she managed to say.

They were going to watch TV, but by the time Agent Iverson got the clock set correctly on the VCR, Kate had fallen asleep. He woke her gently and escorted her upstairs. At her door he told her not to worry about getting up to make him breakfast on Tuesday morning.

"I actually prefer cereal and I'm going to try to get to the office early tomorrow," he informed her. "I think arriving first is my only hope of ever getting to sit down at my own desk."

Kate nodded drowsily. "And the more I think about it, the less I like the idea of you working with Ellis. All that sawdust and paint can't be good for the baby. You should call that decorator Miss Eugenia was talking about and get her to come over. We'll let her coordinate the painting and wallpapering. The inside stuff." Kate nodded again, struggling to remain conscious. "We can talk about it more tomorrow. Go on to bed," he said with half a smile.

Kate watched him until he disappeared down the stairs and wondered if he ever slept.

CHAPTER 4

On Tuesday morning Kate spent an hour on the phone with Happy Goodwin, who agreed to come look around the house the following day. Ellis arrived at 8:30 to work on the baseboards in the nursery, and Miss Eugenia came by on the way to her Literary Guild meeting. She was sitting at the kitchen table, drinking coffee that she had brought herself, when Miss Polly knocked on the back door.

"I know it's not polite to visit so early in the morning, but when I saw Eugenia come over . . ." she began.

Kate forced a smile. "You're welcome anytime."

Miss Polly continued. "Well, I hate to say anything, but I heard that you're hiring a contractor and a decorator to make renovations. I feel obligated to inform you that any changes you make to the Riley house have to be approved by the Haggerty Historical Society."

"Pooh, Pauline Louise! Nobody pays any attention to those old rules anymore. The Johnsons can do whatever they want to this house!" Miss Eugenia answered angrily.

"Land sakes!" Miss Polly gasped. "I'm only trying to do my duty to the community."

"You're only trying to stick your nose in where it doesn't belong."

"I don't mind," Kate intervened before there was bloodshed. "You are both welcome to look at the renovation plan as soon as Mrs. Goodwin has it ready."

Miss Polly looked into the dining room. "Most of your furniture is so . . . modern," she said regretfully.

"I'd love to get some antiques for the house," Kate said before she thought. When she saw their startled expressions, she looked at the almost brand-new dining room set. "I didn't pick that out myself," she said as her mind searched for a reasonable explanation. "My mother did." Kate knew her mother would forgive her, and she couldn't take the blame for the Johnsons' bad taste any longer. "It's fine for a New York apartment, but in this lovely old house . . ." They all sighed in uniform dismay. "Maybe I could tell my mother that the Haggerty Historical Society has taken a personal interest in our home and absolutely insists that it be furnished with as many period pieces as possible. Then I could get rid of our contemporary things without hurting her feelings."

Miss Eugenia nodded thoughtfully. "My sister Annabelle just built one of those new houses on Highway 11, and she's been wanting some modern stuff." The older woman smiled. "She would kill to have authentic New York furniture, and she has some old pieces she might be willing to trade."

"Check the newspaper for estate sales," Miss Polly contributed. "Sometimes you can find bargains if you get there before the 'antique dealers' do." She said the words like other people might say "loan shark" or "child molester."

"Have you looked in the attic?" Miss Eugenia asked. "I doubt if much was left up there, but it's worth a try." She turned, directing her next question to Miss Polly. "Have they sold Geraldine Prescott's estate?"

The other woman shook her head. "Last I heard the heirs were coming in from Savannah over Labor Day to sort through everything."

Miss Eugenia nodded. "I'll look and see what they have. If I remember correctly, there was a nice dining room table and chairs."

Miss Polly bobbed her head. "With a matching buffet and china cabinet. Teakwood, I think."

"Maybe cherry." Miss Eugenia looked back at Kate. "How much can you afford to spend?"

"We've got plenty of money," Kate assured them.

"That's not what we heard," Miss Polly said quickly, then blushed. "Forgive me. That was so ill-mannered of me."

"We did have some financial troubles not long ago, but . . ."

Again, Kate searched for a plausible explanation. "My father is paying for everything until we get back on our feet."

The women exchanged a quick glance, then stood and moved toward the front door.

"Annabelle has a round table that she kept in the entryway of her old house. It would look perfect in here," Miss Eugenia said as they walked through the empty front room.

"If Annabelle is selling that table, I want to buy it," Miss Polly pleaded.

Miss Eugenia dismissed her request with a wave of her hand. "You've got a house full of furniture, Polly. The last thing you need is another table."

"I've always loved that table and you know it." Miss Polly's tone became strident as they walked out the door. Kate could still hear them arguing as they crossed the front yard and went into Miss Eugenia's house.

Agent Iverson called just before lunch and said he was afraid to get out of his chair for fear the old police chief would reclaim it. Kate laughed and offered to bring him a sandwich. He accepted her offer, adding that perhaps she could save his seat while he made a quick trip to the bathroom.

Kate dressed in a nice pantsuit and touched up her makeup, wanting to make a good impression on his coworkers. Then she used the last of the chicken salad to make enough sandwiches for several people. She put the sandwiches in an empty moving box, along with a plate of brownies and a chocolate pie.

The first person she saw when she walked into the office was a woman with an incredible beehive hairdo. Her ample upper body was covered snugly by a black silk blouse, and her thin legs were encased by skin-tight magenta jeans. The woman wore thick makeup and elaborate fake eyelashes. Kate could only assume that she was legally blind since no one would look that way on purpose. The woman stood and introduced herself as Leita, the police dispatcher. She took the box from Kate's hands and told her to follow.

The interior of the police station was dreary. The paint was faded and chipped, mildew stains dotted the ceiling tiles, and cobwebs hung from the corners. The furniture was decades old, and the linoleum was worn through in heavy traffic areas. A young man with acne was sitting at a counter toward the back of a large room, in front of a relatively new-looking computer terminal.

Leita led the way to the door of a small office and went inside without knocking. Kate watched as the other woman put the box of food in the middle of a dented metal desk. Agent Iverson was in a swivel chair behind the desk, and a heavy-set, bald man was sitting across from him, talking on the phone. The phone cord was stretched to its limit, and Kate thought the other man's voice was almost loud enough to be heard in Wyoming.

The FBI agent looked genuinely glad to see her. "It was nice of you to bring lunch." He stood as she walked in. "Here, take my seat," he said, keeping his hand on the arm of the chair.

"That's okay," Kate started to decline, but then saw the desperation in his eyes. "Well, thanks," she relented, sitting down in his chair. Leita took a sandwich from the box as Agent Iverson excused himself for a few minutes. Kate settled comfortably into his chair and looked across at the former police chief. He ended his phone call and introduced himself.

"Just call me Booster," he offered magnanimously. "I'll bet a pretty girl like you is bored stiff in a dull little town like this. Probably miss all the stores and restaurants in New York." He gave her a broad smile and a wink.

"Actually, we like it here," Kate responded coolly.

Agent Iverson returned after a few minutes, looking much relieved, with the young man she had seen earlier close behind him. "Niki, this is Arnold Willis," the agent said. "Arnold, this is my wife."

The patrolman's eyes dipped to Kate's midsection and he blushed a deep red. "Mrs. Johnson," he mumbled, ducking his head.

"It's nice to meet you, Arnold," Kate said kindly. "Please have a sandwich. I made them with some chicken salad that one of the ladies in town brought to us."

"Delicious!" Leita proclaimed as she took a second sandwich from the box and began opening the plastic wrapper. After several minutes of coaxing, Arnold finally accepted a sandwich and then retreated to his counter to eat in privacy. The ex-police chief said that he was meeting some folks for lunch at the town's only real restaurant, a remodeled train depot called Haggerty Station.

"Probably a political powwow," Leita predicted after he left. "I'll give you two kids a few minutes alone," she said with a lilting laugh and returned to her own desk.

"Where's the other policeman?" Kate asked as she watched Agent Iverson eat.

"Winston works the night shift, so he's not on duty until five. He came in early yesterday just to torture me."

"I'm sorry." Kate looked around the dreary room. "It must be terrible to work here."

He shrugged and pulled out another sandwich. "Did Ellis prime a few more inches of baseboard this morning?" he asked pleasantly.

"A couple. And I talked to the decorator in Albany. She's coming to look around tomorrow."

He nodded. "I found a contractor. He's going to send some guys out to give us an estimate in the morning. Unless their price is astronomical, I'll hire them." He asked if she wanted a soft drink and she nodded. He left the room and came back a few minutes later carrying two Sprites. He opened one and drank it without stopping to breathe. Then he got a brownie out of the box. "Agent Thomas is here," he said in between bites.

Kate looked up. "Where?"

"Not right here, but in town. The name he's using is Jefferson Moore, and he started his new job with the street department this morning. I just didn't want you to be surprised if you saw him around." Kate nodded as she took a sip of her drink. "The cable will be installed tomorrow," he continued as Leita's voice spoke over the intercom.

"Sorry to disturb you, but the county sheriff's on line one."

Kate stood. "I'd better get back home and check on Ellis." She walked around the desk and met Agent Iverson in the limited space by the wall. They squeezed past each other, almost touching.

The agent smiled. "Yeah, he might have worked himself into a state of exhaustion by now."

As it turned out, Ellis had not even returned from his lunch with Miss Eugenia when Kate got home. She took her regular afternoon nap, and when she woke, she peeked into the nursery. The handyman had finished priming the baseboards and had about a foot of the crown molding done. Kate praised and encouraged him for a few minutes, then went downstairs to warm up the ham and spinach casserole.

When Ellis left at seven o'clock, Agent Iverson still wasn't home. Kate ate alone and put the rest of the casserole in the microwave to heat up later. As she finished washing her dishes, Miss Eugenia called from the back porch. "I just wanted to come by and see how Ellis is doing on the nursery," she explained, poking her head into the kitchen.

Kate led the way upstairs and flipped on the light switch in the baby's room. She waited for Miss Eugenia's expression of disgust at Ellis's meager progress, but instead, Miss Eugenia sighed with contentment. "Doesn't Ellis do lovely work?" She bent down to run her hand along a smooth baseboard. "Not everyone appreciates a job well done anymore. Most young people are much too impatient. But when you get to be my age, you realize that getting finished isn't all that important."

Kate was ashamed of the critical thoughts she'd had about Ellis. He really was doing a very nice job. They heard the back door slam and a minute later the town's new police chief was standing beside them.

"I see Ellis knocked himself out today," he commented dryly.

"We were just admiring Ellis's meticulous workmanship and saying that patience is almost a forgotten virtue," Kate said quickly.

Miss Eugenia looked at both of them through narrowed eyes. "Some day you'll be old and need people to be patient with you," she scolded. "Hurry up and show me the rest of the house. I don't want to waste too much of your valuable time."

She walked briskly through the adjoining door into the master bedroom. She glanced at the closet and saw Kate's clothes hanging on both sides. Then her eyes swept across the dresser where only feminine articles were displayed. She opened a drawer of the tall chest of drawers to confirm that it was empty.

"I heard the rumors at the Daughters of the Confederacy meeting this afternoon, but I couldn't believe it was true. After all, you are pregnant!" Miss Eugenia eyed them sharply.

"What rumors?" Kate asked warily.

"That the two of you sleep in separate bedrooms," she disclosed with solemnity.

"It's only temporary," Kate explained, glad that they had anticipated this question and were prepared with a reasonable explanation. "I don't sleep well at night because of my pregnancy, so Drew is using the guest room."

"That way I don't wake Niki up early in the morning when I get ready for work," Agent Iverson added.

"They also said that Chief Johnson wears long johns even during this hottest part of the summer," Miss Eugenia continued as if they hadn't spoken. This announcement caused the agent's mouth to fall open in astonishment, and Kate had to control the urge to laugh. "There are several theories on this. Some say that he has bad circulation. Others think it's low blood pressure. The favorite is that he stays cold because he sleeps alone." She looked pointedly at Kate.

Since she had no clear means of defense, Kate decided to act mad. "I suppose Ellis is the one who has been telling people that we have separate bedrooms," she accused. "And to think that we have put up with his shuffling, earthworm pace."

"Humph!" Miss Eugenia made an unladylike noise in her throat. "Ellis would never notice such a thing! And if he did, he wouldn't remember it! I don't know for sure who started the rumors, but my guess would be your nosy neighbor, Miss Pauline Kirby. She can see into several rooms of your house from hers and has plenty of time to snoop. It has also been reported that Chief Johnson has to make his own meals."

"Niki is about to have a baby," Agent Iverson said angrily. "I can't believe that she's being criticized just because I'm trying to be a considerate husband." He rubbed a hand along the back of his neck. "And all of this is absolutely none of anyone's business."

Miss Eugenia studied him for a few seconds, then smiled. "That is absolutely true. What you need is some help." She turned and walked into the hallway.

"What kind of help?" Kate had already decided if her neighbor recommended the psychiatric variety that she was going to give the old busybody a piece of her mind.

"Household help. There are several women in town who supplement their income by cleaning houses. I don't care enough about cleanliness to bother, but Miss Polly has employed a woman named Etta Sue for years. I'll have Miss Polly ask her the next time she comes if she has room for you on her schedule."

Before either Kate or Agent Iverson could respond, Miss Eugenia had let herself out the back door. "We've got to get some curtains on our windows," was his only comment on the matter.

After their evening walk, Kate took a shower and changed into her pajamas. Feeling a little restless, she went into the den and found Agent Iverson watching a baseball game. He politely offered to change to something else, but she shook her head. "Baseball is fine," she assured him, curling onto the couch. She waited until a commercial break to ask about exchanging his furniture. "Would you mind if I got rid of some of the Johnsons' furniture and bought some antiques?" she asked abruptly.

"From who?"

"Miss Eugenia said her sister might have some things she wants to sell."

The agent relaxed against the recliner. "This stuff is comfortable."

Kate looked around the den. "I'll leave this room alone. I meant the furniture in the bedrooms and dining room."

"Do whatever you want."

Kate couldn't tell if he was very interested in the ball game or just not interested in discussing furniture. "I was afraid you might have formed an attachment to something."

"Maybe we could keep that vase that looks like a black fluorescent light bulb," he said without looking up.

"And you seemed fond of that picture frame made out of Coke bottle tops." Kate was encouraged by his attempt at a joke.

"It's a keeper." This time he glanced over at her and almost smiled.

"Did you manage to hold onto your seat after I left the office today?" she asked as long as she had at least a portion of his attention.

"Yeah. But I didn't accomplish much. I can't seem to find any current files. I think Booster must have them at his house."

"Why would he take them home?" Kate was surprised.

"I have an idea that Booster planned to officially resign, but never intended to relinquish control. He probably thought that the boy from New York City would put in token appearances from time to time, but not get involved in the day-to-day stuff."

"So you have been an unpleasant surprise."

"I guess you could say that."

"You should tell him to bring the files back, and if he doesn't, get a search warrant for his house," Kate suggested after a few minutes of thought.

"That won't make him very happy." The agent turned his head to look at her.

"I don't think you and Booster will ever be friends anyway," Kate pointed out.

Agent Iverson considered this, then nodded. "I'll give him an hour in the morning to produce the missing files. Then I'll start throwing my weight around." He returned his attention to the ball game, and Kate settled down to watch. She was asleep before the next batter completed his swing.

* * *

On Wednesday morning Miss Eugenia brought homemade buttermilk biscuits over to eat with her coffee and offered one to Kate.

"I'm eating lunch at the retirement home today," the older woman announced. "But thank goodness it's Wednesday so I can get some gardening done." Kate asked for a second biscuit and said that she had a doctor's appointment at three o'clock. Miss Eugenia told her to come over and report afterwards.

Ellis primed molding in the nursery until noon, then shuffled through the kitchen. Kate offered to make him lunch, but he declined. She asked when he'd be back, intending to explain that she would be gone for part of the afternoon, but he looked up with a blank expression. "Won't be coming back today. It's Wednesday." This was the second reference to the day of the week, but Kate didn't even attempt to get an explanation from Ellis.

Agent Iverson called a little while later. He said that he was on duty all afternoon and wouldn't be home for lunch. Kate offered to bring him something to eat, but he said that Melba Fishburn, the beautician, had brought him a Whopper Combo from the Burger King on Highway 11. "She knew I wouldn't be able to get anything in town since it's Wednesday."

In her haste to advise him against a friendship with Ms. Fishburn, Kate forgot to ask about the significance of Wednesday. "Even I can recognize her type," she cautioned.

"Thanks for the warning," he said as they hung up.

* * *

At 2:30, Kate left the house for her doctor's appointment in Albany. As she climbed into the minivan, she saw a Haggerty Street and Sanitation Department truck parked across the road. Agent Thomas was looking under a manhole cover and she waved at him discreetly. The agent risked a brief, almost imperceptible nod in her direction before returning his attention to the sewer.

Agent Iverson had left detailed instructions for the drive, and she made it to Albany and the doctor's office with no trouble. The receptionist gave her several pages of medical forms to complete, and it required all her concentration to make sure she wrote down the correct information. Exhausted by her efforts, she leaned back against her chair, closing her eyes against the unfamiliar room.

It seemed that for too long everything in her life had been temporary. The apartment Tony had insisted on instead of a real house. The assignment in Chicago that he assured her was only a stepping-stone to bigger and better things. Their brief marriage, which had ended in tragedy and the new marriage that was destined to end from the beginning. As loneliness threatened to overwhelm her, the baby kicked vigorously and Niki's name was announced over the intercom.

Dr. Tremayne was young and personable. He examined her thoroughly and confirmed her due date as October 6th. He told her to set up an appointment in two weeks and to get forms from the receptionist so that she could preregister at Memorial Hospital. She asked him to recommend a pediatrician, and he said he'd have his nurse give her a name.

As Kate pulled into her driveway, she saw Miss Eugenia. Her neighbor was wearing men's coveralls and about a pound of topsoil, and carrying a five-quart ice cream bucket full of ripe red tomatoes. Kate met her by the azalea bushes that separated their property.

"Are these the most beautiful tomatoes you have ever seen?" Miss Eugenia demanded, wiping sweat from her forehead and leaving a dirty smear.

Kate glanced down at the bucket. The tomatoes were nice and plump, but they were also dusted with dirt. An ant crawled lazily across the tomato on top, moved slowly over the edge of the bucket, and up Miss Eugenia's left index finger.

"You've got an ant on you," Kate told her, pointing to the offender.

Miss Eugenia shrugged. "I'm probably covered with them." She flicked the ant carelessly away. "Gardening is one of the true pleasures of life. Come over sometime and I'll show you."

Kate eyed the vegetables, watching for another bug. "Anything that involves dirt and insects is not for me."

Miss Eugenia laughed tolerantly. "I talked to Annabelle at lunch, and she's dying to see the furniture you want to get rid of. She said she has an antique bedroom set that would be perfect for a guest room."

When Miss Eugenia invited Kate for dinner, saying she had made a garden vegetable soup, Kate told her that Happy Goodwin was coming over. She also needed to fix something for her husband to eat.

"You'll never see him until late on a Wednesday," the older lady said, dusting the dirt from her clothes. Kate stepped back a few inches. "When Happy leaves, come on over. I'll send some soup home for the Chief."

Kate changed into the closest thing Niki had to casual clothes and pulled her hair back into a ponytail. She was just walking back downstairs when Happy Goodwin arrived, looking extremely chic in a sleeveless linen dress, her white-blonde hair cut short and tucked neatly behind her ears.

Happy took careful notes as they walked through the house, drew simple sketches of each room, and took small pieces of wallpaper. When they had completed the tour, she said she'd be back on Thursday to present her proposal.

* * *

Kate called the police station to tell Agent Iverson that she was eating dinner next door, but Leita said he was on another line. Leaving a message, Kate walked over to Miss Eugenia's and was startled when her knock was answered by a stranger. Although the woman bore a faint resemblance to Miss Eugenia, she was shorter and more slightly built. Her steel gray hair was cut into a stylish pageboy, and she was wearing a trim business suit.

"You must be Niki," the woman said as she pulled the door open, then added, "I'm Annabelle." They walked through the enclosed back porch and into the kitchen, which was a big, cluttered room with several kinds of vegetables in various stages of decay along the counters. "Eugenia is taking a shower. Have a seat," Annabelle invited, bending over to reach for a plastic grocery sack from under the sink. Straightening up, she began putting shriveled squashes into it. "I don't know why she grows more than she can ever eat." After she had disposed of the worst offenders, she stirred the soup that was bubbling over on the stove.

A short while later, Miss Eugenia rushed in and surveyed the room. "What happened to all my vegetables?" she asked as she pulled a pan of cornbread from the oven.

"I bagged up a few to take home with me," Annabelle said, giving Kate a conspiratorial look over her sister's head.

"You stole my vegetables?" Miss Eugenia protested as she distributed soup bowls on the table. "I was going to can tomorrow!" Turning to Kate, she grimaced. "That's the way it's always been with us. I do all the work, and then she takes what she wants."

Annabelle shrugged as she walked over to turn off the oven and move the potholders away from the burners. When the three women were settled at the table, Miss Eugenia brought up the subject of furniture. It was agreed that when they finished eating, they would walk over to the Johnsons' house and look it over. During the course of the meal, Kate learned that Annabelle was several years younger than Miss Eugenia, although her exact age was never disclosed. She worked as a loan officer at a bank in Albany, was widowed, and was frequently discussed by the Haggerty matrons.

"She dates," Miss Eugenia confided. "Men."

Kate nodded cautiously, unsure how she should respond. "For decades, Haggerty women have just withered away when their husbands died. A woman who wants to continue to live is a novelty," Annabelle elaborated.

"It's been longer than that," Miss Eugenia said thoughtfully. "I would say at least since the Civil War, Haggerty women have suffered with refinement and poise after their men left them, either through death or in other more scandalous ways."

"Silas has been dead for almost twenty years. It would be ridiculous for me to sit at home trying to remember what he looked like," Annabelle scoffed.

"Niki doesn't sleep with her husband," Miss Eugenia contributed, shocking Kate into the conversation.

She knew she turned several shades of red and both women stared. "We have separate bedrooms," Kate defended herself. "That doesn't mean we don't sleep together."

"I slept with Silas when he was alive," Annabelle mused aloud.

"Of course you did," Miss Eugenia nodded approvingly. Kate stood abruptly and suggested that they walk over to her house. She took her guests upstairs and felt like a trespasser as she opened the door to Agent Iverson's room. But he had said she could get rid of the Johnsons' furniture, so she tried to hide her reluctance. She saw the sisters exchange a meaningful glance, but she ignored them and turned the doorknob.

The room was a lot like the agent himself, neat without being fussy. The bed was made, but his tennis shoes were kicked into a corner and the closet door was standing open. Kate had the strangest urge to rub her face on the stiffly starched uniform shirts that hung side by side. A paperback Book of Mormon lay on the table beside the bed. Kate felt certain that somewhere he had a nice set with his real name engraved on the front.

Annabelle loved the furniture and offered to trade the antique set she had for it. "We can drive over to my old house, and, if you like it, we can swap."

"We don't have to go look at your furniture. It's just for a guest room," Kate pointed out casually. "I'm sure it will be fine."

Annabelle smiled. "Well, if it gets here and you hate it, we'll trade back."

Miss Eugenia led the way downstairs. "Let me show you her dining room set."

"I'll bet this cost a fortune," Annabelle said, running her fingers across the glossy surface of the table.

"I don't know what it cost," Kate said flippantly. "And I don't care. It doesn't match the house, so you can have it."

"Oh no, I could never just take it." Annabelle shook her head vigorously. "But I'll try to think of a way . . ."

"I stopped by Geraldine Prescott's house on my way home today," Miss Eugenia announced. "The dining room furniture is in good condition. There was a rug and some occasional tables, but I couldn't see very well because of the glare on the glass."

"Eugenia, it's a wonder you didn't get snake-bit standing in that long grass," Annabelle scolded.

"You looked in their windows?" Kate was horrified.

Miss Eugenia was unrepentant. "You heard Miss Polly say that the heirs wouldn't be here until Labor Day. And I'm sure that Miss Geraldine didn't mind one bit."

Agent Iverson arrived at this point, and the women met him in the kitchen. He looked tired but greeted the sisters politely. Kate heated up his dinner and he complimented Miss Eugenia on the soup. After they left, Kate sat down at the table and asked about his day.

"How did things go with Booster?"

"I told him to get out of my office or I'd get a restraining order against him. Then I told him I wanted every file back by noon since it was Wednesday."

"Wow," she breathed, handing him another piece of Miss Eugenia's cornbread. "What's special about Wednesday?"

"The whole town closes down at noon except the police station."

"Every Wednesday?"

"Yep."

Kate shook her head in amazement. "So, did Booster bring you the files?"

"I had them by ten o'clock, but if I ever need his cooperation for anything . . ." The agent shrugged eloquently.

"Maybe you won't," Kate offered hopefully. "I can't believe there's that much crime committed around here."

The agent nodded, crumbling cornbread into his soup. "Mostly civil disputes, teenage vandalism, and speeding. That's Winston's particular favorite. More tickets were written in Haggerty last quarter than in the rest of the county combined."

"That's bad?"

"It makes it look like we have speed traps set. Winston spends most of his working hours going around to bars and nightclubs out on Highway 76, acting like a big shot. When he gets tired of that, he hides in the bushes at the edge of town where the speed limit changes, catching unsuspecting motorists."

"And you just plain don't like him," Kate added.

"That too," he admitted with half a smile. "All the files Booster had at home were unsolved cases. I think he wanted to make it look like he was doing a better job than he really was." He shook his head and changed the subject. "What did the doctor say?"

Kate gave him a brief report and then told him that she was trading his bedroom suite for Annabelle's antique set. He was relieved to hear that the decorator was coming on Thursday and asked Kate to make sure that blinds were a priority.

"I'm tired of people looking in our windows," he grumbled.

* * *

On Thursday morning Miss Eugenia told Kate that Miss Polly's "help," Etta Sue, could not work the Johnsons into her cleaning schedule. However, a new family had moved into town, and the wife had told Etta Sue that she was interested in lining up a house or two. Miss Eugenia didn't know much about them, but the woman said that her husband had recently taken a job with the Haggerty Street and Sanitation Department. Kate smiled as she wrote down Etta Sue's number so she could call and ask her to have her new neighbor come by for an interview.

Happy arrived on Thursday afternoon to present her detailed renovation plan. The new police chief made a point to be present during her visit, and he told her that he wasn't worried about how much it was going to cost. His only concern was getting the house into livable condition and quickly. He gave her the name of the contractor he had hired and asked her to coordinate her efforts with him.

Kate told Happy about the arrangements she had made to acquire Annabelle's antique bedroom set and the Prescotts' dining room ensemble.

"We want the furniture to match the house," Kate explained as they settled down at the kitchen table.

Happy opened her briefcase and extracted several furniture catalogs. "I recommend that you keep the white upholstered furniture in the living room. We'll mix in some antiques and add a little color with a rug, curtains, and pillows.

"My suggestion on your master bedroom furniture is to buy replicas. This gives you the option of modern comforts like a king-sized bed without detracting from the essence of the house. We can look around for antique furniture for the other two guest rooms, or you can buy reproductions there, too."

"What do you think is best?" Kate asked.

"It's not really that easy to find a complete, antique bedroom suite in good condition. I would probably have to shop around at warehouses and estate sales, possibly buying a few pieces at a time until we filled the rooms. If it was my house . . ." She paused and Kate nodded for her to continue. "I would buy the beds, mattresses, and maybe a dresser for each room from the reproduction companies. The rooms would be usable, and then we could shop around for antique accessories."

"Whatever will be faster," Agent Iverson agreed. Happy handed each of them a furniture catalog. "You pick." He pushed his book toward Kate. "I don't care."

Kate looked back at the decorator. "I don't know enough to choose."

Happy leaned over and pointed out a Baton Rouge series she thought would be nice in the master bedroom. "It's elegant without being feminine." She tapped the picture of a sturdy sleigh bed with her pen. "For one guest room, I'd use the Marie Antoinette line. It is prissy, but . . . it is a guest room. We can paint the walls pale pink and use a crocheted lace bedspread." Kate controlled a smile as she saw Agent Iverson's eyes glaze over with boredom.

"That sounds great," Kate agreed.

"For the other room I suggest Charleston. It's a basic line that will mix well with antiques." Kate showed Happy the catalog of baby furniture and asked for her advice. The decorator seemed pleased with Niki's choice of stores. She flipped through the catalog and in minutes had made her recommendations. Kate watched Happy fill out the order forms, trying not to think about how much all the pieces must cost.

Then Happy went through her room-by-room proposal for paint, wallpaper, drapes, light fixtures, and pictures for the walls. When she spread fabric samples out on the table, Agent Iverson stood, saying he had to get back to the station and he trusted their judgment. After they had picked out material for curtains and bedspreads, Kate asked for a copy of the plan. "You want to check over it and make sure I haven't forgotten anything?" Happy teased lightly.

"No! I trust you completely," Kate assured her. "I just can't remember everything, and I want to read it later when I can concentrate."

Happy squeezed her arm. "You two are dream clients. You have lots of money, your husband doesn't care, and you love everything!" Kate smiled weakly.

Happy went on to say that she thought she could sell Kate's master bedroom furniture to one of her clients on Highway 11. Although the set had probably retailed for around $15,000, Happy said she'd be lucky to get $8,000 for the used set. Both figures were outrageous enough to render Kate speechless.

"I'll go back to my office now and start ordering," Happy said as she repacked her briefcase.

The local paperhanger that Happy wanted to use arrived just then, so she walked him around the house, taking measurements. When they met Kate back in the kitchen, Happy said that she and the wallpaper people would be back on Monday.

On Friday morning Annabelle sent the teenage boy who did her yard work over to help Ellis disassemble Agent Iverson's bedroom set and load it into a rented moving van. The idea had been to take the set over to Annabelle's new house on Highway 11 and then load up the antique suite that was at her old house across town and bring it back. However, Ellis didn't approach this project with any more haste than he did painting woodwork. By lunchtime they still hadn't loaded a single piece onto the truck, and it was dark by the time they left the Johnsons' house and headed toward Annabelle's.

Miss Eugenia came out and stood on the driveway beside Kate as she watched the truck pull away from the curb. "Guess you two will have to manage with just one bed tonight," she murmured, then went inside.

Kate waited anxiously for Agent Iverson to get home, but when she explained the problem, he didn't seem concerned. "I'll sleep on the floor."

"Oh, I'm so sorry," Kate was distraught. "You could sleep on the couch in the den," she suggested.

"I don't want to give Miss Polly any more news to share with the whole town," he said, shaking his head. "And it would be too far away if something happened."

Kate nodded slowly. She was getting so engrossed in Niki's world that she had almost forgotten her life was in danger.

After a quiet dinner, Kate watched a documentary on China for about thirty seconds before she fell asleep. Later Agent Iverson walked her to her room. As she nestled into her comfortable bed, Kate thought about him across the hall sleeping on the hard floor. Sighing into her pillow, she closed her eyes and waited for the freedom from guilt that sleep would bring.

CHAPTER 5

On Saturday morning Arnold picked up Agent Iverson in his battered pickup truck and the two of them went over to Annabelle's old house and got the bedroom furniture. Kate held the door open as they carried the heavy pieces upstairs. Once everything was inside, Arnold helped the agent reassemble the furniture. Kate waited until Arnold left, then went upstairs to see how it looked. "It's wonderful," Kate cried. Without thinking, she sat down on the bed to test the mattress. "Oh, I'm sorry!" she said, jumping back up.

"Keep your seat. Maybe we'll get lucky, and Miss Polly will see us in here together."

After they put the sheets on the bed, Agent Iverson said he was going to work in the yard, and Kate found some furniture polish and started cleaning the antiques. Through the bedroom window, she watched him drag an ancient lawn mower from the storage shed. It took him thirty minutes to determine that it was not going to start. Kate was putting the Pledge back under the sink when he came in and told her that he was going to Wal-Mart to buy a new lawn mower. "Miss Eugenia might have one you could borrow," Kate suggested helpfully.

"I want a lawn mower that was made after World War II," he retorted, dismissing her suggestion. Then he left without asking if she'd like to ride along.

When the agent got home, he assembled the new mower in the punishing heat. Kate tried to get him to come in for lunch, but he refused. Finally she heard the lawnmower crank and looked out to see him walk about ten feet before the motor stalled in the tall grass. He cranked it again and made it about fifteen feet with the same result. At three o'clock a sudden thunderstorm soaked him as he was trying to get the mower back into the crowded shed. When he stomped in through the back door, he was hot, frustrated, and dripping wet.

Kate put a hand over her mouth to keep from laughing. He scowled at her as he pulled off his wet shoes and left them by the door. "This yard is beyond hope," he murmured in defeat, walking to the window. The now short grass was the color of straw. All the hedges were overgrown and intermingled with weeds. The straggly trees drooped in the driving rain. "The only healthy plant out there is the poison ivy."

"I guess you kept your yard in Washington manicured," Kate said as she watched the rain over his shoulder.

"I owned a condo in Washington, so I didn't have a yard," he corrected her mildly. "But I paid my grounds maintenance fee promptly every month."

Kate saw numerous mud puddles forming in dead patches of grass. "Maybe you should have been nicer to that agent in Washington," Kate remarked, and he looked at her blankly. "The one who pretended to be the senator's secretary and bought this house instead of a brand-new place with a well-trimmed yard over on Highway 11."

"Maybe you're right," the agent responded, his eyes narrowing slightly. "She just wanted to move in with me." Kate couldn't muster a response before he turned and walked up the stairs.

* * *

That night they left the house at six o'clock and drove to the bowling alley in a town about thirty minutes away. The rest of the police force, as well as the former chief, was there when they arrived. Seeing that Arnold and Leita looked uncomfortable, Kate had no doubt that Winston and Booster had cooked up something special to irritate the new Haggerty chief of police.

Winston was a nice-looking man in his early thirties. He was tall and a little overweight, like someone who had played football in high school and then stopped exercising. His hairline was receding, but he had a good tan. Booster walked up to greet them as they approached, and she saw Agent Iverson tense as the ex-police chief spoke.

"Please sit here by me, Mrs. Johnson," Booster invited.

"Go get some bowling shoes on, Booster," Leita instructed gruffly. "Our lane is open."

Winston was less cordial, merely nodding to the Johnsons as they joined the group. The teams were divided predictably, Booster and Winston against Agent Iverson and Arnold. Kate and Leita were assigned to keep score. While the agent looked for a ball, Booster walked over and draped his arm around Kate's shoulders. "I think we should make this a little more interesting," he said. "Raise the stakes, so to speak."

Agent Iverson stood silently, staring at the bald man's arm. Kate ducked out of the uninvited embrace. "Why can't we just bowl like always?" Leita asked reasonably.

"I say that whoever wins gets to kiss the Chief's wife," Booster proposed outrageously. Arnold blushed, Winston smiled, and Agent Iverson's lips formed a straight, tense line.

"That wouldn't be much of a prize for me," the agent pointed out through gritted teeth.

Booster laughed. "You've got me there." He considered the problem for a few seconds. "How about this? If you win, Winston will work every Sunday afternoon for the month of September."

"You're on," Agent Iverson said grimly. Kate opened her mouth to protest, but Leita took her arm and led her over to the orange plastic chairs that encircled Lane Six.

The men played three games, and Leita kept a cumulative score. Arnold was not a bad bowler, but the pressure got to him toward the end. Booster was no better, so it was basically a contest between Winston and Agent Iverson. The score was tied at the end of three games so Booster said they would have to play a "sudden death" round. Winston and the agent would take turns rolling balls until someone missed. The tension between them was so obvious that neighboring bowlers turned to watch the men struggle against each other.

They both got strike after strike until finally Winston threw a ball and left one pin standing. Agent Iverson concentrated for several seconds, then rolled his ball down the lane. Kate held her breath as she watched all the pins fall, then let out a sigh of relief. Kissing Winston or Booster was a nauseating thought, but watching Agent Iverson humiliated in defeat would have been worse.

Winston sulked for a few minutes, then Booster thought of a way for them to have some revenge. He walked over to Arnold and patted his back vigorously. "You're on the winning team, boy! Go get your kiss from Mrs. Johnson!" Arnold declined, but Booster pressed.

Finally Agent Iverson intervened. "Leave him alone," he said with finality.

Booster's expression turned nasty. "And what about you, Chief?" he snarled the word. "Aren't you going to collect your prize?"

"I do my kissing at home." The agent tried to pass the challenge off casually.

"But that's no fun for us. I say you kiss her here and now—unless you want to pass the privilege on to the man who came in second." He inclined his head toward Winston.

Without further comment, Agent Iverson took the few steps necessary to reach Kate and pulled her to her feet. Then he pressed warm lips against hers in a hard, angry kiss. "If you've seen enough, I'll take my wife home now," he growled.

Kate had to run to keep up with the agent as he strode furiously across the parking lot. His face was grim as he unlocked the door for her, then went around the car to get in on the driver's side. He backed out of their parking place and turned onto the highway, leaving the crowds and bright lights behind. They rode along in silence for several miles, and then the agent apologized. Kate wasn't sure if he was sorry about the kiss or his loss of temper.

"Booster seemed determined to make you mad," she ventured.

"Booster is obnoxious, but I shouldn't have let him get to me," he said, with a swift glance at Kate. "For a few minutes there, I felt like I really was Drew Johnson, defending my wife."

Kate's laugh was shaky. "It is hard to tell where the Johnsons end and where we begin. There are a lot of things about being Niki that I hate. But sometimes, like when we were talking to Happy—about wallpaper and fabric swatches and beautiful furniture—I loved being Niki. Kate Singleton would have been buying wallpaper from the clearance bin at a wallpaper outlet store and making her own curtains. And at least you won," Kate pointed out. "I would do almost anything to protect my baby, but kissing those two might be beyond my limit."

The agent nodded in the darkness. "I would have sacrificed our cover if necessary to stop them," he said. "Death by hired assassins would be preferable to a kiss from Booster and Winston." Kate smiled in agreement as they passed the Haggerty city limits sign. "Are you hoping for a girl or a boy?" he asked, changing the subject. When she didn't respond immediately, he clarified the question. "I mean, the baby."

Kate was quiet, considering the question. "It seems like it would be harder for a boy to grow up without a father, so I think I want a little girl." Seeing his distressed expression, she hurried to assure him. "I can take care of myself, you know."

"You wouldn't have to if Tony had been more careful," Agent Iverson muttered.

Kate sighed. "Maybe I should have complained about his constant traveling or insisted that he come home more often. If I had made him choose between me and his job, at least I would know—" She paused and took a breath. "But I can't change the past, and there's not much I can do about the present. My baby's future is up to me, and that's what matters now."

The agent pulled the van into the driveway. "I think you are very brave," he told her.

"That may be the nicest thing you've ever said to me," she replied with a smile. Their conversation ended abruptly when Miss Polly's upstairs lights came on, reminding them that they were under her constant surveillance.

* * *

On Sunday morning Kate applied makeup sparingly and wore a dress with a conservative hemline. She felt modest yet presentable when they left for Albany. As they drove along she noticed that Agent Iverson had dared to leave his silk pocket hanky at home. Bishop Sterling looked surprised when they walked into the chapel. "I don't think he expected us to come two weeks in a row," the agent whispered as they took their seats.

"It may send him into cardiac arrest if you pay your tithing," Kate murmured back. Apparently he decided to risk the bishop's health because she saw the agent pick up a donation slip on the way to Sunday School. The topic for the week was correct prayer language, and Agent Iverson appeared comatose by the time it ended. The discussion in Relief Society was livelier, and afterwards the president introduced Kate to her new visiting teachers. They made an appointment to come on Friday morning, and Kate wrote the time in Niki's rapidly filling wallet calendar.

After the meetings, the bishop followed them into the parking lot and pulled Agent Iverson aside. Kate waited most of the way home for him to divulge the nature of the bishop's remarks, but she finally had to ask.

"He wants me to have an opportunity to exercise my priesthood, so next week I'm supposed to stand at the south exit during the sacrament."

His voice was neutral so Kate couldn't tell how he felt about the assignment. "My dad used to love it when he got a chance to participate in sacrament ordinances," she volunteered. "He said he felt like he was personally serving the Savior."

The agent glanced over at her. "I don't have any objection to ushering during the sacrament," he said.

"Good," Kate responded firmly. "Because if you did, I'd have to give you another discourse on pride."

Miss Polly met them by their front steps and asked them to join her for Sunday dinner. She promised that Brother Paul would not be in attendance, but admitted that some career missionaries from Mexico had been invited. Kate and Agent Iverson reluctantly agreed to join her.

The missionaries were much more pleasant than the preacher had been. They were familiar with the Mormon Church and had met hundreds of full-time missionaries during their years in Mexico. They considered themselves experts on the area and occasionally spoke to each other in terribly accented Spanish. Kate watched the FBI agent under her lashes, knowing he understood every word and could talk circles around them if he chose to do so. He caught her watching him during one Spanish comment, and the corners of his mouth curved up in what was almost a smile.

On the way home Kate asked him what the missionary couple had said. "Pass the salt, would you like a roll, that kind of thing," he reported as he held the door open for her.

"Why would they bother saying such common things in Spanish?" she wondered aloud.

The agent raised an eyebrow, a small smile playing on his lips. "I think they just wanted us to know that they hadn't spent all those years in Mexico for nothing." Kate rolled her eyes and turned toward the stairs.

After the meal Kate took her regular nap and then went into the kitchen for a piece of the pie Miss Polly had sent home with them. She found Agent Iverson sitting at the table, looking over files.

"Your unsolved cases?" she asked as she cut a generous piece of pecan pie and put it on a plate.

"Some of them," he answered absently, apparently absorbed in thought. Then he looked up and asked abruptly, "How many car thefts do you think a town the size of Haggerty would have in an average year?"

Kate was surprised by the question, and pleased that he would ask her opinion. She considered it carefully as she put a forkful of pie into her mouth. "Three, maybe four," she guessed.

"Since January of this year there have been nine cars stolen within the Haggerty city limits. All were stolen at night in front of the owner's home." The agent shook his head. "Then again, it could just be an unexplained phenomenon."

"But you don't think so."

"In my experience, there are very few true coincidences."

"Do the cars have anything in common?"

"They are all fairly new and insured."

"Same insurance company?" Kate asked around a mouthful of brown sugar custard.

"No, but that's a good question." He looked at her with something approaching respect. "There is one more thing that they all have in common, and I think that it may be part of why Booster had these files at his house." Kate was paying close attention. "All of the owners had been ticketed for speeding about a month before the theft."

"Winston," Kate breathed. "He's writing tickets, getting the personal information, stealing the cars and then selling them."

Agent Iverson laughed. "It would certainly be easy to fire him if that were true. Unfortunately different officers wrote the tickets. Winston did write most of them, but I told you that speed traps are his hobby."

"Who else has access to the information on the tickets?" Kate asked as she washed off her plate.

"During the day, each ticket is called in to Leita to see if there are any other outstanding warrants. At night there's no dispatcher on duty, so we have to call the county sheriff's office."

They looked at each other. "If the owners of the stolen cars were ticketed at night, then it couldn't be Leita," Kate said hopefully.

"I'll check it out tomorrow," the agent promised as he stacked the files on the side of the table. When he suggested they go for a walk, Kate groaned, then went upstairs to put on Niki's tennis shoes.

* * *

On Monday morning the house was overrun with workmen by eight o'clock. The contractor from Albany came to prepare an estimate on the completion of the kitchen. Kate called Agent Iverson with the estimate, and he gave the go-ahead to start immediately. The wallpaper hanger and an assistant arrived and started hanging paper in the master bedroom. Happy sent an employee to measure windows, and Ellis started priming the door frames in the nursery.

To escape the noise and dust and paint fumes, Kate went into the backyard. Seeing Miss Eugenia at work in her garden, Kate walked over to join her.

"A late freeze this past spring got a couple of my azaleas and I haven't had the heart to dig them up," Miss Eugenia explained, holding up a handful of sticks.

"You certainly have a beautiful yard." Kate looked around at all the flowers and shrubs, the healthy lawn, and the thriving garden.

"It takes hard work and dedication, but a yard tells a lot about the folks that live there."

Kate glanced over at her own dead grass and then turned stricken eyes back to Miss Eugenia, who had seen the direction of Kate's gaze. "Your place has nowhere to go but up," she consoled her briskly. "If you'll clear out the front flowerbed, I'll give you some cuttings from my azaleas. They'll bloom in the spring, and in a couple of years they'll be spectacular."

Miss Eugenia found Kate a pair of gardening gloves and a trowel. Then she led Kate to a small flowerbed at the corner of the house. By lunchtime Kate had cleared a spot about three feet square.

"It's a good thing you're young," Miss Eugenia said when she surveyed her meager progress. "At this rate, Ellis will be through painting the nursery before you plant one flower!"

Miss Eugenia invited Kate to her house for the midday meal and then sent her in to get Ellis. Kate called Agent Iverson at the police station to let him know her plans and to ask if he wanted her to bring him anything. He declined, saying that Leita had gotten him a cheeseburger from Haggerty Station.

Kate was astounded when Miss Eugenia served baked pork chops, scalloped potatoes, cornbread, and a spinach salad for lunch. The older lady explained that traditionally the people of Haggerty ate their largest meal at midday and called it dinner, then ate a lighter meal called "supper" at night.

"So you don't have a lunch at all," Kate said as she poured gravy on her pork chop. "No wonder Ellis always wants to eat with you instead of me!"

After dinner, Kate went home and negotiated her way through

the disaster area. Who would have thought that things would have to get so much worse in the process of getting better? All the furniture in the master bedroom was pushed into the middle of the room, and half the walls were papered. Even though it was a pretty magnolia print, Kate was disappointed that she couldn't take her nap.

As she turned to leave the room, she saw Agent Iverson's bed across the hall. She had eaten more than usual and felt exceptionally drowsy. The soft comforter was just too tempting. She walked in and stretched out on the antique bed. As she dozed off, she pressed her face into the pillow, inhaling the now familiar smell of him. She was awakened some time later by someone calling Niki's name.

Her eyes flew open to see Agent Iverson standing over her. She sat up quickly, embarrassed.

"I only meant to rest for a few minutes," she apologized, glancing over at the clock on the nightstand and seeing that it was almost three o'clock. Then she looked down at her wrinkled tee shirt and grass-stained pants. "I'm a mess."

"I've seen worse," he responded blandly. "Happy's here. She's ordered furniture and all kinds of stuff. She wants to go over it with us. I'll entertain her while you change." She nodded as she climbed off the bed. She stopped at the doorway when she saw the paper-hangers in her room.

"Get your things and bring them in here," the agent suggested practically. He was standing right behind her, and she thought she actually felt his breath on her neck as he spoke. Afraid to face him, she walked to her closet and pulled a cotton dress off a hanger. Then she took it back to his room and changed quickly. Grabbing the comb on his dresser, Kate ran it through her hair without thinking, then dropped it abruptly.

Staring into the mirror at her own haunted eyes, Kate took a deep breath and prayed for composure. She was lonely and vulnerable. Developing feelings for Agent Iverson would be unwise, at the very least, and quite possibly dangerous. Besides, he didn't even like her. He had made it very clear that he was anxious for this assignment to be over so he could get something more challenging. She sighed, hoping that after the baby was born she would regain some emotional strength and be able to ward off these ridiculous feelings. Squaring her shoulders, she turned off the light and left his bedroom.

From the hallway Kate could hear Agent Iverson and Happy engaged in a friendly conversation. She walked into the den and sat beside the decorator on the couch. With her mind still in turmoil, she found it hard to concentrate on their furniture discussion.

Was she getting lost in Niki Johnson? Certainly she was starting to care too much about Niki's house and Niki's neighbors and Niki's pretend husband. Worst of all, she dreaded the prospect of leaving Niki's world behind when things were settled with Tony's enemies.

Happy stayed until the workmen left for the day. Then Kate walked around with Agent Iverson and surveyed the mess. Sawdust covered the hardwood floors and the kitchen was unusable. The master bedroom was papered, but the trim wasn't painted. Agent Iverson said that Ellis might get to it by Easter. The reference to the future made her sad. Where would she be next spring when the trim was painted and the azaleas were blooming in the flowerbed?

* * *

For dinner they ate a chicken casserole that the Methodist preacher's wife had dropped by. While they washed dishes, Agent Iverson told her that he'd checked out the time the speeding tickets had been given to people who subsequently had their cars stolen. While most were written during the day, two had been issued at night.

"That clears Leita," Kate said with relief.

"Not completely," he said, shaking his head regretfully. "She still had access to all of them. I asked Arnold and he said tickets written after Leita leaves are put on her desk so that she can record and file them the next morning."

"So what now?" Kate asked hesitantly.

"Now we wait for another car to be stolen," he answered grimly.

Annabelle called on Tuesday to say that she had devised a plan to get the black lacquer dining room furniture. The contractor Agent Iverson had hired, Dennis Prater, was a friend of Annabelle's who collected antique cars. Annabelle had a vintage truck that had been restored by her late husband. Mr. Prater had asked to buy it several times, but she had refused to sell it. Now she was moving and wouldn't have a place to keep it. So, she would give it to Mr. Prater. He, in turn, would subtract the considerable value of the truck from the Johnsons' bill, and Annabelle could have the dining room furniture, which would look fabulous in her ultra-modern house.

"That is all so complicated. I would be glad to just give it to you," Kate protested.

"That would be unethical. I asked Happy, and she said that furniture is worth over $5,000. It would be absurd to give something so valuable to a stranger."

"Well, trading it for the old truck will be fine then," Kate agreed listlessly.

* * *

Later, the FBI agent posing as Agent Thomas's wife came by for an interview. Miracle Moore was a tall black woman in her thirties with short hair and brilliantly white teeth. She said that she would come for a few hours a day until the baby was born and then all day for a couple of weeks afterwards. Miss Eugenia was pleased with the arrangement and took full credit for finding the "help."

Mr. Prater, the contractor, loaded the dining room table and chairs into his truck at the end of the day on Tuesday and took them to Annabelle. Even though Kate had never liked the furniture, the house seemed even more inhospitable without it.

By Wednesday night, most of the wallpaper was in place, the kitchen was improving, the roof was fixed, and the windows all had blinds at last. Ellis had just finished painting the woodwork in the nursery when the baby furniture arrived on Thursday. Agent Iverson came home from the station early and helped to assemble it. They put the rocking chair together first. Kate sat in it and quietly watched the other pieces take shape. After the crib had been put together and safety-tested repeatedly, Agent Iverson asked Kate where she wanted to put it.

"I thought over there, in front of the windows," she responded tentatively.

"Too much light." Miss Eugenia vetoed this idea with a brisk shake of her head. "The baby would never get any sleep during the day. Put it here." Without waiting to see if Kate agreed, she pushed the crib against a far wall where it would not be in direct sunlight. Kate shrugged.

As the agent unpacked a miniature armoire, Miss Eugenia started to fold a wall hanging, but Kate stopped her. "That goes on the wall," Kate explained, showing her the small plastic loops that were sewn on the back.

"Is that a real antique baby quilt?" Miss Eugenia asked, fingering the yellowed fabric.

"It's a reproduction," Kate explained. "They make it new, then soak it in diluted tea to give it an aged look." Miss Eugenia's eyebrows shot up. "That's what it said in the catalog."

"If that isn't about the most foolish thing I've ever heard" was Miss Eugenia's response.

By the time they had the changing table assembled, Miss Eugenia was grumbling about her arthritis and young people in general.

"Everybody makes such a production out of having a baby these days. You think you need all kinds of expensive gadgets, you wear maternity clothes that have to be dry cleaned, you buy fancy furniture and hang new quilts dipped in tea on your walls." She glared at the wall hanging. "In my day, maternity clothes consisted of a set of loose cotton dresses, we borrowed baby furniture, and everyone actually used old quilts." She shook her head.

Kate looked down at the designer outfit she was wearing and knew that Miss Eugenia probably thought her contemptible. But she was stuck in Niki's life and had to take the bad with the good.

* * *

For the next couple of days the condition of the house continued to improve, but Kate couldn't take any pleasure in it. Occasionally she would feel Agent Iverson's brooding eyes on her. She avoided him as much as possible and went through the motions of her assumed identity. She washed clothes, made sandwiches, and heated casseroles. The house was always full of people. Workmen were everywhere. Happy came by daily to measure walls, hang pictures, and scatter rugs. Ellis puttered from one room to the next, painting woodwork, and Miss Eugenia dropped in regularly to monitor the progress.

Miss Eugenia insisted that Kate learn more about gardening, and by Thursday, she had the flowerbed on one side of the front porch cleared out. Miss Eugenia helped her to choose bedding plants, which they arranged around the azalea cuttings.

That night Kate was particularly discouraged as she stared at the ceiling, waiting to fall asleep. Her life seemed so futile and meaningless. She was fixing up a house that wasn't hers, planting flowers she would never see bloom, and falling in love with a man who didn't belong to her. Restless, she got up and stepped into the hallway.

There was no light shining under Agent Iverson's door. She listened for the sound of the television downstairs, but all was quiet. She tiptoed down to the den, where a street lamp provided enough light for her to locate the Johnsons' unused Book of Mormon. She had it in her hand when Agent Iverson spoke to her from the recliner.

"Kate?"

Startled, she spun around to face him. "Why are you lurking down here in the dark?" she demanded unreasonably.

"I could ask you the same thing," he responded, his features softened by the dim light.

Kate willed her heart to stop pounding and clutched the scriptures to her chest. She watched as the agent's eyes followed the movement. She lifted her chin defensively. "What? Do you think you're the only person in this house righteous enough to read the scriptures?" He gave her a bewildered look and she turned away impatiently. She was not in the mood to argue with him. Once she was back upstairs and had her breathing under control, Kate thumbed through the book until she found the thirty-second chapter of Alma.

Alma said that faith, like her azalea cuttings, would grow through patience and diligence and long-suffering. Kate smiled at the thought of her little flower garden. It was a small piece of order amid the wild confusion of the rest of the yard. Her life was unsettled and her future uncertain, but she knew that there was a home for her somewhere. She blinked back her tears, determined to be faithful and strong. And even though she probably wouldn't be around to see her flowers bloom, she would nurture and care for them. Then, when the time came for her to go, she would leave a little of herself behind in Haggerty.

* * *

The visiting teachers came on Friday morning. Sister Baylor and Sister Armistead brought her a pie, which Kate added to the collection already in the refrigerator. She apologized for the construction mess as they sat in the den and delivered their message. After the lesson they told her that enrichment meeting was on the second Thursday of each month and invited her to attend. They were nice, and Kate felt slightly encouraged after their visit.

Miracle Moore, the FBI agent and temporary housemaid, came after lunch and performed as her name implied. She swept and dusted and vacuumed until the house was spotlessly clean. Kate offered to help, but the woman laughed and said she worked better alone. Kate moved drop cloths for Ellis until he finished painting for the day. As he packed up his brushes, she asked him to open the attic door. He pried the door open and tested the old steps for soundness before he shuffled toward home.

Kate didn't find any heirloom tables or Tiffany lamps in the attic, but she did locate some boxes filled with mementos from Miss Imogene Riley's life. One box contained hundreds of pages of piano sheet music, mostly hymns in various arrangements. She found some photographs in another box, including one taken of the house from the front yard in 1910. Kate set the old picture aside so she could have it framed later. A final box yielded some clothes and handkerchiefs and an old dance card, with a cheerful, if faded, tassel hanging from the corner.

Sitting cross-legged on the plywood floor, her back against a trunk, she studied the little card, reading the men's names that were neatly written in the squares. At that moment, Agent Iverson's head appeared at floor level.

"So, did you find any treasures?" he asked emerging through the hole. Bending almost double as he walked toward her, he took a seat on a stool near Kate.

"Most people wouldn't think so," she said as she showed him the picture and told him her plan to display it somewhere in the house. "I'll bet my mother would love that sewing form." She pointed toward the wicker figure standing in the corner.

"You miss your mother," the agent observed, his voice softening.

Kate leaned back, closing her eyes against the sight of him in the fading afternoon light. "Oh yes, I miss her very much. But it's more a dull ache than a sharp pain. I've had plenty of time to get used to being separated from her. We've basically been apart ever since I moved away to college," Kate sighed.

The agent glanced at the old picture, then back at Kate. "And you really like this place."

She nodded. "The stability of this house and Haggerty in general appeals to me. My parents married young while my father was still in school. It took him forever to finish. He had to sell insurance and wait tables and sometimes even skip a couple of semesters to support us. We were always poor and moved a lot trying to find more space for less money. When he finally got his doctorate, he started teaching at a small college in Utah. My parents bought a house, and it seemed like we were settled at last. A year later my dad found a lump under his arm while he was taking a shower. In six months he was dead. I haven't really felt at home anywhere since then." She forced herself to continue. "Until now."

"How did you meet Tony?" the agent asked, settling comfortably against the dusty wall.

"He came to a dance at the University of Utah with his cousin the weekend before I graduated. Tony had been with the FBI for a couple of years and he seemed so mature. He asked me to dance, and when it was time to leave, he wanted my phone number. I didn't usually have much of an effect on men." She glanced up to see him watching her closely, maybe sympathetically. "But I dated," she said quickly, feeling defensive.

He nodded. "Just not FBI agents."

"No, never anyone that interesting," she agreed. "He called me the next morning and said he was only home for a week and wanted to spend every minute of it with me. I never understood the term 'whirlwind romance' until then." She met the agent's gaze directly. "I was a very dull, predictable sort of girl. Tony was the most exciting thing that had ever happened to me. When he left, I didn't expect to hear from him again. That night the phone rang and when I heard his voice . . ." She shrugged, tears filling her eyes.

"He called me every day and even wrote sometimes." She smiled at the thought of Tony composing a love letter. "He asked me to marry him over the telephone from the Los Angeles airport on his way to Chicago. He flew to Salt Lake on a Friday in time to get the marriage license, and we were married in the bishop's office the next morning. He left again on Monday, and I packed my things and drove to Chicago. I found an apartment, got a job, and saw him when he could get away from his work.

"At first he made it home at least one day a week. Then he would be gone for a whole week at a time, then two, then it was a month or more. It was almost as if he was conditioning me, teaching me to live without him."

"Maybe he was."

Kate shrugged. "I wanted to buy a house, but he said he might be transferred. I wanted to start a family, but he said things were too unsettled. One day I asked him why he'd even bothered to get married since he didn't want anything permanent in his life. He just laughed and said he just couldn't resist me." Kate shook her head. "Tony was like that. When we were together, I would forget all the loneliness, the fear, and disillusionment. He could make me believe that we really did have a future together. But then he'd leave, and I'd start to wonder."

"If the two of you could really be happy?"

"And if I'd ever see him again," she admitted. "I didn't shed a tear at his memorial service and his parents were offended. I guess they thought that I didn't love Tony or that I wasn't sorry he was dead. They didn't understand that Tony left me long before he died, and that I had been grieving since the early weeks of our marriage.

"There I was, stuck in Chicago at a job I hated, living in a dreary apartment with no friends or anyone to talk to. I wanted so much to go home to my mother and I seriously considered it. But she was struggling to raise the girls without my dad and had enough problems. I couldn't add to her worries."

"So you stuck it out," he concluded.

Kate nodded. "I didn't know I was pregnant until a few weeks after Tony died. I was so grateful that the Lord was giving me someone of my very own and letting me keep a little piece of Tony after all. Now I have to concentrate on building a safe, happy life for my child." Her hands went around her abdomen in a protective gesture.

"What about you, Kate? Are you ever going to have a place to call home?" he asked.

She looked at him in the deepening darkness and whispered, "I've learned not to expect too much from life." She hoped he couldn't see her tears.

"You've been unhappy for the last few days," he said after a while.

"I'm afraid," she admitted honestly and Agent Iverson raised an eyebrow. "Not of Tony's enemies. In fact, I feel so safe in this house that I rarely think of the danger. No, I'm afraid of getting too attached to Niki's life. I have to remember that all this—" she waved around the attic, "—is an illusion."

He leaned toward her then. "Mark," he whispered.

Kate wasn't sure she'd heard him correctly. "What?" she asked.

"My name is Mark," he repeated softly.

It wasn't much, just a tiny piece of personal information. But she accepted it for what it was—a gift of confidence. She extended her hand toward him. "It's nice to meet you, Mark." He stared at her hand for a few seconds, then clasped it in his own. Their eyes met and he smiled. "Does this mean we're friends?" she asked.

"I guess so."

"Well," she exhaled deeply. "How about a friendly casserole dinner?"

"Sounds irresistible," he said as he pulled her to her feet, adding, "I hope it's chicken something."

"Sometimes dreams do come true," she reminded him as they made their way down the stairs and to the kitchen.

* * *

On Saturday Mark tried to get out of his appointment at the Albany hair salon. "I could probably go another week," he suggested hopefully as he ducked to look in the mirror above his antique dresser. "Or I could just let the barber in Haggerty cut it on Tuesday."

"I'll bet Melba Fishburn would do it," Kate said from the doorway.

He smiled at her reflection in the mirror. "She's already offered. For free."

"That might not turn out to be much of a bargain." Kate looked over his shoulder into the mirror and put a hand to her own hair. "I could probably wait another week, too. Or just let my hair go back to its natural color."

Mark shook his head in resignation and joined her in the hallway. "Niki would rather die than miss a salon appointment." It was an unfortunate choice of words, and Kate could tell that he regretted them immediately.

She took his hand and examined it carefully. "And Drew would never allow his fingernails to get that unbuffed look," she predicted.

His fingers wrapped around hers. He was so close she could feel the warmth of his body. "Your dossier described you as a nice, quiet girl," he murmured, studying her carefully. "But the better I get to know you . . ."

Overwhelmed by his nearness, Kate took a step back and pulled free of his grasp. "Niki has had an effect on me," she admitted, turning abruptly toward the stairs.

The hair salon was a chain out of Atlanta called The Cutting Edge. Although several men were getting haircuts, Mark was the only one who had his nails done. He braved the stir his manicure caused, joking with the young woman as she trimmed and buffed. But Kate could see the tension around his mouth and knew he hated every humiliating minute of it. Before leaving the salon, Kate made an appointment for manicures again the next Saturday and haircuts in two weeks. Then they went out into the stifling heat.

"Well, that wasn't so bad," Kate said cheerfully as they settled back into the van.

"If I ever see Drew Johnson again, I'm going to break all his buffed fingers, one at a time," Mark said grimly as he pulled onto the street and headed toward the Wal-Mart.

When they got home, Mark mowed the dead grass while Kate put away their groceries. She had bought a roast for Sunday, determined that they would not be forced to eat with Miss Polly again. Mark came in and said he needed to go to the station and take care of some paperwork. While he was gone, Kate mixed up refrigerator roll dough and put it in one of Niki's gold-rimmed crystal bowls. Then she took a chocolate cherry cake out of the freezer to thaw overnight.

She had taken a shower and was curled up on the couch in the den watching the finale of a weeklong *Who Wants to be a Millionaire?* marathon when Mark got home. She told him that Miss Eugenia had brought over something called "pimento cheese" if he wanted to make a sandwich. He reminded her that the next day was Fast Sunday.

"I started my fast at one so it will be a full twenty-four hours," he said, sitting back in the recliner. It wasn't just what he said, but the condescending tone he used that irritated her.

"Don't pat yourself on the back too hard. You might break one of those shiny nails," she advised sarcastically.

"What do you mean by that?" he asked, looking genuinely surprised.

"I fast when I'm not pregnant."

"I never said you didn't. I just said I didn't want a pigmented cheese sandwich."

"Pimento cheese," Kate corrected, "and remember what the Savior said about the Pharisees. If you brag about fasting, you won't get any credit for it in heaven."

Mark's eyes narrowed. "I don't think telling your wife that you don't want a sandwich can be compared to yelling an egotistical prayer on a street corner."

Kate lifted her chin in defiance. "You think I was wrong to marry Tony out of the temple."

Mark sat up straight. "I've never made any judgments about your personal life."

"Yes you have. You think I don't fast or read the scriptures. You think because you went on a mission and pay your tithing that you're better than I am. Well, I paid my tithing, too, when I was working. I read my scriptures every day, and I had a calling in the Primary."

Tears started spilling onto her cheeks. "And I'm not really crying. Pregnant people just do this." Desperate to get away, Kate turned and ran upstairs, leaving him staring after her.

Mark knocked on her door a few minutes later. "Kate? Are you okay?"

"Go away. I'm asleep," she said, burying her face in a pillow to hide her sobs. After a few seconds, she heard his footsteps retreating down the hallway.

* * *

On Sunday morning neither of them mentioned their argument from the night before. Mark did such a good job of standing by the door during the sacrament that they asked him to pass with the deacons the next week.

"Before you know it I'll be saying a prayer," he murmured as they walked to their Sunday School class. The lesson was on respecting priesthood authority, and Mark actually made a few comments.

Afterwards the elders quorum president met them in the hall and told them that a home teacher had been assigned and would be in contact soon. They passed the bishop on their way out the door.

"We want to give the two of you time to get settled in, but after the baby comes we'll talk about callings," the bishop promised as he shook their hands.

"When he realizes how righteous you are, he'll probably call you to be an Apostle," Kate whispered spitefully as they walked to the van.

"Bishops don't call Apostles," he replied, holding the door open for her. Kate sniffed in response and stared out the window all the way home.

Miss Polly was standing on her porch when they pulled up into the driveway. She rushed over and invited them to dinner. When Kate said that she had cooked dinner already, Miss Polly's face fell. Mark took pity on the woman and promised that they would come over for some blackberry cobbler later that evening. Miss Polly left, mildly appeased.

"You've got to stop being so charming," Kate grumbled as he unlocked their front door. "All these women bringing us food and inviting us over to eat is driving me crazy."

"Some people have worse problems," he informed her as they walked inside. He paused as he stepped into the house, nose up, and inhaled deeply. "Roast," he murmured reverently. "It makes me think . . ."

"That Martha Stewart has moved in?" Kate murmured irritably.

"No." He turned to her. "I was going to say it made me think of home." All her animosity toward him evaporated as she looked into his soft brown eyes. They stared at each other for a few seconds, then Kate went into the kitchen to check on her roast. Mark followed, insisting that she let him help prepare the meal.

He took off Drew Johnson's suit coat and tie and hung them over the back of one of the kitchen chairs. Then he peeled potatoes while she put the rolls in the oven and arranged the small pot roast on a platter. With his top button undone and his shirttail hanging out, he looked so adorable that Kate's breath caught in her throat each time she glanced in his direction. The meal was delicious, and afterwards Kate retired for her nap in triumph. Mark Iverson's voice awakened her at dusk. "Kate," he whispered into her ear.

It sounded so wonderful to hear her real name on his lips. She smiled drowsily up at him and murmured, "I always sleep longer than I mean to." She stretched her arms, almost touching his shoulders. "Is it time to go over to Miss Polly's?"

"I've already been and come back," he informed her. "I brought you a piece of cobbler, but right now our home teacher is sitting in the den and he wants to meet you."

After he closed the door behind him, Kate slipped her dress over her head and ran a brush through her hair. When she rushed into the den, a little man in a baggy blue suit stood and extended his hand. He was mostly bald and wore glasses with lenses so thick that they seemed to weigh his head down. He was short, only about five feet, and introduced himself as Brother Stoops. The name was so appropriate that Kate almost laughed out loud.

Brother Stoops sat in the recliner so Kate took a seat beside Mark on the couch, hoping they looked like a happy couple. The home teacher pulled a rolled-up *Ensign* from his inside coat pocket and fumbled through the pages until he found the First Presidency message. For the next thirty minutes, he read in a perfect monotone. He lost his place regularly and had to start back at the beginning of each paragraph. By the time he finished, Kate could have recited most of it. He gave them a yellowed business card printed with his name and phone number.

"I can be here in a few minutes if you need me," he promised. When he asked if they had a garden, Mark said that they had moved in too late to plant one. "You'd be surprised how long the growing season is down here," he said. "You could probably plant some tomatoes tomorrow, and they'd have time to produce before the first hard freeze." Then he told them that he was the ward home storage coordinator and asked if they had a year's supply of basic foods. Kate saw Mark's eyes narrow and decided to answer herself.

"We probably have a year's supply of casseroles!" she reported cheerfully. She was pleased with her witty response, but neither man laughed. When the door finally closed behind Brother Stoops, Kate turned to the agent. He was still sulking. "I guess you have a two-year's supply of everything stored in Washington."

"I never even seriously considered storing food," he replied stiffly. "But if I had a family, I would have. Stupid Drew Johnson," he muttered under his breath.

"How well did you know him?" Kate asked. "Drew, I mean."

"Not well. Most of what I know I learned from his very thick dossier. I met him a few times when he came with his father-in-law to Washington. I think he had political aspirations."

"Do you ever wonder about them? How they're doing with their new life?"

"I think about Drew Johnson every time I put a silk hanky in my pocket or look at my buffed nails or act like I don't take the gospel seriously," the agent answered with resentment.

Kate sighed. "I think about Niki every time I look in the mirror. I never had the time or money for haircuts and expensive makeup, let alone manicures or highlights." She touched her blonde hair absently. "I think about her when I talk to Miss Eugenia or walk through this lovely house. I feel indebted to Niki because I like her life better than I did my own." Kate laughed nervously, sorry that she had been so honest. "I mean, who wouldn't love Haggerty?"

The agent nodded, watching her closely. "Life here is appealing, almost tempting."

"But, it's not real," Kate spoke for them both. "We're not Drew and Niki."

"No," Mark agreed. "Mr. Evans could call at any time and tell us to pack up and go back to our real lives."

Kate didn't want to think about returning to the lonely apartment in Chicago and her monotonous job at the law firm, so she stood up briskly and walked toward the door.

"Did you say you brought home some of Miss Polly's cobbler?" she asked and he nodded. "If you promise not to mention Mr. Evans or Chicago again, I'll split it with you." Then she walked to the kitchen, confident that he would follow.

CHAPTER 6

Mark was off duty on Monday for Labor Day so they agreed to sleep late. The doorbell rang insistently at nine o'clock and they met in the hall, both intending to answer it. Kate was trying, unsuccessfully, to get a floor-length cotton robe tied around her huge stomach. They nodded self-consciously to each other, then walked downstairs together. Brother Stoops was standing on their front porch wearing a brown polyester leisure suit and clutching a dingy white plastic bucket with a "Pure Lard" sticker proclaiming its original contents.

Brother Stoops did not bother with small talk. "I believe that food storage is to the Latter-day Saints what lamb's blood was to the people of Moses. If there is wheat stored in your house, it's a sign to God that His children reside within." Kate looked down at the bucket in his hands and saw the words "Hard Red Wheat—1964" scrawled across the lid. "I couldn't sleep last night, thinking about you over here without so much as a grain of wheat under your roof. I can't give you a year's supply, but I have some extra. I've brought you ten buckets. At least that's a start."

"Oh, Brother Stoops," Kate felt the tears gathering in her eyes. "That is so kind of you, but . . ."

Mark put his hand on her arm. "We can't begin to thank you enough," he said, surprising her with his acceptance of the old man's gift. Kate watched from the porch as the two of them unloaded the wheat from Brother Stoops's dusty pickup truck. When the buckets were all neatly stacked inside, the home teacher waved good-bye and said he'd check on them again soon. Kate was staring at the wheat when she heard the door close.

"Where are we going to put this?" she asked softly.

Mark lifted a bucket and took it into the coat closet. He stepped back out a second later, still holding the wheat. His face was stained with color. "We can't put it in here with the naked people," he said, and Kate had to laugh. His lips twitched as he set the bucket with the others. "I guess we'll just leave it here for now."

Miss Eugenia and Annabelle came over after lunch to invite the Johnsons to the Methodist church's annual Labor Day Picnic that afternoon. Mark told them that they were planning to attend. In fact, the Chief was scheduled to start barbecuing hot dogs and hamburgers there in less than an hour. Miss Eugenia spotted the buckets of wheat and asked the predictable questions.

"I thought people stopped worrying about starving after Y2K," Annabelle commented, walking over to examine the lard containers.

"Our Church has encouraged its members to store food for decades," Mark said.

"Your church wants you to hoard food?" Miss Eugenia looked mildly repulsed.

"We don't hoard it. We just keep extra food on hand in case of emergency."

The sisters were staring at them dubiously. "It's like Miss Eugenia canning tomatoes and green beans in the summer to eat during the winter," Kate explained, trying for an analogy she hoped they could relate to.

"What do you do with wheat anyway?" Miss Eugenia wanted to know.

"Grind it into flour and make bread," Mark replied.

Annabelle considered this. "So, if the world as we know it comes to an end, you'll have bread and Eugenia will have vegetables."

Kate laughed. "We can eat together and cover two of the basic food groups!"

"And if you behave yourself, Annabelle, we might share with you," Miss Eugenia said imperiously. Then she offered Kate a ride to the picnic since the Chief had to go early to cook. Kate accepted, and Miss Eugenia told her they would meet in the driveway at five o'clock.

They made the short trip to the Methodist church in Miss Eugenia's old Buick. The weather was hot, but the sun was starting to sink behind the trees. Miss Eugenia led Kate all around the grounds of the Haggerty Methodist Church, introducing her to innumerable townspeople until they finally reached the back of the building where the barbecue grills were set up. A big patio umbrella had been positioned above the area to provide some shade, but Kate knew Mark had to be extremely hot. As she walked toward him, she heard laughter to her left.

"The Chief looks a little warm." The booming voice of Booster McMillan carried across from a tree about a hundred feet away. "I was expecting a fancy city boy like him to sweat perfume!" The ex-chief laughed at his own joke. "But at least now we know that manicured hands do flip better burgers," he roared again.

Winston Jones was sitting in a lawn chair beside his former boss. Glaring at the men under the tree, Kate leaned toward her husband. Mark was concentrating on the meat spread out on the grill and didn't see her.

"What are those two idiots doing?" she asked in a low voice.

He glanced up at her, then over at his tormentors. "What they do best—causing trouble."

Kate's eyes were pained. "It's not right for you to have to listen to their ridicule," she whispered.

The FBI agent seemed to find her comment amusing. After making sure no one was close by, he leaned forward. "Even back in the real world, I occasionally had to deal with people who didn't like me. I can stand it," he promised.

Miss Eugenia walked over and handed Kate a paper plate with a hamburger bun opened on it. She held her own plate out and asked the police chief to put a well-done burger on the bread. Mark served both women, then Miss Eugenia said she was going to get Niki out of the sun, but promised to send reinforcements.

"Booster and Winston have been making fun of him," Kate hissed as they walked along.

"That type of common behavior usually backfires," Miss Eugenia predicted sagely.

When they passed the welcome booth, she told a woman named Eva Nell that the police chief needed to be relieved immediately. "I happened to notice Booster McMillan and Winston Jones near the grill, and they seemed full of energy. Ask them to spell the Chief," she suggested.

Eva Nell nodded, and Miss Eugenia directed Kate to some folding chairs set up under a striped awning.

When Mark joined them a few minutes later, he had changed his shirt and his nose was sunburned. Kate admired him furtively as he settled into a chair across from her. The moment was ruined when Melba Fishburn sashayed up and stood directly in front of him, almost touching his knees.

"I am so disappointed that you aren't cooking anymore," she announced with an exaggerated pout. "I had my heart set on eating a hamburger prepared by you just for me." She shifted her weight from one sparkly gold sandal to the other. Her shorts were brief and exposed a great deal of nicely shaped leg.

"I cooked for a couple of hours, Ms. Fishburn. Pick any hamburger on the platter, and I'll guarantee you it was grilled by me," Mark said pleasantly.

"I told him to quit being so charming," Kate murmured to Miss Eugenia as the beautician asked Mark's opinion about the best way for a young, attractive, single woman to meet a nice man these days.

"I don't know why you care," Miss Eugenia replied.

Kate was thrown completely off-balance by the comment. "What do you mean?" she demanded.

As Miss Eugenia held up a hand while she chewed a big bite of hamburger, Melba laughed in response to something witty that Agent Iverson had said. Kate looked over and watched the woman shake several bracelets up her arm, then walk away. "I mean that you two don't act like married folks at all," Miss Eugenia answered. Her statement attracted the agent's attention.

"In what way?" he asked, pulling his chair closer to the women.

"In every way and don't think I'm the only one who's noticed. It's not just that you don't sleep together." Kate rolled her eyes. "It's that you never even touch each other." Kate heard a slight intake of breath from the man who was now very close beside her. "Like you're strangers or something." She turned to Kate. "You don't know how he likes his eggs, how much starch he wants in his uniform shirts and you blush like an adolescent girl every time you see him."

"I do?" Kate's voice was strained. Miss Eugenia nodded, scooping up a forkful of potato salad.

"What are people saying about us?" Mark's tone was deceptively calm.

"That you're having marital problems. It's generally assumed that you had an affair with another woman before you came here," she told Mark. "They say you were fired from your job in New York. I heard that you probably would have gone to jail if Niki's father hadn't intervened. He arranged for you to get the job in Haggerty and bought the Riley house for you. You're supposedly trying to save your marriage, but everyone thinks it's just a matter of time before Niki divorces you and moves back home to her parents."

Miss Eugenia's disclosure left Kate speechless.

"I'm afraid that a lot of what you've heard is true." Agent Iverson accepted the blame for Drew Johnson's misdeeds with quiet dignity, and Kate wanted to weep at the disappointment in Miss Eugenia's eyes. "We've made mistakes, but we're trying to change."

Miss Eugenia glanced over at Kate's expensive sundress. "It looks to me like you're making the same mistakes all over again, buying fancy clothes and furniture."

Kate tried to come up with a plausible-sounding explanation. "My clothes were bought before all that," she said, feeling the color rise in her cheeks. "And my . . . father's paying for the furniture."

"You should learn to be satisfied with the things your husband can provide. If you're smart, you'll send those credit cards straight back to your daddy before you get Drew into more trouble," Miss Eugenia advised her gravely.

Mark shook his head. "Niki does have expensive tastes, but she wasn't solely responsible for our financial problems. I have a tendency to be a little . . . proud," he forced the word out. "I didn't want to admit that I couldn't afford our lifestyle. Niki's father wants her to have a nice home, and I figure I owe him that much. But once we get the house fixed up, we'll try to be more independent."

Kate realized that he was doing the best he could to defend her, given the past they had been assigned. His effort touched her deeply, and she wanted to do her part as well.

"Drew's job in New York required him to be gone a lot," she said, choosing her words carefully. "Up until our move to Haggerty, we pretty much led separate lives. I'm afraid I don't really know how to be his wife," she admitted with complete honesty.

Miss Eugenia considered this for a moment. "I firmly believe that people can change, and I've always said that love can conquer all."

"I didn't know you were the one who said that," Mark teased, but Kate could still see the tension around his eyes.

Miss Eugenia studied them both. "You know what would go a long way toward ending some of those divorce rumors?" she asked. "About half the town is watching us right now, and it might do the trick if you were to give Niki a big kiss, Drew— " Kate and Mark exchanged startled looks, "—and I don't mean a little peck on the forehead. If that's the best you can do, you might as well go on back over and cook hamburgers with Booster and Winston."

Mark glanced over his shoulder to see his tormenters sweating over the hot grill. He laughed and turned back to Kate. Their eyes met and she watched his expression change from amused to determined and then to something else harder to define. Her heart pounded as his face moved toward hers. Then her eyes focused on his lips, and suddenly all the loneliness and fear and longing of the last weeks overwhelmed her. She reached up and put her hands behind his neck, drawing him close and changing the quick kiss he had probably intended to give her into something much more.

"Well, I declare!" Miss Eugenia finally interrupted them. They pulled apart, shaken and breathing heavily. "When I said I didn't mean a little peck . . ."

"What in the world is going on over here?" Miss Polly rushed up to them, her face flushed and her chest heaving. "This is a church social," she scolded Mark.

Miss Eugenia jumped to their defense. "They are married, Pauline," she said. "And I don't know why you're objecting. Having to watch a little kiss in public can't compare with looking in their windows, trying to catch the Chief in his long underwear." Miss Polly whimpered at this remark and Miss Eugenia sighed. "It was all my fault anyway. I told them the ladies at the Quilting Club said they never show any affection for each other, and they were trying to improve their image."

Kate sipped lemonade frantically, trying to hide her embarrassment, but Miss Eugenia seemed very pleased with the attention they had attracted. Annabelle joined them a little later.

"I hear you have an X-rated corner over here," she teased as she sat down beside her sister.

To Kate's horror, Miss Eugenia demanded, "Did you see it?"

"No, but I've heard it described in detail several times."

"People are going to talk about us anyway, so they might as well say something that strengthens our cover," Mark whispered to Kate while the sisters conferred. "And I can guarantee you that was the most fun I've ever had in the line of duty," he added, his lips brushing her ear.

"Have you talked to the Prescotts about the dining room furniture?" Kate heard Annabelle ask her sister.

"I'll go by on my way home," Miss Eugenia responded absently.

After they had finished eating, Kate used her swollen feet as an excuse for Mark to take her home. Miss Eugenia dragged them around the entire area again to say their farewells. Back in the cool confines of their house, Kate went straight upstairs and took a shower. Too embarrassed to face Mark, she sat on the bed and tried to relive every millisecond of their kiss. She was jolted from her memories by the sound of a knock on her door.

Reluctantly Kate looked out into the hallway. "I rented *Patriot Games* in honor of the holiday." His hair was damp and his feet were bare. "I've been waiting for you to come down. I was afraid you might be sick."

"I'm not sick, just embarrassed," she replied and he gave her an odd look. "I mean, the way I overreacted to your kiss at the picnic." Walking back to her bed, she sat down on the edge.

"Well, you reacted." He gave her a warm smile as he leaned against the doorframe.

"It's probably my hormones." Kate groped for an explanation. "Like how I cry over nothing and sleep all the time."

Mark studied her. "I've never been married, so I thought that affection between a husband and wife was assumed, but apparently I was wrong. I hope it won't be a problem for you, but I think we're going to have be a little more affectionate in public from now on."

Kate stared at her hands. "If we had met under other circumstances, I wonder if we would have been friends," she said quietly. "I mean, if you had seen me at a Single Adult conference, would you have asked me to dance? Called me afterwards? Even noticed me?"

"I can't say for sure," he hedged slightly. "But I think yes, to all three."

Kate let out a shaky breath and risked a glance at him. "During the entire year I was married to Tony, he never kissed me like that."

Mark Iverson stood up straight. "Then he was more of a fool than I thought," he said softly and went downstairs.

* * *

On Tuesday morning the men came to lay the tile on the kitchen floor. They had to move all the furniture and appliances out of the room, causing even more confusion than before. So when Happy called and asked if she could come over, Kate suggested they meet for lunch at Haggerty Station instead. Mark got a vegetable plate from the buffet, but Kate and Happy ordered chicken salad scooped into a half of a cantaloupe. As they ate, they discussed the status of the house.

When Happy was positive that they were satisfied with her services, she presented them with her bill. The final balance was staggering, but Kate recovered in time to produce one of Niki's credit cards. Mark tried to object, but Kate insisted. Happy was watching them and finally Mark gave in.

"Drew doesn't like being obligated to other people." Kate tossed her head in her best imitation of a spoiled rich girl. "But Daddy wants me to have the best of everything, so we're going to let him pick up Happy's bill," Kate told her husband firmly. *"You* can pay for lunch." Happy laughed as Mark leaned over the table and gave Kate a quick, hard kiss.

"You two are making a habit of public spectacles lately," Annabelle said as she walked past their table carrying a plate of pecan pie.

"Hey, that looks good." Happy pointed at her dessert. "Do either of you want a piece?" she asked her hosts.

Kate shook her head and Mark stood up. "No, thanks," he told Happy. "I've got to get to work."

"All your furniture should be in before the end of the week," Happy said, returning Niki's credit card along with a receipt. "Are you going to be okay?" she asked when she saw Kate's dazed expression.

"I'm not sure," Kate responded with a smile.

"Love!" Happy shook her head in mock disgust.

* * *

Kate had to squeeze through the appliances pushed into the laundry room when she got home. The workmen were packing up their equipment and warned Kate to avoid walking on the tile for twenty-four hours. She watched them weave their way out the back door, then tiptoed across the edge of the new tile floor to the dining room.

The kitchen table and chairs blocked the doorway, but when Kate had maneuvered around them, she saw that the room was full of dusty antique furniture. Miss Eugenia had left a note stuck to the middle of the table saying that Kate owed the Prescott heirs $2,000 and Annabelle's lawn boy $50.

Kate worked her way through the jumble of furniture and found a rug, three occasional tables, and two matching lamps in the living room. A sticky note was attached to each, indicating the price. Anxious to change clothes and lay down for her afternoon nap, Kate walked through the entryway to the stairs. In the center of the room was a beautiful round table. The surface was inlaid with tiny pieces of wood in a complex design. She ran her hand along the glossy wood and picked up the sticky note.

Miss Polly is going to kill me when she sees this, so it will cost you $200 and your firstborn son. Kate laughed as she walked upstairs to start writing checks.

When Mark got home that night, Kate took him through the house and showed him their new acquisitions. He was more thrilled with the kitchen floor than all the antiques put together. Kate offered to heat up a casserole in the microwave that was balanced on top of the washing machine, but Mark said he preferred not to eat anything cooked next to dirty clothes. So they drove into Albany and ate Chinese.

Kate and Miracle spent Wednesday morning polishing the Prescotts' furniture. Ellis worked right beside them on the baseboards in the dining room. They stopped for the day at noon and Kate went upstairs to get ready for her doctor's appointment.

The roads into Albany seemed more familiar as Kate drove to Dr. Tremayne's office. After a short wait, the nurse called Kate back to a room and did an ultrasound. "Do you want to know if it's a boy or a girl?" Dr. Tremayne asked, looking over the nurse's shoulder.

"I had planned to wait until the baby's born," Kate hesitated, studying the monitor. The doctor made some notations. "Can you tell for sure?"

"Yes, ma'am," Dr. Tremayne confirmed.

Kate sighed, deciding that she had enough suspense in her life. "Go ahead and tell me."

"You're certain?" the doctor clarified and Kate nodded. "It's a little girl," he announced with a smile and Kate grinned back. "Have you taken a tour of the hospital yet?"

"I didn't know it was necessary," she responded as she sat up on the examination table.

He gave her a strange look. "It's not required, if that's what you mean. But I strongly recommend it, especially for first-time parents. Why don't you call Memorial and see if they can give you a tour next Wednesday when you come for your appointment? And bring your husband with you."

Kate left the doctor's office and headed home. She passed Happy's shop on her way and pulled into the parking lot. She didn't really have a reason to stop, but she liked Happy and wanted to share her news with someone. She was ushered into a small office where Happy was about to eat a tomato sandwich. She handed half to Kate. "It's only tomato and bread?" Kate inspected the sandwich with suspicion. "No ham or bacon or anything?"

"Try it," Happy commanded. Kate took a bite, then looked up with a smile. "Tomato sandwiches are one of the South's best-kept secrets. So," Happy continued as she bit into her half, "what did the doctor say?"

"It's a girl."

Happy closed her eyes for a few seconds, then smiled. "There are a couple of changes I'll want to make in the nursery for a girl. And now you can start buying baby clothes." Kate stared at the decorator. "I mean, isn't that why you don't have anything, because you didn't know . . ." Happy floundered in confusion.

Kate thought about the baby clothes stacked in her closet in Chicago. Things she had bought out of her grocery money, a quilt her mother had made, and Tony's blessing gown. Seeing that Happy was waiting, Kate searched for an explanation. Tony used to say that the best lie was one that was closest to the truth, so trusting his experience, Kate smiled sadly. "I had gotten a few things before we moved, but in the confusion they were left behind." She sighed. "I just haven't had the heart to buy replacements."

"When did you say this baby is coming?" Happy looked pointedly at Kate's midsection.

"Three weeks from Friday," Kate reported.

"Hmm." Happy glanced at her watch, then picked up the phone. She asked whoever answered where she should go to buy everything for a baby. She paused, then hung up without saying good-bye. "My sister Lucille. Now she probably thinks I'm pregnant," she shrugged. "It will give her something to think about this afternoon besides who is sleeping with who on the soaps. Finish that sandwich and let's go. I hope you've still got your daddy's credit cards because we're about to buy your daughter a wardrobe."

Kate drove behind Happy's little black sports car through the streets of Albany. Finally Happy pulled up to the front of a store called The Baby Warehouse and parked in a handicapped space. It took Kate a few minutes to get her own car legally situated, and by the time she got inside the store, Happy had already enlisted the help of an assistant manager, a cashier with baby experience, and a stock boy.

"You parked in a handicapped space," Kate whispered emphatically when she reached the group.

Happy shrugged. "The worst that will happen is I'll get a ticket."

"No," Kate disagreed. "The worst that will happen is a handicapped person will need that spot!"

Happy considered this and then grimaced. "We'll hurry." She turned to the store manager. "We don't have much time, but we have plenty of money. Kate, give him your credit card." She watched this transaction, then told the manager to wait up front by a cash register. "We'll send the carts up to you one at a time." The man nodded and took his position at register eight. Then Happy instructed everyone else to get a basket and follow her.

Happy filled Kate's basket with receiving blankets and hooded towels, mattress pads and infant gowns, crib sheets and bottles. At this point Kate informed them shyly that she was planning to breast-feed.

"You'll still need bottles," the clerk told her as they pushed on to the next section.

Kate and the stock boy stood back as Happy and the clerk discussed the benefits of cotton versus synthetic fabrics for baby clothes, which brand of diapers was the most absorbent, and whether or not pacifiers caused orthodontic problems. When the first basket was filled, Happy told the stock boy to take it to the front so the manager could start processing their purchases.

Then she picked out a car seat, a swing, two sets of baby monitors, and a ballerina mobile. While the manager and the stock boy put everything in sacks, the clerk whispered that there was a store on the other side of the shopping center that specialized in handmade children's clothes. "They have some lovely things," she confided.

"That will be our next stop then," Happy said firmly.

Kate reclaimed her credit card and signed the charge slip, hoping that Angela had been serious when she said the cards had no limit.

Then she led the way to the van and opened every door so the stock boy could put things inside. When he closed the back hatch, she slipped him $10 and followed Happy down to The Baby Boutique.

Happy walked around the small establishment with the ecstatic owner, selecting various smocked and embroidered outfits. When Happy put an armful of clothes on the counter, Kate looked through them and saw that they were all in newborn and three-month sizes. While Happy examined a pink and white striped romper, Kate reminded her that she was only having one baby and that the child would be in these tiny sizes for a very short period of time.

Happy contemplated this information for a few seconds, then added the striped suit to the growing pile. "And she will look her best on each of those fleeting days," she stated positively. "Besides, I know her grandpa would want her to have one of these." She held up a beautiful christening gown and Kate gasped at the $200 price tag.

Finally accepting defeat, Kate stood by the cash register as Happy ran amok in the baby store. She gave the boutique owner a different credit card, just to be safe, then helped Happy wedge the bags into the limited space available in the van.

"Now you're all set," Happy declared with satisfaction as she slammed the door closed.

"I . . ." Kate couldn't think of an appropriate response.

"Don't thank me!" Happy commanded. With a wave she climbed into her little black car and sped away. Kate left the parking lot at a more sedate pace and turned toward Haggerty.

* * *

Both horrified and thrilled by the obscene quantity of baby items she had purchased, Kate contemplated the day's events, singing along with the radio. She didn't even hear the siren until she glanced back and saw the blue lights flashing very close behind the van. She turned on her blinker and pulled over onto the shoulder. In seconds Winston Jones was standing by her window. He asked to see her license and she fumbled in Niki's purse, handed her fake license to him, and then stared straight ahead, afraid that he would read the guilt in her eyes.

"I clocked you going forty-five in a forty-mile zone," he told her with insincere regret. "Now some people would say that's not really speeding and that I should overlook it. But we take safety in this town very seriously. If someone going forty-five miles an hour in a forty-mile zone were to run over a little child or an elderly person . . ."

"I'm sorry. I didn't notice the change in speed limit," Kate interrupted, hoping he would just give her the ticket and let her get home.

Winston shook his head reproachfully. "It's important to remain alert while you drive, Mrs. Johnson. You should constantly watch for signs that change the speed limit, warn of curves in the road, or notify you that there is a railroad crossing ahead. A car can be a lethal weapon, dangerous as any gun, if not handled properly." He tapped her license against his ticket book.

"I'll be more careful in the future."

"I hope that you will. And I also hope you'll understand that I really have no choice but to write you a ticket. How would it look if I was to let the wife of our new police chief off? People would question my integrity," he added with a sly smile. "And to follow procedure, I'll have to call in the tag number. It's all standard policy."

Kate leaned her head back on the seat. She knew that this not-so-subtle harassment was pure revenge. It took him thirty minutes to clear her tag number, write her a ticket, and return her license. By that time, her feet were swollen and her head was throbbing. As Winston was handing the license back with a smirk, they both heard Mark Iverson's voice calling him over his radio. Winston walked back and pulled the speaker out of the driver's window, watching Kate in her sideview mirror as he answered.

"Yes."

"Do you have my wife detained on Highway 11?" Mark's rage was obvious even over the crackling radio.

"Yes I do," Winston replied with a little less confidence. "I'm sorry to tell you that she was going forty-five miles per hour in a forty-mile zone. I've just finished making out the ticket and will be sending her on her way shortly."

"You called in pursuit fifty minutes ago. An imbecile could write out a routine speeding ticket in less time than that. So you'd better have another reason for keeping my very pregnant wife sitting in a hot car on the side of a county highway for almost an hour!"

Winston's face flushed. "I had to do the routine checks, call in the tag number—"

"You called in my tag number?" Mark's voice was incredulous. "You did a routine check on me?"

"I followed procedure," Winston responded defensively.

"We use those procedures to check for outstanding warrants on strangers. Did you think Niki was an escaped convict?" he bellowed. "You harassed a pregnant woman, and it's going on your record. I might even encourage Niki to file charges against you. If you have a problem with me, we'll settle it between us. But you'd better stay away from my wife. Do you understand that?" Mark didn't wait for Winston to answer. "You will not kiss her, you will not talk to her and if you see her walking down the street, you'd better look the other way. Because if you give me the slightest excuse, I'm going to beat the—" There was an abrupt pause. "You'll be sorry."

Static came through the line, but Winston had no response. After a few seconds, the FBI agent spoke again. "Escort Niki home right now."

"Yes sir," Winston answered hoarsely.

"I'm watching the clock. You've got five minutes."

A Haggerty police car was parked in front of the house when Kate pulled the van into the driveway four minutes later. Winston drove on past without looking in her direction. Mark and Arnold were both waiting in the front yard, and Kate broke into irrational tears. Mark gathered her against his chest and she clung to him.

"Are you okay?" he demanded.

"Yes." She shook her head. Her tears were staining his crisp uniform shirt, but she didn't care. All she could think about was how good it felt to be in his arms.

"Let's get you inside. Arnold, you can take the patrol car back now. And thanks," Mark said to the other man. "You're sure you're okay?" He squeezed her shoulders as they went into the house. Kate nodded, burrowing into his chest. Inside the entryway, he took her chin in his hand and studied her face. Reassured, he pressed a kiss to her forehead.

"When I heard your name on the police radio . . ." His shudder was explanation enough. "I may go ahead and kill Winston after all."

"You two don't mind me," Miss Eugenia instructed as she walked through the front door and toward the kitchen. "I've got cucumbers rotting in the garden, so I'm bringing you a few." Kate eased herself regretfully out of Mark's embrace. "I'll just let myself out the back," Miss Eugenia's fading voice called, followed by the slamming of a door.

Kate felt much better after a warm shower. She joined the FBI agent in the kitchen and saw that he had all the appliances back in place. He had also warmed up a chicken casserole and marinated sliced cucumbers in Italian dressing. Kate complimented him on his ingenuity, but he said he couldn't take credit for the idea. "Miss Eugenia called and gave me detailed instructions," he admitted. As they rinsed their dishes, Kate remembered that the van was full of baby things. "I'll get them," Mark held up his hand and walked toward the front. Kate waited by the door and laughed when she heard his exclamation of dismay. "I'm surprised you were able to get the van up to forty-five miles per hour with this load," he said when he came back in.

Kate preceded him upstairs and opened the nursery door. Mark dropped his first armful of packages on the floor by the crib and went back for another. It took him almost twenty minutes to get everything inside. He collapsed into the rocking chair after his last trip and watched Kate as she sorted through the bags. "I'm guessing the baby is a girl," Mark said when she showed him a white infant gown covered with pink rosebuds. "Either that or a boy who is in for a lifetime of ridicule."

"It's a girl," Kate smiled as she pulled a pink receiving blanket from its plastic wrapper. "Happy took me shopping."

Mark nodded as he looked around the crowded room. "Happy's involvement explains a lot." He stood and extended a hand to her. "It's getting late and you've had a big day." He pulled her up and inertia propelled her into his chest. His arms went around her instinctively. "Maybe if we practice kissing at home we won't be so awkward in public," he murmured, nuzzling her temple.

"It's worth a try." She smiled briefly before his mouth covered hers. When he finally drew back, she sighed. "I'm not sure this is wise," she said drowsily.

"It seems like the more I kiss you, the more I want to," he whispered. Kate pressed her lips to his and the baby kicked hard. Mark spread his hand over her distended stomach. "Do you think she's trying to tell me to get away from her mother?"

Kate laughed softly. "I think she's just saying hello." Mark smiled and pulled her toward the door. "I wonder if Miss Polly was watching us just now," she said when they reached the doorway.

"Next time we'll stand a little closer to the window," Mark replied, turning off the light.

CHAPTER 7

On Thursday the paperhangers arrived right after Mark left for work. Miracle got there at eight o'clock and complained that the workmen were ruining her freshly waxed floors. Ellis came in at 8:30 and chose to prime the woodwork by the front door, which made the paperhangers unhappy. They bickered for about an hour before the furniture people pulled up in the driveway. When they started bringing furniture through the front, disturbing both Ellis and the wallpaper men, Kate ran to Miss Eugenia's back door. Her neighbor was standing in her kitchen, holding her purse and car keys.

"Are you going somewhere?" Kate cried in desperation.

"Bridge Club. What's the matter? Is it the baby?" Miss Eugenia stretched out an arm.

"No, it's just that Ellis and the wallpaper men are fussing about who's in whose way. Then the furniture people came, and they're in everybody's way. Miracle is mad because she had the house all cleaned up, and they're tracking in mud. I can't stand it any more, and I was hoping I could stay over here until they all left."

"Well, you can't sit over here by yourself, but you most certainly can come to my Bridge Club meeting with me."

"I don't know anything about bridges," Kate said morosely.

Miss Eugenia laughed. "Bridge is a card game, and you don't have to know anything about it to watch." Kate called Mark at the police station and explained the situation. He promised to come home and mediate while she went with Miss Eugenia to Bridge Club.

The meeting was being held at George Ann Simmons's house, which was on the other side of the town square, a block from the

Baptist church. During Kate's brief introduction, Miss Simmons made a point of mentioning that her maternal grandfather had donated the property that the church was built on.

The ornate furniture in the living room was pushed against the walls, and four card tables had been set up. Miss Polly was seated at one. She gave them a tremulous smile when they spoke, and Miss Eugenia laughed. "She's just pouting because she's the 'dummy.'"

Kate frowned. She didn't particularly like her nosy neighbor, but it did seem cruel to call her names in public.

Miss Eugenia took Kate around to each table and introduced her to everyone. Then she pulled a chair up beside her own at table three and told Kate not to leave her side. The warning seemed melodramatic, but Kate obeyed. First the ladies questioned each other about everything from soap opera plots to the most effective brand of laundry detergent. When the discussion turned to the new Methodist preacher's wife, someone mentioned her dyed hair. "It's not that I have anything against hair color," a flaming redhead remarked.

"I guess not," Miss Eugenia murmured and everyone laughed.

"It just seems a little worldly for a preacher's wife," the woman continued with a stern look at Miss Eugenia.

"Has anyone heard how Byron Samples and his new wife are doing?" Miss George Ann asked the group.

"I heard they had bought a house in Albany."

"I thought they were looking at a place on Highway 11," someone else commented.

Miss Polly shrugged elegantly. "All I know is that I never received a thank-you note from them for the china dinner plate I gave them as a wedding gift."

"How long has it been since the wedding?" someone asked.

"Six or seven months, I think." Miss Polly answered, placing her cards face up on the table.

There was a universal gasp. "Oh my," the lady on the other side of Miss Eugenia spoke for everyone.

Kate looked at her neighbor in confusion. "Failing to write thank-you notes is an unforgivable sin in the South," Miss Eugenia explained.

"Only thing worse is committing adultery with a close family member," someone else contributed.

"And that's only if you get caught!" a tiny woman wearing a black net hat added from across the room.

"Thank-you notes are what separate us from the barbarians," Miss Polly said very seriously.

"She means the Yankees," Miss Eugenia whispered.

"I'm so sorry, Niki," Miss Polly blushed.

Kate didn't consider herself a Yankee and was not offended by the remark. "I haven't written thank-you notes," she announced anxiously. "And people have given us so much food!"

Miss Eugenia waved her hand. "Do you think I would let you commit social suicide? I've ordered you some engraved note cards, and they should be here soon. We are still well within the proper time frame for your notes."

"What is the proper time to write thank-you notes?" Kate asked as she watched Miss Eugenia expertly deal the cards.

"Never write a thank-you note sooner than a week after you receive something. That seems insincere," Miss Eugenia advised, arranging her hand by suits.

"If I get a 'thank-you' that early, I know they just wanted to get them out of the way," Miss George Ann agreed.

"Two to three weeks is perfect and anything up to six weeks is acceptable. After that . . ."

"It will take years to win forgiveness."

Kate was stunned. "I had no idea."

Someone asked what the specials were at the Wal-Mart SuperCenter, and the subject changed again. The women chatted cheerfully for a few minutes until the games began. Then they turned to Kate.

At first they asked some vague questions about her past, which Kate handled easily. Then, just as she was starting to relax, they unsheathed their claws. How could she afford such expensive clothes on a policeman's salary? Was her father really financing the renovation and furnishing of their house? Was it true that she did not sleep with her husband, and did he have a rare blood disease that caused his body temperature to stay below normal? The questions came in rapid succession, and Kate had no opportunity to answer before the next one was posed. She opened her mouth to offer a defense, but Miss Eugenia stepped in first.

"Agnes, why do you wear such ugly clothes when you have millions of dollars in the bank?" she asked the thin woman to her left. "Why should you care if her father is paying to fix up her house, George Ann? You've lived off your daddy's money all your life. How stupid can you be to ask if she sleeps with her husband, Eva Nell? Didn't you ever find out where babies come from? And there is nothing wrong with the Chief's blood. He's just a Mormon, and they do all kinds of odd things like wear long johns in the summer and save buckets of food even though the Y2K crisis is over."

The women expressed various degrees of outrage over Miss Eugenia's blunt reprimands, but, as the game progressed, they seemed to forget about their anger in their intense determination to win. Kate watched in complete fascination as the elderly women played cards like professional gamblers. At one point, a shouting match broke out at table two over bids, and Miss Polly was eventually reduced to tears when her partner said she was a stupid "dummy."

The games ended at last, and lunch was served buffet-style in Miss Simmons's dining room, with the women appearing to forget the ferocious competition earlier as they now enjoyed the meal. When Kate commented that the key lime pie was especially good, Miss Eugenia whispered for her to be sure to ask Miss Simmons for the recipe.

As they were leaving, Kate did so. Miss Simmons blushed and claimed that the pie had not been one of her best, but eventually went to her writing desk and picked up a recipe card from the stack she had prepared just in case someone should ask. Then she extended it graciously to Kate.

Everyone except Ellis was gone when Kate got home. The old man was grumbling about not getting any lunch, so Kate heated up the chicken casserole from the night before and scooped some cucumber slices onto a plate. She coaxed him into the kitchen, but he steadfastly insisted that he could not eat a meal without iced tea. A phone call had to be made to Miss Eugenia, who brought a jug over within minutes. Kate was irritated with Ellis by the time her neighbor got there.

"Mercy sakes, Ellis! How could I have forgotten you today?" Miss Eugenia cried, and Ellis shook his head sadly as if he couldn't begin to understand her oversight either. "I always fix you a plate after my Bridge Club meetings. The only excuse I can offer is that I'm not as young as I used to be." She patted his hunched shoulder as she poured him a big glass of tea.

Kate was about to mention that Miss Eugenia was not responsible for Ellis's meals, nor was lunch part of his employment agreement with the Johnsons. But before she could form the words, Miss Eugenia had continued, "Niki, did I ever tell you that Ellis's wife and I were best friends all through high school? Then we sang in the Methodist Women's Choir together for almost thirty years. Valera was the best cook in Haggerty. Since her death I have given up eating banana pudding altogether."

"Nobody could make a banana pudding like my Valera," Ellis agreed solemnly.

Kate turned back to Ellis and saw him through different eyes. He was just a lonely old man who missed his wife and didn't have anyone to care about him. Miss Eugenia sat beside him at the table, refilling his glass and instructing Kate when he needed more casserole, a slice of "loaf bread," or the salt.

After Ellis went back to work and Miss Eugenia left, Kate walked around admiring everything that had been done. With the furniture delivered and most of the renovations complete, the house was beginning to realize its potential. Soon it would be a perfect place to raise a family. Kate could feel the baby kicking wildly and wondered when they would have a home of their own.

Mark called as she woke up from her afternoon nap and she told him that he'd done a good job arranging the furniture in the guest rooms. He said that Happy would be by on Friday to look around and evaluate the progress. "I'm sure she'll have her own ideas about where the furniture goes," he predicted. Then he told her that he would not be home for dinner. "Winston has called in sick, so I'll have to make the night rounds for him. It will probably be very late before I get there."

"Can't Arnold help you?" Kate asked.

"I can't send Arnold into those bars and nightclubs out on Highway 76."

"Do you think Winston is really sick?"

"I think he's paying me back for yelling at him over the radio yesterday," Mark answered wearily. "But there's nothing I can do about it. Don't wait up."

Miss Eugenia came over a few minutes later and invited herself to dinner. "I heard the Chief is working late," she remarked, searching through the freezer. Finally she pulled out a dish. "I made this one myself," she said as she put it in the microwave. "It's called Chicken Extravaganza, and I got it out of *Southern Living* last Christmas."

Kate ate too much and ended up with indigestion. She was downstairs taking some antacid when Mark got home at two A.M. He dragged in through the back door, looking exhausted.

"I'm taking some Mylanta," she explained from her seat at the kitchen table. "The casserole I ate for dinner didn't settle very well." He gave her half a smile. "Would you like me to heat some up for you?" she offered.

He shook his head as he unhooked the second button on his uniform shirt. "No, but I'll take a swig of that Mylanta. I ate a cheeseburger at the Dairy Delight." He rubbed his stomach with a grimace. "Then the air conditioner went out on the patrol car and I had to break up three drunken brawls."

"I guess I won't ask how your day was," Kate smiled as she watched him drink the antacid straight from the bottle. She turned on the ceiling fan over the kitchen table and he sat down, raising his head to accept the cool breeze. Kate told him about the Bridge Club meeting, exaggerating just enough to make him laugh. Finally he stood and Kate put the Mylanta on the counter while he checked to be sure that all the doors were locked. They walked upstairs together and paused awkwardly in the middle of the hall. Then Mark leaned down and kissed her gently. Reluctantly she went back to bed. She was asleep in minutes.

* * *

On Friday morning Kate called Memorial Hospital in Albany and set up a tour for the next Wednesday after her appointment with Dr. Tremayne. Ellis arrived at 8:30, after having eaten breakfast with Miss Eugenia. He didn't seem happy that the renovations were almost completed. He told Kate glumly that all the woodwork was finished inside, and he would be working on the back porch until further notice. Miracle came in at nine and started cleaning. She sang as she dusted and swept and polished. Kate went up to the guest room where she was working and waited for a break between verses.

"You don't really have to clean," she whispered as the FBI agent turned to face her.

"What else would I do with my time while I'm here?" Miracle asked in surprise.

"I don't know. You could read or watch television or play games on the computer. It just doesn't seem right for you to be cleaning our house!" Kate hissed.

Miracle threw her head back and laughed. "You are the funniest little white woman I ever met. I can't wait to tell my momma about you." She shook her head and sprayed Pledge on the new dresser. "If word got around that I was coming over to your house every day and playing games on your computer, I might as well shoot you myself."

Kate was startled by her suddenly serious expression. "No one would have to know."

"You've been in this town long enough to see that they know everything about each other." Kate had to concede that information did travel at an alarming rate. "I take my breaks, keep up with my soaps, watch Oprah like any sensible woman. But I have to clean." Kate's expression remained troubled. "Honey, do you think this is the worst assignment I've ever had?"

"I wouldn't want to be a maid," Kate said reasonably.

"Cleaning this nice house is nothing. One time I had to do surveillance in a tenement. You know what that is?" Kate shook her head indicating that she didn't. "It's an old, run-down apartment. The plumbing didn't work, rats and bugs were everywhere. Now that was terrible! Then another time I had to go undercover as a short-order cook. People were yelling at me all day long, complaining that their burgers were burned or their eggs were runny. I couldn't wait for that operation to end."

Kate smiled. "Are you just trying to make me feel better?"

The agent winked. "I was raised in a little town not far from here. My momma cleaned houses to put me through college. It's good, honest work, and I figure if I complained about being a maid, it would be disrespectful to my momma."

. "Does your mother still live nearby?" Kate asked.

Miracle shook her head. "She moved in with my sister a few years ago. She doesn't see too well anymore, and we were afraid for her to live alone."

"Do you miss her when you're on an assignment like this?" Kate's tone was wistful.

"I call her now and then," the agent admitted.

"How did the FBI pick a name like Miracle Moore?" Kate asked, and the agent laughed.

"Miracle is my own name. My momma had seven boys, and when I was born she said 'Lord, thank you for my Miracle!' and the doctor wrote it on the birth certificate."

"You're kidding!" Kate couldn't decide if she was teasing.

"Gospel truth," Miracle promised. They heard a door open downstairs and both jumped. "You'd better go and see who that is. Haggerty ladies don't spend much time with their household help."

Kate found Miss Eugenia in the kitchen. She said she was on her way to the Haggerty Junior Service League meeting but had brought over a jug of tea.

"Keep this in your refrigerator for Ellis and take him some every hour or so. He'll die of a heat stroke if you don't." She wiped the sweat from her forehead with a wrinkled white handkerchief. "If my meeting runs over, will you feed him? Casserole and a salad will be good." Kate nodded. "And bread of some kind." Kate nodded again. "And dessert. He won't eat any supper, so we have to get as much into him as we can at dinner time."

Kate promised that she would feed Ellis. As they walked toward the back door, she dared to ask, "You said you're meeting with the

Haggerty Junior Service League. Is there a Haggerty Senior Service League as well?"

Miss Eugenia laughed so hard she had to wipe her eyes with her sweaty hanky. "There are no ladies in Haggerty any more senior than we are," she was finally able to reply. Kate was embarrassed, but Miss Eugenia squeezed her arm. "I'm not offended. I'd rather be old than dead! Senior citizenship just sort of slipped up on all of us. We never thought to change the name of the group, and now, well, it seems like it's too late."

Happy came in about ten o'clock, so excited she could barely speak. "I have the most fabulous news!" she announced, taking Kate's hands into both of hers. "You'd better sit down for this. It is so . . . so . . . "

Kate pulled her into the den and they sat on the couch. She had learned to hate surprises, but she made herself say, "Tell me."

"I've found you a piano!" Happy screeched. "A baby grand!" There were actually tears in her eyes. "I was walking through a warehouse in Albany and saw this gorgeous piano sitting there," she related breathlessly. "I found the manager and said, 'Who does this belong to?' He said it was shipped here by mistake, and they were supposed to send it back to Pennsylvania. I said, 'Don't you dare touch that piano! I have a client who will buy it for the wholesale price and save the seller the shipping costs!' He made a phone call, and the seller agreed. It's going to be delivered here in just a little while!" Happy leaned back against the plush cushions of the couch. "This is the greatest moment of my decorating career!" She peeked up at Kate. "So far, anyway."

"The neighborhood ladies will be pleased," Kate smiled. "A piano will make the house complete."

"It was a must," Happy agreed. Then she walked around, inspecting the house minutely. As Mark had predicted, she rearranged the furniture in the guest rooms. "Everything should be finished in another week," she said as they worked their way back to the front door.

"We are very pleased with what you have done." Kate looked around the entryway. The walls were freshly papered, and the woodwork was flawlessly painted. In the center of the room stood

Annabelle's round table adorned with a crystal vase full of Miss Eugenia's yellow roses.

"It's been a pleasure doing business with you." Happy tucked her briefcase under her arm. "I don't often get to work with someone so cooperative."

Happy left and Kate conscientiously took Ellis his tea every hour as instructed. She had his lunch heated up when he shuffled into the kitchen at noon, looking around for Miss Eugenia.

"She asked me to feed you dinner," Kate told him gently. The old man sat warily at the table. Kate hovered over him the way she had seen Miss Eugenia do, and after a few minutes he seemed to relax and enjoy the meal. She realized that he wasn't going to ask for anything, so she tried to anticipate his needs. Mark stopped by for a minute just as Ellis was finishing up and said he didn't have time to eat, but would take a plate back to the station. He checked the computer, then rushed into the kitchen.

Kate put generous portions of food on a plate and covered it with aluminum foil. Then she stood by the back door and handed it to Mark as he left. They were close together in the doorway as he thanked her and he pressed a soft kiss on her forehead. "Unless Winston has a relapse, I'll be home around five o'clock."

The piano arrived at one o'clock. Miss Eugenia and Miss Polly followed the movers into the house and watched them set it up, instructing the men as to the exact location and angle that the piano should be placed. Then they took turns playing trilly hymns on the beautiful instrument. As she watched them, Kate ached to touch the keys.

Tired of the endless casseroles, Kate made spaghetti for dinner. She used prepared sauce and frozen bread sticks, but it smelled wonderful. Mark was about thirty minutes late, but she was so glad to see him she didn't mind that the bread had gotten a little tough. While they ate, Kate told him about the piano.

"I wonder how much a baby grand piano costs?" he asked around a mouthful of spaghetti. "Two million dollars?"

"Happy said she got it wholesale," Kate replied.

"Oh good. Maybe it was only one million." Kate smiled and asked about his day.

"Winston is torturing me," he said as he poured a generous amount of dressing on his salad. "He asks me to verify every procedure, makes me read his reports before he'll file them, and even tells me before he goes to the bathroom."

"Surely he'll get tired of that soon," Kate predicted hopefully and Mark shrugged.

After dinner Kate filled the sink with water, and Mark cleared the table. As he put a plate into the sink, their hands touched. Mark's fingers entwined around hers, and she looked up at him. Clearing her throat, she asked him if Niki played the piano.

Mark gave her slippery fingers a squeeze, then pulled his hands out of the water. "She took lessons for several years. There was nothing in her dossier to indicate that she played often or well, but she did love music . . ."

"So I can play the piano."

"Nothing fancy."

Mark went up to take a shower, and Kate walked into the living room. She played the piano for an hour. She was so enthralled with the music that she didn't even see Mark slip in and sit on a chair behind her. When she finally dropped her hands into her lap, he applauded. Embarrassed, she turned around on the bench. "You're very good," he complimented her.

"I'm rusty," she demurred modestly.

"Whatever the piano cost, it was a bargain." He smiled and her heart raced. Then the phone rang, so he walked to the den and picked up the cordless receiver. After a few words, he came back into the living room. "That was Winston. He has a civil disturbance and needs my assistance."

"Winston needs your help?" Kate was incredulous.

"I seriously doubt it," Mark answered, rubbing the back of his neck. "I think this is another step in his plan to drive me crazy."

Kate heard him come in around midnight and met him in the dark hallway. "Is everything okay?"

"Yeah," he said as he walked into his room and flipped on the light. Kate followed as far as the doorway. The agent sat on the bed and pulled off his shoes. "It was a fight at Heads Up." Kate raised her eyebrows. "It's a beer joint out on Highway 76. A woman thought her husband was flirting with her sister. They started a screaming match, and it deteriorated into a brawl and finally a beating."

Kate's eyes followed his hands as he pulled out his shirttail and started unbuttoning his shirt. "How could people stand around and watch a woman being mistreated like that?" she asked as her mouth went dry.

"It was the husband who got hurt. She broke his nose and two ribs." Kate's jaw dropped in astonishment. "The wife's a 300-pound bricklayer, and she beat him half to death."

"Is he going to be okay?"

Mark shrugged. "I guess, but don't waste your sympathy on him. At the hospital he told me he'd been sleeping with the sister for over a year."

"You're kidding."

He gave her a tired smile. "I wish I was." He stretched his arms over his head, pulling his uniform open to expose a white tee shirt, damp with perspiration.

Kate cleared her throat and looked toward the windows. "So you had to help Winston break up the fight?"

"Winston had the fight stopped long before I got there. He could have handled the whole situation himself, but he said he was unclear about when he was supposed to follow all the procedures and when he could skip a few. So he wanted me to supervise." Kate rolled her eyes.

"We tediously interviewed all the witnesses, took pictures of the scene, and estimated damages. Then we went to the hospital and talked to the victim. He said he didn't want to press charges and agreed to pay for everything they broke. So we went back to the station and filled out a report and faxed it to the sheriff's department."

"And none of that could have waited until tomorrow?"

"Most of it, but Winston wanted to be sure that we did everything by the book."

"It was revenge," Kate concluded.

"It was torture." He leaned down to pick up his shoes and took them to the closet.

"Maybe he'll get tired of this childish game soon," Kate said hopefully.

"Or maybe I'll die of sleep deprivation and spoil his fun," Mark grumbled as he walked down the hall toward the bathroom.

* * *

On Saturday morning Kate awoke to the sounds of pouring rain. She placed her feet gingerly on the hardwood floor and padded to the window. Through the parted curtains, she could see that the front lawn was underwater and rain was falling in sheets.

Mark had gone to the station, but he'd left a note on the refrigerator door asking her to call him when she woke up. She dialed the number, and he answered on the second ring. They agreed that the weather was too bad to make a trip into Albany to have their nails done. Kate said she would change their manicures to Wednesday before their hospital tour and her doctor's appointment.

Miss Eugenia rushed in the back door at ten o'clock with a magazine over her head and a bundle clutched to her chest. The magazine was a *Good Housekeeping* from 1972, which she threw into the garbage can. The bundle contained thick vellum note cards with Niki Johnson's name printed in an elaborate script on the front panel. There was a sticky note on the top of the box indicating that Kate owed the printing company $32.50.

Kate got her list of casseroles and other food items that had been given to them since their arrival in town and put it on the kitchen table. Miss Eugenia assembled the supplies. New black pens, stamps, and a dictionary.

"There are two acceptable approaches to the basic covered-dish thank-you note," she said very seriously. "You can use either the complimentary or anecdotal technique. Complimentary would be to say how good the pie was and possibly ask for the recipe. An example of anecdotal would be, 'The Chief ate three pieces of your pie and took another for lunch the next day.' I prefer the second method. It's a little more personal." She looked at the first name on the list. "Now, let's start with Mavis Hargrove." Miss Eugenia dictated as Kate wrote.

When they came to a hamburger casserole made by the young professionals down the street, Kate explained that they hadn't eaten it yet so she couldn't honestly compliment or anecdote. Miss Eugenia nodded. "So you'll tell them that you are saving it until after the baby comes, and that it gives you great peace of mind to know that you have it in the freezer."

By the time Miss Eugenia left, the notes were half done and Kate had the general idea. Mark called at one o'clock to say that a small bridge had washed out on Highway 117. The sheriff's department was going to put out hazard lights on their side of the bridge, but he was going to have to barricade the town side.

He got home thirty minutes later, soaked to the skin. While he showered, Kate heated up some chicken stew Miss Polly had given them. The note taped on the front of the jar said to serve it with cornbread, but in the interest of time, Kate got out a box of saltine crackers instead. She had two bowls of steaming stew on the table when Mark came downstairs. His damp hair was combed back from his face, making him look appealingly boyish. Kate attributed the acceleration of her heart to the baby's constant movement.

As they ate their soup, the rain pounded on the windows but the kitchen felt cozy and safe. In between bites of stew, Mark said that he half-expected Winston to drag him out into the weather for another frivolous reason.

Kate looked at the dark skies and driving rain. "We don't have to answer the phone."

He smiled. "As tempting as that sounds, Winston is just waiting for an opportunity to call Booster in on something. That would make it look like I can't handle my job."

He asked what she had done with her morning and she showed him her stack of completed thank-you notes. While she explained the intricacies of properly expressed appreciation, Mark ran his fingers across the name printed on one of the blank cards.

"Mrs. Andrew Gregory Johnson," he murmured with a frown. "Stupid Drew."

Mark went into his office to check the computer, and Kate sat down on the den couch. She found *Casablanca* on a classic movie channel and snuggled under a blanket to watch it. Mark joined her a few minutes later. He walked up to the couch and leaned close. Kate's heart thundered in her chest as she looked up into his face expectantly.

"Mr. Evans said to give you his regards," he whispered into her ear. She nodded, unable to speak.

He smiled and kept his face close to hers. *"Casablanca?"* He tipped his head toward the television. She nodded again. "Sounds romantic." She shivered under the blanket. "I'll bet the surveillance boys are popping popcorn and getting out their hankies," he said, as if to remind her about the cameras. Then he stood up, and she watched with profound disappointment as he walked over to the recliner and sat down.

She was asleep before Humphrey Bogart said his first line. Mark woke her as the credits rolled across the screen. "I must be very dull company," he commented dryly.

"That must be it. I never used to sleep this much," she told him with a drowsy smile. The rain had stopped, and Mark insisted that they take a short walk.

"Niki would be waiting by the door, praying for the rain to stop so she could rush out for some exercise," he teased as she tied her tennis shoes.

Miss Polly was on her front porch when they circled back around the block. "I wanted to catch you before you started cooking anything for tomorrow. I meant for dinner on Sunday after church to be a standing invitation," the older lady clarified, her hand fluttering to the handkerchief tucked into the neckline of her floral-print dress.

"We ate some of your chicken stew for lunch," Mark told her, walking up to the porch and propping a foot on her bottom step. "I'd been out in the rain, and thought I'd never be warm again. But when I came home and had a bowl full of your soup . . ." He shook his head and smiled at Kate who had come up beside him. "It was like heaven."

Miss Polly blushed pink from her ample bosom to her sweat-dotted forehead. "It's my mother's award-winning recipe," she confided. "It has won countless ribbons at county fairs and church bazaars."

"Well, I can certainly understand why," the agent said.

"So, you'll come tomorrow?" Miss Polly reminded them of her invitation.

Mark looked to Kate, leaving the decision up to her. She remembered Miss Eugenia saying that Miss Polly had been proud of her distinction as the only woman in Haggerty who had fed the new police chief Sunday dinner. So she nodded graciously.

Miss Polly beamed. "Well, oh my! I have a thousand things to do before church tomorrow! It will take hours for me to prepare a meal large enough to feed everyone!" she exclaimed as if the Johnsons had invited themselves. "You will excuse me?" Without waiting for a reply, she rushed into her house.

When they walked into their own yard, Kate stopped beside the van. "I'm having a craving," she announced into the rain-cooled air.

Mark turned to look at her. "Pickles?"

She laughed. "No. I'd like some Oreo cookies with vanilla ice cream on the side. No nutrients and loaded with fat."

He laughed with her. "I'll get the keys."

* * *

His cell phone started ringing as they pulled back into the driveway. After a short conversation, he closed the phone and looked at Kate. "Winston has a problem out on Highway 117."

Kate nodded with resignation. "You go ahead. I can get this stuff inside." Kate looked at the sacks that filled the van.

"No, I'll bring the groceries in and put on a uniform." His expression was grim.

"At least it's not raining anymore," Kate pointed out as she took a sack full of bread.

"Not at the moment," he agreed with a sigh.

She put the groceries away while he changed clothes. "Keep the doors locked," he instructed as he came back through the kitchen. "And don't wait up for me. This could take a while," he added as he picked up his keys off the counter.

Kate followed him to the door. "Be careful." Automatically she reached up and straightened his collar.

He bent down and brushed her lips with his. "I will. If you have a problem . . ."

"I know what to do," she assured him. She watched the van pull away from the house, then dished up a bowl of ice cream and grabbed a handful of Oreos. She turned on the television in the den and watched a rerun with Andy Griffith while she ate. Every few minutes her fingers would stray to her lips as if she could touch the kiss he had left there. At ten o'clock she finally went to bed and never did hear him come in. But he was at the kitchen table on Sunday morning when she went down for breakfast.

"Good morning," he greeted her with a tired smile.

"Another long night?"

"Teenagers having a beer bust in a deserted barn. Winston wanted me to be the one to call the parents, hoping I'd offend someone important."

"Did you?"

"I don't think so. I told them that I would consider this a warning, but if I ever caught their children again, charges would be filed."

"That sounds fair."

"The parents thought so, but if one of these same teenagers drives drunk and kills someone, the town will crucify me," Mark predicted as he walked upstairs.

* * *

Brother Stoops greeted them warmly at the chapel doors, then they found seats toward the back. Sister Baylor came over and set up a visiting teaching appointment for Tuesday. When the bishop walked in, he asked them each to give five-minute talks in sacrament meeting the next week.

"Are you disappointed that you won't be the concluding speaker?" Kate asked as they drove home.

"I'm surprised that he's willing to let Drew Johnson address his congregation at all," Mark responded.

"What will we say?" Kate asked. "What would Drew and Niki say?"

Mark shrugged. "We'll keep it simple. Basically bear our testimonies, their testimonies."

"Drew and Niki have gotten a little more righteous in the past few weeks," Kate said thoughtfully. "I think they love the gospel more than they used to."

He smiled. "I think you might be right." When they walked into the house, Mark took a deep breath of roast-scented air and looked at Kate, a question in his eyes. "I thought we were eating with Miss Polly."

Kate laughed. "We are but I wanted the house to smell like home," she told him. His eyes grew solemn and she tried to lighten the moment. "We can eat it tonight or save it, and I'll cook it again next week!"

Glancing up at one of the tiny, hidden cameras, he took a step back. "I think I'll change my clothes," he said abruptly and Kate watched in confusion as he walked upstairs. Maybe the roast had been a mistake. Maybe he didn't want this house to smell like home, or maybe he just didn't want her acting like a wife.

He was subdued and distant all through dinner at Miss Polly's. The current mayor was a guest and he kept the conversation going with a one-sided discussion of local politics. As they walked back home, Kate commented that she hoped Winston wouldn't call in sick that afternoon. Mark replied that he should be safe. "Taking Sunday afternoons was part of the bet he made at the bowling tournament. It would be against his peculiar code of honor to renege on a bowling wager," he predicted absently.

He looked tired and Kate suggested that he take a nap with her. She laughed at his startled expression. "I mean, take a nap when I do," she amended hastily. Without responding, he walked upstairs and closed the door to his room. Kate didn't know if he took her advice, but she felt much better when she woke up a couple of hours later.

Miss Eugenia came over while they were eating the re-heated roast for dinner. She brought them a teacup and matching saucer that she had found at a flea market. The little white label attached advertised the price as $12, and she kindly said that she wouldn't charge them for her gas. She instructed Kate to put it on the table to the left of the couch in the living room, then she invited them to Annabelle's house-warming party on Saturday. It was to be held around the pool, and after Miss Eugenia left, Mark asked Kate if she had a bathing suit.

"Actually I have two, but I wouldn't be caught dead in either one of them at this point." Her hand moved across her stomach.

"I'll have to dig around and see what Drew has. With my luck, his bathing suit will be made out of paisley silk," he muttered as he climbed the stairs.

CHAPTER 8

On Monday Ellis continued to replace the rotten wood on the back porch. Miss Eugenia brought another jug of tea over for him on her way to the Christmas Bazaar committee meeting. Mark was in a better mood at breakfast that morning. He smiled at several of Miss Eugenia's outrageous comments and just before leaving, he asked Kate to meet him at Haggerty Station for lunch. Kate waited for Miracle to arrive, then left the house and Ellis in the agent's capable hands.

She loaded Mark's uniforms into the van along with some of her own clothes and dropped them off at the dry cleaners, where she proudly informed the clerk that the Chief liked heavy starch to keep the fabric crisp in the humid climate. Mark was waiting by the door when she parked in front of the restaurant, and soon they were eating club sandwiches. Several people came up and spoke to them during the course of their meal, and Kate was pleased to see that Mark seemed popular with the local folks.

When she pulled back into their driveway after lunch, she was astonished to see Brother Stoops in Miss Eugenia's backyard. Her neighbor was on hands and knees in her garden and Brother Stoops was bending over a tomato plant.

"Brother Stoops!" Kate was slightly out of breath by the time she reached them. "I didn't know you were coming to see us today."

"Oh, it wasn't a scheduled visit." His magnified eyeballs blinked up at her. "But I had to make a trip into Albany, and I stopped by here on my way to give you some snap beans."

Kate accepted the bread sack full of vegetables and looked at Miss Eugenia helplessly. "I'll show you what to do with those later," the older woman promised as she rose to her feet. "Elmer has been giving me advice on growing tomatoes."

"Elmer?" Kate was bewildered. Brother Stoops smiled, exposing about an inch of gum above his dentures. "Oh," she said weakly.

"Well, I guess I had best be on my way. Sister Johnson, I'll be back to visit soon. And I hope to see you again as well, Eugenia." Brother Stoops bowed politely to both women.

"Come to see me anytime, Elmer. I know a lot about Mormons now, so I won't offend you by offering you tea or coffee."

"You could never offend me!" he scoffed at the suggestion. "But I'd be glad to see if that cornstarch helps you with your tomatoes. I'll check back in a few days." With a wave, he walked slowly to his dusty pickup truck.

Speechless, Kate looked back at her neighbor. "He sure is a cute little old man," Miss Eugenia said with a chuckle. Kate could agree that he was little and old. Glancing up at Miss Polly's house, Kate saw her other neighbor staring down from a second-story window. "I hate to tell you this, but I think Miss Polly has been watching you and Brother Stoops."

Miss Eugenia put both grimy hands on her hips and squinted up. Miss Polly stepped back and pushed her curtains closed. With a laugh, Miss Eugenia dusted the dirt from her pants. "Good!" she said cheerfully. "It's about time I got my share of the gossip around here. Lately Annabelle's been hogging it all!"

Inside Kate found Miracle polishing a curio cabinet in the living room. "Miss Eugenia sent it over," she said as Kate noticed the $200 price tag hanging from the top shelf. "She said it would look just right over in this empty corner." Miracle continued to rub the wood with the dust rag. It did fit nicely, and the little shelves would be a perfect place to display some of Miss Imogene Riley's things from the attic. She wrote out a check, and Miracle said she would take it by to Miss Eugenia on her way home.

When Mark came in that night, Kate asked him to bring Miss Imogene's things down from the attic. They went through everything together and took out the dance card, a fan, some lace gloves, and a crocheted handkerchief. They arranged them, along with an old

Bible, in the curio cabinet. Kate spread some of the yellowed music neatly on the piano tray.

"There," she said when they were finished. "I think Miss Imogene would be happy with this room now."

"Well, we certainly want her to feel welcome," Mark responded dryly as he leaned against a nearby wall.

Kate looked through the glass at the dead woman's possessions. "Once she was a young girl, full of hopes and dreams. She went to parties and boys signed her dance card. I'm sure she expected to marry and have a family of her own. Instead, she lived in this house her entire life and died alone. It scares me," Kate admitted softly.

"You're not alone," Mark pointed out.

"No." As her hands encircled her stomach, her eyes were drawn to his.

Then the phone rang. He didn't even have to tell her it was Winston, determined to spoil their evening. Kate heard him come in at midnight. She listened to the comforting sounds of him preparing for bed, then turned over and went back to sleep.

* * *

On Tuesday, Sister Baylor and Sister Armistead arrived right on time for their appointment. Kate had just settled them in the living room when Miracle walked through to see if she wanted a casserole heated up for lunch. The sisters watched wide-eyed as Kate instructed her pretend maid. When Miracle left, they began the lesson but were interrupted a few minutes later by Ellis asking how many coats of water sealant he should put on the new porch. He left and they quickly finished the message, then invited her to enrichment meeting on Thursday.

"We'll be making picture frames," Sister Baylor said as her eyes strayed to the table beside her. Miss Eugenia had put an antique frame there with a $55 price tag still attached. Kate tried to hide her embarrassment, and as she walked her visiting teachers to the door, she assured them she would be at the meeting on Thursday night.

When the two women had left, Kate went over to Miss Eugenia's to help can tomatoes. She stared at the assortment of jars covering the kitchen table, which Miss Eugenia said had been sterilized. "These jars are clean?" Kate asked doubtfully, studying the discolored, mismatched collection.

"Of course they're clean." Miss Eugenia swiped a lock of hair from her forehead with the back of her hand. "They're just old. Some of them even belonged to my mother. I need for you to check the rims and make sure that there are no nicks or cracks."

Kate turned back to the jars and ran her finger gingerly across the lip of one. "If you think they might be cracked, why don't you just buy new jars?" Miss Eugenia looked up from the huge pan of boiling water on the stove. "I've borrowed jars, I've found jars, I've been given jars, and I've even stolen a few from Annabelle. But never in seventy-three years have I ever bought a new jar."

Kate pursed her lips. "So new jars are sort of like thank-you notes received more than six weeks after the wedding?"

Miss Eugenia considered this. "Not quite as bad. More like wearing white shoes after Labor Day or serving instant mashed potatoes on Sunday."

"So, if I wanted to can something and bought all new jars, I might be ridiculed but not ostracized?"

"You'd probably get off easy because you're young and a Yankee and have a very handsome husband."

Kate smiled. "Then I'm willing to risk it. I'm going to get new jars that are exactly the same size and have shiny lids." She glanced down at the rusty pile on the table.

"I buy new seals every year!" Miss Eugenia cried defensively.

Ignoring this remark, Kate continued. "Then I'm going to fill them with stewed tomatoes and line them up on my kitchen counters for everyone to admire." She closed her eyes and pictured the jars. "They will match my new wallpaper."

Miss Eugenia's eyes narrowed. "And where are you going to get all these tomatoes?"

"Well, I have a neighbor who has more than she can ever use. But if she won't share with me, I'll buy some at the roadside stand out on Highway 11."

"Their prices are so high!" Miss Eugenia objected and Kate

shrugged. "I already feed half of Haggerty with my hard work. You might as well take advantage of me, too," she finally grumbled.

"At least I'm helping you can!" Kate pointed out cheerfully.

"Goodness knows I can't imagine how I could ever have accomplished anything without you here to insult my jars and talk my ears off," Miss Eugenia said, stirring her tomatoes. Kate laughed as she examined the jars for cracks and chips.

At eleven o'clock Miss Eugenia cleared the table and prepared a meal of fried chicken, potato salad, fresh green beans, and sliced tomatoes. Everything was ready when Ellis shuffled over at noon. The big meal made Kate so tired she could barely keep her eyes open so Miss Eugenia excused her from further duties for the afternoon. Miracle left when Kate got home, so she locked the doors and went up for a nap. Mark woke her at five o'clock, calling to say that Winston was sick again and he would be late. She told him that she needed quart jars to can tomatoes, and he promised to pick up a box at Wal-Mart.

"It seems like you could fire him for calling in sick all the time."

"He says he has a doctor's excuse. I can't fire a man for being sick."

"Can't you get a substitute policeman so that you don't have to work in his place?"

"The city can barely afford the police budget as it is. I could ask the sheriff's department to loan me somebody or I could call Booster in to work a shift, but I don't want to beg."

Kate was anxious to keep him on the phone, so she introduced a new subject. "Have there been any more developments on the car theft cases?"

"All the evidence points toward someone in this office, probably Leita. If there's another one, I'll investigate it fully. For now, I'll just watch and wait."

* * *

On Wednesday morning when Kate walked downstairs she saw the case of jars sitting on the kitchen counter. There was also a note from Mark saying he had gone in to work early. She called the station, eager to hear the sound of his voice. When he answered, she thanked him for the jars and expressed concern about his long hours. He admitted that he was tired, but said it would take a better man than Winston to defeat him. Before hanging up, they agreed that she would come to the station at noon so they could go to their various appointments in Albany.

Miracle arrived at nine o'clock, and Kate carried the jars over to Miss Eugenia's house. Then they spent the morning canning tomatoes, and Kate was very pleased with the result. "They are beautiful!" she exclaimed as she carefully re-packed the box. "I can hardly wait for Ma—my husband to see them." She glanced up, but Miss Eugenia had been too busy staring at Kate's jars to notice the slip.

"They do look nice," she murmured.

Kate placed the last jar in the box and closed the lid. "If I were to give you a box of new jars, you'd have to use them or it wouldn't be polite," she said thoughtfully. Miss Eugenia gave her a sharp look. "And since I owe you for these tomatoes, you wouldn't even have to send me a thank-you note," she said over her shoulder as she hefted the box and walked toward the back door. She heard Miss Eugenia cackling as the door slammed behind her.

Kate lined the jars along the counter but couldn't pause to admire them. She barely had time to shower and change clothes before she had to leave. Ellis was making slow progress toward the door as she rushed into the kitchen, now dressed in a sleeveless cotton pants outfit. Miracle said she didn't want to leave the house empty and would be staying all afternoon, but she promised to put her feet up and watch soaps. Kate grabbed her purse and drove to town.

Leita squealed when she walked into the police station. "Mercy sakes! You are about to pop!" She came around the desk and put her hand on Kate's distended abdomen. "The baby is low and ready. I'd say she'll be here in a few days," she predicted sagely.

Kate shook her head. "I have almost two weeks to go."

"Well, we'll just see about that now, won't we?" the other woman said with a knowing smile.

Winston walked in from the back and gave Kate a speculative

look. "Been keeping under the speed limit lately, Mrs. Johnson?" he inquired.

"At least when I pass through your speed traps," she responded and his face darkened. "How are you feeling?" she asked and he stared back blankly. "I heard that you've been sick a lot lately."

He laughed out loud. "It's kind of you to be concerned about my health, ma'am." He moved closer to her and his eyes narrowed lewdly. "I'd love to discuss it with you, but it's personal and not something I would normally discuss in front of ladies." He turned his gaze to include Leita in the conversation. "If you really want all the details, we could step into the back where we can be alone . . ."

Kate knew he was trying to embarrass her and hated the blush that she felt creeping into her cheeks. "I don't want any details, thank you."

Leita shot Winston a mean look and pulled Kate toward the back. "Chief! You've got company!" she bellowed.

Mark met her just outside his office door. "Did Winston say something to you?" he demanded, eyeing the patrolman angrily.

Kate looked back to see Winston chewing a toothpick and watching them with amusement. Anxious to avoid further conflict between the two men, she said shortly, "I just asked about his health."

They stopped at a Wendy's just outside of Albany for grilled chicken salads, then went to the salon. Mark got his haircut while Kate's roots were touched up. Then they sat next to each other for their manicures. The girl tried to get Mark to let her put a coat of nail strengthener on after she trimmed and buffed, but he refused. On the way out to the van, he said that Drew was about to get too busy for his weekly manicures and Kate laughed.

At the doctor's office, they had to sit for almost an hour before Kate was ushered back to an examination room. Mark stayed in the waiting area while she was weighed and examined, then Dr. Tremayne came out to meet him. "Everything looks good. We'll have a baby soon!" he declared cheerfully.

Afterwards, Mark and Kate toured Memorial Hospital with two other couples who were still months away from delivery. Mark asked several questions and finally Kate looked up at him in amazement. "How do you know so much about childbirth?" she asked.

"I bought a couple of books." Her mouth dropped open in astonishment. He blushed slightly and shrugged. "I believe in being prepared."

It was starting to get dark by the time they got home. Kate apologized to Miracle for being so late, but she said they'd given her a chance to catch up on her stories. Mark insisted that he couldn't face another casserole, so they made hot dogs and ate them in the den. He found a Bette Davis movie, but Kate was asleep before the first commercial. Mark led her up to bed and she had a dim memory of a gentle kiss, but later she thought it could have been a dream.

* * *

On Thursday morning, Miss Eugenia came over early to drink her coffee at the kitchen table while Kate ate her cereal. "Don't forget that today is my Bridge Club meeting." Kate looked up blankly. "You are planning to come with me?"

"I don't play bridge, and I just went last time because of all the construction."

"Well, everyone enjoyed your company and insisted that you come again. It's next door at Miss Polly's house and she's cooking," Miss Eugenia added as incentive. "I figure it's a good idea for us to have at least one person there who is under seventy. Just in case we all have simultaneous heart attacks."

"As seriously as you play, I guess that is a possibility," Kate acknowledged.

"I'll come by at ten and we can walk over together."

Kate dressed carefully and admired her new manicure as she applied her makeup. Fortified by her glamorous appearance, she went downstairs to wait for Miss Eugenia. She reminded Miracle to water Ellis occasionally and locked the front door when she saw her neighbor approaching.

They walked into Miss Polly's living room, and Kate just had time to notice that Annabelle was present before all the old ladies stood and yelled, "Surprise!" Kate tried to retreat, but Miss Eugenia pushed her further inside the room. "You don't have any card tables set up," Kate said, looking around at the pink crepe paper and balloons.

"That's because we aren't playing bridge today. We're giving you a baby shower," Miss George Ann Simmons explained giddily. "Here, open mine first. It's a sterling silver spoon."

"You're supposed to let her open it and see for herself!" a tiny woman reprimanded Miss George Ann crossly.

"Why should she open yours first?" Miss Polly whined. "It's my house."

"You know what all this means, don't you?" Miss Eugenia whispered into her ear as Kate began tearing the paper that covered the silver spoon. "Hours of writing thank-you notes."

When all the gifts were opened and Kate had expressed her appreciation repeatedly, Miss Eva Nell pulled out a camera and made everyone pose. Finally Miss Eugenia said if that camera flashed in her eyes one more time she was going to break it into a million pieces. The camera disappeared and Miss Polly instructed everyone to get something to eat. Kate was starving and loaded her plate.

"Eating for two!" one of the little ladies giggled as she walked past.

"No wonder she's as big as a barn," another commented.

Once they were back in the living room with plates balanced on their laps, Kate nibbled on finger sandwiches and listened to the ladies talk. As they discussed a neighbor's female problems in detail, she got an idea. Putting down her fork, she waited for a lull in the conversation. When the opportunity presented itself, she cleared her throat.

"It's too bad about Winston Jones," she said into the momentary pause. All eyes turned to her, and she felt heat rise in her cheeks. "I mean, about his medical problems," she pressed on bravely.

"Winston has medical problems?" one of the ladies asked without enthusiasm.

"He's been to the doctor twice in the last week, and he's had to miss work, so it must be bad." Everyone was staring at her, waiting. "He said it was personal, something he couldn't discuss in front of ladies . . ." All the old women leaned forward with synchronized baited breath. "So I can only assume that it's . . ."

"A male problem," Miss George Ann spoke for everyone. Kate shrugged eloquently and Annabelle's eyebrows shot up.

"Oh my," Miss Polly breathed, eyes filled with excitement.

Miss Eugenia stood briskly and started stacking the gifts. "Well, we'd love to stay, but Kate takes a nap every afternoon. I'll send Ellis over here to pick up the gifts."

"Nonsense," Annabelle scoffed. "The baby will outgrow everything before Ellis gets it moved. We'll help."

"We've been dying to see the house anyway," Miss George Ann remarked as she lifted the small box that contained her silver baby spoon.

Kate sighed. "I'm sorry I haven't invited you over yet. But it's not really finished and with the baby coming . . ."

"No one expected a formal invitation," Miss Eugenia assured her, giving Miss George Ann a stern look. "But anyone who helps us carry things can take a quick tour."

Miracle didn't bat an eye as a stream of old ladies bearing an assortment of packages walked through the front door and then proceeded to examine the entire house. There were murmurs from every direction. Some were complimentary, others critical. From her seat in the living room, Kate heard several of the ladies discussing Winston's medical problem.

"Congratulations," Annabelle said quietly as she walked up behind her.

Kate looked back and smiled. "Whatever do you mean?" she asked innocently.

Annabelle threw back her head and laughed. "I think you might have succeeded in stopping Winston's absenteeism."

"I hope I at least took some of the fun out of it for him," Kate admitted, smiling.

* * *

Mark rushed home at five to take a shower and change out of his uniform before driving Kate to Albany for her enrichment meeting. He was quiet during the drive while Kate described her surprise party and the Bridge Club's impromptu tour of their house. As they reached the outskirts of Albany, he asked where she wanted to eat. "I'm sort of in the mood for Mexican food," she said.

"Mexican food? Aren't you afraid that it will give you indigestion and keep you up all night . . . ," he began. She looked across at him and they both smiled. "Okay, so nothing could keep you awake, but it just doesn't sound very healthy."

"What do you think Mexican women eat when they're nine months pregnant?" she asked logically.

"You win," he acquiesced. He pulled out his cell phone and called Leita at the station. She recommended a restaurant and gave them directions. Ten minutes later they were eating nachos and waiting for their meal to be prepared. She felt Mark's eyes on her repeatedly and finally asked if something was wrong.

"I wouldn't say that anything is wrong, exactly. But Leita says the whole town thinks that Winston is being treated by a urologist for a medical condition that has left him . . . incapacitated."

Kate choked on a tortilla chip.

"Winston is understandably devastated," he continued as Kate gulped water then stared at him mutely. "He even came into my office and asked for advice." Kate closed her eyes briefly. "I told him that this was the worst kind of rumor. Very hard to disprove," he added with a straight face. "All I could suggest was that he act extremely healthy from now on. No more sick days or trips to the doctor."

"So," Kate asked weakly. "What did he say?" She took another long sip of water.

"He offered to take both weekend shifts for a while." Mark was quiet for a moment, watching her. "I can't help thinking how convenient that rumor was. Winston has been giving me such a hard time, and now all of a sudden he wants to work overtime to prove he's a man. It's like . . ." She dragged her eyes up to meet his. "Someone was looking out for me."

"Almost like a partner?" Kate said shyly.

"Almost like a wife," he corrected, taking her hand in his. Just then the waitress appeared, ruining the moment by slapping hot plates of food on the table and instructing them not to burn themselves. All through the meal Kate caught Mark watching her. She blamed the warmth that suffused her body on the spicy food.

Mark sat in the foyer during the Relief Society meeting while Kate painted her picture frame pink. The sisters were all friendly, but she kept thinking about Mark and the tremor in his voice when he said she was acting like his wife.

At home she took him up to the nursery and put the still damp frame on the baby's dresser, then she showed him all her shower gifts. As she closed the last box, he stood and pulled her into his arms. "Come here," he instructed as he moved her in front of the window. "I want to be sure Miss Polly has a good view," he explained softly as his mouth touched hers. "Thanks for your help with Winston," he murmured a few minutes later.

"How did you know it was me?"

"I just knew."

"Serves him right." Kate pressed her face into the warm hollow of his neck.

"It couldn't happen to a nicer guy," he agreed, stepping away. "Do you need me to tuck you in tonight?" he asked.

"Unfortunately, I think I can manage," Kate admitted and he laughed as he closed the door behind him.

* * *

Mark was sitting at the kitchen table talking to Miss Eugenia when Kate came down for breakfast. She was swollen and attributed this condition to her unwise choice of Mexican food the night before. When she opened the refrigerator, Miss Eugenia exclaimed. "Mercy me! That baby could come any minute. Look how puffy your lips are!" Kate's fingers flew to her mouth, remembering the long kisses she and Mark had shared in the nursery. She felt the blood rising in her face and turned away quickly.

"Puffy lips are a sign of impending labor?" Mark asked Miss Eugenia anxiously.

"Among other things," the older woman murmured thoughtfully.

Kate filled her bowl with cereal and walked stiffly to the table. "Going in late today?" she asked Mark.

"Yeah, I figure Winston will probably be there around the clock for the next few weeks, so I'm going to take it easy."

Miss Eugenia chuckled again. "Poor Winston, so young to be sterile."

"You heard he was sterile?" Mark asked in surprise. "I heard . . ." He looked from one woman to the other. "I heard it was something else," he finished lamely.

"Rumors develop a life of their own in Haggerty. By noon he'll probably be an amputee," Miss Eugenia predicted.

Mark left with a smile on his face, and Miss Eugenia invited Kate to attend the Weight Watchers meeting with her and Annabelle that morning. "I didn't know you were on a diet," Kate said as she washed her cereal bowl.

"Oh, we're not, but we've been going off and on for almost twenty years and have made friends there. So we go once a month just to see everybody," Miss Eugenia answered blithely. "And it's a great place to get recipes."

Kate declined the invitation, saying that she needed to sort through the baby things.

"Everything needs to be washed in Ivory Snow and rinsed with Downy," Miss Eugenia said from the door. She held up her hand as Kate started to question her. "It's just one of those things. I'll pick some up at the Wal-Mart on my way back from Weight Watchers."

Since people kept telling her that the baby was coming soon, Kate spent the morning packing her suitcase for the hospital. Then she looked through the baby's clothes and pulled out all the newborn sizes. She had a stack of tiny things ready to wash when Miss Eugenia got back.

"I'll need all the blankets, sheets, towels, wash cloths, bibs, and even those bumper pads." The older woman waved toward the crib set that Kate already had neatly attached to the baby's bed.

"Why do we have to wash all that?" Kate complained.

"Anything that will touch the baby's skin must be washed. Otherwise, she might get a rash," Miss Eugenia insisted.

The one-hour project Kate had expected lasted well into the evening. Around six Mark called to say he would be a little late since the sheriff wanted to talk to him about a few cases.

When Kate finally put the last baby item back in the nursery at eight o'clock she was exhausted. She had missed her nap and was too tired to even eat. Miss Eugenia was pale with fatigue, but Kate didn't have any sympathy to spare as she watched the old woman hobble across the backyard and into her own house.

She changed clothes and fell into bed, but her eyes flew open at nine o'clock when she heard a noise in the hall. She got up and crept hesitantly to her door. She yanked it open and came face to face with Mark Iverson. His chest was bare and the towel he was clutching around his waist exposed a good deal of one leg as well. He looked as stunned as she felt.

"I'm sorry!" she gasped. "I heard a noise."

"I'm the one who should apologize. I thought you were asleep." Beads of water clung to his flexed muscles as he held the towel tightly in place. His neck and arms were deeply tanned, but his pale shoulders and torso were evidence of his regard for his temple covenants. Had Tony ever seemed so attractive to her?

"Good night," he whispered as he stepped into his room. Kate stared at his door for a few seconds before she turned and went back to bed.

On Saturday morning they carefully avoided each other. Mark worked outside while Kate folded and refolded baby clothes. Finally, at lunchtime she went out to the garage where he appeared to be trying to organize the tangle of tools, spare parts, and leftover construction supplies that were piled inside. "Making any progress?" she asked as she came up behind him.

He lifted his head and wiped the sweat from his brow. "If you have to ask, I guess not," he remarked guardedly.

"I've made some sandwiches for lunch." She examined a rusty saw. "I thought you might be ready to take a break."

He thought for a few seconds, then nodded. "I'll be there in a minute."

Kate watched from the kitchen window as he closed up the shed and walked across the yard. He came in through the back door and stopped by the sink to splash water onto his face and neck. Kate pulled her eyes away and stared outside.

After lunch Mark offered to take her to Wal-Mart to buy a roast for Sunday. She said she also needed to get some canning jars for Miss Eugenia. While they rode to the store, she explained the old jar situation and succeeded in making him smile before they reached the parking lot.

* * *

After they got back from Wal-Mart, Kate made a pound cake to take to Annabelle's party, using a no-fault recipe Miss Eugenia had given her. By the time she and Mark arrived, a few minutes late, several people were already in the pool. Happy was there with her husband. They were sitting close together in a secluded corner and didn't seem aware of the other guests. Annabelle pointed them out to Miss Eugenia and mentioned that their marriage seemed to be doing fine. There were a few other young people in attendance and several of their neighbors from Haggerty. Annabelle insisted that Mark take off his shirt and get into the pool.

He tried to decline her invitation. "I thought I would just sit here by Niki," he hedged.

"What? And disappoint all these old ladies?" Annabelle waved toward the matrons sitting under umbrellas along the fence. "The only reason most of them came was because I told them they'd get to see you in a swimsuit."

Mark's complexion darkened. "If that's why they came, they're in for a big disappointment." Kate watched helplessly as he peeled off his T-shirt, wishing she had the strength to disagree with him.

Annabelle squinted at the rapidly setting sun. "There can't be many ultraviolet rays left, but we'd better not take a chance with all that white skin." She squeezed a blob of sunscreen into Mark's palm and tossed the tube to Kate. "Your wife will take care of your back."

Kate felt very conspicuous as she squirted some of the lotion into her hand. Slowly she reached forward and touched Mark. His skin felt warm beneath her fingers, and as she rubbed firmly, he sat perfectly still. When Annabelle walked past them a few minutes later, she laughed. "I wanted you to protect him from cancer, not rub off three layers of skin."

Kate dropped her hands to her lap, embarrassed. Mark looked over his shoulder and smiled. "Thanks," he said as he stood. Then he leaned forward and whispered into her ear. "And I can assure you that back rub was well worth a few skin cells."

Kate watched with pleasure as he swam around the pool. She glanced at the widows and saw that they were equally enthralled. A teller from Annabelle's bank arrived, and Mark played with her children until their hostess commanded everyone to get out of the pool to eat. Mark dried off with the towel Kate had brought, then held out his hand and pulled her up. She accepted his assistance reluctantly, trying to pretend that his bare chest had no effect on her.

After dinner they enjoyed a short fireworks display and then a man played the guitar. Several couples danced while the musician sang romantic ballads. Kate and Mark were content to sit quietly in the shadows. At some point he reached for her hand and laced his fingers through hers.

As they drove home, Kate leaned her head drowsily against the cool glass of the van window. She realized with a sense of wonder that for the first time in years, she was completely satisfied with her life.

* * *

As Kate dressed for church on Sunday, she nervously rehearsed the simple testimony that Mark had composed for Niki to give in sacrament meeting. It had been a while since Kate had given a talk, which added to her anxiety. Impersonating Niki in everyday life had become almost effortless, but the prospect of pretending to be someone else in front of a large congregation of strangers was daunting.

She found Mark in the kitchen eating breakfast. She fixed a bowl of cereal and shared her concerns with him. He reassured her while she ate Raisin Bran. "Just stick with what I wrote down for you. It will be over before you know it."

The bishop met them as they walked into the chapel and insisted that they sit on the stand. When the time came for Kate to speak, she stood and gripped the side of the podium, reciting the words printed neatly on the page before her. Mark gave her a smile as they passed on his way to the microphone. He read his talk from a prepared script as well. He thanked everyone for their kindness and expressed gratitude for all his blessings. Then, at the very end, his head lifted and he looked out into the congregation. "I am also thankful for my wife." There was a second's hesitation and then he continued, "I can't imagine my life without her."

When he sat back down beside Kate, he kept his attention elsewhere. He wouldn't meet her eyes during Sunday School and seemed relieved when he could leave her to go to priesthood meeting. In the car on the way back to Haggerty, Kate forced him to talk by asking questions that required more than a yes or no answer. They discussed the investigator in their Gospel Essentials class who was preparing for baptism, and Mark told her that Brother Stoops would be bringing them some peaches later that week.

At home Kate turned off the roast, and then they walked next door. Miss Polly had a bad cold, so the meal was served quickly, and she and Mark prepared to leave immediately afterwards.

"Is there anything we can do to help you feel better?" Kate asked as they walked toward the door.

Miss Polly shook her head with a sniff. "I'm going to take some Tylenol Cold and go to bed," she informed them.

Back in their own house, they went upstairs to change clothes. Then, instead of taking her regular afternoon nap, Kate went down to the den. Mark looked up in surprise when she came through the door. He had his scriptures open in his lap.

"Researching the ten tribes?" she asked as she stretched out on the couch.

He looked uncomfortable with her presence. "I thought you'd be asleep," he replied, ignoring her question.

She shrugged. "I decided to keep you company instead." He closed his scriptures and faced her. "There's something I've been wanting to ask you," she began slowly. "It's a personal question and I'll understand if you don't want to answer." The agent nodded warily.

"Since you are extra righteous, well-educated, and a returned missionary who pays his tithing . . ."

"Why wasn't I married?" he said, anticipating her question. She nodded. "I dated a girl for several years, and we planned to marry eventually. She was a communications major, and after she graduated she got an offer to anchor a morning news show in Cincinnati. Since I was assigned to the Washington office, she had a decision to make. She didn't choose me."

"She made a big mistake," Kate assured him loyally.

"She probably doesn't think so. The last I heard she was married and making a six-figure salary."

"I'll bet her husband doesn't have an extensive collection of silk pocket hankies," Kate pointed out with a smile.

"I imagine you're right about that." He rubbed the back of his neck. "Anyway, after Trisha, I didn't have much interest in dating for a while. Then there was the FBI agent in Washington."

"The one who pretended to be Niki's father's secretary and bought us this house?" Kate watched him closely. "And wanted to move in with you?"

Mark nodded. "When I finally got out of that situation, I carefully avoided women. So, that's why I was still single when we met."

"Why did you start working for the FBI?" Since he had answered one personal question, she decided to press for more information.

"It's all I've ever wanted to do, for as long as I can remember."

Kate smiled sadly. "That's what Tony said, too."

Mark's expression darkened. "Tony's career in the FBI was like a fairy tale. He finished college, applied, and got a field assignment right away."

"Mr. Evans liked him," Kate acknowledged.

"Well, I guess nobody liked me," Mark shrugged. "I started applying with the Bureau as soon as I graduated from high school. I was told that the best way to get into the FBI was to major in accounting. So I did. I added a Spanish minor when I got back from my mission and graduated summa cum laude, but the FBI still turned me down. They suggested that I get a law degree." He sighed. "So I did."

"You have an accounting degree and a law degree?" Kate was

impressed.

"And I'm fluent in Spanish. It still took me two years to get a job, and even then they stuck me in Washington reading other people's mail and eavesdropping on Spanish phone conversations. They wouldn't give me a chance at an undercover operation."

"Is that why you get mad every time Tony's name is mentioned? Because he got better breaks than you did?"

"No," Mark exhaled slowly. "Tony was exceptionally adept at undercover work, I have to give him that. He knew how to blend in and he was incredibly brave. Of course, that fearlessness eventually cost him his life. Most people have at least some sense of self-preservation, but not Tony. He risked everything all the time."

"If he had cared more, he might have risked less," Kate suggested sadly. "If I had been a little more like Niki, then maybe . . ."

"You were pretty enough before they turned you into Niki Johnson," Mark said sharply and Kate smiled at his harsh kindness. "Tony was reckless, and nothing you could have done would have changed anything."

Kate sighed. "He never knew about the baby. Maybe that would have made a difference." Mark didn't comment. "It's a miracle, really. He was fanatical about preventing pregnancy, but after our last weekend together . . ." She shrugged at the obvious result.

Mark glanced toward one of the tiny cameras above the door. "Maybe he was trying to protect you," he said quietly.

"From what?" Kate asked. "Raising a child alone?"

Mark looked away. "He did have a very dangerous occupation."

Kate watched him, waiting for him to pursue the topic, but he didn't. She fell asleep on the couch and woke up several hours later with a terrible headache. Mark had heated up the roast and she ate a little, then took two Tylenol and went to bed.

* * *

Some time later she was awakened by . . . what was it? It sounded like a commotion in the hall. She rose from her bed and tiptoed toward the door, filled with trepidation. She didn't know if she was more afraid of an intruder or another encounter with Mark wearing only a towel.

Turning the knob slowly, she looked out to see that Mark's door was slightly ajar. Warily she crept across the hallway and into his room. Mark was in his bed, lying perfectly still. She saw a shadow move to her left and turned instinctively.

A horrifying sight met her eyes. Tony was standing at the far side of the bed, his FBI revolver pointed straight at Mark's head.

Kate moved toward him, her arm outstretched. "Tony!" Her voice echoed eerily in the dark room. "Tony!"

He didn't give any indication that he had heard her. She tried to grab his arm, but he pushed her aside and released the safety on the gun.

"No!" she cried. When he didn't respond she ran to the window and pushed it open. "Help me please!" she called into the night.

She saw lights come on in Miss Eugenia's house, then turned back to Tony, who was still in his original position. Mark lay motionless in the bed and a new terror gripped her. She ran over and grabbed Mark's shoulder, shaking him gently.

"You've killed him!" she yelled at Tony. "You're the one who is supposed to be dead, not him! You're supposed to be dead!"

"Kate!" a voice called firmly, pulling her from the nightmare. "Kate! It's okay," Mark's voice soothed her. She reached up and clung to him, pressing her face against his chest as she listened to the reassuring sound of his heart beating. He stroked her hair until her breathing became regular and even. "You were dreaming about Tony," he said miserably.

Kate controlled a shudder and snuggled closer to him. "Tony was standing in your room with his gun pointed at your head. It seemed so real." She shook her head. "I called out the window for help and even saw the lights come on in Miss Eugenia's house," she whispered. "I thought you were dead."

He lifted her face to his. "Well, as you can see, I am very much alive and you have nothing to be afraid of." She nodded although she knew she was right to be frightened. In her dream and in her heart, she had chosen Mark over Tony, and in the long run that might prove to be more dangerous than a hired assassin's bullet.

CHAPTER 9

On Monday morning Kate woke up achy and tired. She took more Tylenol and then went downstairs without getting dressed. Miss Eugenia was at the table and informed her that the Chief had already gone to work. "He said he would call at noon and to please remember to pick up the dry cleaning. He's almost out of uniforms," she added and Kate nodded dully, forcing a few bites of cereal down her throat. Miss Eugenia left for her Garden Club meeting as Miracle arrived. Kate spoke briefly to the agent, then went back to bed.

She woke up a couple of hours later feeling marginally better. A shower revived her even more, and by the time she was dressed she felt almost normal. Mark called while she was drinking a glass of orange juice to tell her that there had been a wreck out on Highway 76 and he was on his way over there. "It's a bad one, so I probably won't see you at lunch, but I'll be home for dinner."

Determined to ward off a return of her dismal mood, Kate picked up her keys from the counter and told Miracle that she was going to the dry cleaners. As she walked around the corner of the house, she noticed a man standing near the end of their driveway. His face was unfamiliar, but there were still a lot of people in Haggerty that she didn't know. He continued walking away from town as Kate climbed into the van and drove down Maple Street, intent on her errand.

When she had picked up the dry cleaning, she followed the same route back to the house. As she pulled into the driveway, the stranger was nowhere in sight, but she made a mental note to tell Mark about him. It required two trips to get all the clothes inside, and as she was hanging Mark's uniforms in his closet, she suddenly realized that her purse was still in the van.

Pushing her hair away from her face in a weary gesture, she trudged outside. Stepping onto the gravel driveway, she saw that the driver's side door of the van was open. Shocked by her carelessness, she rushed forward. The noise of her approach startled the stranger, who had been crouched under the steering column of the van.

Too surprised to be afraid, Kate continued to walk toward the car. "What are you doing?" she demanded before she thought about the wisdom of confronting him. Their eyes met briefly, then he moved away from the van and started to run.

Kate took a step to the right, intending to avoid him, but instead placed herself directly in his path. Their violent contact sent her sprawling onto the grass. Kate stared up into the clear October sky as the man escaped into the alley behind the house. In seconds Miss Eugenia's face appeared above her. "Are you hurt, dear?" she asked in an unusually gentle tone.

"I really don't know," Kate answered vaguely. "My back aches, and I think my water has broken."

"There isn't much doubt about that," Miss Eugenia confirmed, glancing down at Kate's wet clothing.

Miracle joined them then, her eyes round with shock. "Are you okay, Mrs. Johnson?" she asked breathlessly.

"She's going to be fine. Could you get us a couple of blankets and some pillows from the house?" Miss Eugenia asked the agent. "We're going to be making a trip to the hospital."

As Kate digested this information, more footsteps pounded toward her. She saw the shiny black shoes and her heart lifted, thinking that Mark had come. Then she heard Winston Jones's voice. "What's going on here, Miss Eugenia?"

"Niki was pushed down by a man who tried to steal her car," the older woman said calmly. Winston cursed under his breath and looked toward the alley. "The man got away, and there's no point in trying to find him now. We've got to get Niki to the hospital."

"Drew is helping with a wreck out on Highway 76," Kate informed them drowsily as Miracle came out of the house with an armful of pillows and blankets.

"That's where I was headed," Winston confirmed. "It's a bad one. Several people were killed."

"Well, if the Chief's tied up, you'll have to drive us, Winston," Miss Eugenia instructed. "Miracle, hand me a quilt to put around her. Then spread the other blanket on the back seat of the police car and arrange the pillows."

Kate allowed herself to be wrapped in soft cotton, then felt strong arms lift and carry her to the patrol car. The pain in her back increased steadily. Winston climbed in behind the wheel and Miss Eugenia took a position in the passenger seat. "Which hospital?" Winston asked, glancing in his rearview mirror.

"Memorial," Miss Eugenia supplied. "Use your radio to call Leita," she advised the policeman. "Have her call the hospital to let them know we are coming. Then she can notify the Chief."

Winston spoke into the microphone, following Miss Eugenia's instructions. He turned on his flashing lights as they sped toward Albany, and Kate concentrated on the pain. "Leita says the hospital wants to know the name of your doctor," Winston called back to her and she told him. The roads were bumpy, and the patrol car's suspension system was badly in need of repair. The upholstery smelled like stale cigarettes, and Kate began to feel nauseous.

After what seemed like an eternity, they pulled into the emergency entrance at Memorial Hospital. Gentle hands pulled her onto a stretcher, and Kate turned her face into the crisp, clean sheets as the pain enveloped her again. When the agony receded temporarily, she could hear the pounding of Winston's shoes against the tile floor as he walked beside her.

Finally they stopped and a nurse helped her change into a hospital gown. Then she was examined and given medication for the pain. When the anesthesia started to take effect, she pushed up on an elbow and focused her eyes on Miss Eugenia.

"Are you feeling better?" the older woman asked anxiously.

"A little," Kate forced the words through parched lips.

"Winston has gone to help at the wreck so Drew can come to the hospital. He should be here soon. And I've called Elmer," Miss

Eugenia continued and Kate stared blankly. "He said he was your household teacher and that I should call him when you had the baby," she explained.

"Wake me up when Mark gets here," Kate requested as her eyelids drooped.

"Who is Mark, dear?" Miss Eugenia's forehead wrinkled in an effort to understand.

"Drew. I mean, when Drew gets here."

* * *

Kate slept for a while and when she opened her eyes, Miss Eugenia was gone and Mark was standing beside her bed. His shirt was soaked with perspiration, and his face looked haggard. "I'm okay," she struggled to reassure him.

"Brother Stoops is here," he said. She saw him take something out of his pocket and show it to the home teacher. Then she closed her eyes as they conversed quietly. "We're going to give you a blessing now." Mark's voice penetrated her drug-induced sleep. She felt the pressure of their hands on her head. The home teacher sealed the anointing and then Mark said her name. "Kate Lynn Iverson," he began. She heard him bless her with comfort and the strength to deliver her child safely before her mind drifted and she dozed off.

Later Mark spoke again. She forced her eyes open and saw that he had put on a blue hospital gown and mask. An unattractive paper cap covered his cute haircut, and she had to smile. "Do you have a medical degree, too?" she asked, drowsily.

He smiled back. "No, but I'm going with you to the operating room anyway. The baby is turned wrong, and they are going to have to do a cesarean."

"Don't faint," Kate instructed as her eyes fell closed.

Through the fog in her mind, she felt the bed rolling through the hospital hallways. Occasionally she would hear a voice or feel someone touch her. Finally she heard Mark whisper that she had a baby girl. "She's beautiful, just like you." She knew that this remark was probably for the benefit of the nurses in the room, but she smiled anyway.

* * *

When Kate woke up hours later, she saw Mark sitting in a reclining chair by her hospital bed. The cap and mask were gone, but he was still wearing the blue gown over his police uniform. Nestled in his arms was a tiny bundle wrapped in a white blanket. "Well," he said quietly when he saw Kate watching him. He stood and smoothly moved the baby into the crook of his arm. "Let's go over here and meet your mom," he said as he approached the bed.

"Oh," Kate breathed as she pulled back the blanket and looked at her daughter. Her eyes were closed, the soft black lashes resting against her little cheeks. She had dark hair and her hands were clenched in tiny fists. "She's perfect."

"From head to toe," Mark agreed. "I watched the pediatrician examine her." Kate nodded vaguely as she ran her finger across the baby's face. "What are you going to name her?"

"Emily," Kate answered firmly.

"You sound certain," he said, smiling.

"I am," she agreed. "Emily is a strong name."

"Just right for a Haggerty baby."

"Yes," Kate whispered. The little hand opened and grasped her finger.

A nurse came in and Mark excused himself. The nurse helped arrange the baby for her first feeding. Everything went well and Kate was encouraged by the time Mark got back. "She opened her eyes for a few minutes," Kate reported proudly.

Mark settled the baby into her cradle and then pulled his chair up close to the bed. Taking Kate's hand, he pressed it against his cheek. "What a day," he murmured.

"Winston said the wreck was a bad one." Kate concentrated on speaking clearly, trying to ignore the feeling of his whiskers against her palm.

"Two people dead, three more in the hospital," he confirmed. "And speaking of Winston, he's called forty times to check on you. If he didn't have to be at the station while I'm gone, he'd be pacing the hall outside your door," he grumbled. "The way he's acting, you'd think he was the baby's father . . ." Mark began, then his eyes filled with pain. He took a deep breath. "I learned about irony when I studied literature in school, but I never understood it until now."

He glanced over at the sleeping baby. "When I was given this assignment, I thought there was no one I would hate being any more than Drew Johnson. He was vain, lazy, and dishonest— completely contemptible in every way. But if it meant we were just a regular family, that we had been married for a couple of years, and Emily was my daughter . . ." He was silent for a few seconds. "I'd be willing to actually be Drew Johnson."

Kate reached out and pushed the hair back from his forehead. "This may not be the right time to have this discussion, but at least there are no surveillance men watching," he said as he looked around the room. "First, I want you to understand that I'm not asking for any kind of commitment. I know that my feelings for you are unprofessional, and Heaven knows I've tried to fight them. But the truth is, I'm in love with you."

"Oh, Mark," Kate breathed.

"I understand that it's too soon after Tony's death. You will probably never forget him completely, but I hope that in time maybe . . ." His voice trailed off and he looked up at her. "I think you have feelings for me, too. I won't push you, Kate, and we won't rush into anything. But I would like to try to be a husband and a father, if you'll let me."

Kate wiped the tears seeping from her eyes. "I loved Tony, I really did," she whispered.

"I know."

Kate struggled to explain. "With Tony, his job always came first. We never really had a chance to get to know each other, let alone work out a relationship. My feelings for you are so different. You remember the other night when I dreamed about Tony?" Mark nodded. "I wanted him to be dead because he was dangerous to you or at least a threat to our future together." Kate was ashamed to say the words, but knew she had to be honest. "That's when I knew that I loved you, but I was afraid . . ."

A nurse coming in to get Emily interrupted their discussion, and Mark stepped out while the woman talked to Kate about her incision.

After the nurse left, Kate dozed off again. Later she heard Mark unfold the recliner into a narrow, uncomfortable-looking bed.

Kate woke up several times during the night and fought the fatigue for a few seconds to savor the sight of Mark's face relaxed in sleep. When the nurse brought Emily in for the two o'clock feeding, he stumbled to his feet and went into the hall, saying that he needed to stretch. The nurse smiled tolerantly as she settled the baby in Kate's arms. "He'll get used to this before you know it. They all do."

At dawn Mark said he couldn't live with himself another minute and had to go home to shower and change clothes. Kate asked him to bring her suitcase when he came back. "In the confusion, we left it behind. And I never did put in my toothbrush or makeup. All that stuff is in—" The nurse walked in, and Kate stopped speaking in mid-sentence.

He nodded. "I'll be back with everything in a couple of hours."

Kate took a shower and put on a clean hospital gown. Then the pediatrician came by and confirmed that Emily was healthy. Dr. Tremayne made his rounds and said that she could go home the next morning. Mark was gone longer than the two hours he had promised, and by eleven she was getting worried. He finally came in carrying her suitcase. His face was grim and Kate knew that something had happened. "What's wrong?" she demanded.

He put her suitcase down and closed the door. Then he sat in the chair by her bed and leaned very close. "Pat Roper, the agent who took your place in Chicago . . ." he paused and Kate nodded warily. "She didn't go to church on Sunday or to work yesterday. The surveillance guys got worried and went in last night. They found her dead. Shot."

A sob escaped Kate's lips. "Do the criminals think I'm dead?" she asked, struggling for control of her emotions.

"They'll know her identity soon." His reluctance to continue was obvious, but she held his eyes with hers. "They cut off her left hand," he said reluctantly, and Kate leaned her head back against the pillow as the room spun around her.

"Why would they do that?" Kate asked and heard her voice as if it were far away.

"Some employers require positive proof that a contract has been fulfilled," he explained. "If they didn't know Agent Roper's identity before, they will as soon as they check her fingerprints. Then they'll begin an all-out search."

"What does that mean for us?" Kate asked numbly.

Mark exhaled deeply, rubbing the back of his neck. "For you personally, it means that you can never, ever be alone," he emphasized.

Kate considered this. "Ellis is almost always at the house, and Miracle will be there all day for a few weeks. Agent Thomas is around, and we have the surveillance men watching the cameras."

Mark shook his head. "I doubt that Ellis could protect you from a mosquito, and Miracle goes home at night. There is a limit to the amount of time Agent Thomas can spend near our house without causing suspicion. So another set of agents is on the way. They'll pose as my parents and move into the house with us for as long as we can get away with it."

"So we are in danger."

"We are on alert," he hedged.

"Will we have to move, change our identities again?" The thought filled Kate with dread.

"Not yet. Our covers are solid. There's no need to panic. In fact, that would just draw attention to us. You'll have plenty of protection, and you have the additional comfort of knowing that Miss Polly never takes her eyes off our house," he added, attempting to lighten the mood.

She tried to smile. "How will the criminals go about trying to find us?"

"Computers. They'll look for women who meet your description."

"Who just had a baby." Kate realized the significance of this.

"Yes. That will narrow the field for them considerably. The baby makes us vulnerable in many ways. It would probably be better for everyone if she went—"

"Please, don't even say it." Kate put a hand gently over his mouth. "I can't bear the thought of sending my child to strangers."

He took her hand and laced his fingers through hers. "It would be temporary."

"How temporary? Until she's a month old? Two months? Two years?" Kate shook her head vigorously. "It's too much. I can't do it."

He gave her a worried look. "We may not be able to protect her. She would really be much safer, and I'm sure my parents would take care of her for a little while."

"Emily stays with me, us," Kate said firmly and Mark finally nodded his acceptance. "When they find the record of her birth and that I fit the description, what next?"

"They'll probably send someone to Haggerty to take pictures and talk to folks."

"Do you think our friends would tell strangers personal information about us?"

"They won't ask our friends. They'll ask the mailman and the dry cleaners and maybe even the Baptist preacher."

"What can people who don't know us tell them?"

"If we act like who we are supposed to be."

"What do you think they'll say?" Kate asked softly.

"I think they'll say that we seem like a nice young couple. Most will say we're a little odd, wear flashy, expensive clothes, and spend money like crazy."

"All of which fits our cover."

"Some may say that there were rumors we don't sleep together," he reminded her grimly.

"They might dismiss that as a temporary marital rift stemming from Drew's problems in New York."

"I doubt if these people dismiss anything."

"So, if they hear that things may not be as they should with the Johnsons . . ."

"They'll come to Haggerty."

"What will we do then?"

"We'll be on our guard. Mr. Evans is working hard to put these people in jail. He had hoped to get enough evidence to convict them on the money-laundering and drug-trafficking charges, but he says he can try to get them for Tony's murder. Once they are in jail, the threat to you will be over."

"So we're going to be okay?" Kate whispered.

"I can't tell you that. All I can say is that I will do everything in my power to protect you and Emily," Mark promised. He turned and looked out the window at the warm Georgia sunshine. "I'm worried about the people of Haggerty. They're all so trusting. Ruthless criminals could come in and slaughter the whole town."

"You have to warn them," Kate insisted.

"I can't do that without blowing the whole thing wide open."

"You can't just leave them unprotected."

"I have a plan. I've been meaning to start a safety campaign anyway, and I can use the attempt to steal our van as an excuse. We'll have some classes on self-defense, pass out flyers warning people to keep their doors locked and report strangers to the police immediately. Winston, Arnold, and I can even go door to door, making sure that people are complying."

"Someone could still get hurt."

"It's the best I can do," Mark said wearily.

A nurse came in and Mark left. Kate changed into a nightgown from her suitcase and brushed her teeth. Knowing that Niki would be dying to get some cosmetics on, Kate applied a little makeup before getting back into bed. They brought Emily in for a feeding, and Mark got back in time to burp her.

"I've been thinking about the car thefts," Kate began as he paced the room patting the baby gently. "You said that every time a ticket is issued, it's called in to Leita so she can check the driver and car." Mark nodded. "If the ticket is written at night when she's not there, it's put on her desk so she can record and file it." He nodded again. "If she records all the tickets, chances are she submits some kind of report to someone else. Probably monthly, which would account for the delay between when the ticket is issued and when the cars are stolen."

Mark stopped pacing and stared at her. "That's true."

"So you need to find out if she makes a report and if so, where she sends it."

"I most certainly will." He placed the sleeping baby in her plexiglass bed.

"Record and file. I did a lot of that at the law office where I used to work. If you record before you file, there has to be a reason." He nodded again, thinking. "And it didn't make sense that Leita would try to steal the police chief's van," Kate pointed out. "So, now you can solve this case, and our attempted robbery will be the last theft in the chain." She leaned back and looked at him proudly.

"I'm not sure the incident with our van was related to the others," he said slowly.

"What do you mean?" Kate was disappointed.

"The man you saw may have been trying to get fingerprints from the van, not steal it."

"That would mean that they've already found us!"

"Agent Roper didn't go to church on Sunday, but she could have died as early as Friday night. She told her surveillance team that she had a cold and was going to stay in all weekend, so they didn't get concerned until Monday."

"They may have been looking for me since Friday," Kate realized grimly. "Three days is a long time."

"They may have sent someone to take pictures and get prints," Mark nodded.

Kate raised her eyes to meet his. "I am so scared."

"You've got the Bureau to protect you."

Tyler Thornhill's words echoed in her mind. He had said that Mr. Evans cared more about the operation than the people involved. He claimed that Tony's life had been dispensable and that Kate's might be as well. But Mark's eyes were tender and his tone sincere. So Kate smiled and tried to forget her doubts.

* * *

Miss Eugenia was dying to see the baby and make sure that she was being properly cared for, but said she was afraid to drive in Albany. So instead she called about once an hour to check on Emily and give unsolicited advice. Kate was amazed to find out that Miss Eugenia was scared of anything, but told her they would be home early on Wednesday morning.

After lunch, Brother Stoops brought them some roses from his yard. He seemed subdued, and after he left, Mark explained, "I had to tell him who we are."

"Of all the people we are lying to, you chose to tell Brother Stoops the truth?" Kate was astounded.

"He helped me give you a blessing. I was performing a priesthood ordinance, so I felt I should use your real name."

Kate tried to think back to the hours before Emily's birth. She remembered seeing Mark and Brother Stoops, talking quietly. Mark had taken something out of his pocket. "You showed him your FBI credentials?" she asked and Mark nodded. "How did he take the news?"

"Pretty well, actually. He accepted the explanation I gave him and didn't ask me any questions."

"He was uncomfortable during his visit today," Kate pointed out.

"Probably because he didn't know what to call us. I know I feel silly every time I call you Niki."

Late in the afternoon Winston came into the room carrying a teddy bear almost as big as he was.

"I can't thank you enough for getting me to the hospital in time," Kate began as he propped the bear in a corner.

"Yeah, I guess I owe you," Mark growled. His attitude toward this obligation was obvious.

Winston ignored them both as he looked into the tiny crib. "This is her?" he asked, bending down.

Mark made a sound of derision, but Kate nodded. "That's her." She watched as the big man reached a finger out to touch Emily's silky hair. "Would you like to hold her?"

Panic clouded his features. "Oh, no. I never held a baby before. I'd probably drop her."

"Yeah, you probably would," Mark agreed uncharitably. "We really appreciate the bear and the visit, but Niki's real tired—"

Kate looked up at him, appalled. "Drew!"

Winston laughed. "It's okay, Mrs. Johnson. I understand why the Chief wouldn't want me here, and I guess you really are tired. I just wanted to see for myself that you were both all right."

He moved toward the door. "Winston Jones, you sit down in that chair right now." Kate pointed to the recliner and did her best impression of Miss Eugenia. She walked carefully to the baby bed and lifted Emily. Seconds later she had the baby settled in Winston's shaking arms.

"She doesn't weigh anything at all!" he exclaimed.

"Almost nine pounds," Kate disagreed.

"You better take her back, Mrs. Johnson," he begged. "Before I break her."

"You won't break her," Kate laughed as she scooped the baby up. "And when she gets big enough to understand, I'll tell her that you played a crucial role in her birth."

Winston blushed from his too-tight collar to the edge of his receding hairline. "It was an honor, ma'am," he assured her. He stood and looked longingly at the door, but forced himself to continue. "I'm not proud of the way I've acted since you came to Haggerty. I shouldn't have given you that speeding ticket, and I'm sorry that I made you sit in the heat for so long," he said with sincerity. "My behavior at the bowling alley and then later, when you asked about me being sick—"

"Don't worry about that, Winston. I'm not proud of everything I've ever done or said either. Let's just put the past behind us and start fresh." Kate held out her hand, and Winston eyed it nervously. Then he turned to his chief.

"I'll give you permission to touch her, just this once," Mark said.

Winston shook Kate's extended hand briefly, then backed out of the room. "Well, what do you know about that?" Kate said after he left.

"I know that having Winston as a friend might be worse than having him as an enemy. Now he'll be hanging around the house, wanting to hold Emily and buying her atrocious toys." Mark eyed the giant bear in the corner.

Kate laughed. "Winston's not so bad."

"No, Winston isn't 'so bad.' He's worse."

After dinner, Mark's FBI-assigned "parents" came to the hospital to visit. Leaving Kate and Emily in their care, Mark went home to check the computer and pack an overnight bag. When he got back, he looked grim. "The autopsy is back on Agent Roper. She died on Friday afternoon."

"So they've had almost four days," the agent posing as Mrs. Johnson remarked solemnly.

Mark nodded and looked back at Kate. "Mr. Evans wants you to wear a little patch." He held up a small zip-lock bag with a tiny black dot inside. "It's adhesive and sticks directly to your skin."

"Put it under your arm, just above the bra line," Mark's "mother" advised.

"It would help us track you if we got . . . separated," Mark explained hesitantly.

Kate took the plastic bag and went into the bathroom. When she had the dot secured, she returned to find all the FBI agents gathered near the bed. Once Kate was settled, Mark continued.

"I've started Haggerty's new safety campaign. Leita printed posters, and we're putting them up everywhere. I'm speaking to the Methodists on Sunday and hopefully to the Baptists tomorrow night. Arnold and Winston will canvas door to door in their spare time. I guess we're as ready as we can be."

"So now we wait?"

"We wait," Mark agreed. "Mr. Evans says that if we see anything to indicate that the criminals have found you, he'll move in and arrest them with what he already has."

"So there won't be a shoot-out, and we won't have to move," Kate clarified and Mark nodded. "And if Mr. Evans arrests the people who are trying to kill me, we won't need to be Drew and Niki anymore?"

Mark turned his eyes to meet hers. "Probably not."

* * *

Mark took Kate and Emily home on Wednesday morning. Her short-term in-laws and Miss Eugenia met them at the front door. Miss Eugenia immediately took Emily from Kate's arms.

"Oh, what a fine girl!" she exclaimed. "I'll take you straight up and show you the nice new room we've got waiting for you." She made little cooing noises as she walked toward the stairs. Still standing at the door, Mark spoke with the other agents briefly before they went to the kitchen, where Miracle was preparing lunch.

In her own room, Kate changed back into a nightgown. Miss Eugenia walked in from the nursery and handed her the baby. Kate sat gingerly on the bed and started feeding Emily. "She is a beautiful baby," the older woman smiled. "And Drew's parents seem nice enough."

Kate looked up. "I don't know them well. It's going to be awkward living with them for a while."

"How long are they going to stay?"

"At least a couple of weeks," Kate reported with a grimace, and Miss Eugenia laughed.

"Good. With them in the house, you and Drew will have to stay in the same room."

Kate hadn't really considered this, but when Mark brought in her suitcase and the giant bear, she mentioned it to him. After a brief discussion, he agreed that they probably should stay together.

"I'll set up a cot over here." He pointed toward the windows. "I hope I won't make you uncomfortable, but it wouldn't be wise to leave you and the baby alone."

"I got used to sharing a room with you at the hospital," she pointed out. "And I like to watch you sleep." His head shot up. "You're so cute when your mouth is open, and drool is running out both corners."

He scowled at this remark. "I'll try not to slobber tonight."

* * *

Mark addressed a large crowd at the Baptist church that evening and stressed the need for increased safety awareness. He went back to work on Thursday, leaving the three FBI agents with Kate, but called to check on them at least once every hour. When he rushed into the house at five, he said he felt like he'd been gone for days.

"Did you miss me?" he asked Emily as he lifted her from the bassinet.

"Actually, I think she did. No one else burps her quite as well as you do." Kate watched with pleasure as he paced around with her daughter clutched to his chest.

"Well, I'm here now," he murmured to the baby. As he walked, he told Kate that he had traced Leita's monthly ticket log to an office at the county courthouse in Albany. He had turned the case over to the sheriff's department, and they already had a suspect.

"So much for your one big case," Kate teased.

He smiled. "I couldn't have solved it without your help."

Kate accepted his praise graciously. "You would have eventually figured it out, but hundreds of other people may have lost their cars first."

Brother Stoops came by on Thursday evening to see them for a few minutes and then spent two hours with Miss Eugenia in her garden. The visiting teachers came on Friday and brought a nice meal. Miss Eugenia was impressed and told them they would be receiving a thank-you note soon. Casseroles and pies and baby gifts arrived on almost an hourly basis from the generous people of Haggerty. Even Agent Thomas paid a visit on the pretense of checking the Johnsons' sewer lines.

On Sunday morning Mark spoke to the Methodists about the importance of locking their doors and watching for strangers. Miss Polly prepared a wonderful dinner and served it on the Prescotts' antique dining room ensemble to make it more convenient for Kate. Miss Eugenia ate with them and quizzed the visitors. After their neighbors went home, the older "Mr. Johnson" said the FBI should hire Miss Eugenia to do their interrogations.

When Mark came home on Monday night, he said that Booster McMillan was claiming that the safety campaign was his idea and using it to promote his candidacy for mayor. "I hate to think that I'm doing anything to help Booster," he muttered.

"Well, look on the bright side. Booster is helping you to put Haggerty on guard," Kate pointed out, trying to console him.

* * *

Two weeks passed without unusual incident. There were no strangers reported in Haggerty and no robberies or car thefts. Mark was encouraged but said they couldn't afford to let their guard down.

Nevertheless, as the days passed, they started to relax as their days fell into an easy routine. Kate and Mark both learned the basics of baby care, and Emily thrived. Often during the night Kate would wake up to see Mark rocking the baby gently, trying to delay the time when she would have to wake up to feed her.

When Emily was three weeks old, Mark took Kate for a checkup with Dr. Tremayne, who said that her incision was healing nicely. On the way home from Albany, they stopped at a roadside fruit stand, and Mark walked around showing Emily all the brightly colored vegetables while Kate bought a big pumpkin for Halloween. When they got back to Haggerty, Mark dropped Kate, the baby, and the pumpkin off at the house, then went to check on things at the station.

Miracle had cooked a pot roast for dinner and was taking the rolls out of the oven when Kate walked in. At the sight of the pumpkin, the FBI agents became as excited as preschoolers and volunteered to carve the jack-o-lantern while Kate fed the baby. They were just lighting the candle inside when the police chief walked in and casually kissed his wife, ignoring the other agents and the cameras. Then he went upstairs and took a shower, returning a short while later, wearing Drew's designer blue jeans and an expensive polo shirt.

While they were eating dinner, Miss Eugenia appeared at the back door and walked into the kitchen. Taking a plate from the cabinet, she dished herself a little of everything.

"I just had to come over and tell ya'll what Miss Polly did at the Women's Choir meeting today," she began as she scooped an ample helping of carrot salad onto her plate. "Afterwards we had pie and coffee. Somebody mentioned they'd seen in the paper where another one of those snake-charming preachers was bitten to death last Saturday. One thing led to another and soon we were talking about Mormons."

Kate and Mark both looked up simultaneously. "The ladies went straight from snake handlers to Mormons?" Mark asked dubiously.

"Well, not straight," Miss Eugenia smiled. "I think they talked about some religion that doesn't allow its members to bathe in between." Mark nodded in resignation. "Anyway, one of the ladies said that Mormons built temples and sacrificed babies on altars."

"Why would anyone believe such an awful thing?" Kate gasped.

Miss Eugenia shrugged. "Who knows? Of course, I was about to say that this couldn't be true, but before I could swallow my blackberry cobbler, Miss Polly was up on her feet. She pressed her hand to her chest—" Miss Eugenia stood and demonstrated, "—then with tears in her eyes, she said that was the most horrible lie she had ever heard."

Kate lowered her fork, listening in amazement as Miss Eugenia continued. "George Ann Simmons said how in the world did Miss Polly know it wasn't true since she had never been inside a Mormon temple in her life. Miss Polly stood there bold as brass and said she didn't have to go inside a Mormon temple to know that they didn't kill babies. She said she was well acquainted with Drew and Niki Johnson who were Mormons and that was proof enough for her."

Miss Eugenia concluded her story with a broad smile, and Mark grinned back at her. Kate burst into tears, and Mark looked at her worriedly. His "parents" exchanged an anxious look while Miss Eugenia continued to eat.

"What's the matter, Niki?" Mark asked.

"That was just so sweet!" Kate sobbed. "And Miss Polly, of all people!"

Miss Eugenia shoveled another mouthful of black-eyed peas into her already crowded mouth. "Don't worry about her," she said as Kate excused herself and hurried upstairs. "It's just hormones. She'll be back to normal in no time."

* * *

Two days before Halloween, Mr. Evans recalled the agents who were posing as Mark's parents.

"I hate to let them go," Mark told Kate as he ate his cereal that morning. "But Mr. Evans is right. They've been here for almost four weeks, and it's starting to look suspicious. Since Niki's father is a public figure, we can't use agents to pose as her parents. Mr. Evans said he'd try to think of a plausible excuse to send someone else."

"It's been a month and nothing has happened," Kate said hopefully. "Surely, if these people are as powerful and resourceful as you say, they would have found me by now if they really wanted to."

"Rumor has it that the contract on your life has been canceled," Mark reported, "but Mr. Evans said his source wasn't very reliable."

Kate remembered Tyler's objections to the original information. "Worse than the drug addict who reported the contract in the first place?" she asked.

"They might just be watching, waiting for us to let down our guard," he said grimly as the two other agents walked into the kitchen carrying suitcases.

Miss Eugenia and Miss Polly walked in to bid Mark's "parents" farewell, effectively ending the conversation about hired killers. After saying good-bye to her neighbor's parents, Miss Eugenia invited Kate to the Bridge Club meeting the next day.

"I couldn't leave the baby," Kate declined.

"Leave her? I want to show her off! I'll pick you up at 9:45," Miss Eugenia insisted.

The house seemed quiet that night without the other agents. Kate expected Mark to move back into the guest room now that his temporary parents were gone, but when it was time for bed, he settled on the little cot in her room as usual. She smiled as she fell asleep, grateful for his comforting presence.

* * *

At the Bridge Club meeting, Emily was passed around and admired, then Kate took her to a back bedroom to feed her. When she returned, the games were well underway. During lunch the discussion worked its way around to a lady in Haggerty whose husband had suffered a stroke a few days before. They agreed that meals should be taken in, and a heated argument broke out between Miss George Ann and Miss Polly, who both wanted to make a sweet potato pie.

Miss Eugenia finally intervened. "I declare! Both of you make one. She can put one in the freezer!"

Kate was tired by the time they got home. Miracle met them at the car and helped get Emily up to the nursery. Miss Eugenia followed Kate into the kitchen to check on Ellis, who had completed the back porch and was now re-grouting the tile in the guest bathroom.

"I brought you a plate," the older woman told the handyman as he shuffled forward. "Why don't you come over to my place and eat it? I'd like some company while I make peanut brittle." She turned to Kate. "Oh Niki, here's a recipe for Chicken Extraordinary. It's a simple casserole, but it heats up nicely."

Kate stared at the card. "You want me to make this?"

"Of course. For Miss Gladys Norcross, whose husband had a stroke. I'll take it over myself tomorrow when I deliver my potato salad."

Tears welled in her eyes as Kate realized the significance of the card in her hand. "Oh, Miss Eugenia!" she said, her voice cracking with emotion.

"There, there. No need to make such a fuss over a little casserole." Miss Eugenia's tone was matter-of-fact.

"I'll have it ready first thing in the morning," Kate promised fervently.

"Well, I won't pick it up until eleven on my way to the quarterly poetry reading at the retirement home," Miss Eugenia replied blandly as she followed Ellis outside.

When Mark came home, Kate showed him the recipe card. "Do you know what this means?" she asked, extending the card for his review.

"That you will now begin to contribute to the gross overabundance of casseroles cooked in this town?" he teased lightly as he walked across the room bouncing Emily.

"It means that I am *accepted.* I am 'a Haggerty lady.'" The words caught in her throat and tears threatened again.

"Congratulations, Kate," he whispered as he bent to kiss her.

"I feel hopeful for the first time in years. I think that maybe everything is really going to be okay," Kate dared to predict.

"Let me put Emily down so I can take advantage of this good mood you're in," Mark said as he laid the sleeping baby in her bassinet. Then he pulled Kate into his arms and kissed her again.

"So what do you think? Are we safe?" she asked breathlessly a few minutes later.

Worry clouded his eyes. "I think that you are the most beautiful woman in the whole world," he said, evading her question.

Kate shook her head. "That's Niki."

He put his hands on both sides of her face. "I never see Niki when I look at you."

"Who do you see?" she asked.

He bent close to her ear. "I see Kate Iverson, my wife and the woman I love."

"Oh, Mark," she whispered, her voice trembling.

"We'll wait another week, then I'll tell Mr. Evans to move in with what he has. Once this is settled, we can forget all about Niki and Drew." He nuzzled her ear. "We could go away for a weekend."

"Like a honeymoon?" Kate whispered.

Mark looked into her eyes. "It will be a new start."

"A *real* start," Kate corrected, and he kissed her again.

CHAPTER 10

On Halloween morning, Mark left early, telling Kate that it would probably be very late before he got home. All the policemen were planning to work through the night to keep the trick-or-treaters safe and discourage teenage pranksters from doing any serious damage. Kate assembled her casserole, poured it into a pan, and had it wrapped with aluminum foil by 8:30 A.M.

Miss Eugenia came by to get it a couple of hours later. Kate was feeding Emily at the kitchen table and her neighbor pulled up a chair, saying she had a few minutes to spare. "How many trick-or-treaters will we have?" Kate asked when Miss Eugenia said she needed to buy some Halloween candy. Since there were no children in the neighborhood, Kate couldn't imagine they would see very many.

"Oh, we'll have droves!" Miss Eugenia exclaimed. "People drive in from several of the surrounding communities and bring their families here since our houses are close together. You'd have to walk ten miles to get a handful of candy in that subdivision over on Highway 11."

"I don't have enough candy then," Kate said as she put Emily up on her shoulder.

"I'll pick some up for you. Or, better yet, why don't you ride with me to the poetry reading, and we'll stop by the store afterwards?"

"I couldn't trust Emily to be quiet during a poetry reading," Kate declined with regret.

"The way those old women read, it would be a blessing if Emily cried so loud they couldn't be heard," Miss Eugenia confided. "But Miracle is here to keep an eye on the baby. You could leave her for an hour or so."

The idea of being out of the house did sound inviting, and she wanted to see if Wal-Mart had a costume for Emily. So she called Mark and he said to go ahead. Nothing much was happening at the station, and he'd come home for lunch to help Miracle with the baby.

Kate changed clothes, dabbed on some extra makeup, and rode off with Miss Eugenia. They took the food to Mrs. Norcross, then drove to the retirement home. The poetry reading was even worse than Miss Eugenia had predicted, but the old folks were nice, Kate thought. On the way home, she bought ten bags of candy and a tiny ballerina outfit that could be worn as pajamas after Halloween.

By the time they were headed back to Maple Street, Kate was uncomfortably aware that she needed to feed the baby. She waved good-bye to Miss Eugenia and went inside where Miracle was eating a tuna salad sandwich.

"Where's Mark?" she asked, piling her purchases on the counter.

"Chief called and said something had come up, and he couldn't come home. Isn't this the cutest thing!" she exclaimed as she pulled Emily's costume from a sack. "Baby's sleeping. I just checked on her a few minutes ago." Miracle offered to make Kate a sandwich.

"Thanks, but I had cookies and punch at the retirement home. What I need right now is to feed Emily whether she's hungry or not," she told the agent, heading toward the stairs. Kate flipped on the light in her bedroom and tossed Niki's purse on the bed. She glanced over into the bassinet, but Emily was not curled up there. She went across to the door that adjoined her room with the nursery and walked inside. The baby crib was also empty.

"Miracle!" she called down the stairs. "Where did you lay Emily down for her nap?" She waited for a few seconds as she heard the agent's footsteps approaching the landing. She had not even thought to worry until she saw Miracle's face peering up at her from the bottom of the stairs.

A knot of dread started to form in Kate's stomach. "Where's Emily?!" she demanded.

"I laid her in the bassinet," Miracle answered slowly.

All the blood rushed from Kate's head, and she grabbed the banister to keep from falling. Miracle started up the stairs as Kate staggered dizzily down the hall. There was no baby in the bassinet, but under the little pink receiving blanket were two airline tickets from Albany to Miami in the names of Mark and Kate Iverson.

Miracle was visibly shaken, but Kate was amazingly calm. "Call Mark. Tell him to come home immediately." As Miracle turned to do as she had instructed, Kate took out a suitcase and began to pack.

Mark rushed in five minutes later, breathing hard. "They took Emily?!" he asked frantically.

Kate handed him the tickets. He opened the front flap of hers, and an Illinois driver's license fell out. It had Kate's biographical information and Pat Roper's picture.

"They put our real names on the tickets to scare us," Mark said, frowning. "And they sent the license, so we'd know they were the ones who killed Agent Roper." His voice shook slightly.

Kate zipped the suitcase closed. "You need to pack quickly. I'm going to have to change my dress." She motioned vaguely toward the milk stains on her chest. Hoping a dark color would be more practical, she chose a black pantsuit from the closet and walked into the bathroom. A few minutes later she found Miracle in the kitchen. Mark's overnight bag was by the back door.

"He's on the computer," Miracle informed her miserably as Kate put her small suitcase beside Mark's. "We're supposed to meet him in the office."

Kate didn't bother to look away when she reached the office and found Mark typing numbers and letters on the keyboard.

"Miracle, would you go over and ask Miss Eugenia to come," Kate said from the doorway. Mark looked up sharply, but didn't countermand her. Miracle glanced between them, then went out the back door. "Do you think they have the baby at the airport?"

"Probably, yes."

"I should have sent her to your parents like you said," Kate whispered. "This is all my fault."

"If anyone's to blame, it's me," Mark disagreed wretchedly. "I was supposed to protect you both."

Kate took a deep breath. "There's nothing we can do about it now. We have to get to the airport and find Emily. Then you can make a trade. I'll go with them, and you'll take Emily somewhere safe." Just saying the words made Kate's chest convulse with pain.

Miss Eugenia hurried in at this point, pale and terrified. Mark finished typing and turned off the console. "Miss Eugenia," he said grimly. "I guess Miracle told you that Emily has been kidnapped." The old woman bobbed her head as he stood and closed the door. "There are no cameras in here," he explained, turning back to face them. "We don't have time for a lengthy explanation. All I can say is that we are not Drew and Niki Johnson. I am an FBI agent, and we were given those identities because Kate's life is in danger. Now we need your help."

Miss Eugenia examined them both. "I knew things weren't right over here." She stared hard at Kate. "And you never looked like a Niki."

"Miss Eugenia, I want you to go over to your house and call Winston at the police station. Tell him that you need him to come immediately. Don't give any details over the phone, but make sure he understands that it is an emergency." Miss Eugenia nodded. "Have him take you to the airport." Mark wrote down some information on a small piece of paper and extended it to her. "Go to this gate. Miracle will stay here to answer the phone and relay messages."

"It's me that the kidnappers really want," Kate explained quietly. "Mark's going to try to get Emily out of there, and he'll need help with her on the drive home."

"I'm going to try to get us all out of there," Mark corrected.

"If you do that they may kill us all," Kate objected sharply. "Emily's safety is the priority here. Promise me that you will do as I said, or I won't let you come with me," she threatened desperately.

"And just how do you propose to stop me?" he shot back angrily.

"I'll think of something," she promised.

"Rather than fight between ourselves, we should work together." Miss Eugenia's age-spotted hands grasped Kate's icy cold ones. "And Emily's safety is the most important consideration." This she directed toward Mark.

"I think I should be the one to go with you to the airport in case there's trouble. Miss Eugenia can stay here and answer the phone," Miracle spoke up.

"We don't know what we'll find at the airport. I want someone there who can get Emily out fast and without us if necessary. Miss Eugenia can pass as a relative and will draw less attention. I think we're better off with her." Nevertheless, Mark's grimace suggested that he would have preferred the agent's presence.

"I'm trained for situations like this, and I'm licensed to carry a gun," Miracle argued.

Mark would not be swayed. "Winston has a gun and he'll be wearing a uniform, which will give him credibility with the airport officials if anything goes wrong," he said firmly.

Kate was frustrated by the amount of time they were wasting. "I'm going upstairs to pack the diaper bag, and I'll drive myself to the airport if we can't get things settled quickly," she said and turned toward the door.

Miracle's dark hand reached out and stopped her. "I'll pack the diaper bag. You two get your things loaded into the van."

"Put some of those sample bottles of formula that they sent home with me from the hospital," Kate instructed her. "Emily will be hungry."

"Let's go," Mark said, taking her arm and leading her to the door. Miss Eugenia hurried across her yard to her house to call Winston, and Mark loaded the van while Kate fastened her seatbelt. Several more precious minutes ticked by before Miracle ran out of the house with the diaper bag. When she had given it to Kate, Mark started the car and pulled into the street.

Kate looked straight ahead and tried to keep her mind blank, clear of paralyzing emotion. Mark turned onto Highway 11, headed toward Albany, and increased his speed.

"Can't you go any faster?" Kate complained when he leveled off at eighty miles per hour.

"Killing ourselves won't help Emily and getting pulled over by a sheriff's deputy will only delay us more," he responded calmly. As Kate breathed slowly and deeply to calm herself, he continued, "Agent Thomas's sanitation truck was parked in the alley behind the house. If the kidnappers got past him, he must be dead."

"No!" Kate put her hands over her face.

"I want you to realize that these are not reasonable, rational people we're dealing with. They are killers, and a few more deaths on their conscience won't mean anything."

After several torturous minutes, they finally reached Albany, and Mark had to slow down to negotiate the heavier city traffic. His fingers gripped the steering wheel so tightly that his knuckles turned white. At 1:30 he pulled in front of the airport and parked in the loading zone. A security guard stepped up to the van as Kate was climbing out.

"I'm sorry, but you can't park here," he said with authority.

Mark handed Kate the diaper bag and flipped open his FBI credentials. "We're on official business, and this van is U.S. Government property. Keep an eye on it."

The startled man stared after them as they went into the terminal. They searched for Emily as they walked but saw no sign of her. When they reached the designated gate, they checked their luggage as carry-ons. Kate struggled to control her trembling hands as their tickets were stamped by a stern-looking airline employee with steel-gray hair pulled into a tight, no-nonsense bun. After a cursory glance, the woman pointed to the door that Kate hoped would lead to her daughter. Picking up their bags, they crossed the portable bridge into the plane.

The first-class compartment was empty, and they hurried through to the coach section. On the left-hand side of the front row sat a man holding Emily. Kate's relief was so profound that her knees buckled. Mark's hand at her elbow steadied her as they took their seats on either side of the man.

"Give me my baby," she hissed, reaching for the child.

"We have some talking to do first." The man held Emily tightly, and she started to cry.

"You're making a scene." Kate glanced around at the other passengers who were stowing bags and settling into their seats. "Give her to me so I can feed her."

The man seemed to consider for a second, then released his grip. Emily slipped into Kate's hands, and Kate clutched the baby to her chest, trying to quiet the pitiful wails.

"If you've hurt that baby . . ." Mark whispered fiercely from the window seat.

The man laughed. "You'll do what? Stare me to death?" He was very pleased with his response. Mark and Kate exchanged a quick glance, then she turned her attention back to the baby. Tossing a receiving blanket over her shoulder, she unbuttoned her shirt and in seconds the baby was calm.

"I'm willing to go with you quietly," Kate told the man over Emily's head. "Let Agent Iverson take the baby off the plane, and I'll cooperate."

"You'll cooperate anyway." The man pushed the point of a gun into her side.

"No, that's where you're wrong," Kate disagreed fiercely. "If we're all going to die, it might as well be right here and now. In the confusion, one of us might be lucky enough to escape." Kate took a deep breath. "However, I'm willing to trade my life for theirs."

"Well, isn't that sweet," the man sneered. "But my instructions were to bring you both. If I show up without either one of you, I'm a dead man. So sit still, or we'll go ahead and have that showdown you were talking about."

Kate bit her lip. Mark was on the other side of a man who had a gun, and he couldn't help her. Somehow she had to find a way to get Emily off the plane to Miss Eugenia and Winston. She watched as the stewardesses stacked canned drinks and crackers in the tiny kitchen. One laughed and said that she could hardly wait to get to Miami. She was off for two weeks and needed the break.

A tone sounded and the pilot's voice reverberated throughout the cabin. He introduced himself and gave the time and temperature in Miami, with the prediction that they would arrive at 3:45 EST. He advised everyone to prepare for takeoff. The airline employee who had stamped their boarding passes walked onto the plane and spoke to the stewardesses. Kate heard the woman say that the plane was cleared for departure and they were about to secure the doors.

At the comment that they had an unusually large crowd for an afternoon flight, one of the stewardesses said that maybe everyone was trying to get home for Halloween. They all laughed and the older woman waved good-bye. Kate leaned forward as she turned to go.

"Excuse me," she said loudly enough to get their attention. The two stewardesses and other airline employee all looked at her. Kate was afraid to stand, but twisted in her seat away from the man with the gun. She hoped that her body would shield the baby if her desperate plan didn't work. She motioned for the women to come closer, and they approached cautiously.

"We're traveling to Miami for a family emergency—" She waved vaguely to include Mark and their kidnapper. "I was going to take the baby, but I've just realized that she's running a fever. There is a tall, gray-haired lady in a Halloween sweatshirt waiting at the gate to watch our plane leave. Could you give the baby to her and explain?"

The stewardesses looked at each other, and the gray-haired airline employee shook her head. "Oh no, ma'am. I couldn't possibly do that. You'll have to take her off yourself."

Kate pleaded with her eyes. "Please. I can't miss this plane, but the baby really needs to stay here."

The older woman glanced over her head at the man with the gun. Kate felt the hard steel dig viciously into her back. With one smooth motion, she transferred the baby into the woman's arms. "Here's her diaper bag," she added, looping the strap around the startled lady's wrist.

"The plane is ready to go," one of the stewardesses said anxiously.

"Please," Kate whispered, tears welling up in her eyes.

The woman nodded reluctantly and started toward the exit. Kate watched as she turned and looked back once before she ducked through the doorway and out of the plane. Kate shuddered with relief and slumped back against her seat. The stewardesses watched Kate nervously for a few minutes before beginning their pre-flight routine.

"That was very clever," the man whispered. "One more stunt like that, and I'll kill you both."

Kate nodded, trying to hide her fear. "I told you I'd go quietly once the baby was safe." She glanced over at Mark, but the man with the gun blocked the agent from her view. All she could see of Mark was his clenched fists on the armrests.

As they pulled away from the terminal, Kate looked across the aisle and out of the plane. Vaguely, through the airport windows, she could see Miss Eugenia pressed against the glass with Emily in her arms. Closing her eyes and fighting back tears, Kate said a silent prayer of thanks.

The flight seemed endless. Kate resisted the thought that she might never see her baby again and clung instead to the knowledge that Emily was safe with Miss Eugenia.

They arrived in Miami five minutes ahead of schedule. When the other passengers stood to leave, the man put a restraining hand on Kate's leg. "We'll be polite and let everybody else get off first."

When the plane was almost empty, he nudged Kate with the gun. "Get up slowly and get your bag. No quick movements, and don't say anything to anyone or you're dead."

Kate followed his instructions carefully. She was afraid that if she looked at Mark, she would dissolve into tears, so she kept her eyes away from him.

When they stepped into the busy Miami airport, the man told them to walk in front so he would have a clear line of fire if they did anything stupid. Mark reached over and took Kate's hand. The man noticed the gesture and laughed. "So that's the way the wind blows," he chuckled. "It will be interesting to see what everybody thinks about that."

Mark squeezed her hand in a vain attempt at reassurance as they pressed into the crowds. As they approached the security checkpoint, their abductor leaned between them. "The airport folks think I'm with the CIA and kindly allowed me to keep my government-issue revolver during our flight. I'm going to have to give it up for a minute." Kate looked into his menacing eyes. "But if anything happens, I'll make sure both of you get a bullet in the head."

He put his gun in his shoulder holster as they piled luggage onto the small conveyor belt. "CIA," the man said, showing a badge to the bored security guard before handing over his gun and walking through the metal detector. In seconds he had the gun back. He led Mark and Kate toward the front entrance of the airport, where two other men joined them. An all-terrain vehicle was waiting for them in the passenger loading area.

As they rode along, the other men communicated mostly in Spanish. Kate's legs started to cramp. Then she thought of Emily and her milk let down, soaking the front of her shirt. When one of the men noticed this, he made a comment and the others laughed. Kate felt Mark stiffen, and she put a hand on his arm. Their lives depended on both of them being alert and staying calm.

Finally they turned off the highway onto a two-lane road. Several miles later they pulled onto a gravel trail and drove far back into the woods. A tall metal gate with barbed wire wrapped around the top appeared from out of nowhere. The guard at the gate looked into the car through the driver's window, then he waved them inside.

The road changed to smooth asphalt as they rounded a corner, and a huge mansion came into view. Kate caught a glimpse of the ocean behind the massive structure. The lawns were manicured to perfection. Flowers of all colors were carefully arranged in beds along stone-paved pathways and sidewalks. The house itself was made of marble with eight columns across the front like an ancient Greek temple. Several men were loitering on the walkway, and one of them stepped forward to open the door when the car pulled to a stop. Kate got out, closely followed by her abductor. Two of the men fell into step behind Mark as they climbed toward the house.

"Mr. Morris welcomes you to his home," a man standing beside the large double doors greeted them, as if they were invited guests.

Mark stared mutinously over the man's head, but Kate nodded stiffly at the man, who continued, "My name is Mr. Chavez, and I will get you settled. After your journey, I'm sure you are tired and wish to refresh before dinner. Mr. Morris has planned a lovely meal in your honor."

They followed him into an enormous foyer and up a spiral staircase along the far right-hand wall. Finally, he stopped at a door and ushered them into a luxurious suite with an ocean view. "I hope this will be acceptable to you," he said with a pleasant smile. The driver of the car reached around Mr. Chavez and deposited their suitcases on the floor beside them. "Dinner is at seven and the dress is black tie," their guide provided helpfully.

Kate glanced at Mark, then back at the little man. "We packed in a hurry. We didn't bring evening clothes with us," she responded, a note of sarcasm in her voice.

Mr. Chavez smiled indulgently. "Mr. Morris keeps an extensive selection of formal wear on hand for just such a contingency. If you'll give me your sizes, I'll have something sent up." Once he had the needed information, Mr. Chavez left them.

Seconds later, Kate began to shake uncontrollably. Mark swiftly closed the distance between them and pulled her into his arms. He didn't promise that everything was going to be okay. Instead, he gently stroked her hair. When her shivering subsided, she looked up into his face. His expression was bleak, and did nothing to console her.

"What are we going to do now?" she asked.

He leaned down and spoke into her ear. "This room is certainly bugged," he whispered. "Probably cameras, too."

She eased out of his embrace, and Mark led her through a set of French doors onto a small balcony. The sound of the waves provided some privacy. From where they stood, Kate could see three different swimming pools.

"All we can do is see what they want from us," Mark said. "Once we actually meet Mr. Morris . . ."

". . . they'll never let us go," Kate finished for him. He took her hand as they watched the magnificent waves.

"Emily is with Miss Eugenia," Kate said softly. "I could see them through the window at the airport."

Mark squeezed her hand. "That's something then." A man came out of the house and stood on the terrace below them. Mark pulled her back inside, suggesting that she take a shower and try to rest for a little while. He accompanied her to the bathroom door and looked around.

"Start the hot water and let the room fill with steam. Then you can undress in the shower," he advised. She nodded, and taking a bathrobe from her suitcase, she went into the bathroom and shut the door.

After a long shower, Kate curled up on the bed and tried not to cry. Mark woke her a couple of hours later. His hair was wet from his shower and he had on most of a tuxedo. "Mr. Chavez brought it by," Mark explained. He pointed to a black beaded evening gown spread out on the other bed. "That's for you."

"Do I have to wear it?" Kate asked as she touched the dress. It wasn't exactly immodest, but it was certainly more daring than anything she normally wore.

"I think at this point it is to our advantage to be cooperative."

Kate picked up the gown and walked into the bathroom. It took a little while to fix her hair, brush her teeth, and apply fresh makeup. She couldn't reach the zipper and had to ask for Mark's help. When she was ready, he examined her closely and pronounced her "spectacular." Uninterested in her appearance, Kate simply glanced at Niki's watch and saw that it was a few minutes before seven o'clock. Mark shrugged on his coat, and they waited by the door until Mr. Chavez came for them.

It seemed like they walked for miles through the elaborate house before they were ushered into a banquet hall. Several round tables covered with floor-length white cloths and set with glittering crystal dotted the room. They weaved through the smaller tables toward a long banquet table at the front of the large room. A flower arrangement dominated the middle of the head table, and chairs were lined up along the far side. As they approached, Kate had a vague impression of a short, heavyset man with dark hair sitting just to the left of the flowers, but all her attention was focused on the man seated next to him.

The blood drained from her face as Kate locked eyes with those of her husband, Tony Singleton. His hair was lighter, bleached by the sun. His skin was darker, tanned and glowing with health. His face registered the same shock she felt as he dropped his arm from around the shoulders of the lovely blonde woman seated beside him.

"What is she doing here?" he demanded, half-rising from his chair. "Our deal was that you leave her completely out of this!"

The man beside him put a restraining hand on his arm. "Tony! Didn't I tell you that I had a little surprise for you tonight?"

Tony smirked. "Yeah, but you're such a liar, Everett!"

The heavy man smiled. "Well, this time you can see that I told you the truth. I have given you quite a surprise, true?"

"You could've given me a stroke!" Tony corrected with a lazy smile. He sat back down in his chair. "But I don't understand."

"I guess you could say that your wife is the final test, so to speak, in our efforts to make sure that you don't know anything about the missing and, oh so incriminating, computer chip."

"I told you I don't know anything about that chip!" Tony said in exasperation.

"Yes," the man named Everett nodded. "You have told us that on numerous occasions, but I thought the presence of your lovely wife might jog your memory."

The blonde leaned forward, a petulant look on her face. "You said she wasn't even pretty," she examined Kate critically.

"I said she wasn't as beautiful as you are," Tony corrected her, then glanced back at Kate and grimaced. "She looks better than she used to, I can tell you that." Several men standing behind Kate laughed. "But no one can compare with you, my darling," he said and kissed the woman full on the lips. Kate stared at him in horror, unable to comprehend what was happening.

"So, you still insist that you don't know where the chip is?" Everett Morris returned to the original subject.

"I've told you a hundred times. Gino had it."

The large man nodded sadly. "And Gino is now very dead, and his secrets are buried with him. We had hoped that the chip would turn up, but it has been months now and . . . nothing." Everett Morris shrugged expressively. "I believed you when you said you would give me the chip if you could but, nevertheless, I have asked some of our friends to bring your wife to me. The FBI thought that I had ordered her death and so they hid her, but not well enough as you can see. You know Special Agent Mark Iverson?" Tony shrugged. "A pencil pusher. Accountant." He dismissed Mark with an impatient gesture.

"It might interest you to know that this pencil pusher has been sleeping with your wife." Tony looked up sharply. "Their cover was to pose as husband and wife. It seems that they both enjoyed the role." Tony's eyes narrowed. "How do you feel about that?" the big man pressed.

Tony turned to face Everett Morris. "I wouldn't have thought I'd care," he answered thoughtfully. "I don't want her." The men in the back of the room laughed again. "But she is my wife, and I guess I don't want anyone else to sleep with her either," he scowled at Mark as Kate closed her eyes against the pain.

Her eyes flew open when Mr. Morris clapped Tony loudly on the shoulder. "Poor Tony!" Turning back to his reluctant guests, he addressed Kate. "And what about you, Mrs. Singleton? Do you know anything about the missing computer chip?"

Kate shook her head mutely, and Mr. Morris studied her for a few seconds. Then he turned to Tony. "Several months after your untimely demise, your wife gave birth to a daughter."

"Impossible!" Tony objected vehemently. "I was always extremely careful!" His expression changed, and a curse broke from his lips as he looked back at Kate. "There was an . . . accident the last weekend I was home." She nodded, too scared to be embarrassed. "You had a baby?" he asked her directly.

Kate cleared her throat. "Four weeks ago." Tony rubbed his eyes, then looked back at Everett Morris.

"That doesn't change anything." His voice shook slightly. "My future is here with you."

"You don't care about your own flesh and blood?" Mr. Morris asked gently.

Tony met his eyes. "I care, but I've come too far to go back now." He took the blonde girl's hand. "And I can have more children."

Mr. Morris nodded approvingly. "You are a practical man. In life sometimes difficult choices must be made."

"I've already made mine." Tony held the man's gaze.

The older man turned back to Kate. "I will guarantee your daughter's safety if you will tell me where the chip is."

"I would do anything to protect my daughter," Kate said firmly. "But I don't have any computer chips."

"If I had stolen the chip and sent it to Kate, she would have already given it to the FBI and you would be in jail," Tony grumbled irritably.

The man ignored Tony's remark and continued to question Kate. "Since he left Chicago for the last time before his 'death,' Tony mailed you nothing? No letters, gifts, anything?"

"Nothing." Kate's word both condemned and exonerated him.

Mr. Morris leaned back with a smile on his face. Mark took half a step toward Tony. "Why?" he asked. "Why did you do it?"

Tony didn't respond to Mark. Instead he turned to Kate. "All this started before I ever even met you, you know. After my first few assignments with the FBI, Mr. Evans decided that I had a 'gift' for undercover work. He called me in and told me that he had an operation that was perfect for me. His plan was to bury me deep in the heart of Everett's organization. Once there, I would be able to collect enough evidence to close him down."

Tony tapped his fingers on the table restlessly. "By that time I had seen the way the Bureau works. The field agents take all the risks while the bosses sit in nice offices and get all the credit. With the kind of assignments I was getting, I knew I probably wouldn't live long enough to get one of the good jobs. I was tired of red tape and paper work and answering to other people. I wanted to make some serious money and live in style." Kate stared at him in amazement, unable to reconcile his words with the man she thought she had known.

"Tony contacted me and told me the whole plan as Evans had outlined it to him," Mr. Morris took up the story. "He hoped that I would pay him back for the information by giving him a job in my organization. But I suggested he stay with the FBI and accept the new assignment. He could go deep undercover and give the FBI little bits of unimportant information—just enough to keep the operation alive, you understand. At the same time, he could pass on all kinds of useful tips to us and protect my business enterprises from serious scrutiny."

At this point, Tony spoke up again. "The plan was to milk the operation for as long as possible and stage my death at the end. This would cripple the FBI's investigation into Mr. Morris's organization and discredit the Bureau in the process."

"But then a computer chip was stolen from my home in Key Biscayne," Mr. Morris said. "It contains a complete list of all my employees. Some of these people work openly in my organization. Others are employed by police departments, the armed forces, governors, senators, and even the FBI. If this information was to get into the wrong hands . . ."

Tony nodded. "It also details transfers of illegal funds—dates, times, places. Whoever has that chip can destroy us," he said grimly.

Mr. Morris glanced at Tony, his eyes narrowed. "Few people had access to the chip," he said in a thoughtful voice. "One was a man named Gino, and he was our major suspect. Tony and my grandson Ross were also possible culprits. Containment was our first concern, so we closed Tony down with the FBI by staging his death. He and Ross and Gino were all restricted to the premises at Key Biscayne and put under twenty-four-hour surveillance. They went nowhere, did nothing without an escort. A few days later, Gino was dead by his own hand. All indications are that he stole the chip, intending to sell it to one of our competitors or the government; when the theft was discovered, he committed suicide."

"He probably destroyed the chip before he killed himself," Tony said and Mr. Morris smiled.

"That's Tony's favorite theory because it clears him completely," Mr. Morris told Kate and Mark. "However, Gino was watched continuously before his death, and afterwards we examined his body minutely. We searched his room, his car, everything. The chip was nowhere to be found."

"Maybe he flushed it down the toilet," Tony suggested.

"We routinely strain the sewage at all my residences," Mr. Morris said, and Tony laughed. "We are especially security conscious at Key Biscayne because of the sensitive information stored there. We take every precaution. All mail is screened, phone calls monitored, garbage checked. There is no way that anyone could have gotten that chip out of there. And yet . . . it is gone."

"If it hasn't shown up in almost a year, I think we should stop worrying about it," Tony proposed.

"Perhaps you are right," Mr. Morris agreed as he took a sip of wine. "I guess that we no longer require your wife's presence."

Kate's legs were aching, and she didn't know how much longer she could stand. Tony gave her a speculative look, and she hoped he would make a plea for their lives.

"So, are you going to have them tortured for the evening's enter- tainment?" he asked instead. Kate recoiled, actually taking a step back.

Mr. Morris chuckled and shook his head. "No, I'm not in the mood for blood and gore tonight, but I'm afraid they will have to be eliminated." Kate's knees buckled, and Mark's arm went around her for support. The blonde had been sitting in bored silence during the conversation, but she smiled at this remark.

"It's a shame. I was hoping there was some way she could be allowed to live, especially since there is a baby to consider," Tony mused idly. "But at least the child will have the extra insurance I bought at the airport right before my 'death.'"

Mr. Morris snapped his head around. "What airport and what insurance?" he demanded.

Tony shrugged casually. "I went to the airport with Cosmo to pick up some guys from Costa Rica last year. It was in the middle of the night, and everything was closed. But I saw this insurance booth, and I guess I felt guilty about Kate, so I filled out the card and put it in the box."

Mr. Morris turned to the man who had escorted Kate and Mark to Miami. "You let him do this?" he asked angrily. "I told you no mail, no correspondence of any kind!"

Cosmo stepped forward nervously. "He didn't mail nothing. He put it in the box for the insurance company to pick up. I watched him write it, and all he put on it was his name and stuff."

"You're sure he didn't write any notes on the card?" Mr. Morris asked suspiciously.

"What? Like 'I'm an undercover agent for the FBI. Take this card to the president immediately'?" Tony scoffed.

"He didn't write nothing on it but his name and address," Cosmo reaffirmed.

Mr. Morris relaxed against his chair. "It was just a card? You didn't have to put any money with it or give them a credit card number?"

Tony shook his head. "Nothing. The first week's premium was free, and I knew I'd be dead in a matter of days. It was an easy way to give Kate an extra thousand bucks."

"It went straight to the insurance company—not to your home or office?"

"It went into a little box." Tony shrugged. "I don't know how often they check those things. It could still be there for all I know."

As the men talked, Kate took several deep breaths, fighting the nausea that rose inside her. The day before the FBI notified her of Tony's death, an envelope had come in the mail from an insurance company she had never heard of. In the envelope had been the card Tony was referring to. He thought he had done something nice for her, but in reality the policy had never been in force because he didn't fill out the card completely.

"I don't like it, but I guess there was no harm done," Mr. Morris said as he turned back to Kate and Mark. "I regret that your visit with us now must come to an unhappy end. But you have seen my face, you have heard our secrets. You know that Tony is alive." As he shrugged, a waiter walked past Kate and leaned over the table to refill the wineglasses. Mr. Morris gave him an irritated look. Tony covered his crystal goblet absently, but the blonde accepted a glassful.

"Cosmo," Mr. Morris directed, "please take care of our guests."

Mark squeezed Kate's hand as the blonde laughed and put her arm around Tony possessively. Tony smiled at the girl and leaned forward. Pulling a small red carnation from the flower arrangement on the table, he tucked it into the lapel of his tuxedo. Mark tensed as Cosmo stepped forward, gesturing toward the door with his gun. Kate couldn't resist one more glance at her husband.

Tony moved so quickly that she didn't realize he had grabbed a steak knife from the table until he buried it into Everett Morris's chest. The older man's eyes widened in surprise, then he nodded his acceptance. "My mind told me not to trust you, but my heart . . ." His voice trailed off as he slumped forward. Gunshots reverberated around the room. Mark pushed Kate to the floor, then rolled with her under the table.

The door burst open and Kate could hear the pounding of heavy footsteps. More shots were fired, filling the room with moans and screams and crashing furniture. Kate could feel Mark's ragged breathing against her ear. She shuddered under his weight, expecting at any moment for someone to pull back the tablecloth and fire bullets at them.

Finally the cloth was thrown to the side, and the waiter who had poured the wine stood over them. Seeing the automatic weapon in his hand, Kate could feel her heart sink. Then she noticed that his other hand was extended toward them.

"It's all clear, Iverson," he said and Mark shifted off of her. He crawled out carefully and then pulled her after him.

Kate stood slowly and surveyed the devastation. Broken dishes and shattered glass covered the floor. Tables were overturned and bullet holes riddled the fabric-covered walls. Everett Morris was still in much the same position as when the shooting started; a small red circle had started to form around the steak knife in his chest. Several more bodies were lying all over the room. Men holding guns walked between them, checking for signs of life. The blonde was slumped against a far wall, sobbing loudly.

Kate's eyes moved back to Tony. His face was down on the table, and she could almost believe that he had fallen asleep except for the large puddle of blood spreading under his cheek. Instinctively she stepped toward him. His left hand was clutching the soiled tablecloth. The right was outstretched, his wedding band glittering in the chandelier light. Without hesitation, she reached for his fingers. They were limp, but still warm as she brought them to her lips and whispered his name.

"He'll be taken care of." An agent stepped forward and brought a hand-held radio to his mouth. Depressing a button, he spoke. "Riva here. Let me know when it's secure." A voice responded immediately, and he turned back to Kate. "We need to get you out of here before reinforcements arrive." He addressed the room in general. "Let's go. You guys first." He waved to a group of men by the door. "Pollate, you and Fields follow us."

Kate watched numbly as the agents raised their weapons and went carefully out into the hall. Kate stayed close to the man with the radio. They negotiated the long corridors, passing more bodies slumped in death. Kate was trembling by the time they reached the front steps, and she had to wipe continuously at the tears that wouldn't stop falling from her eyes.

"I do have some good news for you," Agent Riva said as he led her to a Jeep parked at the curb. "Your baby is fine."

Kate reached out to touch his arm. "What can you tell me about her?"

Agent Riva held the door while Kate got into the backseat and then he slid in beside her. She was vaguely aware of Mark as he climbed into the front with the driver, but her attention was riveted on the man who had the information about Emily.

"Your policeman friend took her to the police station in Haggerty and wouldn't let the Resident Agent from Albany inside. He shot at some sheriff deputies when they tried to break down the door, so the SAC from Chicago offered to talk to him. The policeman said he'd never heard of a Mr. Evans in Chicago and wouldn't release the baby on his say-so."

Mark twisted around to face them as the Jeep pulled away from Mr. Morris's house and started down the drive. "Several different people called and authorized him to release the baby to the agent from Albany, but your friend wouldn't do it. Finally they said they would have the Director patched through."

"The Director of the FBI?" Mark asked from the front seat.

Agent Riva grinned. "Yeah, but that cowboy said he didn't watch much news and wouldn't know the Director of the FBI from the man in the moon. He said the only public figure he would recognize on the telephone was the president of the United States. So the Director called the White House and the President talked to your friend."

"Winston talked to the President?" Kate breathed as she and Mark exchanged a glance.

Agent Riva nodded. "After his conversation with the Commander-in-Chief, your policeman friend let the Resident Agent into the station, but he still refused to give him your daughter. He said he was responsible for her safety and anywhere the baby went, he and the old lady would go, too. So the agent from Albany brought them all with him to Miami."

"Emily's here?" Kate seized upon his words.

The agent smiled. "At a hotel near the airport. We'll be there soon."

Kate nodded and leaned back against the seat.

Agent Riva was in a talkative mood. "Oh yes, the whole town of Haggerty's been on the national news all day. The mayor has gotten a lot of mileage out of this situation. They say he's up for re-election soon and now that he's recognized nationally, he'll be sure to win. That is, unless he decides to run for governor instead," the agent laughed.

Kate forced a smile. She looked out the window and saw a couple of children dressed in Halloween costumes. It made her sad to think of the bags of candy she would not be distributing to the trick-or-treaters in Haggerty.

When they finally pulled in front of a large hotel, the agent escorted her inside. Mr. Evans was waiting in the lobby and greeted her warmly.

"Kate!" He took her hand and patted it vigorously. "I'm so glad to see that you are all right." He looked behind him toward the elevators, then nodded to the agent. "Your friends have your baby in a suite upstairs. Agent Riva will take you to them."

Kate started to walk past him, but he stopped her. "We can give you a few minutes, but then I'm afraid we're going to have to go over everything that happened. Important details may be lost if we wait too long."

His tone was regretful, but his eyes uncompromising. Kate remembered Tyler's assertion that Mr. Evans put operations ahead of the safety of his agents. Then she thought of Tony, bleeding onto the white tablecloth. She nodded coldly and walked away without comment.

CHAPTER 11

At Kate's knock, Winston opened the door of the hotel room and she threw herself into his arms, startling the poor man. "I don't know how I can ever thank you!" she cried against the tightly stretched fabric of his uniform shirt.

Winston patted her back awkwardly. "It's okay, Mrs. Johnson. Everybody's okay."

"Her name is not Mrs. Johnson," Miss Eugenia corrected from a chair across the room. Kate released the policeman and walked over to take the sleeping baby from her friend.

"My name is Kate," she told them simply.

"And Drew is really Mark," Miss Eugenia continued knowledge- ably. Kate sat in a chair and watched Emily's chest rise and fall in peaceful sleep. Tears started falling down her cheeks again, and Miss Eugenia spoke up in alarm. "Oh don't cry, dear. You're safe and sound now."

Kate pulled a handful of Kleenex from the box beside her chair and dabbed her eyes while Miss Eugenia began an account of every- thing that had transpired since they parted in Haggerty.

"Winston picked me up in his patrol car and turned on the siren, so we got to the airport faster than you would believe. Then we went to the gate just like Mark told me. I searched everywhere but didn't see you or Emily or anyone who looked like a criminal. I was begin- ning to think we may have gotten to the airport before you did, then that strange woman came off the plane carrying Emily, and I was so afraid for you."

"The kidnapper wouldn't let me or Mark leave the plane," Kate explained. "Sending Emily with the ticket-stamper was the best I could do. Thanks for standing in the window so I could see that you had her."

"Humph!" Miss Eugenia sent Winston a meaningful look. "He fussed at me all the way to Haggerty about that."

Winston spread his hands. "Miss Eugenia called and said that she had an emergency. When I got to her house, she told me that the Chief was really an FBI agent, the Mafia was trying to kill you, and Emily had been kidnapped. For all I knew, everyone in that airport was armed and dangerous. When the stewardess woman brought Emily off the plane, all I could think about was getting her somewhere safe," he appealed to Kate. "I told Miss Eugenia to follow me out, and when I turned around, she was climbing onto the window sill." Winston shook his head in dismay. "It's a miracle she didn't break her neck and Emily's, too."

Miss Eugenia was about to make another comment, but Kate interrupted. "It was a big responsibility, and I appreciate you more than I can ever express," she said, trying to mollify Winston. "But while my life was in danger, my only comfort was the knowledge that Emily was safe." Kate sighed as Miss Eugenia and Winston continued to glare at each other. "So you left the airport and went to the police station," she prompted in an effort to distract them.

Winston nodded. "It was the best place I could think of. It would take a bomb to break through those cinderblock walls."

"Then the FBI agent from Albany arrived and tried to get the baby," Kate prompted him again.

"I didn't know who he was," Winston pointed out angrily. "I watch TV enough to know that criminals can get fake IDs." Kate struggled to concentrate as he described the siege at the police station and his subsequent conversation with the president of the United States.

"Actually," Miss Eugenia said with a snort. "All he said was, 'Yes sir.'"

"I said plenty more than that," Winston objected vehemently.

"Humph!" Miss Eugenia laughed. "The president said, 'Officer Jones,' and you said, 'Yes, sir!' Then he said, 'This is the President of the United States,' and you said, 'Yes, sir!' He said, 'Let the FBI agent into the police station,' and you said, 'Yes, sir!'" As tired as she was, Kate had to smile.

"Yeah, well, you should have seen Miss Eugenia on that plane ride from Albany," Winston said, remembering that the best defense is a good offense. "She'd never been on a plane before, and I thought they were going to throw her out the door before we crossed the Florida state line. She kept asking to talk to the pilot. She told the stewardess she didn't think he was going the right way!" Winston rolled his eyes. "Her food wasn't warm enough, and there was no water in the toilet."

"Well, there wasn't!" Miss Eugenia cried in self-defense.

"Then we hit some turbulence, and she started screaming like a stuck pig."

"I most certainly did not," she said disdainfully. "It was merely a ladylike cry of distress."

"They could hear you in Hawaii!"

Miss Eugenia smoothed her skirt primly. "Be that as it may, I can assure you that I will not leave the ground on my way home. If the good Lord intended for people to fly, He would have given them wings."

"Why didn't He give us wheels if He intended for us to ride in cars?" Winston asked impertinently.

Miss Eugenia turned narrowed eyes toward him. "I have had just about enough out of you. You will never be too old for me to thrash, Winston Jones," she reminded him.

Kate quickly asked about the news coverage, and they were off again, describing the mayor and his numerous interviews, Booster's vain attempts to get in front of a camera, and Miss Polly with three of her most recent blue ribbons pinned to her chest as she talked to reporters.

Emily woke up, anxious to eat, so Kate took her into the bedroom. She felt ridiculous in the black evening gown but didn't have any clothes to change into. After Emily was full, Kate gave her to Miss Eugenia, then went into the bathroom and splashed some cold water in her face. An agent came for her a few minutes later, and she had no choice but to follow.

He took her to a small conference room in the hotel where eight or nine men were already seated around a table. Mark sat in a far corner, still wearing his borrowed tuxedo. Kate recognized the waiter from Mr. Morris's house sitting next to Mr. Evans, the SAC from Chicago. Mr. Evans pointed to an empty chair beside him, and Kate sat down.

Clearing his throat, Mr. Evans began, "First, I want to express our heartfelt sorrow for Tony's death," he said. "I know that you will mourn for him all over again, and I very much regret the additional pain this has caused you." Kate nodded, and he glanced at the papers in front of him.

"Agent Dodson, since you were in the house, tell us what you can." This instruction was directed toward the waiter, who leaned forward, resting his elbows on the table.

"A few days ago, the cook told me the boss was expecting important guests. He said he thought it was Everett's daughter and his favorite protégé. They called him '007.' I didn't know it was Agent Singleton. They arrived mid-morning today, and I saw him for the first time when I served lunch."

"Did he recognize you?" Mr. Evans asked.

The waiter nodded. "He knew who I was when he saw me." Agent Dodson smiled at the memory. "His reaction to me was slight, but it was there. There were cameras all over the place, and someone running the tapes later might have caught it. So, instead of trying to hide it, he called me over and said I looked familiar. He asked where I was from and if we'd ever met."

"What did you say?"

"I stuck with my cover, told him I was from Detroit, and used to work for the Marinaro family. He dismissed me, and as I walked off, I heard him tell the man sitting next to him that no one could ever forget a face as ugly as mine. Then they both laughed."

"Tony was the best," a man from across the table commented with reverence.

The waiter bowed his head briefly, endorsing this remark. "They were in meetings all day, and the cook said more guests were coming for dinner. I figured it was just some more thugs. But when I saw Agent Iverson, I called the emergency number."

Mr. Evans turned to Mark. "Dodson was wearing a wire. I listened to the tape on the ride over here, and we're working on a transcript now. They were going to kill you both."

"Yes, no matter how it all worked out," Mark agreed.

Kate leaned forward. "Did you know that Tony was still alive?" she asked Mr. Evans.

"I didn't know for sure. The video they sent us was very convincing, but any time you don't have a body, you have to wonder."

"You didn't tell me there was any doubt."

"Why give you false hope?" Mr. Evans dismissed her question. "I saw no advantage in telling you that Tony could still be alive, but it was my duty to protect you."

"And salvage the operation," Mark added cynically.

"If possible," Mr. Evans admitted. "The real question is whether or not Tony had turned."

Kate gasped. "You believe all those things he said about working for Mr. Morris?" She was shocked and dismayed. "He saved our lives! Surely that proves which side he was on."

"Actually, it doesn't," Mr. Evans said regretfully. "All it proves is that he felt some remaining loyalty or responsibility to you. Tony's cover was to fake a turn, but there is a lot of money in crime, and some crucial information was leaked to Morris. Then there's the matter of the missing chip that contained the evidence we needed to close them permanently. The whole operation centered around it, and it's gone without a trace."

Mark looked pensive. "So, if Tony was working for Morris, he didn't take the chip and never intended to give it to us. But if he was still undercover, he did get the chip and somehow he must have gotten it out."

"Which would mean we have missed something," Mr. Evans acknowledged.

"Are you saying that the computer chip would clear Tony?" Kate asked.

Mr. Evans nodded. "I guess so, yes."

A woman walked in to distribute copies of the transcript, and all conversation paused while everyone scanned it. Kate stared straight ahead. She already knew what it would say.

"How did they get the baby?" Mark asked over the sound of turning pages.

"They killed Agent Thomas, then used mirrors on some of the outside cameras. They came through a bedroom window, took the baby, and were out before the surveillance team noticed anything."

"It was well planned then?"

"Yes. They've probably been watching for days, maybe weeks."

"Morris claimed that there was no contract on Mrs. Singleton's life. He said he had given orders to have her brought in, not killed," the waiter pointed out.

Mr. Evans grimaced. "Our source on the matter was not the most reliable person. It is possible there never was a contract."

"If there was no contract, why did they kill Agent Roper?" Mark asked.

"There could have been a contract, and Morris just lied to Tony," the waiter proposed.

Mr. Evans nodded. "I believe they thought for several weeks that Agent Roper was Kate Singleton. Otherwise, we would have seen some evidence of a massive search. They finally got past her surveillance team and killed her, just as Morris ordered. They took her left hand so Morris could show Tony and test his allegiance."

"Why would they want to show Tony my left hand?" Kate asked, trying unsuccessfully to hide her horror.

Mr. Evans answered reluctantly. "He would have recognized it immediately because of your wedding rings." Kate shuddered. "He wanted to see how Tony would react."

"If he remained loyal, knowing that Morris had killed you, they would trust him," Mark explained, facing her for the first time. His tone and manner as he spoke were cool and professional.

"It is my opinion that Kate's death was an integral part of Morris's plan for Tony from the beginning," Mr. Evans declared. "She was a loose end that had to be taken care of. They got to Agent Roper and thought they had been successful."

"But when they checked the fingerprints and found out they had killed the wrong woman . . ." Mark spoke again.

"They started an all-out search for Kate. They found her, watched until an opportunity presented itself, and then moved in," Mr. Evans finished.

A man looked up from the transcript. "According to this, Tony had been a virtual prisoner for months, which would explain why he hadn't made contact with anyone," he said thoughtfully. "And what was that stuff about the insurance policy?"

Kate blinked as all eyes turned toward her. "Tony filled out a card in the airport. It was a gimmick where they give you a $1,000 policy with the first week's premium free." There was some mumbling around the table, but this was quickly dismissed as unrelated.

Mr. Evans turned back to Kate. "I realize that all this has been a terrible shock to you, but I'd like your opinion on Tony's state of mind. How did he seem to you?"

Kate felt tears pool in her eyes and hated herself for showing weakness in front of these men who doubted Tony. "When he would come home—" Kate cleared her throat and forced herself to continue, "—before, it would take him a day or two to get back to himself. For a while he was distant, different."

"Still under," someone contributed.

Mr. Evans nodded in agreement. "An undercover agent, especially one as good as Tony, sometimes gets so involved in his role that it takes some time for him to come out of it."

"To remember who they really are," Mark added.

"That's part of what concerns us about Tony. We're afraid that he might have gotten lost in his cover," Mr. Evans explained for her benefit.

"Tonight he was not at all like the man I knew," Kate continued, trying to hold back the tears. "But when he mentioned the insurance policy, I think he was trying to tell me that he loved me."

There was an embarrassed silence.

Mr. Evans cleared his throat. "How well did you actually know your husband?"

Kate blushed, humiliated and angered by the question. "It's no secret that Tony and I never had much time together. His job always came first. But I was his wife." She raised her chin slightly. No one contradicted her, so she continued. "Tony didn't fill out that insurance card to give me an extra thousand dollars. Tony never concerned himself about details. I paid the bills, filed the insurance claims, and figured the taxes. Tony barely knew how much he made in a year, let alone how much insurance we had. It's absurd to think that Tony was walking through an airport and suddenly decided he needed another $1,000 of life insurance."

Some of the men were staring at her with open skepticism. Others, like Mark, were looking elsewhere. She searched the room for an ally. "He couldn't contact me directly, but I think he saw the insurance as a way to let me know he was thinking of me. He loved me," she insisted. "And I'll never believe that he was a criminal. He was devoted to the FBI, he hated drugs, and he never gave a thought to money."

"There are other complicating issues," Mr. Evans said reluctantly. "I didn't want to have to bring them up—"

"Then don't," Mark suggested angrily.

"I think that it's about time you told me the whole truth," Kate said, ignoring Mark and looking directly at Mr. Evans.

"It may not have been just money and power that convinced Tony to choose crime as a way of life. You saw Morris's daughter at dinner tonight," he asked pointedly.

Kate nodded, remembering the intimate way the girl had touched Tony, and the now familiar knot of dread formed again in her stomach. "You think they had a relationship."

"I'm fairly certain of it," Mr. Evans confirmed. "It can take years for an undercover agent to gain the trust of a man like Morris. Tony saved a lot of time by using Celeste."

"The FBI asked Tony to start a romance with Mr. Morris's daughter?" Kate asked, incredulous.

"The FBI does not ask agents to do anything illegal or immoral. In extremely important or sensitive cases like this one, however, agents are occasionally given latitude to do whatever they think is necessary."

"So, you're saying that Tony became involved with this woman just a few months after our marriage?" She could barely get the words past her lips.

"Possibly even before you were married."

Kate felt the room spin around her and clutched the table for support. He continued, "We've never understood exactly why Tony married you when he did. He was a very smart agent, and I feel that there has to be a reason—"

"Other than love." Kate interrupted him.

"He would have waited until after this operation was over, unless . . ."

Kate stared at him. "You think he married me to *strengthen* his cover for this operation?"

"Not at all." Mr. Evans regarded her steadily. "Your marriage did not help his cover with Morris."

"Then why?"

"The only plausible explanation is that his marriage to you was intended to win our trust," he answered.

"You think he married me to keep the FBI from getting suspicious about him working for Mr. Morris?" Kate croaked.

"I'm sorry. Yes, I do." Everyone was silent for a few awkward seconds. "Which brings me to another difficult subject. The surveillance team said that you and Agent Iverson seemed very . . . friendly, especially during the past month. Since Tony was not dead at the time of your marriage . . ."

"Mark and I are not really married," Kate stated bluntly. "I figured that out all by myself."

"So, that's not going to be a problem?" Mr. Evans pressed, and Kate gave him a frosty look.

"Nothing happened," Mark spoke tersely from across the room. "I slept on a cot in her room as a security measure."

Kate shook her head. "If you had doubts about Tony's death, why did you let us think we were married?"

Mr. Evans looked uncomfortable. "It was absolutely essential to the whole plan that a legal marriage be recorded for you and Agent Iverson. I didn't know that Tony was alive; I just wasn't sure that he was dead. No one could have predicted that a romance would develop between the two of you." He waved toward Mark. "It was assumed that you would want to have the marriage annulled once we had eliminated the threat to your life."

Kate felt that he had shown a callous disregard for their feelings, but did her best to hide her emotions. "I'd like to speak to Agent Thomas's family," she said, taking a deep breath. "He was a good man and died trying to protect me. I want to express my appreciation and my sorrow for their loss."

"Under the circumstances, it would probably be better for you to just write them a note. Send it to my office and I'll get it to them," Mr. Evans directed. "Tony's body will have to be autopsied, then it will be released for burial. You may want to talk to his parents and decide where to have the body shipped."

"Tony has a grave," Kate corrected him. "And what circumstances are you talking about?"

Mr. Evans shook his head regretfully. "Since there is some question as to Tony's loyalties at the time of his death . . ."

"You're going to steal his grave!" Mark demanded furiously from his corner.

"We are not stealing anything." The SAC looked mildly perturbed by Mark's outburst. "But until Tony's name is cleared, he cannot be buried with FBI agents who died honorably."

"Tony may have been working for Everett Morris, but he still had honor," Mark responded. "He warned me."

"Warned you of what?" Mr. Evans asked impatiently.

"That he was about to make a move. Just before he stabbed Morris, he took a red carnation from the flower arrangement on the table and stuck it into his lapel." Everyone looked up in awed silence, and Mark addressed Kate. "In our field office we have a signal for extreme danger. It's the color red."

"If any one of the team members wore red, it was a signal that all he— uh . . . that all heck was about to break loose," another man added.

"That doesn't prove anything," Mr. Evans said to Mark. "We've already established that Tony wanted to protect his wife, if he could."

Kate stood up, exasperated. "Am I free to go?" she demanded. Mr. Evans nodded. "No more cameras or other people's clothes or false identities or pretend husbands?"

Mr. Evans sighed. "I think you will be safe without our protection. Everett Morris is dead, and you have proven beyond any doubt that you do not have the missing computer chip. I don't expect his successors to bother you. Despite the controversy surrounding the last few months of his life, Tony was still employed by the FBI and is entitled to back pay, plus death benefits and insurance. It should all add up to quite a bit of money. Enough for you and your daughter to live comfortably." Kate stared. "Tony's personal items will have to be searched, then they'll be returned to you."

"What about the apartment in Chicago and our things there?" she asked.

"That's a crime scene so it's sealed for now, but I did bring your purse with me." He leaned down and picked up the old, brown bag from the floor and pushed it toward her.

"What about Niki Johnson's jewelry, the credit cards in her name, and her clothes . . . ?"

"She won't want the clothes back," Mr. Evans spoke with certainty. "Destroy the credit cards. The accounts will be closed tomorrow. You can leave the jewelry with me and keep any cash." He paused, but Kate made no comment. "We will be glad to do anything we can to help you resettle," he offered. "You might want to take a few weeks to consider your options. Once you decide on an area of the country, let me know. We'll help you find a house, a job, and whatever else you need."

Kate piled Niki's jewelry on the table and stepped back. "Thank you anyway, but I don't want any help from Tony's enemies." Mr. Evans started to protest, but she held up her hand. "Because if you think Tony was working for Mr. Morris, then that's what you are." She looked around the room, but no one would meet her eyes. "Tony was a good man. There are aspects of his life that I don't understand and decisions he made that I don't agree with, but you'll never convince me that he was a traitor to the Bureau. I'm sure that eventually you will find your computer chip, and his innocence will be proven even to your satisfaction. At that time you may contact me with a complete and detailed apology. Until then, I don't want to hear from you. Any of you."

Kate turned and walked toward the door. As her hand grasped the knob, she glanced over her shoulder. "When you finish pillaging through my apartment, call me at my mother's house. I'm sure you have the number."

So exhausted she could barely walk, Kate trudged toward her hotel room. Miracle was there, waiting with Winston and Miss Eugenia. Kate gave them a brief explanation, leaving out several sensitive and humiliating details. Then she expressed her gratitude for all they had done and told them she was going to bed. The baby was asleep in a small traveling crib, and the suitcase she had packed before leaving Haggerty was sitting by the bathroom door.

She showered, enjoying the hot water and its numbing effect on her brain. As she put on a nightgown afterwards, she saw the tiny tracking disc under her arm. With a firm motion, she pulled it off and threw it in the garbage. Then she walked into the bedroom, lifted the baby onto the bed beside her, and fell into a troubled sleep.

* * *

Early the next morning Kate made plane reservations, then she called Tony's parents. Unsure of how much information the FBI had given them, she simply suggested that they might want Tony to be buried near their home in Salt Lake rather than in Washington, D.C. Then she told them that she was going to her mother's house and would contact them as soon as she arrived.

The next call was to her mother in Utah. At the sound of Jeanine Taylor's voice, Kate started to cry, and over the long-distance lines, she could hear her mother's sobs mingling with her own.

"They kept telling me that you were okay, but I was so worried," her mother said.

"I know you were, Mom, and I'm sorry. But we really are fine," Kate assured her mother, "and you have a beautiful granddaughter named Emily who is anxious to meet you."

"You're coming here then?"

"My plane arrives at the Salt Lake airport at 5:30 tonight."

"I'll be there to meet you," her mother promised.

"Thanks, Mom," Kate said gratefully.

Miss Eugenia called room service and had their breakfast charged to Mr. Evans. While they ate, she told Kate that Winston had rented a car and was driving her back home. "It's good that you're going to Utah for a while. You need to spend time with your mother."

"I don't know what the future holds," Kate said quietly. "I feel numb inside, and I can't concentrate on anything."

Miss Eugenia nodded. "After a few weeks, you'll be able to think and feel again."

Kate looked up, knowing that her misery showed in her eyes. "I'm not Niki Johnson. I don't have a house in Haggerty."

Miss Eugenia studied her carefully. "No, you're not Niki, but you can live anywhere you want to. Stay with your mother until you're ready to make a decision. If your mother gets tired of you before you decide, I guess you can come visit me."

Kate smiled tearfully. "I'm very grateful for your offer."

When Winston appeared at the door, Miss Eugenia told him to load up the car. "We'll drop Kate and Emily off at the airport on our way home," she informed him, as she helped Kate pack up the diaper bag. "Now I wonder where Miracle is? I haven't seen her at all this morning."

"I told Mr. Evans that I didn't want to have anything else to do with the FBI," Kate admitted. "She was probably told to leave us alone."

"Humph!" the old lady said as she zipped the bag closed.

Winston went down to pull the car around to the front door while Kate and Miss Eugenia followed at a slower pace. When they reached the lobby, they saw Miracle standing by the elevators. "I'm going with you," the agent said simply.

Kate waved her away. "I made it very clear to Mr. Evans last night that I am through playing games with the FBI."

"I'm taking some vacation time," the agent insisted and Kate looked at her sharply. "This isn't official business, it's personal. It's dangerous for you and the baby to go off alone. Even with Everett Morris dead, the contract on your life might still be active." Miracle patted her side. "I'm licensed to carry a gun, even on airplanes."

"I can't let you do this," Kate tried to argue.

"Of course you can," Miss Eugenia spoke up. "If Miracle wants to take a vacation and she just happens to be staying near your mother's house . . ." She shrugged eloquently.

"I'm going, Kate," the agent repeated. "Whether you want me to or not. So we might as well work together."

"Am I ever going to be free of you people?" Kate whispered in exasperation.

"What do you mean by 'you people'?" Miracle demanded.

"Nosy people, you and Miss Eugenia, specifically," Kate smiled.

Walking through the doors, Kate couldn't resist one last look around. Despite her instructions to the contrary, she had thought Mark might come to say good-bye, but he was nowhere in sight.

Everyone was brave as they said their farewells at the airport. Miracle was on the same plane with Kate, but several rows in front of her, so they didn't have a chance to talk. They changed planes in Dallas, and after they were in the air, Miracle handed Kate a large manila envelope. "Mr. Evans asked me to give this to you." Kate shifted the baby onto her lap and took the envelope. "Tony's things."

Kate unhooked the clasp and looked inside. She found his wallet, a watch she'd never seen before, and at the very bottom, his wedding ring. She dug it out and slipped it on her left index finger. "I think it had to mean something that he was still wearing this," she whispered.

Miracle nodded. "I think so, too, honey."

* * *

The plane arrived in Salt Lake on time, and Jeanine Taylor was waiting at the gate. Kate had expected the reunion with her mother to be emotional but was surprised at the intensity of her feelings. As they embraced, tears clogged her throat, and Miracle had to introduce herself.

"My name is Miracle McDonald and I'm a friend of Kate's. I came along to help with the baby and things," she explained vaguely. Jeanine continued to hug her daughter tightly until Miracle finally took Emily out of Kate's arms. "And this baby the two of you are smothering is your granddaughter."

When Kate finally pulled away from her mother, she reintroduced Miracle and they went to collect their baggage. After that, they went to the main entrance where Jeanine had left her car parked in a restricted area. A ticket tucked under the windshield wipers blew in the cold November wind.

"Give me that," Miracle commanded as she snatched the paper from Jeanine's fingers. "I have connections."

After Miracle had them safely in the car, she said she'd call them later and waved good-bye. Leaning back against the seat, Kate allowed herself to enjoy the security of being in her mother's care. When she was settled in the guest room of her mother's small home in Orem, Kate put Emily to bed and called the Singletons. Tony's mother said that his body would arrive the next morning. They had talked to the bishop and were planning a graveside service for Friday.

"Would you like to come meet your granddaughter?" Kate asked as the conversation dwindled.

She heard Sister Singleton sob. "We would very much like to see her, but would you mind coming here? We're not up to going anywhere."

Kate was ashamed that she hadn't realized how hard this would be for them. They had already lost their son once before. Now they were burying him for the second time.

* * *

After Emily woke up, Kate dressed her in the nicest outfit Miss Eugenia had packed. When Miracle called from her hotel room and learned of Kate's plans for the afternoon, she insisted on driving her to the Singletons' house. Since Kate didn't have transportation of her own, she gave in without a fight. Although Kate wanted to introduce her to Tony's family, Miracle said she would wait out front.

Several other cars were parked on the street, and Kate was glad to see that the Singletons had friends and relatives offering support. Tony's older sister Jessica opened the door. Kate had not seen her since the wedding almost two years before.

"Kate," she greeted her cautiously, her eyes wide with curiosity.

"Jessica," Kate answered politely. "This is Emily."

"She has Tony's eyes," Jessica commented as she led Kate into the living room. Several people Kate didn't know were assembled there,

but Tony's mother welcomed her warmly. She studied the baby carefully, then looked up at Kate.

"She's the image of Tony at this age," his mother pronounced
tearfully. Hearing this, Kate smiled to herself. She personally thought
Emily bore a strong resemblance to her own baby pictures.

Sister Singleton looked at Kate anxiously. "Mr. Evans said she was
kidnapped?"

Kate nodded. "It was a terrible ordeal, but we're safe now. I don't
know how much they told you . . ." she paused. Not much, she gathered, from the look on Sister Singleton's face. Just then Tony's father
walked into the room and came up behind his wife. "But Tony saved
my life." Kate swiped at the tears that ran down her cheeks. "I wish
you could have heard all the other agents talking about him. They
admired him very much."

Sister Singleton reached up and grasped her husband's hand over
the back of the couch. "He saved your life?"

"The man who kidnapped Emily was going to kill me. Tony
stabbed him with a steak knife." There was an audible gasp from
around the room, and Kate hoped that by telling them, she hadn't
gone too far. But she looked into their haunted eyes and knew that
they needed to hear the truth. "The man's bodyguards shot Tony just
as the FBI came into the room."

"My poor boy," Mrs. Singleton sobbed.

"He died bravely. You should be very proud." Kate's mouth was
firm, refusing to consider any doubts about his loyalties. She stayed
for a while, watching as Tony's family took turns holding the baby.
There were pictures of him everywhere, and she could almost feel him
near as she comforted his parents.

* * *

When Kate looked out the window on Friday morning, she saw
that it had started to snow. She borrowed boots and gloves from her
mother and asked if Emily could stay at home with her during Tony's
funeral. As Kate pulled on her coat, the doorbell rang. Seconds later
Miracle walked in wearing a black suit. A dark, fleece-lined trench

coat was folded over her arm.

"Do I look official?" she asked awkwardly.

"What do you mean?" Kate asked, bewildered.

"I mean, do I look important enough to represent the FBI at Tony's funeral?" Miracle said.

"The FBI doesn't want to be represented at Tony's funeral." The words were bitter in Kate's mouth.

"No reason for his folks to know that," Miracle shrugged. "Let's go. Being late for a funeral is impolite."

The service was brief and poignant, much like Tony's life had been. When it was over, Kate watched as Miracle walked over to the Singletons and introduced herself. "My name is Special Agent Miracle McDonald," she said solemnly. "On behalf of the Bureau, I would like to express our deep regret for your loss. Your son was a fine man and an exceptional agent. I consider it a great privilege to have known him."

When the Singletons thanked her for coming, Miracle shook their hands gravely. "Mr. Evans would be here if he could," she said, lying through her bright white teeth.

Miracle and Kate went by Jeanine's house to collect the baby, then drove to the Singletons'. While friends and family ate a meal provided by the Relief Society, Miracle told fables about Tony's exploits at the FBI. "You might say that boy is a legend," she smiled at the crowd gathered around her.

On the way home, Kate accused her of stretching the truth. "I can't believe all of the feats you attributed to Tony were substantiated."

Miracle laughed. "I didn't swear on a stack of Bibles, and I did say he was a 'legend.'" Miracle's eyes became serious. "Those people need something to hold onto. If that means stretching the truth a little . . ."

"You're a good woman," Kate told her with a smile.

"Now, you ain't lying," Miracle agreed with a huge grin.

CHAPTER 12

Miracle stayed for a week and then went back to Chicago and her next assignment with the FBI. Kate kept busy, pretending to be a part of her mother's household. She visited the Singletons regularly, cleaned, cooked, washed clothes, shopped for groceries, and tried to re-establish a relationship with her sisters.

Thirteen-year-old Kacie was easy to approach, and within a few days Kate had learned everything there was to know about life in the seventh grade. Kendall was a senior in high school and less open, so Kate took her to the mall and invested $150 in gaining her friendship. Her sister Kelsey was a totally different proposition. She was a junior at Utah Valley State College, who worked part time at a shoe store and studied for several hours every day at the library. Kate rarely saw her and when she did, Kelsey did not encourage familiarity. Kate offered to buy her clothes, but Kelsey coldly refused. When Kate tried to talk about school, her sister answered in monosyllables. Finally Kate gave up and left Kelsey alone.

As Thanksgiving drew near, Kate helped her mother prepare for the big meal. Kate and Emily moved into Kelsey's room, to accommodate their grandparents, who drove down from Idaho. This forced Kate and Kelsey to speak at least occasionally. The whole weekend was hectic, and when their guests left Monday, Kate immediately started packing her things to move back to the guest room. She was almost finished when Kelsey and Kacie came in together.

"Kelsey's got to get ready for a big date," Kacie explained with a sly smile.

"A *big* date?" Kate repeated.

"Get out of my room," Kelsey instructed her youngest sister, then added reluctantly for Kate's benefit, "We're just going to the movies."

"But you're going with someone special?" Kate guessed. She had her answer when Kelsey blushed crimson. Kate set aside the receiving blanket she had been folding and concentrated on her sister. "What's his name?"

"Travis. Travis Pearce. He's a senior at UVSC, majoring in biology. When he graduates this summer, he wants to get a master's so he can get a job at a pharmaceutical lab," Kelsey blurted, as if unable to help herself.

Kate studied her sister closely. "You really like this guy."

"He's nice and we've been dating for a while. He—"

"He's a nerd!" Kacie called from the hallway.

"He's smart and a little awkward in social situations," Kelsey explained defensively.

"I'm a little awkward in social situations, and I'm not even all that smart," Kate tried to tease her into relaxing. Kelsey's serious expression melted and she gave a small smile.

"He's really a great person. He's ambitious and righteous and . . ." Kelsey's voice trailed off in embarrassment.

"And . . ." Kate prompted.

"I think I love him," Kelsey whispered. She shut the door firmly, then turned, and leaned against it. "How do you know for sure if you love somebody?" she asked.

Kate had been looking for an opportunity to develop some sisterly closeness, but she was unprepared for this deeply personal question.

"Love is hard to explain," she began vaguely, hoping Kelsey would be satisfied with banality. But Kelsey, who never asked for help from anyone, was waiting expectantly, and Kate knew she would have to do better. Closing her eyes, she tried to remember.

"When you really love someone," she began again, "you think about him all the time. No matter where you are or what you're doing, he never completely leaves your thoughts. When you're apart, you want to be with him. When you're together you're conscious of every move he makes, every word he says, and every breath he takes. Just the sight of him makes your heart race and your mouth go dry. And when he touches you, the rest of the world disappears."

Kate opened her eyes abruptly. "That's what I thought," Kelsey said softly.

Kate grabbed her suitcase with trembling hands and rushed to the door. "I've got to go," she explained briefly as she hurried to the guest room. The baby was still asleep, so she stretched out on the bed and covered her eyes with a pillow. For weeks she had refused to let herself think about the FBI or Niki Johnson or the time she spent in Haggerty. But when she was describing love to Kelsey, she wasn't remembering her marriage to Tony. She was thinking of Mark Iverson, and that terrified her.

He was part of the enemy, one of the people who thought awful things about Tony. He didn't say good-bye at the hotel in Miami, and he hadn't called her once during all the time she'd been at her mother's house. She knew that things were left unfinished between them, but she had buried her feelings for Mark along with all the other things she couldn't face—like Emily's kidnapping, Tony's betrayal, and the memory of his face as it lay in a growing pool of blood.

After her conversation with Kelsey, Kate grew more restless as each day passed. She tried to slip back into the routine she'd developed before Thanksgiving, but as much as she loved her mother and sisters, she wasn't really home. She tried to close her mind against her memories of Mark and Haggerty with dwindling success.

Sensing her discontent, her mother attempted to help by finding a house for rent across town. "It's been redecorated recently," she said, pointing to the ad in the newspaper. "It says 'small,' but how much room do you need? And you'd just be a few minutes away from me and the girls."

Kate's mother had some additional news as well. "I called the doctor to make an appointment for Emily on Friday morning. Selena Wallace—she's the receptionist—told me that Jeff Baxter is divorced and back in town. I thought we might invite him over for dinner on Sunday."

Jeff and Kate had dated sporadically during high school, and Kate recognized this as a blatant attempt to create a social life for her. The thought of meeting men and eventually dating made Kate shudder. Walking toward the front windows, she looked out at the falling snow.

"If you rent that house, you can be all moved in by Christmas," her mother said hopefully.

And then Kate knew. She couldn't stay in Orem. Nor was there anything for her in Chicago. The only place she had ever felt that she belonged was Haggerty, Georgia, and that was where she needed to go. She wanted Emily to be a young Haggerty lady, schooled in the art of thank-you note writing, tomato canning, and bridge playing. She wanted nosy neighbors and a collection of casserole recipes. She wanted to see her azaleas bloom in the spring.

"I can't stay here," she said, turning to face her mother. "I have to go back to Georgia."

"No!" Jeanine cried. "It's so far away!"

"It's home to me, Mom. I won't be happy anywhere else."

"Oh, Kate. I thought I finally had you home again," she murmured softly in a voice plaintive with regret.

"You do, Mom," Kate embraced her mother tenderly. "I'll just be a few states away, that's all."

* * *

Kate made her plane reservations for Monday, December 4th. She felt good about her decision, but she dreaded breaking the news to Tony's parents. She waited to tell them until the Sunday night before her departure. They accepted her decision bravely, saying they wanted her to be happy. She stayed with the Singletons all that evening, to give them as much time as she could with their granddaughter.

When Kate got home, she considered calling Miracle but decided against it. Miracle might feel obligated to share any information Kate gave her with Mr. Evans, and she didn't want the Bureau involved in her life. She had intended to warn Miss Eugenia that she would be arriving the next day, but the hour was late and Kate didn't want to wake her. So she went to bed, hoping that her old neighbor liked surprises.

On Monday morning, Jeanine took Kate and Emily to the airport and wept pitifully as they boarded the plane. Kate regretted the pain she was causing her mother, but she pressed on with determination. Their flight was uneventful, and they arrived in Albany just as it was starting to get dark. Kate rented a car at the airport and drove toward Haggerty.

As she passed the city limits sign, she reached over with one hand to tuck the receiving blanket close around Emily's ears and rolled down her window. Then she took a deep breath of crisp Haggerty air. Winston was parked under a tree, and she waved as she drove by at exactly forty miles per hour. She laughed at the look of surprise on his face when he recognized her.

Red bells with metallic gold bows hung from the street lamps and utility poles in town, and white Christmas lights decorated the trees. Everything looked so charming that Kate drove around the square twice. She could see Leita through the windows of the police station, talking on the phone. The owner of the drug store was locking his doors so Kate knew it must be close to five o'clock. As she turned down Maple Street, she saw Miss Polly's house ablaze with lights. Then suddenly, there was home. She stopped the car in the middle of the road and looked at the old Riley place. Although no Christmas decorations had been put up, the windows reflected the twinkling colors from Miss Polly's house. There was a lamp on in the living room, and the house looked cozy and warm.

Emily started to fuss, so Kate pulled into the driveway and took the baby to Miss Eugenia's back door. The house was dark, and Kate had to knock several times before she got an answer.

"Well! Look who's here!" Miss Eugenia said as she stepped back to let them in.

"I should have called," Kate apologized belatedly as she put the diaper bag down.

"Nonsense, have a seat." For once the table was clean, uncluttered with baking ingredients or rotting vegetables. As Kate sank gratefully into one of the tattered chairs that encircled Miss Eugenia's kitchen table, her tired brain registered this unusual condition.

"How's your mother?" Miss Eugenia asked as she took the baby from Kate's arms.

"She's fine and I enjoyed my visit, but the longer I stayed, the more I got to thinking about Haggerty and wondering what was going on here."

Miss Eugenia's laugh was dry and scratchy. "Nothing much happens around here. Miss Polly took four ribbons at the Founders' Day Pie contest, and Rita Wilcox dropped dead at Bridge Club two weeks ago."

As Kate gasped in horror, Miss Eugenia continued, "The worst of it was that she was just about to complete 'a grand slam.'" Kate stared at the older woman blankly, who quickly explained, "That's the highest score in Bridge. Before Rita could fulfill her last bid, she collapsed and we had to call an ambulance. By the time the paramedics got there and took her body out, Eva Nell had cleared away all the cards. So now we'll never know for sure."

"Why would anyone care about cards when Mrs. Wilcox was dead?"

"A grand slam? I'll bet even Rita was begging St. Peter to let her take a peek!"

"Miss Eugenia!"

"It's true. Cards like that are once in a lifetime, and if Eva Nell hadn't been on the opposing team, she would never have moved them." Miss Eugenia shook her head in disgust.

Kate looked around Miss Eugenia's kitchen. There was not a single cake or casserole on the counters, nor was there a Christmas decoration in sight. Kate's eyes swung back to Miss Eugenia.

"Okay, what's going on? You're always cooking something, taking a dish somewhere, or rushing from one meeting to another, and your house is never this clean. Something is wrong, and I want to know what it is."

"Nothing is wrong. I just can't do Christmas," she muttered.

"What do you mean? You can't do what?"

"Have it. Not without Charles."

"Charles?" Kate repeated stupidly.

"My husband, Charles. When he died, everyone told me that if I never let myself have a spare moment, I'd adjust to life without him. It was true. As long as I never stopped to think, I could pretend that everything was fine. Then you came along, and my life seemed full again." She held Emily a little closer. "But then you left. When Thanksgiving came, I helped Annabelle with dinner. Her son and his family was driving down from Birmingham. But when we put all the food on the table, I looked up and there was no Charles." She shrugged hopelessly. "Somehow I made it through Thanksgiving, but then Christmas was staring me in the face, and I decided that enough was enough. I can't do it anymore. I'm not having Christmas."

Kate nodded with understanding. She and Tony had never spent a major holiday together, so she was used to Christmas and Thanksgiving without him. But she remembered how awful family celebrations had been right after her father died.

"It takes time, but you'll adjust," Kate predicted. "How long have you been a widow?"

"Seems like forever," Miss Eugenia responded. "Almost a year."

Kate didn't try to hide her shock. "I assumed that it had been years . . ."

"I couldn't talk about it. I still can't." Miss Eugenia's voice shook slightly. "He retired ten years ago, and after that we did everything together. Gardening, fishing, canning, cooking, even trips to the doctor. He didn't care about whether the house was clean or if my fingernails were painted." Kate glanced down at her own fresh manicure. "He loved to dig around in the dirt, loved sitting for hours in the sun, and he loved me." Her voice was low and her eyes were full of pain.

"How did he die?" Kate asked gently.

"Stroke. Sudden and massive. Fine one minute, dead the next."

"Most people would say he was lucky."

"Most people weren't his wife." They sat in silence for a few minutes. "So, are you back to stay, then?" Miss Eugenia asked finally.

"Yes, ma'am." Kate cleared her throat. "I want Emily to speak with a Southern accent."

Miss Eugenia nodded approvingly. "You're perfect for Haggerty. You make a decent casserole, and you're a natural busybody."

Kate decided to overlook this last remark. "I wanted to buy the Riley house from the government, but when I called Mr. Evans's office, they said it had already been sold. So, I guess I'll see what's available over on Highway 11." Kate watched for Miss Eugenia's reaction.

"Over my dead body!" the older woman objected heatedly.

Kate laughed as her eyes strayed toward the window. "Nobody's moved into our house yet?" she asked wistfully.

Miss Eugenia shook her head. "Haven't seen anybody new over there yet."

"I need to get my clothes. And Emily's."

"The back door's unlocked."

"I thought our things might have been put in storage."

"As far as I know, everything's just like you left it," Miss Eugenia said softly. "Leave Emily with me and go on. I can tell you're dying to."

Kate stood. "I won't be gone long," she promised, and in a matter of seconds she was climbing up onto Ellis's new back porch. When she tried the doorknob, it turned easily in her hand. As the smells of fresh paint and old wood assailed her, she closed her eyes, savoring the feeling of coming home.

The kitchen was spotlessly clean, just the way Miracle always kept it. Kate ran a hand along the counter and saw a bowl and spoon rinsed off and sitting in the sink. Almost as if . . . She heard a sound from behind her and turned to see Mark's familiar form fill the doorway. His hair was windblown and his cheeks red from the cold.

"You're here," she whispered, half expecting him to disappear.

"Winston called and told me he saw you driving into town." He studied her. "You look good," he said finally.

She touched her hair. "I haven't had it permed or colored lately," she said. "But I still get my nails done every week."

"Niki's legacy." His eyes were warm.

"How are they? Do you know?" she asked.

"The real Johnsons?" Kate nodded. "Niki's father is up for re-election next year, and Drew resigned from the FBI to work on his campaign staff. I'm sure the senator is paying him a huge salary out of political contributions," Mark reported. "How's Emily?" His voice was gentle.

"She's good. Getting big."

"I've missed her."

"She's missed you, too. I don't think she's had a good burp since October." He smiled and her heart skipped a beat. Dragging her eyes away, Kate looked around the kitchen. "I wonder when the new owners will move in."

"I'm the new owner," he told her softly. "Mr. Evans gave me a good deal on the place, furniture and everything."

Kate was astounded. "Why would you want a house in Haggerty?"

"I've been reassigned to the Resident Agency in Albany."

"Did you finally get your big field assignment?"

"No, I'm back to pencil pushing again. Checking tax returns, corporate ledgers, bank statements, phone records, an occasional check fraud."

"After Miami I thought that they would give you a good assignment."

"They offered me anything I wanted."

"Then why would you settle for an office job in Albany?" she asked, mystified.

"Because it was close to home." Their eyes locked. "And I knew that eventually you would come back."

"How did you know?" Kate breathed.

"Well, there's the unsettled matter of the ten tribes," he reminded her tenderly.

Kate took a ragged breath. "Do you still think Tony was a traitor?" Her eyes begged him to give her the answer she needed.

"I'm undecided."

She hadn't expect this response and had to consider it for a few seconds. Then she nodded. "I guess I can accept that." She moved closer to him. "You never called me." She tried to hide her pain.

"I thought you needed some time alone to grieve for Tony and sort through your feelings," he answered gravely.

"So, where do we go from here?" she whispered.

He took a step, stopping right in front of her. "I guess that depends."

"Depends on what?" she asked as his hand came up to touch her cheek.

"On this," he answered, his lips touching hers. He pulled her close, and she lost all concept of time until the back door slammed shut.

They jumped apart as Miss Eugenia walked in carrying Emily. "You two can stay over here hugging and kissing the whole night for all I care, but this little girl is hungry."

Kate eased out of Mark's arms and took the baby into the den. She heard Mark telling Miss Eugenia the whole story, starting out with Tony's assignment to go undercover in Everett Morris's organization. When the baby was finished eating, Kate went into the kitchen and handed her to Mark. He arranged Emily in her regular burping position on his shoulder, covering her little forehead with kisses. Then he paced back and forth as Kate took a seat beside Miss Eugenia.

Mark buried his face in Emily's neck. "I've dreamed of this smell," he whispered, breathing deeply.

Miss Eugenia leaned forward and spoke directly to Kate. "I caught him sniffing the Ivory Snow on several occasions." Kate laughed as a blush crept up Mark's neck. "So, from what Mark says, you two aren't really married. You thought you were, but your first husband wasn't dead, and now he is." Kate winced at this blunt itemization of the painful events, but nodded. "Based on the way you were kissing a while ago, I would guess that you do want to be married."

"It seems a little soon after Tony's death," Kate said hesitantly.

"Pooh! Life is too short. You've been grieving for the first one for a year, and I say that's long enough. He'd want you to move on."

"I'd like to believe that," Kate sighed. Mark had stopped walking around and was watching her closely.

"He'd want Emily to have a father, a real family," Miss Eugenia continued. "So, you two should get married immediately."

"It will take some time." Kate looked up at Mark.

"You don't have any time! You can't let anyone in Haggerty know that you weren't really married before!" Miss Eugenia insisted vehemently.

"Why not? We told you everything and you understand."

"I am a very open-minded, progressive Southern woman," she informed them. "The other folks here can deal with the idea that the two of you were living under assumed identities to hide from drug dealers. That's like something off of television and will only increase your popularity in town. They can forgive you for spending some time at your mother's house after your ordeal in Florida. But if you try to explain to them that you were never legally married to Mark, that Emily is not Mark's child, and that your real husband died only a few weeks ago in a messy gun battle . . ." Miss Eugenia shook her head. "I don't think the town can handle all that."

"We'll have to lie, then?" Kate asked.

"You just don't have to tell them every gory detail." Miss Eugenia stopped, seeing that Kate was unconvinced, then she tried again. "It's for their own good, really. You might shock one of the old folks into cardiac arrest with the awful truth, but if you and Emily just move back in here like nothing ever happened . . ."

"I can't stay here with Mark until after we're married," Kate protested weakly.

"You've been living together for months, and you weren't married."

"But we thought we were." Kate glanced over to see the amusement in Mark's eyes.

Miss Eugenia considered this for a moment and then nodded. "I guess I'll have to move in here with you. We'll tell everyone it's because Miracle's gone, and you need help with the baby, but really I'll be your chaperone."

Kate thought about the empty house next door that awaited Miss Eugenia and the trouble she was having with the holidays.

"It's the only sensible solution," she agreed. "But it may take a couple of weeks. Weddings are a little complicated in our church. We'll want to get married in the Atlanta temple and that will require interviews with our bishop and the stake president and . . ."

"Don't tell me! You'll give me a headache. If you had to belong to an exotic church, why couldn't you join one of the snake-charming congregations in Walapoosa? I'll bet they get married close to home like sensible people," Miss Eugenia complained. Taking a deep breath, she regarded them both. "So, can you get all your waivers and dispensations and interviews or whatever taken care of by the week before Christmas?"

Kate struggled to keep a straight face. "I think so." Mark smiled into the baby's neck.

"That will be perfect then. You can get married on the Friday before Christmas. Invite your parents to the wedding in Atlanta. We'll say that Mark has business there, which will certainly be true," Miss Eugenia said firmly as if anyone had disputed this point. "After the ceremony, you'll all drive back here for a big family Christmas."

"I guess that will be okay," Kate agreed warily.

"It will be more than okay. You and Mark will get married in your cathedral . . ."

"Temple," Kate corrected absently.

"Whatever." Miss Eugenia dismissed her comment. "Until you are legally husband and wife, you will be closely chaperoned, and since we're all staying over here, I won't have to find the sheets that fit the bed in my guest room. I'm going home to pack, but I'll be back before you know it. So behave yourselves," Miss Eugenia ordered, then strode purposefully from the room.

When the back door closed loudly behind her, Mark carried Emily upstairs. He put her in the bassinet and Kate tucked a blanket around her. "You're sure no one can get in here again?" she asked tensely, looking out onto the quiet street.

"I had a new security system put in. The windows are locked and there are motion detectors on the sills," he replied solemnly.

"You don't mind if Miss Eugenia stays with us for a while?" Kate asked, turning back to face him. "The holidays are lonely for her without her husband, and I think she was looking for an excuse to get out of her house."

"I probably won't even notice a difference. She's always over here anyway."

Kate stared at her hands. "Are you sure you want to marry me?"

"More sure than I've ever been about anything in my life," Mark said gently. "And I want to adopt Emily so she can be sealed to us."

"I want that, too."

Mark cupped her face with his hands and looked into her eyes. "We don't really have to rush this, Kate. We can have announcements printed, order flowers and plan a real reception. Haggerty will get over the shock eventually."

Kate laughed tremulously. "I don't care about the wedding. I just want to be your wife."

Mark pulled her into his arms. "Then I'll call the bishop and see when he can meet with us. I hope he has a sense of humor."

"We didn't really do anything wrong."

"We told too many lies to count, and I had some thoughts, but since they were about the woman I thought I was married to, maybe he'll go easy on me," Mark disagreed with a smile.

"If you use that phone, you can keep an eye on Emily," Kate responded primly, indicating toward the nightstand. "I'll go see if I can find something for dinner."

"If you look real hard, you may be able to find a casserole or two," he called after her.

Kate didn't even try to pick and choose between the foil-wrapped dishes stacked in the freezer. She just took one out and pre-heated the oven to 350 degrees. She was making a salad when Mark came down the stairs carrying the portable bassinet.

"So, what did the bishop say?" Kate asked as he put a piece of carrot in his mouth.

"We both have appointments with him on Wednesday night. Assuming they go well, we'll meet with the stake president next week. If we pass our interviews, we can go ahead and get a marriage license." He walked up behind her and wrapped his arms around her waist. "You know we'll have to get blood tests."

"I made it through childbirth. I think I can stand a blood test." She smiled and leaned back against him for a few seconds. The timer went off and he released her to pull a steaming casserole from the oven.

Miss Eugenia returned as Kate was putting their dinner on the table. She dragged in a battered suitcase and a large-capacity coffee maker. Mark took the suitcase up to a guest room while Miss Eugenia assembled her coffee maker on the counter. Once it was plugged in, she took her seat at the table. "What's for dinner?" she asked with a satisfied smile.

"Casserole," Kate replied dryly.

Miss Eugenia took a bite and analyzed it carefully. "Chicken Divine. I'd say Miss Rowena Duke made it. She always uses too much sour cream."

Kate rolled her eyes at Mark as he walked back in and sat down. While they ate, Mark filled Kate in on town politics. "Winston's the acting police chief," he said between bites. "Mayor Witherspoon was re-elected, and Booster moved to Walker County."

"I think that Winston Jones might just amount to something yet," Miss Eugenia mused as she ate a second helping of casserole. After the kitchen was cleaned up, they all went into the den. "Rosie O'Donnell is hosting a Christmas special tonight," Miss Eugenia announced, taking possession of the remote control and settling herself in the recliner. Mark pushed the bassinet into a relatively quiet corner and then sat by Kate on the couch.

"I'll need to take my rental car to the airport tomorrow," Kate said. "Then I'll have to make arrangements for permanent transportation."

"Your dream van is parked at the agency office in Albany," Mark said with a smile. "Mr. Evans threw it in with the house." He took her hand and held it against his lips. "I'll drive the rental car in tomorrow and bring the van back." They were quiet for a few minutes, then Mark leaned over and whispered into Kate's ear. "I've dreamed about this. You here with me."

"It's good to be home," she replied with a smile.

"And in a couple of weeks, we'll really be married."

"Isn't it funny how for so long I didn't feel like your wife when I thought I was, and now I know I'm not, but I feel like I am."

"Give me a little while to think that through." He kissed the tip of her nose.

"Shhh!" Miss Eugenia commanded from the recliner.

An hour later the program was over and Miss Eugenia was snoring loudly. "I can't believe you actually stayed awake during an entire Christmas special," Mark commented as he carried the bassinet upstairs.

Kate opened the door to her room and followed him inside. "Either it was pregnancy that made me sleepy or you're getting more interesting," she said thoughtfully and he kissed her.

"I guess I'd better go get our chaperone," he murmured reluctantly.

"I guess you should," Kate agreed, tracing her finger along the corner of his mouth. When he closed her door behind him, Kate fed the baby and left her in the bassinet while she took a shower. After changing into pajamas, she pulled Emily up beside her in the big bed and fell asleep, secure in the knowledge that Mark was only a few feet away.

* * *

On Tuesday morning Miss Eugenia had breakfast ready when Kate got downstairs. Mark was finished eating, so he took Emily while Kate ate her scrambled eggs. After Mark left for work, Miss Eugenia told Kate to get dressed and ready for company. "Who's coming?" Kate asked.

"By now the whole town knows you're back, and most of them will find an excuse to drop by. I'll probably have to store some of the casseroles at my house," Miss Eugenia said as she walked by, shaking her head.

As Miss Eugenia had predicted, they had visitors all day long. The Baptist preacher brought them a Bible, saying he felt it was his Christian duty to make sure they had one for the baby's sake. Miss Polly delivered pumpkin bread and the Bridge Club ladies made chicken casseroles. The Methodist preacher's wife brought a potted plant, and Melba Fishburne came empty-handed, just hoping to see the ex-police chief.

"Now that he's working in Albany, I never see him," she complained.

"We'll tell him you came by," was the best response Kate could muster. Melba resisted their best efforts to get rid of her, offering to perm Kate's hair or paint her nails. She finally left when Miss Eugenia said they needed someone to help wash dishes.

"Why did you turn down a free permanent and manicure?" Miss Eugenia asked when they closed the door behind her.

"Do you think I would let that woman get near me with sharp instruments or toxic chemicals?" Kate demanded and Miss Eugenia laughed.

After lunch Leita brought over a baby afghan she had crocheted herself and a certificate from Arnold to have Emily's first shoes bronzed. Winston rolled in a bicycle that Emily would be able to ride in about ten years, and the mayor presented Kate with a tiny gold-toned key to the city. By dark Kate was exhausted, but Miss Eugenia looked years younger.

Annabelle walked in with a coconut pound cake just as they were sitting down to dinner, and Kate insisted that she stay. While Miss Eugenia cleared the dishes, Annabelle pulled Kate to the side.

"I'm so glad you're back. I was really starting to worry about Eugenia," she whispered. "It's like you're the granddaughter she never had." At that moment, the subject of their quiet conversation rushed by, carrying the baby.

"I guess I'm the only person in this house who can change a diaper," Miss Eugenia grumbled as she climbed up the stairs.

"I've tried to explain about 'stay dry linings,'" Kate said, and Annabelle shook her head.

"Nobody's ever been able to tell Eugenia anything!"

After the baby was fed and asleep, Kate called to tell her mother about the wedding. Jeanine Taylor was not completely surprised. "I thought there must be someone. Otherwise, you would have been willing to at least try and settle here."

Kate gave her the dates and then ended her call. Mark took the phone from Kate's hand and called his parents, but the conversation didn't go as smoothly. Kate finally left the room when she could tell that he was having trouble answering their questions in front of her. She waited in the den with Miss Eugenia, and he joined them fifteen minutes later.

"They aren't happy," Kate stated grimly.

Mark rubbed the back of his neck. "They'll get used to the idea," he assured her.

"I'm not what they wanted for you. A woman who's been married and has a child."

"No," he admitted honestly. "But they're all coming to the wedding, and once they meet you, they'll love you."

"Like you said, they'll get used to the idea anyway," Kate responded morosely.

"And if they don't ever like you, so what? They live in Texas. You'll never see them," Miss Eugenia contributed philosophically from the recliner.

On Wednesday morning Kate called the Singletons. Their dismay was obvious, and Kate tried to reassure them by promising that her marriage would not affect their relationship with Emily. That evening they met with the bishop. He was very gracious during Kate's interview. He had talked to Mark first so he already knew all the details. He told Kate that he was pleased to have them in his ward, whoever they were.

On Thursday morning Miss Polly, Miss George Ann Simmons, and Miss Eva Nell Talbot all came to call. Kate watched nervously as the ladies settled themselves around the living room.

"You have a seat, Kate," Miss Eugenia whispered. "I'll get some refreshments." Kate watched in horror as Miss Eugenia walked out, leaving her alone with the Haggerty matrons.

They exchanged pleasantries for several minutes. Kate told Miss Polly that she had seen her on television, and the older woman blushed with pleasure. Then she expressed sorrow over Mrs. Wilcox's death at the Bridge Club meeting and the women took turns giving detailed accounts of the event. Miss Eugenia returned with coconut pound cake and coffee on a tray. As she distributed food, the ladies got down to business.

"We have decided to revive the Haggerty Historical Society," Miss George Ann announced.

"Your renovations to this house brought to our attention the need for a committee to make sure that changes made by new homeowners don't affect the integrity of the original structures," Miss Eva Nell further explained.

"You did a lovely job on this house," Miss Polly hastened to add.

"But what if you had wanted to close in the front porch and make a sun room?" Miss Eva Nell hypothesized.

"You mean, if someone bought one of these old houses and wanted to make a structural change, the Historical Society could stop them? Even though they owned the house?" Kate asked incredulously.

"There are laws protecting historical buildings," Miss George Ann nodded.

"The Society would have to approve all major changes," Miss Eva Nell agreed.

"This has never been challenged in court," Miss Eugenia said as she took a seat beside Kate. "The threat of George Ann's wrath has been enough so far."

Kate smiled, but Miss George Ann was not amused. "Can't you be serious for just a few minutes, Eugenia?" she demanded. After a sip of coffee, she smoothed her tightly stretched skirt. "Anyway, the purpose of our visit today is to ask you to join the Historical Society."

Kate blinked at Miss George Ann. "Me?"

Miss George Ann smiled. "As Pauline said, we've been very impressed by the way you restored your home. You've modernized it without destroying any of its charm."

"Happy Goodwin really deserves the credit for that," Kate said with complete honesty.

Miss Eugenia waved a hand. "They just want someone in the Society who doesn't drink Ensure or wear Depends," she said, earning glares from her fellow members.

"I don't know what to say." Kate felt tears gathering in her eyes.

"Say yes!" Miss Polly suggested with a huge smile.

"Yes!" Kate laughed along with the other ladies.

"Wonderful!" Miss George Ann proclaimed. "Now, as a new member, we'd like to invite you to participate in our annual Historical Society Holiday Parade of Homes." Kate waited expectantly. "We select a few appropriate houses and ask their owners to open their doors to the public for one night during the Christmas season. We post flyers and send invitations to the officials of surrounding towns.

It's a way for people to see how lovely these old homes are."

"Actually, this annual event has not taken place in decades," Miss Eugenia muttered.

"We thought renewing the tradition would be a good way to generate some interest in our neighborhood."

"Show the young folks from Albany that they don't have to buy out on Highway 11."

"And increase our property value," Miss Polly admitted, then blushed violently.

"I'd be delighted," Kate accepted cheerfully.

"I knew you'd want to help," Miss George Ann said primly. "You will need to submit a description of your decorating scheme for us to review."

"To avoid duplication."

"You'll be asked to serve light refreshments."

"Punch and cookies."

"Or cake and coffee."

"Just let us know which so we can be sure that no one else serves the same thing."

"Your house will need to be open to the public from seven until nine on that night," Miss George Ann clarified.

Kate nodded. "What night is it?" she asked belatedly.

"Two weeks from Friday on December 22nd."

"Oh no! That's . . ." Kate began.

"Kate and Mark have family coming for Christmas. They'll all be arriving that day," Miss Eugenia said, breaking into the conversation.

"Will that be a problem then?" Miss George Ann turned worried eyes back to Kate.

"I don't see why," Miss Eugenia answered for her. "It will give everyone in Haggerty a chance to extend a friendly Southern welcome to the visitors." Kate gave Miss Eugenia a doubtful look. "Don't worry. I've got this under control," Miss Eugenia promised her confidently.

Kate watched in numb silence as the women finished their cake. When they left, she voiced her concern to Miss Eugenia. "There will be so much going on that weekend. The wedding and my family and Mark's family."

"Look on the bright side. With so many other people in your house, you won't have to spend much time alone with your new in-laws," Miss Eugenia replied blithely. "Now, we need to decide on the refreshments so we can make them up in advance. Pound cake and coffee would be easy," Miss Eugenia proposed.

"I don't want to serve coffee," Kate said with unusual firmness. "Mark's parents don't think much of me as it is. I don't want to look like I don't follow the Word of Wisdom."

Miss Eugenia gave her a suspicious look. "Okay, we won't have coffee so that Mark's mother will think you're smart. Punch and cookies will be just as easy. We'll start making cookies on Monday." Looking over the room, she frowned. "We've got to get some decorations up around here. It's two weeks until Christmas, and you don't have so much as a holly leaf."

Kate refrained from mentioning that Miss Eugenia's house was equally devoid of holiday cheer. "We don't own any decorations, and since we will be inviting in the public . . ."

"Happy," Miss Eugenia said suddenly. "I'll bet she would decorate for you. Call her and see if she has time. If she agrees, tell her George Ann needs a copy of her plan right away."

Kate made her phone call, and Happy said she had plenty of free time. "Nobody wants to redecorate during the holidays, so this is a slack period for us. I never had thought of it before, but this might be a good sideline for me. How much can I spend?"

Kate thought about Tony's back pay and the insurance money that was now sitting in her checking account. "I won't give you a limit."

"We're not using Daddy's credit card anymore, are we?" Happy asked regretfully.

"No, I'm paying for it myself. But I want this house to look spectacular."

CHAPTER 13

After dinner on Thursday night, Kate asked Mark to list his family members so that she could buy Christmas gifts. "You don't really have to get individual gifts for everyone," he said when his list was complete.

"I'm hoping to buy their love," Kate replied with a brave smile.

"Hey, it might work." He kissed her soundly.

"Don't distract me. I've got more lists to make."

The weather was nice on Friday, so Kate took the baby and went Christmas shopping in Albany. She made her choices carefully and returned to the van often to drop off packages. Her last stop was the Hallmark store, where she bought wrapping paper and ribbons. As the sun set, Kate drove home, exhausted but exhilarated. Miss Eugenia held the baby while Kate made trip after trip to the van, lugging in her purchases.

"Gracious sakes alive! Did you just buy one of everything?"

Kate laughed and asked what they were having for dinner. Miss Eugenia had baked pork chops and homemade biscuits. Kate stacked the gifts in the dining room, then sat down to feed Emily. Mark walked through the door just in time to burp the baby.

"Happy came by while you were gone and left her sketches." Miss Eugenia waved a wooden spoon toward some papers on the counter. "She said she was going to use poinsettias and gingerbread men," Miss Eugenia added as Kate skimmed the proposal.

As they sat down to eat the delicious, non-casserole dinner, Miss Eugenia told Mark that Happy needed three Christmas trees by

Monday. "What in the world is she going to do with three trees?" Mark asked irritably.

"She's going to use them to decorate your house for the holidays," Miss Eugenia informed him sharply. "And don't come home with little, scrawny trees. We want everything to look perfect."

On Saturday morning Kate got up early, and she had Emily dressed by the time Mark got back from borrowing Arnold's truck. Then they drove all around the county until they found three perfect trees. Mark maintained a sullen silence during the entire process, and when they got home, he stalked into the den, saying only, "Call Happy and tell her the trees are on the porch. I'm not carrying them one more inch."

Deciding he needed some time alone, Kate fed the baby in the kitchen, but when Emily was ready to be burped, she walked into the den. Mark was staring at a documentary about earthworms. He made no comment, but took the baby and put her on his shoulder. When Kate looked in later, both were sound asleep.

After his nap, Mark was more pleasant. He made his special Texas Chili for dinner and then they all watched *It's a Wonderful Life.* He made fun of Kate for crying, but his eyes were suspiciously red when the movie ended.

As they said good night in the hallway between their rooms, Mark apologized for his foul humor that morning. "I wanted us to have a quiet, simple Christmas, but instead we'll have three trees, both our families, and half of Haggerty in our house."

"I shouldn't have agreed to be a part of the Parade of Homes," Kate apologized.

Mark pulled her into his arms. "As long as we're together, I guess it doesn't really matter how many other people are around or how many Christmas trees we have," he relented and she smiled, relaxing into the embrace.

Kate was nervous about going to church on Sunday. She expected things to be awkward, but the bishop met them at the door and welcomed them warmly. After sacrament meeting, Sister Baylor and Sister Armistead rushed up and gave Kate a hug. "We thought you had moved without saying good-bye," Sister Baylor told her sadly.

"We're glad to have you back," Sister Armistead added with a smile. "We'd like to come visit on Tuesday." Brother Stoops set up an appointment for that very afternoon, and his eyes positively glowed when he found out that Miss Eugenia was a temporary houseguest.

Miss Polly was standing on their front porch when they parked in the driveway and insisted that they eat Sunday dinner with her. Miss Eugenia included herself and Ellis Harper in the invitation. Kate was amazed by the tenderness she felt when she saw the old man again. She asked if he'd been busy, and he said that he hadn't had a job in over a month. She glanced at Mark and then told Ellis to come to their house first thing on Monday morning.

"What do we have that needs to be fixed?" Mark whispered when the conversation moved on.

"If necessary, I'll break something myself," Kate answered firmly. "Poor Ellis, stuck at home alone during the holidays!"

Mark laughed and Miss Eugenia smiled in approval.

After lunch they walked back home and Kate went upstairs to feed the baby. In the process they both fell asleep. Mark woke Kate at three, saying that Brother Stoops was there. "Not that he really wants to see *us.* "

Hearing the laughter that drifted up from downstairs, Kate said, "We may have to chaperone Miss Eugenia for a change!" Sitting up on the side of the bed, she promised to come down as soon as she fed the baby.

When she joined them in the den, Kate noted that Miss Eugenia had abandoned her usual seat in the recliner for a place beside Brother Stoops on the couch. "Oh, Elmer!" she exclaimed loudly. "You are such a card." Kate and Mark exchanged glances.

The home teacher smoothed his few remaining strands of hair and laboriously read the First Presidency Message from the *Ensign.* The topic was "Keeping Focused on the Savior," and when Brother Stoops finally closed the magazine, Miss Eugenia clapped with enthusiasm. "Why, Elmer, I do declare that was as good a sermon as any I've heard preached from a pulpit," she praised him lavishly.

"Thank you, Eugenia, but I can't take credit for these words. They were written by the prophet of our church."

"Well, you read them mighty nice." She patted his thin knee. Then she offered him a piece of the peanut butter pie that Miss Polly had sent home with them after lunch.

When Brother Stoops left, Miss Eugenia went up to her room and Kate heated the roast for dinner. As Mark set the table, she asked if he thought there was a romance budding between Miss Eugenia and their home teacher.

"Oh, I think they're both just lonely," Mark said, taking both of her hands in his.

Kate wasn't convinced. "I don't know. If she had been sitting any closer to him, she would have been in his lap. And the first time they met, she told me she thought he was cute."

"Brother Stoops?" Mark asked incredulously.

"Elmer," Kate confirmed.

Mark pulled her close and nuzzled her neck. "I wonder if you'll think I'm cute when I'm old," he murmured.

Kate considered this, trying to ignore Mark's lips on her neck. "Maybe a cute old man isn't an impossibility after all," she said softly and Mark laughed. "Speaking of cute old men, Ellis will be here tomorrow morning. Have you thought of something he can do, or will I have to break something?"

"The shed out back is full of stuff that needs to be sorted through and organized," Mark proposed as he put the roast on the table.

"He can't work outside!" Kate protested. "It's cold."

"He could spray the attic for bugs."

"I don't want him exposed to dangerous pesticides!"

"Well, I guess he could sit in the den and watch television."

Kate laughed. "I was thinking he could paint the cupboards in the butler's pantry."

Mark looked up in surprise. "I thought we were going to replace those to match the ones in the kitchen."

"We can replace them just as easily after they've been painted, can't we?" Kate ignored his amused expression and called Miss Eugenia down for dinner.

Ellis was eating breakfast when Kate walked into the kitchen the next morning. Kate explained his cabinet painting project, and he nodded as Miss Eugenia refilled his coffee cup. Kate had finished her pancakes and was rinsing her plate when Happy arrived. She had two assistants, a truckload of poinsettias, and a variety of other decorations with her.

"Looks like you found some good trees," she said breathlessly as she dropped her purse and briefcase on the kitchen table. When Miss Eugenia offered Happy some breakfast, the decorator shook her head.

"I'd better get the boys started," she replied, leading her assistants to the front of the house. Kate wrapped Christmas gifts for a couple of hours and watched Happy work. She bossed and fussed and praised just often enough to keep her helpers from quitting.

At one point Happy paused at the door of the dining room and surveyed the wrapping paper and ribbon that Kate had spread out on the table. "I'll have all this cleaned up by the night of the Open House," Kate promised.

Happy shook her head thoughtfully. "I was just thinking that it might look quaint to leave it. People like little personal touches."

Kate looked down at the paper scraps doubtfully. "Are you sure?"

Happy nodded. "'Real life' is in style this year."

After lunch Kate took Emily to the pediatrician in Albany for a checkup. The doctor gave the baby her first shots and warned Kate that she might run a slight fever. When Kate got home, Miss Eugenia was on the phone and the house looked like something out of a Christmas issue of *Southern Living*. Happy had rearranged the wrapping paper rolls and ribbon remnants on the dining room table so that even they looked elegant.

Kate wanted to call Mark after she fed the baby and put her down for a nap, but Miss Eugenia was still on the phone. Finally Kate was forced to use the cell phone.

"She must be talking to Brother Stoops!" Kate whispered into the small receiver. "Maybe he's asking her out on a date!"

Mark refused to take the situation seriously. "If so, we're going to have to give her a curfew."

* * *

When Mark came in that night, he surveyed the elaborate decorations with dismay. "Even after my previous experience with Happy, I'm amazed by this," he said, fingering the pine boughs wired to the stair railing. "If anyone has an undiagnosed evergreen allergy, they're dead," he added with a grimace.

The visiting teachers came on Tuesday morning while Kate was bathing Emily, and Miss Eugenia entertained them for a while. By the time Kate walked into the den, both ladies had a piece of chocolate layer cake and a tall glass of milk. They presented a lesson about gaining strength through adversity. Every time they quoted a scripture, Miss Eugenia demanded to know the reference. The third time they told her the scripture could be found in the Book of Mormon, Kate made up her mind to ask Mark if Miss Eugenia could have his old paperback copy now that he had his real set back.

A little while later, Mark called to tell Kate that her furniture and other personal items from the apartment in Chicago had been shipped to the Bureau office in Albany. "I'm not ready to look through that stuff yet," Kate told him.

"There's a storage place not far from the office. I'll rent a unit and put all of it in there." They moved to more pleasant subjects, including Miss Eugenia's interest in the visiting teacher's message and Kate asked him about his copy of the Book of Mormon.

"Do you really think she'll read it?" he asked skeptically.

"I don't know for sure, but she was impressed by the verses that my visiting teachers quoted. I'm counting on her curiosity," Kate said with a smile.

When they ended their conversation, Kate got the book from Mark's room. She took it downstairs and placed it on the counter beside Miss Eugenia. "Why are you giving me this Mormon Bible?" the older woman asked, looking up from the vegetable soup she was stirring.

Kate smiled. "You asked my visiting teachers about those scriptures, and I thought you might like to read them for yourself."

"I don't want to read it! Methodists have lost their souls for less!" She shook her head in horror. "I was just surprised that the things your church ladies read sounded like something out of the Bible," she finally admitted.

"It's about the people in ancient America."

"I thought it was about Joseph Smith."

"It's not."

"Humph!" She eyed the book with interest.

"If you ever feel brave enough to risk your soul, start reading in Mosiah. I've marked it for you," Kate said casually.

Miss Eugenia put down the soupspoon. "I'd better put this up before someone sees it and gets the wrong idea." She grabbed the book and rushed toward the stairs.

Ellis came into the kitchen at twelve, and Kate served him lunch. After they were through eating, she settled in the den, planning to watch television. Miss Eugenia came in and turned off the set.

"I like that program," Kate protested. "They give you very useful tips about things, like how to make curtains out of sheets."

Miss Eugenia looked around the room. "I thought you liked the curtains Happy ordered."

"It would be a good thing to know," Kate replied stubbornly.

"Well, you can learn to make curtains after Christmas. Right now we need to go over the plans I've made for next weekend." She waved a stack of notebook paper in her hand. "You leave for Atlanta on Thursday morning." Kate nodded. "On Friday, you and Mark will get married again." Miss Eugenia pointed to her list. "That's the easy part. Once the wedding is over, you'll all drive back to Haggerty, which should put you here about one o'clock. The Bridge Club will provide a light lunch, then Mark's family will go over to Annabelle's." Kate raised an eyebrow. "She's going to spend Christmas with her son in Birmingham, and she volunteered her house for some of your guests. I thought if we put Mark's family over there, they could all be together."

"That was good thinking." Kate was impressed.

"Of course it was. Everyone will have a little while to freshen up before the Parade of Homes. The cookies will be made in advance and frozen. I have a recipe for sparkling punch that looks like champagne." She held up her hand when she saw that Kate was about to object. "It's nonalcoholic." Kate nodded again. "The Methodists will bring breakfast to both houses on Saturday morning. It will be easy to serve things like biscuits, fruit, and breakfast casseroles."

"I didn't know there was such a thing as a breakfast casserole," Kate said in surprise.

Miss Eugenia gave her a disdainful look. "There is a casserole for everything." Taking a deep breath, she continued. "On Saturday, Miss Polly will serve everyone dinner at her house."

Kate gasped. "That's too many people for Miss Polly to handle all by herself!"

Miss Eugenia waved her hand. "She just wants to show off. Let her do it. Then supper on Saturday night will be provided by the Relief Society ladies from your church. They said they wanted to help, so I gave them Saturday night. They'll serve their meal at Annabelle's to cut down on the traffic over here. Then Winston will take care of breakfast on Sunday morning."

"How in the world will he do that?"

Miss Eugenia smiled. "He's been dating every available woman within driving distance, trying to disprove the rumors about his lack of virility. He's particularly friendly with the manager of Hardee's out on Highway 76. He said she'll fix biscuits, and he'll deliver them in the patrol car."

"Won't that cost him a fortune?"

Miss Eugenia shrugged. "I imagine he's getting a discount. Now, the Baptists will bring in dinner after church, and we'll warm up casseroles for Sunday evening. Christmas dinner will be at Haggerty Station."

"Haggerty Station is open on Christmas Day?"

"Of course not, but you're paying them an outrageous amount to make an exception."

Kate walked over to Miss Eugenia and touched the old hand that grasped the scribbled pages. "You have gone to so much trouble. All of you. The whole town."

"Everyone likes you, and we want to make a good impression on your families."

"I don't know what to say," Kate felt tears gathering in her eyes.

"Then don't say anything. Feed your baby and come into the kitchen. I need help with a batch of cranberry cookies."

After dinner, Mark showed Kate a key from Mike's Mini-Storage. "I'm going to put this in the middle drawer of the desk," he told her as he walked down the hall. "When you're ready to look at the stuff from your apartment, let me know."

Kate nodded. "I'll save a few of Tony's things for Emily and send the rest to his parents. But I'd rather wait until after the wedding and the Open House and Christmas . . ."

"There's no rush," Mark told her gently.

On Wednesday morning the Historical Society ladies came over to examine the house. Not surprisingly, Happy's decorations passed inspection. That evening Mark and Kate had their interviews with the stake president, and both left the stake center with temple recommends. On the way home, they stopped at the store to get the ingredients for Miss Eugenia's sparkling punch. At home, Mark stacked their purchases in the butler's pantry while Kate put the baby to bed. Later Kate heard Mark walking down the hall and stuck her head out. "Do you think I should check on Miss Eugenia?" she whispered. "It's only nine o'clock and she's already in bed."

"Maybe she was tired," Mark suggested. "I know I am after lugging in a hundred bottles of ginger ale."

"I'm just afraid that she's depressed about her husband again."

"Forget about Miss Eugenia and try to get some sleep." He kissed her senseless, then pushed her gently into her room.

On Thursday morning, Kate and Miss Eugenia made hundreds of cookies. After lunch they made divinity and fudge for the upcoming Relief Society enrichment meeting. While the candy cooled, Kate invited Miss Eugenia to come with them that evening. "I'm looking forward to some peace and quiet around here while you're gone," she declined ungraciously.

By the time Kate got downstairs on Friday morning, Miss Eugenia already had a batch of cinnamon oatmeal cookies in the oven. "We're running out of freezer space over here," the older lady announced as Kate poured herself some cereal. "When these are done, we'll have to take them to my house."

Emily smiled and blew bubbles while they cooked. "She's getting so big," Miss Eugenia commented as she took the last batch from the oven. "Blink your eyes and she'll be in school. Before you can turn around, she'll be married with children of her own."

"I want things to stay like they are," Kate murmured.

"Well, they won't. You can't stop time."

"But ten years into the future, you might . . ." Kate struggled for the right words.

"Not be alive? That's true, but there's nothing either one of us can do about it. So, we'll make the best of every minute we have together. I learned that from Charles's death." She started scooping cookies into a Tupperware container. "Now, wrap Emily up so we can take these cookies next door."

The temperature inside Miss Eugenia's house was uncomfortably cold. Miss Eugenia turned on the furnace, and in minutes warm, scorched-smelling air circulated through the room. Kate watched patiently while the older woman wedged plastic tubs and bulging plastic bags into the upright freezer. When all the cookies were situated, Miss Eugenia turned to go, but Kate reached out and stopped her.

"Wait a minute," she said, gathering her courage as Miss Eugenia's eyebrows shot up. "Before we leave, I want to see pictures of Charles. I'd like to see how he looked when you first got married and later when he was old. I want to get to know him."

Miss Eugenia regarded her solemnly for a few seconds, then she nodded. They walked into the cluttered living room, and Kate spread a quilt out for Emily while Miss Eugenia dragged an old shoebox down from the closet shelf. As Kate studied each photograph, Miss Eugenia narrated. "This is a picture of our graduating class." She pointed to herself and then to Charles.

"You were beautiful!" Kate exclaimed, then blushed.

Miss Eugenia laughed. "I wasn't always old and wrinkled!" Kate picked up a photo of a young couple standing outside the Methodist church. "That was taken a few days before we married. And this was Charles in our first car . . ."

Kate examined every picture, growing closer to Miss Eugenia with each look into the past. "You had a wonderful life together," Kate said finally and Miss Eugenia agreed. "In our church we believe that marriage can last throughout eternity and not just 'until death do you part,'" Kate told her quietly. "That's why Mark and I are going to Atlanta. If we marry in the temple, we're sealed together forever."

"I wish the Methodists believed that," Miss Eugenia sighed. "I asked my preacher how Charles and I would feel when we see each other again, and he said that in heaven we won't even remember that we used to be married. According to him, I won't feel any different toward Charles than I will toward all the other angels."

"I hate to speak unkindly of your preacher, but that is a lie," Kate told her with conviction. "We will remember every minute of our lives on earth."

Miss Eugenia shook her head and started to pack up the pictures. "I do want to thank you for the book you gave me. It's been entertaining reading." It took Kate a few seconds to realize that she meant the Book of Mormon. "Charles and I used to read every night before we went to bed, but I lost the habit after he died."

"Is that what you've been doing in your room every night? Reading the Book of Mormon?" Kate demanded and Miss Eugenia nodded. "I was afraid that you were sick or depressed or worse." Kate exhaled deeply. "You said you liked it?"

"Oh, the characters are so vivid. Elmer and I are reading along together, and we confer regularly. He is partial to King Benjamin, and I'll admit he had some good things to say, but I don't particularly enjoy being reminded that as a sinner, I'm worse than dirt. I preferred the stories about the boys who went on missions into strange lands full of ferocious Indians. That would be so exciting."

"And dangerous," Kate said mildly.

"They converted kings and confounded unscrupulous lawyers . . ."

"And got thrown in jail," Kate added with a smile.

"I guess my favorite character is Captain Moroni. 'I seek not for power, but to pull it down. I seek not for honor of the world, but for the glory of my God and the freedom and welfare of my country!' Now there's a man I could vote for!"

Kate stared at her neighbor. "You've memorized scriptures from the Book of Mormon."

"I haven't memorized anything, I just remember what he said," Miss Eugenia corrected. "But if Moroni were a real man, I would have some hope for the future of this country."

"Captain Moroni was a real person. He's just dead now."

Miss Eugenia shook her head. "I'm willing to say that it's an interesting book and that Joseph Smith must have been a very smart man to write it. But I don't believe it's actually scripture."

"Joseph Smith did not write the Book of Mormon. He translated it."

"So you say."

"You might need to pray about that." Their eyes held for a few seconds, then the baby started to fuss. Kate picked her up and stood. "I'd better get back home."

"I'll be right behind you," Miss Eugenia promised, and Kate left her alone with her memories.

* * *

Kate had looked through Niki's old clothes and found a dress that she could wear for the Parade of Homes. But it was bright red, and Kate wanted something more subdued for the temple. So on Saturday, Mark took Kate shopping in Albany. The malls were crowded and the lines were long, but Kate finally found a pale green suit and shoes to match. She and Mark ate lunch at a sandwich shop in the food court and watched the people go by, then Mark called Miss Eugenia on his cell phone. He offered to bring her something back for lunch, but she said that Elmer had stopped by with foot-long hot dogs.

On Sunday the bishop announced the Historical Society's Open House and encouraged anyone with questions to talk to Kate. People surrounded her after the meeting, asking for directions and other details. They ate dinner with Miss Polly and then accepted her invitation to attend the Christmas Cantata at her church that evening.

Miss Eugenia accompanied them, saying she would protect them from the overzealous Baptists. When they walked through the doors of the big sanctuary, Brother Paul greeted them eagerly.

"Don't get your hopes up, Preacher. They've just come to hear the music," Miss Eugenia told him bluntly. Miss Polly had saved them seats toward the front and was so pleased to have guests. "She gives a whole new meaning to the phrase 'tickled pink,'" Miss Eugenia said unkindly, eyeing Miss Polly's blotched skin as they sat down.

* * *

On Monday morning Miss Eugenia complained that Ellis had the whole place smelling like paint and told him to work outside until after the Open House. The weather was warmer, so he could rake the leaves in the front yard. Once he was out of the way, Miss Eugenia said that every room had to be given a final once-over. She collected cleaning supplies and told Kate to follow her up to the back guest room. Taking the baby, Miss Eugenia settled herself into a comfortable chair, and while Kate cleaned, Miss Eugenia pointed out spots she had missed. Kate was ready to complain about the arrangement until they came to Mark's room, where she found she didn't mind dusting his dresser, folding his clothes, or changing his sheets.

That evening Kate gave Mark a description of her day after Miss Eugenia went upstairs for the night. "She's impossible to please. I'm ready for her to pack her bags and go home."

"That won't change things much. She knows the way back," he teased.

"I found out why she goes up to her room so early every night. She's reading the Book of Mormon and discussing it with Elmer Stoops," Kate reported. "But she's reading it like it's a novel instead of scripture. Maybe I made a mistake by starting her in Mosiah."

"You've got a seventy-three-year-old Methodist reading the Book of Mormon. I don't think anyone would criticize your methods," he smiled.

On Tuesday morning Miss Eugenia said they had to start cleaning downstairs. While Kate was on her hands and knees scrubbing the kitchen, Miss Eugenia announced that she had finished the Book of Moroni. "I started back at the front, and I don't know why you didn't want me to read about Nephi. He's a wonderful young man!" she said reproachfully.

"It's not that I didn't want you to read about Nephi." Kate pushed her hair back in exasperation. "I just didn't want you to get bogged down in the allegory of the olive trees."

"You didn't think I would be able to understand it?" Miss Eugenia challenged. "I'll have you know that I have spent a lifetime deciphering unfathomable doctrine. There is nothing in that book that I can't figure out."

Kate had to laugh. "Then you're better qualified to read Second Nephi than us Mormons."

This seemed to please the old woman. "I'll look at it tonight," she promised, closing her eyes and resting her head against the chair. Kate worked in silence, thinking Miss Eugenia had gone to sleep. She was startled a few minutes later when her neighbor made a comment. "I could accept the Book of Mormon as scripture if Joseph Smith said he just found it, buried in that mountain or something. But I can't believe all that talk about angels and gold plates and inspired translation. And his claim that God appeared to him in a forest is ridiculous."

"It was a grove."

"Same difference."

Kate sat back on her heels and looked at her friend. "Why can't you believe that the plates were preserved by the hand of the Lord and then given to Joseph Smith to translate?"

"Too farfetched." Miss Eugenia dismissed the idea with a wave of her hand.

"Do you believe that Moses parted the Red Sea?" Kate demanded and Miss Eugenia nodded reluctantly. "Do you believe that Jesus turned water into wine, healed the sick, and even raised the dead?" Kate continued to press.

"Of course."

"Then why can't you accept that an angel gave the gold plates to Joseph Smith?"

"I don't know," Miss Eugenia said irritably. "The people in the Bible seemed holier than folks today, I guess. It's more reasonable that God would speak to them." Kate lifted an eyebrow as she waited for her neighbor to explain. "Well, look at the mess we've made of the world," Miss Eugenia pointed out. "I'll bet if the Lord ever looks down here, He shudders in horror."

"Miss Eugenia!"

"It's true. He's given up on us."

"He never will. That's why He appeared to Joseph Smith and then sent an angel to give him the plates. So that we could have the Book of Mormon to give us strength and hope."

"Well, if I ever was to be able to get past all my reservations about Joseph Smith, I still couldn't be a Mormon."

"Why not?"

"If the people of this town got wind that I was even considering it . . ." She shivered at the thought. "All the preachers in Haggerty would wear down my grass coming to talk me out of it. I'd be asked to resign from my clubs and organizations. My friends would shun me, and if no one could bring me back to my senses, they'd put me in the loony bin, or worse."

Kate laughed. "What could be worse than the loony bin?"

Miss Eugenia leaned forward and confided quietly, "The Retirement Home."

"I thought you liked going to the Retirement Home," Kate whispered.

"I don't mind visiting, but I wouldn't want to live there!" she hissed. "If they locked me in a little room away from my flowers and fruit trees and garden, well, they might just as well give me a lethal injection." Miss Eugenia shook her head. "Besides, my body needs several cups of coffee a day to keep rigor mortis from setting in."

By late afternoon Kate finally had the house clean enough for Miss Eugenia. She took Emily into the den and collapsed on the couch. "Kate!" Miss Eugenia called from the kitchen.

"You can kick me out of the Haggerty Historical Society if you want to, but I'm not cleaning one more thing today!" Kate answered mutinously.

Miss Eugenia walked to the door. "I just wanted to know if you would like to have Chicken Elegant for dinner."

Kate scowled. "Since when do you care what I want?"

Miss Eugenia sniffed. "I certainly will be glad when your hormones level off. It's difficult to live with someone so moody." With that remark, she turned and walked stiffly into the kitchen.

CHAPTER 14

When Kate got downstairs on Wednesday morning, Mark was just finishing up a plate of pancakes. "Every muscle in my body aches," she told him grimly as she poured syrup. Mark gave her a sympathetic look, but Miss Eugenia suggested that if a little cleaning made her sore, she might want to consider a regular exercise program to get into shape. Kate stuck her tongue out at the old woman's back.

"I do declare, Kate, there's no need to be childish," Miss Eugenia said as she turned around and caught her. "Now quit dawdling over your food so we can clean up this kitchen. I just realized that we haven't made any peppermint cookies."

"I thought we'd made every kind of cookie there is," Kate said as she stuffed some pancakes in her mouth.

Miss Eugenia ignored her comment. "I've finished the first batch of dough. You need to roll it out and cut them like so." She demonstrated on the other end of the table.

"I'd better get to work," Mark stood and kissed Kate, then headed for the back door.

"Coward," Kate muttered as she watched him leave. She slowly chewed her pancakes and then took her time feeding Emily while Miss Eugenia waited impatiently. "Babies do have to be fed," she told her houseguest.

"Especially when there is work to be done," Miss Eugenia mumbled.

"I have worked myself to death for two days for this Open House . . ." As the words left her lips, Kate gasped.

"What?" Miss Eugenia demanded.

Kate suddenly realized she had forgotten to take Niki's red dress to the cleaners. It had been packed in a box for months, and the wrinkles would be too stubborn for a warm iron. But even though the dress had to be cleaned before the Open House, Kate didn't want to admit her oversight to Miss Eugenia. Glancing at the clock, she calculated that if she got to the cleaners right away, they could probably have the dress ready by Friday afternoon.

"I've got to run a few errands," she told her neighbor abruptly. Miss Eugenia started to object, but Kate shook her head firmly. The old woman muttered under her breath as she went back to mixing cookie dough.

Irritated with herself for being so careless and convinced that it was somehow Miss Eugenia's fault, Kate got the dress and loaded Emily into the van. It only took a few minutes to arrange for the dress to be cleaned, but almost an hour for Kate to escape from the customers at the dry cleaners who wanted to admire the baby, wish her a Merry Christmas, and ask personal questions. By the time she got home, Emily was ready to eat again.

Kate was just starting on the cookies when Miss Eugenia came downstairs. "I've got to go to my house for a while and show Ellis where to hang my outdoor lights," she told Kate. "Emily can come with me." She scooped the baby up out of her swing.

"She's being good," Kate complained, unhappy about the prospect of Emily being out of her sight.

Miss Eugenia walked over and examined one of the candy canes she had just made. "I think you'd better save all your concentration for the cookies," she suggested as she carried the baby through the back door.

* * *

Kate was taking the first batch of cookies out of the oven when the doorbell rang. Wiping at the flour on her hands, she went to answer it. Standing on her front porch was Tyler Thornhill.

"Tyler!" Kate screamed in welcome. She gave him a big hug, trying not to get flour on his suit. "You look wonderful. All tan!"

"That's what a couple of months in Afghanistan will do for you," he said with a wry smile. "Now you're the one who looks great. Who would ever guess that you've just had a baby? And very domestic too." He glanced at her flour-covered hands. "You look like the typical happy homemaker."

"I am happy, Tyler. I really am. Come in," she said, pulling him into the foyer and down the hall toward the kitchen. "I love being a housewife." She rubbed her aching back and remembered the grueling days of deep cleaning. "Well, most of it, anyway. Try a cookie," she insisted.

"Not bad," he murmured as he chewed.

"So, what brings you to Haggerty?" she asked, cutting out more cookie dough.

"I've been reassigned to Orlando. This was sort of on the way, so I decided to stop by." Tyler nibbled his cookie and watched her arrange little pink candy canes on the pan.

"Orlando, huh? You can buy season passes to DisneyWorld!"

He tried to smile. "It's an okay assignment, I guess."

"What's the matter, Tyler?" She put the cookies in the oven and gave him her full attention. "You seem sad."

"You fell in love with Iverson," he said bluntly and she nodded. "If they had let me protect you, maybe . . ." he began, but Kate interrupted him.

"No, Tyler. Under any circumstances, you and I would never be more than friends."

"I guess we'll never know," he replied stubbornly. Dusting a few crumbs off his hands, he looked up at her. "I've had some time between assignments, so I've been trying to find that missing computer chip."

Kate's throat tightened with emotion. "Oh Tyler, you want to clear Tony's name."

"He was my partner." Tyler shrugged. "I know that Tony got that chip out somehow; we just never found it. It took a lot of doing, but I finally convinced Mr. Evans to give me everything on the case. He turned over every tape, every file, every scrap of paper, and I think I've finally found something."

"What?" Kate leaned forward on the table.

"I concentrated on that last conversation you had with Tony before he died. I looked for things that didn't make sense or seemed out of place. The only odd thing was Tony's mention of the insurance policy he bought for you in the Miami airport." Tyler scooted his chair up closer to the table and explained earnestly. "He was under guard after the disappearance of the chip. He had been strictly forbidden to have any contact with the outside world. By filling out that insurance card, he flagrantly disobeyed Everett Morris, but he got away with it and he should have been satisfied. So why did he mention it that night?"

Kate looked down at her hands. "At the time I thought he was making fun of me," Kate admitted. "But later, after he killed Mr. Morris, I decided that he was trying to tell me he loved me and maybe that he was sorry."

"I read your explanation in the transcript, and at first I agreed with you. The minute he saw you walk in, he knew he was going to have to kill Everett Morris. He also knew that when he did, his own life would be over. It seemed reasonable that he would say something to let you know how he felt since he couldn't tell you openly." Tyler touched her hand. "And Tony did love you, Kate. Despite all the things he did as part of his cover. He told me right after he married you that he shouldn't have dragged you into his messed-up life. He knew it was selfish, but he said he just couldn't help himself."

Tears welled in Kate's eyes. "Thank you, Tyler."

"Mr. Evans knew it, too," Tyler said resentfully.

"Knew what?" Kate asked in confusion.

"He knew that Tony loved you very much. That's part of the reason he hid you here in Haggerty. He had serious doubts about Tony's 'death,' and he wanted to smoke him out."

Kate was stunned at this information. "He used me as bait?"

Tyler nodded grimly. "That was one of the reasons I was so opposed to the whole plan."

"There wasn't really a contract on my life?" Kate asked.

"Well, I guess there was, but there were other ways to protect you—the most obvious being to arrest Everett Morris with the considerable evidence they already had against him. But Mr. Evans wanted more."

"The chip?"

Tyler nodded. "That last night you saw Tony, he knew he wouldn't ever be able to explain his actions to you, but killing Morris to save your life was the ultimate expression of affection. Mentioning the policy was not only unnecessary, it was extremely dangerous. Tony was anything but stupid and I kept looking for a reason, an important reason. I went to the Miami airport and found the insurance booth, thinking he might have left the chip there. I had the stall dismantled, checked inch by inch, and there was no chip. So then I contacted the home office to find out what I could about the policy. They said that the policy had never been issued. The card was returned to the home address because it wasn't filled out completely."

Kate bowed her head. "I didn't have the heart to tell him he had made a mistake," she admitted. "Then, when Mr. Evans said the policy wasn't relevant, I didn't tell them either. Why malign Tony any more than they already had?"

"Tony was very thorough, but like you said, not particularly thoughtful about personal details. It was out of character for him to fill out a card applying for insurance. Tony did something odd, and that should have been a flag to everyone." Tyler's eyes shone with excitement. "Let's say that Tony didn't betray the FBI. He's working undercover in Mr. Morris's organization, and he gets an opportunity to steal the chip Mr. Evans wants. He needs to get it out, but before he can, the theft is discovered. He's put under twenty-four-hour surveillance. A few days later, Cosmo has to pick up some people flying in from Costa Rica, and he takes Tony along. When he left the house at Key Biscayne, Tony had to know that this might be his only chance to get the chip out, one way or another." Kate nodded her encouragement and Tyler continued.

"So Tony is walking through the airport with one of Morris's most dangerous professional killers, and he sees the sign advertising a measly $1,000 life insurance policy. But when he walks over to that booth, he isn't thinking about buying insurance. He sees that the first week's premium of a penny is already glued on the card, and he sees it as a means of getting that chip out of his possession and on its way to Mr. Evans." Tyler paused in triumph before asking Kate, "Does it make any sense that Tony would go to the trouble to fill out that card and then fail to list all the required information?"

Kate shook her head.

"What was missing?" Tyler asked.

"His social security number," she whispered.

Tyler's eyes narrowed. "He left it off on purpose."

"But why?" Kate asked in confusion.

"Because he knew that without the social security number, a policy couldn't be issued. The company would probably send it to him at his home address, asking for the necessary information. It was the only way he could mail something to you without sending it directly."

"Oh gosh." Kate leaned back in her seat, trying to remember the day she had opened the mail to find the card. It was in a regular legal-sized envelope, along with a letter asking Tony to fill in the missing number and return it. She had put it in with her bills, intending to ask Tony about it when he got home, but she'd never had the chance. After she'd been notified of Tony's death, she had come across the card again while looking for insurance policies. She had stared at the words, neatly printed in his handwriting, for hours. "How small did you say the chip is?"

"Smaller than a dime."

She closed her eyes, picturing the card in her mind. The name of the company was Life Partners. There were several lines of instructions, then the blanks to be filled out by the applicants. A shiny penny was glued to the bottom, just above the signature line.

Kate opened her eyes and squeezed Tyler's hand. "The penny on the card was upside down," she said, "and I remember thinking it was odd that the company would go to the trouble to use shiny, new pennies, then glue them on crooked."

"That's where the chip is," Tyler said eagerly. "He somehow managed to get it under the penny."

"He used his gum," Kate whispered. "I thought it was just my imagination, but the card smelled vaguely like spearmint."

Tyler threw back his head and laughed. "Tony was too smart for the FBI and organized crime put together! Where is that card now?"

"It should be in the expandable folder with the rest of our bills, policies, and warranties. Mr. Evans shipped our things here, and Mark put it all in a storage unit in Albany."

"I think you need to take me there," Tyler said, standing.

"Do we have to go right now?" Kate asked as she took the cookies from the oven.

Tyler nodded. "That chip has already cost several people their lives, and if I figured out where it is, someone else is eventually bound to. Besides, all the doubts about Tony and his loyalties will be settled when Mr. Evans gets the chip."

Kate put the cookie dough in the refrigerator. "I'll call Mark and have him meet us."

"No!" Tyler objected strongly, then he laughed. "We don't know for sure that the chip is there, and I don't want to look like a fool if I'm wrong. And if I'm right, I want all the credit," Tyler explained with a charming smile. "So, just get the baby and we'll go."

"I'm not taking the baby out in this weather." Kate pointed toward the window where a cold rain had started to fall.

"It's not that bad," Tyler cajoled. "You can wrap her up in a blanket."

Kate shook her head. "I'll see if my neighbor can keep her. Otherwise, you'll have to share the glory with Mark." Tyler was not pleased. "I'll get my coat and be right back," she promised.

Kate walked up the stairs and into the master bedroom. She pulled her raincoat down from its hanger and pushed an arm into it. As she turned around, she was startled to see Tyler standing just inside the doorway.

"I said I'd be right back," she told him, suddenly a little uncomfortable.

"Nice house." He looked around the room, offering no excuse for his bad manners.

Kate brushed past him and walked down to Mark's office. As she opened the desk drawer to get the key for the storage unit, she saw a pencil and a flash of memory staggered her. The insurance card had been neatly filled out in pencil. Rubbing the key, she remembered that there had been a random pencil mark on the policy application. She had thought it was accidental, but Tyler had said that everything about the card was significant. The card was Tony's messenger, and she couldn't afford to ignore anything.

She concentrated, trying to recall exactly where the pencil mark had been. The image of the card came clearly to her mind. The mark was faint, but precise, beginning and ending under only one word. The word Tony had underlined was "partner."

"Did you find it?" Tyler asked impatiently from the doorway.

Kate tried to keep her voice steady. "It's right here." She held up the key with an orange tag attached. Without giving him a chance to object, she picked up the phone and pushed "2" on her speed dial. "I'll let my neighbor know we'll be gone for a little while," she said, turning to face Tyler so he wouldn't be suspicious.

"Heeello!" Miss Eugenia hollered into the phone.

"A friend of mine from Chicago has dropped by, and he needs something out of my storage unit," Kate explained quickly. "Can Emily stay with you for a little longer?"

There was a brief pause on the other end of the phone. "I thought you were baking cookies," Miss Eugenia said finally.

"I was, but this is a very good friend, so I'm going to leave my cookies for a while. We won't be gone long."

"Okay," Miss Eugenia answered warily.

"And would you call Mark and ask him to pick up my dress from the cleaners before they close?" Tyler was getting restless, so she said good-bye and hung up the phone.

"Let's go," he said, pointing toward the front of the house where his car was parked. Kate climbed in and fastened her seat belt. Her hands were trembling and she tried to still them. He asked a sudden question and startled a little scream from her.

"Oh, Kate," Tyler said regretfully. "You're not a very good actress. I was hoping to get the chip and disappear, but now I'll have to take you with me."

"What do you mean?"

"I can feel your fear, Kate."

"I can't leave my baby!" she cried.

"I tried to get you to bring her with us. You insisted that she stay with the neighbor."

"Please, Tyler. I'll show you where the chip is, and then you can go. I won't tell anyone until you've had a chance to get away."

He shook his head sadly. "You haven't dealt with bad guys much, have you, Kate?"

Tears started to fall down her cheeks as she prayed that Mark would understand her message. "Where will you take me?" she asked.

"Miami, I guess."

The car was quiet except for the sobs that Kate could not control. "Oh, Tyler. You were the one working for the criminals?"

Tyler sighed. "I never had any choice. I'm part of the family and not just in the business sense. Everett Morris was a third cousin on my mother's side," he said as he pulled onto the highway headed toward Albany.

"He was your cousin?" The horror was obvious in her voice.

"It was a shock to me, too, I can assure you. He changed his name years ago and never had any open contact with my family. My dad runs a very successful car dealership in Tallahassee. Too successful, I guess you could say. We had everything. Nice house, cars, clothes, boats, and a cabin on the beach. I just thought my dad sold a lot of cars. It never occurred to me that he was laundering money for the mob.

"Both my brothers joined the business after college, but I was the idealist of the family. Instead of selling cars, I wanted to work for the FBI and fight crime. When I graduated from law school, my cousin Everett came to see me. He explained that the clothes I had on, the food I ate, and the education I had just received were all paid for by the same crime I was hoping to fight. He said that he had always intended for me to follow in my father's footsteps, but after some consideration had decided that having me in the FBI was a good idea. He said I'd be his ace in the hole, just in case.

"He even pulled some strings to help me get hired. I worked in New York for a while, then was transferred to Chicago and teamed up with Tony. When Mr. Evans told Tony that he was going to be working on a big operation, they gave me some cases I could handle without a partner and shut me out. Mr. Evans is paranoid about secrecy so I had no idea Tony was going in deep with my own family until Everett told me about it. He said Tony had approached him about joining the organization, and I told him no way, something stinks. But Tony was very convincing, and after a while, I started to wonder. Everett decided to play along and see what happened."

"Before long Tony leaked Everett some information that messed up a couple of big drug busts. I didn't know what to think, but regardless of whether Tony was trying to destroy my family or join it, there was a good chance he was going to end up dead . . ."

As they entered Albany, Tyler looked at the address on the storage tag and entered it into the laptop computer propped between them on the seat. The instructions popped up, and a few minutes later they were pulling up in front of Mike's Mini-Storage.

"And then Tony stole that stupid chip. We all knew he did it, but Everett had a soft spot for Tony. He preferred to believe his own grandson was guilty rather than Tony. So he put the three people who had access under house arrest. Everett had his people search every-where for that chip but couldn't find a trace of it." Tyler shook his head. "It's taken me months to track it down, and all the time it was right under our noses."

He pulled a gun halfway out of his coat pocket to show it to Kate. "You go first," he instructed as he opened his door.

They stepped out into the rain and walked along the gravel road until they came to the unit with a number that corresponded to the tag. Kate was soaked to the skin by the time they stooped under the metal door. The inside of the unit smelled musty and there was little light from the overcast skies. The old, familiar furniture was pushed against one wall. Tyler cursed when he saw all the identical boxes stacked neatly on the other side of the storage unit.

"Pick a box and start looking," he said as he walked over to the boxes and ripped the packing tape off the first carton. "I don't guess I need to tell you that your life depends on your cooperation."

Kate shook her head and started opening another box. After a few unsuccessful minutes, Tyler looked up. "How did you know, Kate? Did I give myself away?"

Kate shook her head as she dug slowly through a box of magazines. "Tony told me."

Tyler's face registered his shock. "Tony?"

"On the insurance card. He underlined one word—'partner.'"

Tyler sighed. "Everett always told me I'd never be half as good as Tony was." He glanced up at Kate. "It didn't hurt my feelings. Tony was the best."

"Tony's dead," Kate reminded him harshly.

"Yes, well, sometimes even geniuses have weaknesses, and you were Tony's."

Kate pulled up the flap on a box and knew immediately that she had found the one they were looking for. The expandable folder wasn't on top, but she recognized other things from their desk and felt sure the file was underneath. Once Tyler had the chip, Tony's reputation and her life were both in great danger, so Kate stalled. She knew that she had been searching the same box for too long when Tyler looked up.

"Find something, Kate?" he asked as her fingers touched the accordion side of the brown file.

"I . . ." Kate began just as car wheels screeched outside. Gravel hit the metal door of the unit, and Tyler sighed.

"Oh, Kate. Why did you have to complicate things?" he asked as Mark ducked under the door. The light was behind him, making him a perfect target. "Is that the kind of approach they taught you at Quantico, Iverson?" Tyler asked. "No wonder you're still a pencil pusher."

Mark ignored Tyler's insult. "Kate, are you okay?" His eyes searched for her in the dim light.

"I'm fine," she reassured him.

"I was hoping to get out of here without ever having to lay eyes on you again, Iverson. Just how did you find us?" Tyler asked casually.

"Our neighbor called and said that Kate was supposed to be baking cookies, but she had stopped suddenly to get something out of storage for a good friend from Chicago. She also said that Kate wanted me to pick up a dress at the dry cleaners before they closed." Mark's empty hands were in plain sight, but Kate could see the bulge of his gun under his left arm. Somehow she had to even the odds.

"Kate never leaves Emily," Mark continued. "And she has never asked me to pick up the dry cleaning. In Haggerty everything closes early on Wednesday, so it wasn't just a small favor. She knew I'd have to leave work early in order to do it." Mark was providing a lot of details, and Kate wondered if he was trying to buy some time. "All of these odd things happening at once made me suspicious." Mark inched a little farther into the rental space.

"So I dropped everything and drove like a maniac to Haggerty. I got to the dry cleaners just as the owner was locking up. He said he couldn't imagine why Kate would ask me to pick up that dress today since she had just dropped it off this morning and knew it wouldn't be ready until Friday. By then, I was sure something was wrong so I asked to see the dress. Can you guess what color it was, Thornhill?"

Tyler smiled sadly. "I guess it must have been red."

"Extreme danger," Mark agreed, nodding.

"She's smarter than I thought," Tyler conceded. "But really, she's only made things worse because now I'm going to have to kill you. Kate, of course, will be coming with me as a shield and a hostage. I think you've found the file, Kate. Get out the card and hand it to me."

Kate glanced at Mark, and he nodded without taking his eyes off Tyler. Kate looked inside the folder at the card with the upside-down penny that smelled like spearmint. As she touched it, she knew she couldn't just give it to him. Tony had died for this scrap of paper, and she couldn't let that be for nothing. As her mind raced, she saw a paperweight in the box beside the file. Slowly she pulled the card out with her left hand while her right hand closed around the heavy glass.

"Slide it over here," Tyler instructed, watching Mark.

Instead, Kate pulled out the paperweight and flung it at Tyler. It landed wide right and short—but it distracted him long enough for Mark to pull his gun. Now it was a standoff.

"That was stupid, Kate!" Tyler hissed. "You bring me that card before I start shooting."

"Don't move, Kate," Mark said calmly.

The two men studied each other, their faces glistening with rain and sweat. "You can't win here, Iverson," Tyler threatened. "You might as well give me the chip, and at least Kate will live."

Mark remained silent, and Tyler's face showed his panic. "Don't think I'll lose my nerve," he shouted. "My whole family will go to jail if that chip gets into the wrong hands. I have no choice."

Mark still refused to answer. "And don't count on my feelings for Kate," Tyler yelled, sounding almost hysterical. "Drop the gun, Iverson!"

Kate watched both men in the fading light. All Mark needed was a split second to gain the advantage, and his silence was getting to Tyler.

"Don't make me kill you!" Tyler called to Mark. Kate saw the gun tremble slightly in Tyler's hand, and she realized he was afraid.

She took a step toward him, gaining a portion of his attention. "You're not a bad man, Tyler," she said quietly. "You're really as much a victim in this as I am."

"Be quiet, Kate. You don't know what you're talking about."

"I know that you care about me and that you loved Tony. You can't help who your family is." Tyler shook his head as if to clear it. "You're not a killer." A few tears slipped out of Tyler's eyes, adding to the moisture already on his cheeks. "Enough people have died. Put down your gun, and we'll go away together. No one will ever find us."

Tyler laughed pitifully. "Iverson won't let me take you," he snorted.

"Yes he will." Kate took another step. "I can convince him."

Mark didn't respond. Tyler's shoulders twitched and his eyes cut toward her nervously. "Please, Kate. Don't . . ." His hand relaxed, lowering the gun slightly, and Mark charged forward.

"Drop the gun, Thornhill!" Mark ordered from only a few feet away. Tyler shook his head and the sound of a gunshot reverberated through the cramped space. Kate screamed, her eyes closing automatically. When she forced them back open, she saw the men, still in the same position as before, now crouched with guns pointed at each other. She didn't know who had fired until she saw Tyler's finger move again, his gun hand recoiling slightly as a bullet ricocheted off the metal door of the storage unit.

"Come on, Iverson," Tyler said desperately. "End this."

Kate's eyes swung back to Mark. He shook his head sadly. "I can't."

"It's a clear case of self-defense!" Tyler screamed. "Kate's life is in danger!"

Mark just shook his head again. "Put your gun on the ground, and kick it to me. It's over."

A harsh laugh burst from Tyler's lips. "I should have known a pencil pusher like you wouldn't have the guts." Slowly Tyler stood straight, pointing the nose of the gun toward his own head.

"Tyler!" Kate and Mark both screamed in unison, rushing toward him.

A triumphant smile spread across Tyler's face as Mark's fingers wrapped around the gun. "Thanks for the fingerprints," he whispered as his gun went off. Kate watched Tyler and Mark slump to the floor, vaguely aware of the blood and gore that now stained the couch from her apartment in Chicago. Her mouth opened, and she started screaming uncontrollably. Her mind registered that Mark was still moving just before it shut down completely and darkness engulfed her.

* * *

When she opened her eyes, she was in the back seat of a police car. The door was ajar and she could see Albany City policemen milling around in the cold rain. A coroner's van was backed up to the storage unit. Bright artificial light shone from inside. Kate felt nauseous and laid her head back down.

A few minutes later Mark leaned into the car. Rain was dripping off his hair onto the unfamiliar raincoat that covered his shoulders. She smiled at him, so grateful that he was alive and unhurt.

"Do you feel up to giving the police a statement?" he asked gently. Kate nodded and pushed herself into a sitting position. Blinking back dizziness, she was careful not to look toward the storage unit or the black van that was parked in front of it.

"I've explained to the policemen that what happened here is related to an ongoing FBI investigation. Therefore, the details are considered classified information," Mark said, sounding very much like a man with a law degree. "All you need to tell them is how Tyler died."

His eyes held hers for a few seconds before a soaking wet Albany policeman climbed into the front seat and twisted around to face her. He looked miserable as he flipped open a notepad and pulled a pen from his uniform pocket.

"I'm ready when you are." The officer waited for her to begin.

"Tyler said he was going to kill Mark. He didn't really want to," Kate appealed to the policeman. The man stared at her, unmoved. "But he felt he had no choice." Kate sighed, realizing that Tyler wasn't likely to get sympathy from anyone. "I threw a paperweight at Tyler to distract him so that Mark could get out his gun. They stood forever, pointing guns at each other. I was begging Tyler not to kill Mark, but he started shooting anyway. He missed, and Mark ran toward him. They struggled," Kate looked up. "Then Tyler's gun went off. It all happened so fast. They both fell, and I didn't know if Mark was hurt . . ."

"How do you know that it was Agent Thornhill's gun that they were struggling over?" the policeman asked, looking up from his notes.

"I saw Mark's revolver fall to the ground when he rushed Tyler," Kate said, and the policeman made some more notes on the damp paper. Mark's cell phone rang, and he stepped out of the car to answer it.

"I guess that's all then," the officer said briskly, closing his pad. "A simple case of self-defense." Kate nodded, grateful that the man had accepted her explanation without mentioning suicide. The policeman smiled. "Well, maybe not simple. We have an occasional shootout around here, but it's not usually FBI agents trying to kill each other."

Mark ducked back into the car and handed the cell phone to the policeman. The man said yes several times, then gave the phone back to Mark. As he replaced it in his pocket, Mark spoke to the officer. "So you'll have your superior call Mr. Evans as soon as you get back to the station?" The man nodded. "And until then, you and your men won't discuss the details of what you've seen here with anyone." The man nodded again and turned to Kate.

"Your statement will be typed up, and we'll ask you to come in and sign it sometime next week." He moved toward the door. "I'm sorry for your trouble, ma'am." He tipped his hat and disappeared into the gray afternoon.

"Let's get you home," Mark said tenderly, reaching for her hand. Once he had her settled in his agency car, Kate closed her eyes. She needed to feed Emily, and her head was pounding. Mark negotiated through the light traffic and turned onto Highway 11 toward Haggerty. When he reached the speed limit, he turned to Kate. "Tell me what happened."

Kate opened her eyes and took a deep breath. "I was making peppermint cookies. Miss Eugenia had taken Emily because she said I needed to concentrate. The doorbell rang and there was Tyler, standing on the front porch." Kate cleared her throat and forced herself to continue. "I was glad to see him."

Mark nodded. "You had no reason to be suspicious of him."

"He told me he was on his way to a new assignment in Orlando. He had been trying to find the missing computer chip and clear Tony's name. Mr. Evans gave him all the paperwork on the case, and he thought that the insurance policy Tony had applied for in the Miami Airport was significant. He had contacted the company and found out that no policy was ever issued because the card wasn't filled out completely."

Mark looked over sharply. "The policy was never issued?" he repeated.

"No, they returned the card to me."

"So you had it all along?"

"Well, I didn't exactly have it. The card was in a file with other important papers in our apartment."

"Mr. Evans said they searched your apartment minutely. They couldn't have missed that card!"

"It was just a scrap of paper stuck in between insurance policies and warranties."

Mark's lips compressed into a tense, angry line. "You didn't tell Mr. Evans that the card wasn't filled out completely."

Kate winced at this. "They said the policy was irrelevant."

"They wouldn't have thought so if they had known that the card was returned to you."

Tears welled in Kate's eyes, but she blinked them back. "It didn't seem important, and I thought it would make Tony look bad. They were already saying such awful things about him . . ."

"It's okay, Kate. You didn't miss any more than a team of experienced FBI agents," he comforted her gently. "So Tyler told you the chip was on the card?"

"He knew the card was somehow the key to finding the chip. He went to the airport in Miami and saw that the cards had a penny glued on the bottom . . ." Mark slapped the steering wheel with the heel of his hand, startling her. "The penny was upside down on the card Tony filled out, and it smelled like spearmint." Mark lifted an eyebrow and Kate added softly, "It was Tony's favorite flavor of gum."

"He stuck the chip under the penny with his gum?" Mark asked.

"I think so." Kate extended the damp, crumpled card toward him.

Mark pulled off the road near the city limits sign and took the insurance card from her hand. Kate watched as Mark gently removed the penny and exposed the computer chip, embedded in hardened chewing gum.

"I'd like to have the card back," Kate said, tears spilling down her cheeks. "After all this is over."

Mark faced her with tortured eyes. "If they had sent some thorough pencil pushers in to search your apartment instead of a bunch of he-men, all of this could have been avoided. Emily wouldn't have been kidnapped, and Agent Roper, Agent Thomas, and even Tony might still be alive."

Kate shook her head. "There's no point in trying to assign blame. We all have to share it." Mark put the card, along with the penny and the computer chip, into his shirt pocket. He checked the traffic and pulled back onto the road.

"Tyler said that Tony really did love me," she told Mark tremulously as they drove. "He also said that Mr. Evans used me like bait to find out if Tony was still alive." She waited for Mark to deny the charge, but he didn't.

"I never really doubted that Tony loved you," he answered instead. "What I can't understand is how he was able to leave you." He stopped the van in their driveway and reached up to touch her cheek.

Miss Eugenia stepped off the front porch into the rain, her arms flailing. "Are you okay? Is everything all right?" she demanded as Kate opened her door.

"We're fine," Kate answered.

"Thanks to you," Mark added with a weary smile.

Miss Eugenia grabbed Kate's arm. "We'll all catch our death of cold if we stand around out here in the rain chitchatting," she scolded, as if they had been the ones to meet her on the driveway. "For goodness sake, let's go inside!"

Kate and Mark left their wet shoes and coats by the back door, then walked into the kitchen. Winston was sitting at the kitchen table, but stood abruptly as they entered. "Miss Eugenia said you were in some kind of trouble, but I didn't really think . . ." He was clearly startled by their bedraggled condition.

"You didn't really think. That is the truth. Now sit down and finish your coffee while they change clothes." Miss Eugenia walked to the stairs with Kate and Mark. "I called Winston to come over and protect the baby in case there was trouble. He drove up expecting to find armed gunmen on the roof. When I tried to explain that his presence was just a precaution, he said I was a nervous old woman wasting his valuable time," she hissed quietly.

"You did the right thing," Mark assured her.

Miss Eugenia eyed the bloodstains on his neck and collar. "You two get cleaned up," she instructed, turning back to the kitchen. "Emily is hungry," she added for Kate's benefit.

Kate went into the master bathroom and stripped out of her wet clothes with trembling hands. A hot shower finally stopped her shivering. When she got downstairs, Mark was already sitting at the table. His damp hair was brushed back from his face, and she had the strongest urge to go over and clutch him to her chest. Her hand actually reached toward him, but Miss Eugenia brought her back to reality. "The baby just dozed off. Sit down and eat this soup. Then you can feed her."

Kate accepted the steaming bowl and gratefully spooned some into her mouth. "This is wonderful," she said in between bites.

"I called Miss Polly and told her you'd been caught out in the rain," Miss Eugenia explained. "She sent this chicken soup to ward off a cold."

She refilled Mark's bowl and asked Winston if he'd had enough. When Mark pushed back from the table, Miss Eugenia sat down. "Okay, so tell us what happened."

Kate continued to eat while Mark related every gruesome detail, completely ignoring rules about classified information and ongoing FBI investigations.

"So, was the chip there?" Miss Eugenia asked when Mark reached the end of the story.

"Oh yes, it's there." The men exchanged a long glance and Kate's eyes narrowed.

"What now?" she asked.

Mark cleared his throat. "I'll have to take it to Atlanta tonight."

"Tonight?" Kate felt tears threatening again.

"I'm meeting Mr. Evans at the Bureau Office in Atlanta to review the chip. We don't really know how much data it contains or how valuable the information is."

"It was important enough for Tony to die for," Kate said soberly.

"And if anyone realizes that we have it . . ."

"They'll kill us, too," Kate realized and the shivering returned.

Mark nodded grimly. "I've asked Winston to drive me to the airport in his patrol car, and then I'll take the 7:00 flight to Atlanta."

"That's in two hours," Kate said, looking at the clock and then at his overnight bag sitting by the back door.

"I'll meet you at the temple tomorrow night at six," he promised. "I do have one little piece of good news." Kate's lips trembled as she waited. "Miracle is on her way from Chicago. She should be here in a few hours." Kate mustered half a smile.

"So, after you meet with this Mr. Evans man and give him that darn computer chip, all of this shooting and kidnapping will finally be over?" Miss Eugenia demanded.

"I hope so . . ." Mark began.

"I hope so, too, because I'm tired of having to worry about people trying to kill you." She shook her head as if they had brought it all on themselves. "And if I ever meet Mr. Evans, I might just give him a piece of my mind. The very idea of having you leave Kate when she's in danger."

"Mr. Evans is sending Miracle to protect Kate and Emily. This chip is my responsibility, and I have to take it in. Believe me, no one wants this case closed any more than I do," Mark assured her as he stood. "If you two will excuse us for a minute?"

He didn't wait for a response, but pulled Kate from her chair and into the living room. When they were alone, he drew her into his arms. "You were incredible today," he whispered. "So smart and brave, and I love you so much." He pressed his cheek against her hair.

"I love you, too." Kate struggled in vain to control the emotion in her voice. "When I left the house with Tyler, I thought I would never see you again." She held him tightly.

"It's almost over now," Mark murmured close to her ear. "And soon we'll be married forever."

"Keep your fingers crossed on that. Things haven't been going well for me lately," she said woefully, and Mark laughed and kissed her hard. Then he stepped back and led her into the kitchen. Winston was standing by the back door wearing his coat and worrying the brim of his police hat.

Mark picked up the sleeping baby, then covered her little face with kisses. She woke up with a wail, and he handed her to Kate. "See you tomorrow," he said.

"I'll take good care of him, Miss Kate," Winston promised as they turned to leave. If she hadn't been so upset, Kate would have been pleased that he addressed her as he would any Haggerty lady.

* * *

Kate couldn't bear to put Emily to bed although Miss Eugenia promised that holding the baby as she slept would spoil her and probably make her little muscles ache. So they all settled in the den and tried to watch television until Miracle arrived at 9:30. She grinned broadly as she walked through the door.

"Where's my baby?" she asked before greeting anyone else. When she spied Emily on Kate's lap, she leaned down and picked her up.

"This can't be my girl! She's twice as big as my little Emily!" Miracle exclaimed.

"Of course that's her. What do you think? We traded Emily in for another baby?" Miss Eugenia asked irritably.

"Sounds like somebody got up on the wrong side of the bed." Miracle winked at Kate.

"Somebody is tired of all this cops and robbers stuff. It's almost Christmas, and we have a wedding and an open house to get through. I wish we could just concentrate on that without people waving guns in our faces."

"Somebody waved a gun in your face?" Miracle was instantly serious.

"Not yet!" Miss Eugenia cried in exasperation. She pushed herself to her feet. "I'm going to bed. Tomorrow's going to be a big day."

After Miss Eugenia had hobbled up the stairs, Miracle sat in the recliner and smiled at Kate. "So, Agent Singleton is not only cleared of any wrongdoing, he's a hero."

Kate smiled back. "I guess that is the one bright spot in all this."

"There are several bright spots. You and Mark are about to get married, you've got a real nice house, you've got me and your crabby neighbor as lifelong friends, and if you want a career as a Special Agent for the FBI, I'll bet you could get a job."

Kate laughed. "That's the last thing I want."

Miracle stood and handed the baby back to Kate. "Well, Miss Eugenia is right about one thing. Tomorrow is going to be a very big day. Tell me where you want me to sleep, and go on to bed."

"Miss Eugenia is in the yellow room. Mark is in the hall across from me. You can take the pink room. Miss Eugenia made me clean all the rooms so thoroughly you could eat off the floor."

Miracle laughed. "Well, if you need anything, just holler."

"You can count on that," Kate promised grimly as they climbed upstairs.

CHAPTER 15

Everyone got up early on Thursday morning and ate a bowl of cereal for breakfast. Miracle loaded the suitcases into the van while Kate dressed Emily. Then Miss Eugenia rushed them off before eight.

"If you'll leave, I can start getting this house ready for tomorrow night," the old woman grumbled as Kate climbed into the backseat beside Emily. Miracle helped pass the time during the long drive by relating stories from her childhood. At some point, Kate dozed off and woke up as they entered the Atlanta traffic.

They had just settled into the hotel when Kate's family arrived at one o'clock. After dropping off their luggage in the suite across the hall, the Taylors all piled into Kate's room for a visit. Jeanine took charge of the baby.

"So, where's Mark?" Kate's mother asked as she teased a smile out of little Emily.

"He had some FBI business to take care of," Kate told them reluctantly. Everyone looked up in surprise. "You'll get to meet him at the temple tonight," she promised.

Kacie got a king-sized bag of peanut M&M's out of the snack cabinet and plopped down on the bed beside Kate. She then proceeded to bring her sister up to speed on romance in the seventh grade, including the fact that she liked a boy named Sean, but he had given no indication that he shared her feelings.

"Well, he'd be crazy not to like you," Kate said firmly.

"That's what I think, too," Kacie concurred.

"How are things with Travis?" Kate asked Kelsey, who was standing by the windows looking out at the Atlanta skyline.

Kacie made a face and said she was going back to their room to watch television. Kelsey waited until she had left before replying. "I think he's going to ask me to marry him."

"Congratulations!" Kate gave her sister a hug.

Emily started to fuss, so Kate settled in a chair to feed her. Kelsey said she thought she'd call Travis, and Jeanine went over to check on Kacie. Kendall was sitting cross-legged on the bed, watching *Friends*. When they were alone, she looked up at Kate and rolled her eyes.

"Don't you like Travis either?" Kate asked.

Kendall shrugged. "He's okay. Kind of a know-it-all and Kelsey acts dumb around him, but I guess that's what love does to you," she said with teenage wisdom.

"How about you. Any boyfriends?"

"No time for that. I have to make good grades so I can get a college scholarship."

Kate was impressed. "Where do you want to go?"

"Far away," Kendall admitted before she thought. Kate laughed, and Kendall blushed deeply. "It's not that I don't love Mom or anything. It's just . . ."

"I understand completely," Kate assured her.

The phone rang and Kate picked the receiver up, pleased to hear Mark's voice, asking if they had arrived safely. After a brief conversation, he said he had to go but would see her soon. Kate put the baby down in the middle of her bed and asked Kendall to watch her while she took a shower.

"Are you nervous?" Kendall asked as Kate looked through her suitcase.

Kate shook her head. "Not really. I just want it all to be over. I want to settle down to everyday life as Mark's wife and Emily's mother."

"Is he great? Mark, I mean."

"Of course!" Kate confirmed. "I think he's wonderful. Now you might think he's boring and a nerd just like Travis."

"What did you say about Travis?" Kelsey demanded suspiciously as she came through the door.

"I said that nobody has to love him but you. I hope you all like Mark, but I'm the only one who is marrying him."

After a shower, Kate spent an hour in the bathroom working on her hair and makeup. When she was completely dressed, Kate studied herself in the mirror. The woman who stared back was not plain old Kate nor glamorous Niki, but someone in between. Smiling, Kate squared her shoulders and walked out to face her family.

* * *

They left for the temple with Miracle at the wheel of the van. When they arrived, Mark was standing by the front door. Kate had intended to greet him calmly, but she couldn't resist giving him a good solid kiss, which thoroughly shocked an elderly couple walking past.

Mark and Kate escorted Miracle and the girls down to the Annex, where one of his sisters-in-law was already sitting with four little boys and a baby girl. Mark made quick introductions, then Miracle offered to keep the Iverson children during the temple session. The mother seemed reluctant, but when Mark reminded her that Miracle was an armed FBI agent, the woman finally agreed, apparently assured that the children would be more than safe. Then Mark and Kate walked to the temple lobby, where Mark's parents were waiting.

The Iversons were standing as a group just past the reception desk. Sister Iverson was tall and thin with short, dark hair. Her brown eyes were guarded and her expression strained. Her husband stood quietly behind her, but he smiled when they were introduced. The brothers and their wives were a jumble of gloomy faces.

Jeanine rushed up and took charge of Kate for the next couple of hours. The endowment session required all of Kate's concentration, and she only caught glimpses of Mark across the room, surrounded by his brothers. Finally they were reunited at the veil and walked to the celestial room together.

Holding her closely, Mark whispered, "By this time tomorrow, you'll be my wife."

Kate sighed happily, then saw her mother surreptitiously blotting her eyes with a lace handkerchief. "I think she's missing my dad." Kate nodded toward the corner where Jeanine was standing.

"Or maybe she can feel his presence." Mark brought her fingers to his lips as Kate blinked back tears of her own.

After changing clothes, they all met in front of the temple, and Brother Iverson suggested that they go out to eat at a nearby restaurant.

"I can't, Dad," Mark declined. "I have to get back to the Bureau Office."

"Why?" Kate stared at him in disbelief.

"This is a very big case, you know that, Kate." His voice was pleading. "The director himself is flying in tomorrow, and we need to harvest all the information and have it decoded before he gets here. The more people involved, the greater is the risk of leaks, so Mr. Evans doesn't want to involve too many people. That means . . ."

"That means he's making you work even though he knows we're getting married and that your family has driven all the way from Texas to see you," Kate said. Then she saw the exhaustion in his eyes and relented. "I know you're just trying to do your job." Kate touched his face gently. "He will let you come to the wedding, won't he?"

"He's seen you angry before. I don't think he'll risk it again," Mark teased lightly.

"Not if he's smart." Kate was only half joking.

He kissed her quickly, then walked with his parents to the assortment of vans they had traveled in. Kate watched as Brother Iverson put his arm around Mark in a brief hug. The other men joined them and stood close together in earnest conversation.

Kendall came up beside Kate. "I do think Mark is cute," she said. "For an old guy." Kate had to smile.

Kacie walked over and looked toward the group of Iversons. "They look like the Baldwin brothers," she contributed. Kate didn't see any similarity between Mark's brothers and the famous actors, but the Iverson men did share a strong family resemblance. The second brother, Jeff, glanced up at that moment and gave Kate an annoyed look over Mark's shoulder. "They are a little crabby, though," Kacie added.

Back in their rooms, they ordered pizza and bought canned drinks from the hotel vending machines. "Why don't we stay up all night watching old movies?" Kacie suggested as she jammed her mouth full of pizza. "Like a spend-the-night party?"

"Kate's got a big day tomorrow!" Jeanine protested. "She needs her sleep!"

"I'll sleep when you've gone back to Utah. I want to enjoy every minute of your visit," Kate answered firmly. She put Emily into the portable crib supplied by the hotel and called Miracle. "Put on your pajamas, and get over here. We're having a slumber party, and the first one to close her eyes gets toothpaste smeared all over her face."

By two o'clock the next morning, everyone except Miracle and Kate had fallen asleep in various locations. "Looks like those extra hotel rooms were a waste of money," Miracle commented as she surveyed the area.

"How come you're still awake?" Kate asked as she stood and stretched.

"My FBI training allows me to function without sleep for indefinite periods of time," Miracle claimed, and Kate laughed. "But since you're an undisciplined civilian, you need to find an empty bed somewhere and get some rest."

Kate shook her head. "It will be time to feed Emily in about an hour and I'm so nervous, I don't think I could sleep anyway."

"Not having second thoughts, are you?" Miracle raised an eyebrow.

"Oh no. Not about marrying Mark. I know that's what I want," Kate assured her. "But his family has been so unfriendly, and it's hard to forget about Tony and Tyler and Miami and—"

"First, you're marrying Mark, not his family, and second, you may never forget the past, but you've got to put it away for a while. Later on, you'll have time to take out your memories and examine them," Miracle advised. She took the last piece of greasy pizza from the box and held it up. "You want this?"

Kate assured her that she didn't. Miracle shrugged and started to nibble on the chewy crust. "Never have found anybody I wanted to spend my whole life with," she mused quietly. "In spite of everything that's happened to you, I'd say you're a mighty lucky girl, and you shouldn't let anything spoil your wedding day."

Kate reached over to touch her hand. "You're a good friend."

"I know that's right!" the other woman agreed with a grin. "Now sit there in that chair and try to sleep for an hour or two. I'll keep an eye on our girl."

* * *

When Kate woke at six, she didn't have time to think about anything but getting her clothes on. She and her family arrived at the temple without a minute to spare. The ever-grim Iversons were waiting in the balmy morning air in front when Kate and her family walked up. Mark was not with them.

"Maybe he's come to his senses," Kate said in a poor attempt at humor. Sister Iverson gave her a dark look, and Jeanine suggested that they go on in.

As Miracle walked the Taylor sisters and the Iverson children to the Annex, Kate's mother said, "It will take you longer to get ready anyway, so it's a good thing you'll have a head start."

With her mother's help, Kate put on the simple wedding gown she had rented. When she was dressed, Jeanine led her before a full-length mirror. Kate glanced at herself, then met her mother's gaze. "Mom, I want you to go see if Mark is here, because if he really didn't show up, there's no way I'm going out there to face his parents."

Her mother nodded and slipped out the door. She was back in less than a minute with a big smile on her face. "He's here?" Kate breathed.

"All dressed and waiting for you."

Once they were kneeling at the altar, Kate clasped Mark's hand tightly, as if a firm grip could keep her from losing him as she had lost her father and Tony. Mark smiled and returned a steady pressure with his hand. She listened as the temple president spoke of love and marriage and eternity. By the time he pronounced them husband and wife, Kate had no feeling left in her fingers, but Mark was hers forever.

After accepting congratulations, they moved toward the door of the sealing room. "I'll meet you by the recommend desk," Mark whispered as they separated.

Kate changed back into her suit and hurried out to the lobby where Mark was waiting. Together they walked outside where both families had gathered. Kate took Emily from Kelsey and held her close. Several cameras flashed at once.

"So, are you really married?" Kacie breathed.

"I'm really married," Kate confirmed.

"I wish I could have seen you in your dress," Kendall said regretfully.

"We'll have another bride in the family soon. She'll have a big wedding with the dress and flowers and a reception," Kate predicted and Kelsey blushed.

Since an agent had dropped Mark off at the temple, he planned to ride home with Kate and her family. After confirming that there would be room for him in the van, he went back to his parents to tell them about a rest area on the edge of Atlanta, where they could all meet after checking out of their various hotels. In the meantime, the Iverson brothers and their wives were standing together in a cluster not more than a few feet from Kate. While she waited for Mark, she heard his brother, Jeff, complaining about how difficult it had been to get all his children's Christmas presents into the van without them seeing everything.

A woman's voice agreed that it had been a bad time of year to travel. "I was supposed to sing a solo in the ward Christmas program on Sunday, but I had to call and cancel at the last minute," she said regretfully.

Both became aware of Kate's presence at the same moment, and although she was tempted to walk away, she squared her shoulders instead.

"I guess it was inconsiderate of us to get married right before Christmas," she said evenly. "I hope you will accept my apology for the inconvenience." They continued to stare and she tried to continue, "We'll do our best to make the holidays enjoyable for you . . ." In the face of their hostility, she floundered and let her voice trail away.

The brothers exchanged a look as Mark walked up and spoke to

Kate. "Is something wrong?" he asked, noting the moisture in her eyes.

Kate gave him her best imitation of a smile. "I'm just happy," she said.

They started toward the van where Kate's family and Miracle were waiting. As she leaned over to climb into the van, Kate glimpsed a small, neatly dressed man standing beside a dark blue sedan parked right outside the temple gates. Her heart sank as she stepped forward to get a closer look. Mark's eyes followed her gaze, and he muttered under his breath.

"Is he ever going to leave us alone?" Kate whimpered.

"Go ahead and get in." Mark pointed toward the middle seat beside Emily. Jeanine sat in front, and Miracle settled behind the wheel. Mark perched on the edge of Kate's seat as they rolled slowly down the hill and parked beside the blue car. Then Mark got out and faced Mr. Evans.

"I thought you said you could handle it from here," Mark said brusquely.

"I've run into a complication. We've cracked the code, but part of the information is written in Spanish. I need you to translate, or at least look at it and tell me if any of it is important." He looked into the van and met Kate's eyes. "I'm sorry. I promise I will have him home in time for your party tonight."

"I'm not sure that I can depend on your word," Kate answered bluntly.

Mr. Evans winced but held her gaze. "I know that you cannot begin to understand the scope and importance of this case. We have uncovered the names of hundreds of people in very influential positions who are on the payroll of organized crime. A federal judge has been working since late last night on search warrants and indictments. This is bigger than me, bigger than Mark, and bigger than you. I regret the timing, but it cannot be helped. You have my word that Mark will be home tonight even if I have to drive him there myself."

Kate nodded. "I'll trust you."

Mark leaned in through the open door and gave her a quick kiss, then walked around the sedan and got in the front seat. Mr. Evans pulled open the driver's door, then looked back at Kate. "And Mrs. Iverson, I owe you a complete and detailed apology for my suspicions about Tony and his loyalties. Until I have time to compose a proper one, I hope the words will do."

Kate accepted his apology with a brief nod. "The words are enough," she acknowledged. "Just make sure Tony gets plenty of glory for all this. It will help his parents."

The man nodded, then slipped into the car and drove away. Everyone was subdued on the way back to the hotel. They packed up and checked out quickly. When they reached the rest area, the Iverson vans were parked in a neat line, waiting for them. Kate got out and spoke briefly to Mark's father. She told him that the FBI had detained Mark and that he would join them as soon as he could. When she got back in the van beside Emily, they drove caravan-style toward Haggerty.

Although she was tired, Kate did not sleep. She watched for familiar landmarks, thinking about Mark and Mr. Evans working together in Atlanta. It was beginning to look like they would never be free of the little man. Then she thought about the Iversons, driving stoically behind the van, and wondered if she would ever be accepted as a member of Mark's family. She was thoroughly depressed by the time Miracle pulled the van in front of the house.

Miss Eugenia met them in the driveway for introductions. She complimented Jared and his wife on their handsome sons, then told Mark's pregnant sister-in-law that she was carrying her baby high, so it was sure to be a girl. Turning to Jeff, she warned that his son was going to require expensive orthodontic care if they didn't put a stop to his thumb-sucking.

After that, she started giving instructions. "Everyone come in and have some lunch." She waved toward the front door where Miss Polly and several other members of the Bridge Club stood, all wearing aprons. "I'll get Mark's folks fed. Kate, you take your mother and sisters up to their rooms."

Turning back to the Iversons, Miss Eugenia addressed Mark's mother directly. "Suzanne, your family will be staying at my sister's place. It's a monstrosity over on Highway 11, but it has lots of room. She's visiting her son for the holidays, so you'll have the whole house to yourselves," she added and Mark's mother smiled appreciatively.

Kate scowled, thinking that she hadn't managed to get anything close to a smile from "Suzanne" yet. Seeing Kate still standing in the entryway, Miss Eugenia scolded her. "Mercy me, Kate! I thought I told you to take your family upstairs." When Kate turned to comply, Miss Eugenia hollered after her. "I've moved over to my house and Miracle is staying with me, so all three of the guest rooms are available."

Kate nodded and trudged upstairs, dragging her suitcase. The door to Mark's bedroom was open, and she noticed immediately that all his things were gone. Leaving her family to choose their own rooms, she walked into the master bedroom and opened the closet. Mark's clothes, mixed with some of Drew Johnson's expensive suits, were hung on the left side. She pulled open a drawer of the tall chest and found his socks. She smiled, knowing that one of the drawers now contained his "long-johns," and he was going to be furious when he found out that Miss Eugenia had moved them.

She was about to put up her toothbrush when Miss Eugenia rushed in and stopped her. "Keep everything in your suitcase. You'll need it tonight." Miss Eugenia stepped closer and bent her head to Kate's ear. "After the Open House, you and Mark are going to drive to a nice little bed and breakfast in Willow Falls for a short honeymoon."

"But we have all this company . . ." Kate started to protest.

"And they will all be well taken care of. You and Mark need some time alone."

"But what about Emily?" Kate's mind filled with objections.

"She takes an occasional formula bottle just fine."

"But—"

"Miracle and I will stay awake and stare at her all night long. She'll be perfectly safe."

"But won't people suspect something if we disappear?"

"Who? By the time you leave, the Haggerty folks will be home in bed, and with so much confusion over here tomorrow, even Miss

Polly won't notice that you're missing!"

Kate felt tears threatening. "Miss Eugenia . . ."

"Pooh! I don't have time for sentimentality. You can thank me later!"

"I was going to ask if you found sheets for the bed in your guest room."

Miss Eugenia threw back her head and laughed. "Actually, I never even looked. I borrowed some of yours, and they fit that bed just fine." Kate had to smile as she closed her suitcase and followed her neighbor downstairs.

The kitchen looked like a cookie bomb had exploded. "I've got to pick up my dress at the cleaners," Kate told Miss Eugenia as she surveyed the room in wonder. "There must be a thousand cookies in here."

"More like fifteen hundred," Miss Eugenia corrected. "And I already told Winston to get your dress." She shoved a chicken salad sandwich into Kate's hand. "Eat now because this is the last chance you'll get for a while. And if the temperature will just drop about twenty degrees, we can light a fire." Miss Eugenia rubbed her hands against her apron. "I hate to think about a cold fireplace at the Open House."

The back door slammed and Winston came in carrying a silver punch bowl and Kate's red dress. Miss Eugenia grabbed the punch bowl and started rinsing it in the sink. He handed the dress to Kate and she thanked him.

"You've saved my life again," she teased him just to watch him blush.

He complied, turning a lovely shade of Christmas red. "Temperature's dropping, Miss Eugenia," he reported gruffly. "Down to about fifty now."

"Praise be!" the old woman exclaimed as Winston left to change clothes for the party. Miss Eugenia put the punch bowl on the counter and took a long sip from her coffee mug. Out of the corner of her eye, Kate glimpsed something white in the cup.

"What's that you're drinking?" she demanded.

Miss Eugenia looked uncomfortable for the first time since Kate had known her. "I'm just having a little eggnog. It's Christmas time, in case you've forgotten."

Kate scrutinized her mercilessly for a few seconds, then walked over to the expensive coffee maker. There was no coffee in the pot, and it was cool to the touch. Miss Eugenia shrugged. "Too much caffeine makes you jittery."

"Really? I've never heard you express any concerns about caffeine before."

"Well, I'm not getting any younger, and I have to be cautious with my health. Now enough of this nonsense. You need to go upstairs and get ready."

Kate walked up close to her friend. "One of the many weird things Mormons believe is that ordinances can be performed for people after they die." Miss Eugenia's eyes widened. "So if you never find the courage to join the Church while you're alive, I'll wait until you're dead. Then, with Annabelle's permission, I can have you baptized."

"She'll never agree," Miss Eugenia gasped.

"Oh yes she will. She doesn't believe that anything Mormons do can affect the eternities. Besides, I have all that stuff of Niki's to bribe her with. The long, black vase and that picture frame made out of old Coke lids," Kate taunted. "I even have some statues of naked people in a closet." Miss Eugenia closed her eyes in defeat. "I'm sure that she and I can make a deal, and by the time you learn your way around heaven, you'll find out I've turned you into a Mormon."

Miss Eugenia stepped back a foot.

"Charles, too," Kate continued. "Then Mark and I will seal you together for time and all eternity." The old woman's hand trembled slightly as she put her coffee cup full of eggnog on the counter. "Not that you'll have to accept any of the work we do for you. If you'd rather spend the eternities singing in a choir than married to Charles—" Kate lifted her shoulder in an elaborate shrug, "—the Lord won't force you to be happy."

With that, Kate tucked her dress over her arm and hurried to her room. Her mother was in the nursery with Emily, so Kate took her second shower of the day and then dressed carefully. While drying her hair and re-applying makeup, she listened for Mark's footsteps in the hall or the sound of his voice.

When she was completely ready, she stared out the nursery window into the night. Christmas lights twinkled everywhere. Even Miss Eugenia's house was lined with large, outdoor bulbs. Cars had started to park along the street, and Kate could see people standing on the porch of Miss George Ann's house. But, still, there was no sign of Mark. With a sigh, she closed the blinds and went downstairs.

Jeanine Taylor sat in the kitchen, bouncing Emily on her lap. The baby looked like an angel in her snow-white dress smocked with tiny Christmas trees at the bodice. Kate lifted the baby into her arms and cuddled with her for a few precious minutes.

"During the Open House, the girls and I will be responsible for Emily," Jeanine said. "We'll stay close so you can show her off, but you'll need to concentrate on your guests." Kate and her mother smiled at each other over the baby's head.

"I see you've received your instructions," Kate commented, her eyes twinkling.

Her mother grinned back. "She's something else, your Miss Eugenia. She'd make a good Army sergeant." Jeanine squinted her eyes, studying her daughter. "You look good, Kate. That dress is so stylish."

Kate laughed, thinking that Niki wouldn't be caught dead in last year's dress. "It came from New York," she explained vaguely.

Jeanine smoothed the soft fabric on Kate's arm. "Well, it's perfect. Now you just stand wherever Miss Eugenia told you to, and we'll take care of the baby." Emily was gently removed from her arms, and Kate immediately started to miss her soft warmth.

Miss Eugenia rushed in, waving her arms. "I just saw a crowd of people walking down the sidewalk toward us. Everyone get into position." She took Kate's arm and dragged her to the entryway, just in front of the round table.

"It's not seven o'clock yet," Kate protested, hoping that Mark would arrive before their guests.

Miss Eugenia gave her a withering look. "Should I ask everyone to wait on the porch for five minutes?"

"Of course not. I just wish Mark were here," Kate responded lamely.

"Mark will be here when he can. Consider it your first duty as his wife to make excuses for him, and believe me, that's a skill you should develop. It will come in handy during years of married life. Now—" Miss Eugenia moved Kate a little to the right, "—I'll stay with you to make introductions, and Miss Polly will replenish the food table."

The large group of people headed toward the house turned out to be the Iversons. Miss Eugenia settled them all in a corner of the living room. "We won't ask you to stand with us for two hours, but we'll want you close by so folks can meet you," she explained. "If the children get tired, put them on any bed upstairs."

Jeanine and her daughters walked in from the dining room. Emily was propped on her grandmother's shoulder, cooing and smiling. Kate's heart tightened as she watched her mother speak to Suzanne. When Mark's mother asked to hold the baby, Kate stepped forward involuntarily, but by the time Kate reached them, Emily was settled happily on Suzanne Iverson's lap.

"She's beautiful," Suzanne murmured as Emily gripped her finger and tried to pull it into her mouth.

Kate clasped her hands together to keep from reaching for Emily. "Yes."

"Mark said your first husband was an FBI agent, too."

"That's not something we want to discuss in front of the people of Haggerty," Kate replied stiffly. "But he was a good man, and by this time tomorrow, he will probably be a national hero," she added. Then she couldn't stand it anymore and held out her arms for the baby.

"Why don't you let Emily stay with me for a little while?" Mark's mother suggested. "I like to be on good terms with all my grandchildren."

Tears clogged Kate's throat as she watched Mark's mother smiling down at her daughter. "He's going to adopt her," she managed finally.

Suzanne lifted her eyes and smiled at Kate for the first time. "I know. And I'm sorry if I have seemed unfriendly. This was all just such a shock . . ."

Kate decided to give the Iversons one more chance. "I know it was sudden and that I'm not the wife you would have picked for Mark."

"It's nothing personal. We just thought he'd marry someone . . ."

"Without a baby and a dead husband."

"Yes," she admitted. "That's why the whole family came."

"To look me over?"

"To try and talk him out of it," she replied honestly. "But we couldn't. He loves you and Emily. Mark has always been sensible, and if he's chosen you, then I'll trust his judgment. I hope you will be very happy together."

"I think I could be happy forever if he would just walk through that door," Kate admitted, as she felt tears gathering again. Hearing a commotion in the entryway, Kate walked over to investigate. As she turned the corner, she saw the man she had learned to trust, grown to love, and married twice standing in the doorway. As she flung herself into Mark's arms, she was vaguely aware of Mr. Evans in the background. The tears she had restrained all day escaped down her cheeks. "I was afraid you weren't going to make it."

"I'm here," he soothed, pulling back to look at her. "Oh, Kate, you look too good to be true, almost dangerous," he teased, touching the neckline of her bright red dress. "You're not trying to tell me anything, are you?"

She laughed. "Not tonight. I just wore it to match the poinsettias."

"I apologize for keeping your husband so long," Mr. Evans said, clearing his throat, "but he was very helpful. Watch the news tomorrow. It will please you, I think."

More guests started to come through the door, and Kate could see Miss Eugenia gesturing frantically for them to join her.

"I'll be on my way." Mr. Evans touched his forehead and stepped out the door. "Merry Christmas."

"Merry Christmas to you, too," Kate returned solemnly, clutching Mark for dear life.

"I do declare! If you don't let go of that boy, you're going to cut off his circulation," Miss Eugenia exclaimed from across the room. Embarrassed, Kate released her hold. "You look like death warmed over," Miss Eugenia addressed Mark, and Kate suddenly noticed the dark circles under his eyes and the tension lines around his mouth.

"I haven't slept much in three days," he admitted, shrugging out of his overcoat.

"Go up and change into something more presentable." Miss Eugenia eyed his wrinkled suit with distaste. "And run a razor over your face. Then get back down here."

"Come with me," Mark murmured to Kate as he moved toward the stairs. Their fingers entwined and she followed him.

"She can't go anywhere! She has guests!" Miss Eugenia objected strongly.

"We won't be long," Mark said, defying her smoothly.

Kate looked back down at Miss Eugenia's astounded expression. "I guess I'll consider helping him get ready for the Open House to be my second duty as his wife," she said as she continued up the stairs.

In their own room, Mark pushed the door closed and locked it. Then he pulled her into his arms and crushed her against his chest. "I can't believe we are finally alone," he whispered.

"That's only if you don't count all those people downstairs."

"It seems like forever since I've been able to just have a simple conversation with you," he murmured, his mouth close to her ear.

"Miss Eugenia is trying to give up coffee," Kate related breathlessly.

"Now that is remarkable." He smiled down at her.

"And after the Open House, they are sending us off to a little bed and breakfast in Willow Falls." She half expected him to object, but he didn't.

"That's the best news I've heard lately," he said with a sigh.

"You just want to go somewhere quiet so you can get some sleep," Kate teased.

"I'll admit that I'm looking forward to that," Mark agreed, holding Kate tightly. "I wish you could have seen all the stuff that was on that chip. Everett Morris had employees everywhere. He had people in police departments, on the staffs of senators and governors. He even had a couple of people in the White House. Tony sacrificed everything to get the chip out, but he has brought down a huge crime organization. Because of him, tonight this country is a safer place. He has made a difference in this world, and I envy him."

Kate pressed closer to Mark. "All of us can make a difference in this world by voting and paying tithing and storing wheat and fulfilling callings and raising strong, healthy, well-adjusted children. Your mark on the world may not be as dramatic, but it will be just as important," she assured him.

"Maybe so, but one day I hope to see Tony again and thank him. For everything," he smiled at Kate. "Now, I guess I'd better change and get back downstairs before Miss Eugenia comes after me." He trailed little kisses along her jaw, then pushed back slightly. "And if you stay in here while I change, we may never make it to the party at all."

Kate's eyebrows rose. "Well, Agent Iverson, I do declare!" His laughter followed her as she walked down to join their friends and family.

ABOUT THE AUTHOR

As a child, Betsy Green spent many wonderful days in a small town in South Alabama, where her father was born and raised. That town was the inspiration for Haggerty, she says, as were the "genteel and gracious" Southern women who influenced her young life.

Although born in Salt Lake City, Betsy Green currently lives in a suburb of Birmingham, Alabama (Bessemer), with her husband Robert (Butch) and eight children. She is the secretary for the kinder-garten campus of Hueytown Elementary School and serves in the Primary presidency of the Bessemer Ward. *Hearts in Hiding* is her first published novel.

Readers can email her at <u>betsyb8@yahoo.com.</u>